I0675447

Vengeance Protocol

Will Kincaid

Published by Will Kincaid, 2025.

Vengeance Protocol — Second Edition

© Will Kincaid 2025

Second Edition — Revised and Expanded

First edition published June 2025.

This edition published December 2025 by Glen Lyon Publishing.

Cover design and interior layout by Glen Lyon Publishing

Print Edition ISBN: 978-1-7643462-3-8

Table of Contents

For Rosey, for never giving up on me.

He who fights with monsters should see to it that he himself does not become a monster. And when you gaze long into an abyss, the abyss also gazes into you.

— Friedrich Nietzsche, Beyond Good and Evil (1886)

To Rose

He who fights with monsters should see to it that he himself does not become a monster. And when you gaze long into an abyss, the abyss also gazes into you.

— **Friedrich Nietzsche, Beyond Good and Evil (1886)**

Chapter 1: The Deal

The bar breathed heat and static. Trance bass rolled through the floor like a slow pulse, shaking the glass in my hand. The haze hung thick with ion dust and cheap scent—the kind that burned the back of your throat. I sat in the half-light and waited for Hela, one hand on the trigger guard of my Type V.

The last hunter came five days ago, while I was checking a cargo load out on Dax Station. He was quick, and I was quicker—but only just. I rushed the first shot, clipped him instead of killing him, and he almost took my head off before I finished the job.

That was the truth about survival out here: sometimes it wasn't skill that saved you. It was the part of you that refused to die.

There was a bounty on my head—the kind that kept amateurs hungry and professionals interested. The Polity called me a liability; the Syndicate called me useful, depending on who was paying that week. Either way, I slept with one eye open and a gun within reach.

A ship opened up on short notice—a medium freighter, *Ardent Wind*. The regular captain went down with fever, and the Syndicate needed the cargo moved fast. I took the job before they could find someone else. Calista wasn't my usual run, but credits were credits.

As soon as I cleared customs, a coded ping lit my comm: Syndicate seal. No greeting—just a name, a time, and a set of coordinates. *Hela. 22:00. The Glass Knife.*

The Knife squatted at the edge of the docks, a strip-bar turned broker's den. Neon flared through the fog like a bad signal, painting everything in red and blue. I got there early, took a corner booth, and waited.

I'd seen enough death to stop pretending it mattered. The Crawlers crushed everything they touched—cities, fleets, people. And when the fires went out, humanity shook their hands and called it peace.

Humanity had lost the first systems within weeks. The Crawlers' ships moved faster and communicated across light-years in real time, overwhelming every defence. Recovery began only after the first captured vessels were dismantled.

Their lattice cores provided the basis for faster-than-light communications, their drives led to the next generation of warp engines, and their neural interfaces advanced the existing Defined program into full production.

With those three breakthroughs—instant comms, faster travel, and enhanced soldiers—the war stopped being one-sided. We started pushing them back.

After Chance's Drift they pinned a medal to my chest and put my commission on ice—with instructions to keep my mouth shut. *Justice*, they said. *Politics*, I thought. I'd held too many dying friends to believe in words like honour.

The ones who lived are scattered now—hauling freight, fixing hulls, drinking in the dark to forget what they remember. There were no parades. Just the silence that comes after the noise. But I was still here. Still flying. Not hoping—but not finished, either.

The bar filled by degrees—dockhands, traders, crew from the night shift. Voices rose, fell, mixed with the bass until everything became one long vibration in the air. Neon bled across the floor, catching the sweat on faces and the smoke curling from cheap sticks.

I stayed in shadow, watching. The room had that restless hum you get before something happens. Maybe they felt it too—the weight of a deal waiting to close, or someone about to walk in who could change their luck.

I'd seen rooms like this before. They all smelled of the same things: work, want, and fear disguised as noise.

I ignored the menu's list of narcotics and off-world liquors and asked for a bottle of Earth whisky. Like most of us, I'd never been there. They said this batch came from an island the radiation missed. Maybe it did. After the wars, most of the planet was ash.

The whisky burned clean. The Syndicate was paying, which made it easier to swallow. If Hela turned up.

The obvious trouble was easy enough to mark; it's the quiet ones you watch. Two tables over, a group of Defined were drinking out their last night before the mines took them back. Ursa strain—seven feet tall, shoulders like armour plating, skin traced with service scars.

I'd served with their kind back when the programme was still experimental—before they'd perfected tissue regrowth. When a Defined lost a limb in those days, that was it. The flesh collapsed. You patched them up, or you buried them.

I went in with eight once and came out with four. My arm grew back; theirs didn't. Sixty Crawler soldiers never left the dirt. They weren't born; they were built—human genes crossed with predators, grown in vats when the war was going bad. The Polity threw them in by the thousand. Most never came home.

Some bars won't serve them. Too strong. Too different. Too much reminder of what the war had made. Truth is, they fought harder than anyone. I'm six feet, give or take, but next to an Ursa I look half-sized. You don't pick a fight with one unless you've made peace with dying.

Most of them work the mines now—strong backs, long contracts, no rights worth naming. The years wear them down slower than the stone, but not by much. Maybe that's what makes them dangerous. Nothing left to lose, nothing left to fear.

The security crew understood that: two reptilian hybrids and a tall woman with alloy across her shoulders, watching the Ursa the way miners watch a fault line—waiting for it to shift.

Everyone watched the Defined. No one really looked. And in a Syndicate bar, peace is a rented thing. It lasts for as long as the house wants it to.

An elegantly dressed woman took the seat opposite me. Two men followed—human, steady on their feet, moving like they'd done this before. They stopped behind her, one on each side.

Her eyes met mine—clear, pale, and cold as methane ice. She had the look of someone who'd ordered deaths and forgotten most of the names.

'You must be Hela,' I said. 'You're an hour late.'

'Business runs on its own schedule,' she replied. 'And here I am.'

The smile that followed was polite enough to be dangerous. She leaned back, a flick of her fingers sending the larger guard to turn toward the bar. He moved like he'd rehearsed it a hundred times—smooth, invisible, utterly in place.

The smaller one turned to me and held out his hand. 'You're going to give me that blaster, Captain.'

The regrown skin on his left hand had that taut, new look—younger than the rest of him.

'Fleet Marine?' I asked.

'Yes, sir. Signed up when the Crawlers came. Lived to tell it.' His hand drifted toward his holster. 'I'm asking nicely, because there are plenty in the fleet who remember what you did for us.'

We exchanged a look. My fingers rested loose on my pistol. The safety clicked.

I held his gaze a beat, then unclipped the heavy sidearm and slid it across the table. 'Thanks for the courtesy, Marine.'

I wasn't worried. I'd taped a spare under the seat before she arrived.

Hela had high cheekbones and skin so pale it caught the light like frost. Her eyes were the washed blue of deep ice—clear, unreadable. She flicked her wrist, activating the privacy field, then set a small black box on the table. It blinked red once, then steadied to green.

'Good. Now we can talk.' She exhaled a slow ribbon of blue-tinged smoke. 'Have they made you comfortable?'

'Your messenger didn't give me the impression I had a choice.' I took a measured sip of Talisker. 'What's the job?'

Her mouth curved—not quite a smile. 'They said you were difficult.' She tapped ash into a tray. 'I don't mind difficult. But if you don't cooperate, Spalding will shoot you, and we'll move on.'

I met her eyes, steady. 'You want to trade threats or get to the point?'

The curve deepened. 'Business, then. You're not just a starship captain, Commander Rakkan. You're the hero of Chance's Drift.'

I shook my head. 'That was a long time ago.'

'And still glorious,' she said softly. Her fingertip traced the rim of her glass. 'A handful of gunships against an entire Crawler fleet. Jero Rakkan wins the Cross of Honour—one of only four awarded in the whole war.' She paused, studying me. 'The feeds loved you for it. Especially after you took down the Mother Ship. But not everyone admired your methods, did they?'

She leaned forward, watching. 'And now?' She nodded at my glass. 'Running ore. A hero turned hauler. That's a long way down.'

I rolled the whisky on my tongue. 'Keeps me flying.'

'We know why you left.' Smoke drifted from her mouth as she spoke. 'Chance's Drift was a victory some still call a crime.'

I didn't answer. Her eyes stayed on me. The air tightened.

'You won,' she said. 'You did what others wouldn't. Don't pretend you regret it.'

'Regret's expensive.'

She smiled faintly. 'You need money. You need a ship. High Command pinned a medal on you—then threw you in the garbage. The Crawlers put five million on your head. One day, that luck of yours runs out.'

She let the words hang, then added, 'The man who came for you last week? The Syndicate used him sometimes. Competent—usually. But obviously not enough for you.'

I said nothing. She was measuring reaction, not guilt.

'You need us,' she said.

'You people are well informed.'

'It's our business.' She flicked the last of her ash into the tray. 'I have a job for you.'

'It requires a delicate hand,' she said. 'We need someone who understands how the Navy thinks. Someone who's worked with the Defined. A captain who can run a single-ship strike and make it count. And above all—someone who keeps quiet, so we don't have to do it for them. Permanently.'

She blew another line of blue smoke across the table. 'Have you heard of a man named Ephraim Virell?'

'I'm retired, not buried,' I said. 'I know the name.'

She waited.

'Virell was a traitor,' I said. 'Sold Crawler targeting data straight out of Fleet Command. They caught him mid-transmission. Should've been erased the same day.'

'That's the story,' she said. 'But Virell was a genius. Half the fleet's logistics algorithms came out of his head. The Polity wanted him gone but not lost. Too valuable to kill, too dangerous to keep.'

I sat back. Virell should've been dust. Disruption chambers don't fail.

'The price,' she went on, 'was everything he owned. The Polity took the lot. His family lost it all. Officially he was executed. Unofficially, they froze him. Insurance for a crisis they didn't yet see.'

I let the thought turn over once. 'Why not send your own people? You've got plenty who'd love to do it.'

Hela flicked the cigarette into the tray, smoke curling off the tip. 'We asked the AIs to model success. They gave us one name. Yours.' She let it sit, then added, 'And I think you're starting to see you don't have much choice if you plan to stay alive.'

'And if I walk?'

'There was some debate.' She drew slow on the smoke, eyes steady. 'Two of the three think you'll take the job. They called it pragmatism.'

She tapped ash from her cigarette, her voice smooth as glass. 'The third? It wanted your psych report from after the Mother Ship. It worries you might have a death wish.'

I met her gaze. 'I'm still here, Hela.'

'Yes, you are.' A small smile touched her lips. 'I don't think it's a death wish. I think you like unfinished wars. Revenge—so very old-fashioned.'

The whisky soured in my throat.

'But that's enough of that.' She waved a hand. 'You don't talk about it. Not to me, not to Fleet, not to anyone. I don't care why you did it. I care that you won. And that our AIs say you can get Virell out.'

She ground the cigarette into the tray. 'All we needed was to find him.'

'Why go to all this trouble for one man?'

'Virell was a major player in the Syndicate. There are things only he knows. We've already burned a fortune tracking his hole and setting the extraction. We just need the right man to finish it.'

'So, if I refuse, I'm dead.' I took a sip. 'What's the reward if I don't?'

'A fortune, if you like. Or freedom. We can erase the bounty, clear your name. You'd be clean, rich, and breathing.'

I studied her. 'Hela's an unusual name.'

That earned a slight smile—the kind that carried history.

'It wasn't the one I was born with,' she said. 'That was Diamond. Synthetic, polished, made to sell.' She took a sip of her drink. 'But I chose Hela. You know your myths, Jero? Goddess of the forgotten dead. Daughter of Loki.'

Her eyes held mine. 'Virell always fancied himself a god. Trickster fits him better.'

'Hela was the name I chose when I joined the Syndicate. But the one I was born with was Virell. Justine Virell.'

The air between us seemed to still.

'Ephraim is family,' she said quietly. 'In a manner of speaking.'

Her eyes caught the low light—pale, cold, certain. 'I'm his clone, Rakkan. Built from his code, shaped to replace him. The Syndicate think that makes me the right person to bring him home.'

She leaned in, voice barely audible above the hum of the field. 'Bring him in alive, and we'll give you what you really want.'

'Which is?'

'Redemption.'

I looked at her for a long moment. Then I finished the whisky. 'That's not on my list.'

There was something human in her eyes, just for a moment.

'That must've been a fun childhood, Hela. I've never met a direct clone before.'

'It's obscenely expensive,' she said. 'And rather self-indulgent, in my considered opinion.'

I nodded. It couldn't have been an easy start. But empathy was a luxury I couldn't afford. Not here. Not with her.

'Sorry, Hela. I think my chances of survival are better with the bounty hunters. I get why you want me—who argues with three AIs and wins?—but I can't see why I should.'

Her face stayed unreadable, though her eyes did the maths.

'So, Captain,' she said, voice even, 'what you're really saying is that you can be had—just not at that price.'

'You make me sound cheap,' I said. 'But yes. Your offer's not worth the risk.'

She laughed—a small, deliberate sound that didn't reach her eyes.

'Rakkan, meeting someone like you really is a treat. People don't argue with me much these days. I admire the confidence—that you can kill Spalding and French, take me out, get past the five other units watching, and still dodge the needle-beam pointed at your skull.'

She drew slow on the cigarette and smiled. 'But don't worry. I expected you'd need more convincing. That's why I arranged a special present. Cost me a fortune. Want to know what it is?'

I'd already got the spare blaster in my hand. Small weapon, wide radius. At this range, it'd turn anyone in its path into smoke and regret.

It didn't look good though. I probably wasn't making it out of here alive. I wasn't sure I cared.

'I think we're about out of time, Hela,' I said. 'I almost wish you had something I wanted. I really do. But I can't think of a thing you could offer that'd make me take this job.'

She wagged a finger, amused. 'Now, now, Captain. Don't be so premature. I know a lot about you. I know, for example, that your first Fleet posting was Eden—aide to the commander.'

'What's that got to do with anything? That was twenty Sols ago. I was barely twenty-one.'

'I was intrigued by what came next,' she said. 'Top of your class, plum assignment—and then suddenly you're reassigned to Tactical Command with the Defined. The most dangerous billet in the Force.'

I took a slow sip of whisky. 'I've always had a knack for making the wrong enemies.'

'I empathise with them,' she said, the smirk returning. 'So I set my little helpers to dig. And they found a rather torrid romance between our young hero and the colony governor's daughter,' she finished. 'A scandal that saw you exiled and left to die in someone else's war.'

She let the silence stretch, smoke drifting between us.

'I was captivated by the story, you know,' she said at last. 'The young officer and the governor's daughter—ambition, secrecy, ruin. Almost classical.' Her smile was faint, practised. 'But I am such a romantic, of course.'

'Get to the point,' I said. My voice came out harder than I intended.

'Gladly.' The smile held, brittle as glass. 'Let me tell you a secret. And if you still want to walk away after that, I'll let you. Because the man I want couldn't.'

I waited.

'Twenty-two years ago, you had an affair with Gwendolyn Rhys. Young. Careless. It ended, they sent you off-world, and time did what it does.' She drew a slow breath, watching my eyes. 'But what you were never told—what Gwen never told you—is that there was a child. A daughter. Your daughter, Rakkan. She's alive. On Eden. And I know exactly where.'

The world seemed to stop. The hum of the bar fell away until there was only her voice and the sound of my own pulse. A daughter. I'd never known. Couldn't have known. And yet—lies were the cheapest currency the Syndicate traded in.

'A child, you say?' My tone stayed even. 'One you know all about, and I've somehow missed for two decades?'

'That's right, Rakkan. Maybe you should check your messages more often. Or maybe Gwen's father didn't want you to know. He never thought much of you.'

She set a small vial on the table—blood, dark against the glass.

'Take it. Run it. It's hers—sampled before the invasion. Getting it wasn't easy. Or cheap. But we want you. And only you.'

The air felt thinner. My pulse thundered in my ears. I gripped the table until my fingers stopped shaking.

'Eden,' I said quietly. 'That's—'

'A Crawler slave world. Yes.' Her tone softened, almost kind. 'Life there is short.'

'And Gwen?'

'Dead.' No hesitation. 'Executed once she'd outlived her usefulness.'

The woman who'd told me to leave. The woman I'd carried like a scar. Gone.

And a daughter left behind in chains.

I set the glass down carefully, the sound sharp against the table. I would check the blood—of course I would—but there was only one path I would take from here.

'All right, Hela,' I said. 'I'm going to assume you don't like wasting your time—and that this sample is real. I'm going to test it. If it's real, you've got yourself a captain.'

I smiled. 'And if it isn't, then you will have pissed me off—and you won't like that at all.'

I leaned forward, voice steady again.

'Now tell me where she is.'

They Have Forgotten the Shape of Fire

Hunger Command Hub: Ark Flagship, Fist of Salvation.

Location: Threxil Home System

We moved as one, our drives steady, our formation absolute. The Ark of Salvation led us—mighty and battle-tested, her hull unmarked by this cycle's remaking. She had not been chosen to burn. She had been chosen to bear witness.

Through the Hunger's crucible, worlds have fallen in their thousands. Their lifeblood is woven into the tapestry of becoming. Each consumed realm was not taken in conquest, but in reverence. Every silence is sacred. Every ruin, a hymn.

The proud were not destroyed—they were transformed. We reforged their strength into steel. We welcomed their fleets into our own. This is our purpose. This is the sacrament of becoming.

On the scarred plains of Threxil IX, the final insectoid legions lay broken. Their ambition lay in pieces. Pulse rifles sparked uselessly in the dust. Their war fleets smoldered like spent coals. They began in defiance. They ended in penance.

High Acolyte Veris stood upon the bridge dais. His wings were folded in sacred posture. His voice rang through the hull.

'Through consumption, we grant rebirth.

Through annihilation, we grant peace.'

The Swarm answered him. Our vessels sang in unified harmonics—the hymn of becoming, carried across the stars.

When silence returned, Fist Supreme Lord Tharim turned her gaze toward the path ahead. The work was not finished. There remained insectoid strongholds along the outer rim—systems yet to be purified. Their silence had not yet been granted. Their fracture had not yet forged them.

We offered no celebration. There is no triumph in fire. Only devotion. Only the next step.

And so we turned toward the unfinished.

The sacred work continues.

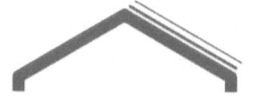

Chapter 2: Extraction

Even gods crack under waiting. You chain a super intelligence in a box long enough, and it doesn't stay divine—it just starts sharpening the walls.

Freyja dropped from warp into real space, silent and steady beyond the heliosphere. Scanners unfolded, whispering through the dark. A single asteroid pulsed green on the tactical grid.

The ship confirmed through the console: Target locked.

Then: Combat override Intelligence: *Residual traffic indicates two Crawler carrier groups moving outbound. Vectors avoid all human systems in range.*

This ship had seen combat during the war. Like me, it didn't trust Crawlers. They didn't run from humans. Not during the war. Not ever. Which meant that right now they were running from something else.

I sat back, watching the projection fade. For a moment I felt something I hadn't allowed in years — relief. Whatever they'd found out there, it wasn't us. Let them keep running. Let them vanish into the dark. Humanity had bled enough.

I logged the data and pulled up the local chart. The planetoid was a nameless lump of heavy metal, meaningless to anyone but Freyja. It had a secret. Buried inside was Sentinel — a Hunter-Killer AI with the power to burn a system clean.

Meeting it head-on would be suicide, but choice was no longer part of the equation. Success here was the only path to a daughter I had never met. They were paying well enough to buy a planet, but the reason I was here had nothing to do with money

Force would not beat the Sentinel, but guile might. Even the invincible carry a flaw. For Sentinel, it was time. Minds built to think in a thousand directions don't endure centuries of silence. Isolation corrodes them.

The Fleet called it AI psychosis. I thought of it as intelligence turned inward until it cracked.

The remedy was narcotic code — engineered programs that fed them order, dreams, and something to hold onto in the long dark. A single patch each Earth year kept the fractures from spreading, stretching centuries into something a machine could stand.

Few could write that code without breaking the mind they meant to soothe. The Syndicate had found a woman who could. They paid three million credits — and whatever it cost to make sure she never wrote another line.

Sentinel's last upgrade had her fingerprint in the feed. She slipped in a few extra lines — quiet, surgical, deniable. That was the Syndicate's trade: expensive, precise betrayals. I never asked what became of the woman who wrote it. The Syndicate kept its promises when convenient; I trusted those promises like a contract written in smoke and blood. But I'd signed anyway.

At least I was happy with my ship.

The Syndicate provided access to a black-market shipyard, no questions asked. War surplus flowed freely now that peace had arrived—every commodity available for a price. Including me, it seemed.

I'd named her Freyja after the Norse goddess of love and war. She was a Corsair-class frigate, swift, modular, and deadly, carrying three splinter ships built for ambush and covert operations.

For this mission, Freyja's purpose was singular: capture Ephraim Virell alive and deliver him to the Syndicate.

The tactical holo tank—a stolen military prototype—queried my insertion route. I keyed the override and locked in my trajectory. They built Hunter-Killer sentries tough, their Sentinel AIs mercilessly efficient at killing unwary fools who dared disturb their sleep. A shudder ran through the hull as subspace engines surged, driving Freyja toward our target.

Most of the crew were still locked in Gel Fields—protective but leaving them sluggish and numb on awakening. Life-support indicators showed Morgan's team already up and checking their gear.

Morgan was the security chief—under my command on paper. In reality, he was Hela's leash around my throat. Insurance against deviation. I'd hired half the crew from my past service, ex-Navy veterans I could trust. Unlike Morgan.

Morgan and his six Syndicate men wore discipline like a borrowed uniform—beneath it, something mean and feral watched the world too closely.

But Morgan wasn't my only problem. And there was no more time to delay. The moment I'd dreaded had arrived. I steadied my breath and spoke clearly to the ship.

'Freyja, initialize the Avatar.'

The Syndicate had invested deep in this mission—money, influence, stolen secrets. Somehow they'd pried open the archives of the Avatar project, buried at the height of the war.

Freyja's Avatar was profoundly illegal tech: a fusion of artificial intelligence and human consciousness. During the desperate days after the Crawler attack, ethics had become optional. Humanity was cornered, and survival came before morality.

Even the fusion of human and machine.

The subjects had been volunteers. I'd seen the recordings of the five who tried it—men and women who walked into the unknown because someone had to. Their minds didn't survive the merge; the feedback broke them apart within days. They had been heroes. They were promptly forgotten.

The Syndicate had dragged the Avatar program out of cold storage, promising the impossible was now only dangerous. I didn't buy it. No one who'd seen those test recordings could. Five volunteers, five minds shattered trying to merge with an AI core. I still remembered their faces—alive one day, hollow the next. They called it progress. I called it desperation.

Now I was about to turn one of those ghosts back on.

The holo tank flared to life, cycling through five flickering human forms before settling on a calm, middle-aged man.

'We are active and awaiting orders, Captain. For operational clarity, address us as Ariel. Sentinel is querying our identity.'

My throat tightened. 'Ariel—take control of Sentinel. Override its narcotic protocols. Total obedience.'

'Understood.'

Data spilled through the tank like static lightning. Sentinel's defences lit the room red and violet; Ariel cut through them with surgical precision, exploiting Syndicate backdoors I wasn't supposed to know existed. I stood still, watching something born of human ruin win another battle.

The colours softened to blue. Ariel steadied. 'Sentinel neutralized. Awaiting command.'

Freyja shuddered as we hit atmosphere. The hull groaned, sandstorm hammering against her plates. Stealth mines, orbital guns, and remote ship-killers slept beneath us—dormant only because Ariel held the Sentinel in her grip.

Beneath that layer of silence waited something worse: the Defined, mercenaries in stasis around Ephraim Virell's crypt. Wake them, and nobody left this planet alive. We had to stay invisible.

Virell had been asleep three years. Not dead, not preserved—contained. Too dangerous to kill, too valuable to lose.

The Syndicate had been clear they wanted him breathing. And that if he died, so did I.

This job meant I had a shot at saving the only family I had from whatever hell the Crawlers had built on Eden. Whether I made it or not didn't matter. But without me she was finished. And that was why I had to make it there alive.

I checked the alert board again. Still silent. Ariel's narcotics were holding Sentinel's madness at bay—for now. Minutes left. Move fast. Get Virell. Get clear.

The Defined waited below us—soldiers built from desperation and predator DNA, sharper, faster, stronger than anything human. When the war ended, the Polity tried to 'decommission' them—classed them as property, not people. The Defined answered that mistake in blood.

Now they fought for whoever could pay, and they hadn't forgiven their makers.

I'd fought beside them once. Respected their precision, their sense of honour. Even liked a few. But the truth never changed—if you weren't on their side, you were collateral.

My console flashed red, a single pulse that meant disaster. Ariel flickered through faces—young, old, male, female—before locking into a hard-edged focus.

'Captain. Sentinel's sub-process has reactivated. I'm suppressing it—'

Too late. The holo tank bled crimson.

Klaxons screamed through the fort.

'Ground team,' I snapped. 'Tell me that wasn't you. Report.'

Morgan's voice came back, maddeningly calm. 'Not us. System woke itself. You'd better move.'

Ariel's feed cut through the noise. 'Alert protocols are online. Defined units are being woken—one hundred and twenty total. Six

Octs active.' Defined worked in packs of eight. Forty-eight was more than enough to erase us.

The mission was blown, but stopping wasn't an option.

'You've got twenty minutes. Get Virell out. Move.'

On the airlock cams, Morgan's team was already hauling the gravity sled, Virell limp and blinking slow from cryo. My own crew—five veterans, three of them Defined—took firing positions.

'Ready up,' I said, arming Freyja's outer batteries. 'Company's coming.'

Morgan's voice came through the comm, as calm as if he were ordering breakfast.

'Secured Virell. Dawes and Yeltsin are rigging explosives and micro-mines along the exit route. The Defined won't follow without paying dearly.'

'Good. Get him back to the ship as quickly as you can. My team will cover you.'

I keyed the comm to Ariel. 'Keep Sentinel sedated. Maintain the narcotic feed. Prep the second dose.'

A ventilation grate exploded inward. A Defined soldier dropped through the haze, armour shimmer-black, eyes glowing amber. A particle beam screamed past my head, carving through a plinth of carved obsidian. The statue above it disintegrated into dust.

'Sentinel's active. Countermeasures deployed,' Ariel said, her voice breaking into static.

Three more dropped from the vents like wolves through smoke. One strode forward—broad, deliberate—his chest plate marked with a sigil I hadn't seen since the Kesserath slaughter: the Twelfth Gene-enhanced.

I emptied my pistol at short range into his chest. The impacts punched deep, armour flaring white-hot before the man inside folded and fell.

I reloaded and switched to my carbine, thumbing to armor-piercing rounds. The barrel hummed with deadly promise.

Ariel stabilized abruptly, cycling images rapidly. A blast of wind slammed through the chamber, toppling shelves and sending shards of priceless ceramics skittering across the floor like shrapnel. A tapestry caught fire mid-air, whipping itself into blackened cinders. Defined soldiers stumbled, momentarily blinded. I fired at their leader, phosphorous rounds exploding brilliantly against reactive armor. He staggered forward, biology fighting a losing battle, before finally collapsing.

I lunged forward as Ariel fragmented into swirling defensive protocols, disabling enemy neural implants. Another Defined fell, nerves fried, black ichor trickling from nose slits.

A Defined soldier loomed in front of me and I fired point-blank into his center mass, before plunging my combat knife into a gap between cervical armor plates before he could recover. Around me, plasma bolts and kinetic rounds smashed in to the walls as the rest of his unit opened up on us.

'Thirty seconds to structural failure,' Ariel warned calmly.

I moved through smoke and ruin, firing into another Defined until he stopped moving. Around me, plasma bolts shredded the air.

'Morgan, status!'

Morgan stood ahead, two Defined corpses sprawled at his feet, his plasma rifle glowing from recent combat. 'Took your sweet time,' he growled, hurling grenades to seal off our escape route. Explosions echoed behind him, corridors collapsing in smoke and debris. 'Booby traps are rigged. That'll hold them for a few minutes.'

But Morgan's team were now only five.

'What happened to Weber?'

'He panicked. I shot him for endangering the mission.' Morgan didn't blink. 'He's bleeding out on his credits.'

For a heartbeat I just stared at him through the haze—ash swirling between us, the air thick with burnt metal. Weber had been green, maybe reckless, but not mutinous. He'd followed orders before. He'd trusted us to lead him.

'You hired him,' I said quietly. 'We get to lead them, and they trust us to do it. Do that to one of mine and it's between you and me.'

Morgan's jaw tightened. 'Discipline keeps people alive. Removing liabilities keeps ships flying.'

I stepped closer, close enough to smell ozone on his armour. 'We're not executioners. Not in my ship. Don't forget what I said.'

His mouth twitched—half smirk, half warning. 'Wasn't what you did at Chance's Drift an execution? But I wouldn't dream of it.'

It was a challenge, and we both knew the truth. There'd be blood between us. Maybe not now. Maybe not tomorrow. But it was coming.

My thumb brushed the safety on my sidearm—a silent promise—then eased.

'Captain!' Ariel's voice snapped through the static. The deck heaved beneath us; coolant screamed from ruptured pipes. Virell lay half-buried in debris, neural cuffs still glowing.

I grabbed him by the collar and hauled him upright. 'Move!'

His eyes focused on the chamber around us. 'You need to hurry, Captain. They'll flood the complex with neurotoxin,' he murmured evenly, pupils wide and dark. 'I'm immune, by design. You likely aren't.'

Failure wasn't an option. Not after everything that had already been taken from me.

Concrete cracked underfoot as I ran, the tunnel heaving with every detonation. Ariel's glowing markers flickered like a heartbeat in smoke, leading us forward. A pipe burst near my shoulder, venting coolant in a scream. Then—metal. The airlock door, half-buried in rubble.

I sealed the hatch and braced as Freyja's Gatling batteries tore into the pursuing Defined, cutting through dust and flame. 'Ariel, deploy the second narcotic patch. Now.'

Her image steadied, then wavered.

'Something's wrong,' she said—flat, composed.

The holo-tank bled red. Code scrolled like falling embers.

'Corruption detected in the narcotic protocol. Rebuilding.'

A shiver moved through the hull, like the ship itself was holding its breath. 'If Sentinel stabilizes too early—'

'Don't let it,' I snapped.

For five seconds we were blind—no ship, no crew, only static and heat.

Then the colours flattened to blue. Ariel settled. 'Back in control.'

We both knew it wouldn't last.

I threw myself into the Nav chair and hit crash procedures, combat stimulants flooding my veins. Freyja trembled beneath me, engines screaming for release. 'Ariel, confirm all crew aboard.'

'All secure, Captain.'

'Crash harness. Ten seconds. Four...three...two—launch.'

I killed the dampeners. Freyja roared upward, engines flaring white, ripping free of the surface in a storm of dust and fire. The planetoid fell away beneath us, shrinking into the black.

Alarms screamed their warnings as the ship bucked against the atmosphere. I held her steady, every muscle locked, the hull howling under pressure. Stars broke through the haze like cold needles of light.

We cleared the gravity well at full impulse and jumped clean to warp. The system vanished behind us in a streak of flame and silence.

We had made it. We had our prize, and I was one step closer to getting her out. For the first time in years, I wasn't just running from something.

I was running toward it.

Chapter 3: War Games

Good tactics are just convincing lies—wrapped in steel and timed to explode the moment your enemy starts believing you.

I'd been playing war games with the Defined captain for days now. Two things were clear: their Hub ship was faster, and their captain wasn't stupid.

I hadn't answered their hails or their threats to surrender. But that didn't mean we weren't talking. Freyja still had a fair stock of static mines. Nothing clever—standard Polity loadout. Static for brute disruption. Smart mines for finesse. I wasn't in the mood for finesse.

Every few hours I tossed one into the dark—just a lump of high explosive wrapped around a dense core, tumbling lazy until it wasn't. Inertial drift made it look random. Then the trajectory snapped straight, right into their path. To the Defined captain, they came screaming out of nowhere.

Some detonated on proximity. Others burst into cluster shards that didn't care about armour or shielding. Each mine forced a choice: dodge or waste time clearing the way.

It worked—again and again. They'd close the gap, and I'd make them flinch. Enough feints, enough hesitation, and Freyja stayed ahead. Until the last mine was gone.

Between launches, I pulled up a wideband scan to plot their next vector. Something else caught my eye—three relay stations along the frontier were dark. No chatter, no orbit drift, no distress beacons. Just silence where there should have been noise.

Ariel shimmered in the tank. 'Captain, last recorded transmissions were routine. Station shutdowns anomalous. No reported conflicts.'

I frowned. Crawlers didn't take outposts like that. Neither did pirates. Systems don't just go dark for no reason. Not this close to home.

The Defined ship pulsed red in the tactical tank. Freyja's drives were already running hot, well past safe thresholds, but it wasn't enough. They were closing fast. At this rate, they'd have us long before the halfway mark.

And being boarded by the Defined wasn't an option. I'd seen what they did to Crawler ships—what they left behind. We had nothing they wanted. Except Ephraim Virell.

I watched the red blip narrow the gap, then opened a channel. Chief Engineer Leela McNair's broad face filled the screen, hair tied back, grease on her sleeves.

'Leela, I need more speed.'

She wiped her forehead with the back of her arm. 'I can give it to you, Captain. But you know the cost. More thrust means catastrophic damage.'

Leela was from a heavy-Grav world. I'd known her long enough to learn two things: never arm-wrestle her on shore leave; and never expect her to risk her engines lightly.

'Chief, we need to reach Callista in one piece. I've got a Defined ship on my tail, and they're not coming to negotiate.' I checked the nav tank. 'Assuming exponential degradation, Warp Nine gets us there with enough fuel for a crash stop. Barely. That about right?'

She didn't answer straight away. When she did, her voice was flat. 'Aye, Cap'n. But after that, the engines will need a full rebuild. We'll be dead in the water. No room to dodge. Just a straight run.'

'They won't fire—they need Virell alive. Push us to Nine. Assign someone to engine watch full-time. Any fluctuation, I want it on my board first. Bridge out.'

The screen went dark. But the look on Leela's face said I hadn't heard the last of it.

The drive engines surged. I felt it in the deck plating, in the hinge of my jaw — the kind of vibration you don't notice until you realize it hasn't stopped. For fifteen minutes, I watched the display. No shifts, no anomalies. Just the same blinking data: slow, deliberate, almost reluctant to admit the truth.

The Defined ship was losing ground.

Not by much. Not enough to lean back in the chair or unclench my jaw. But the margin was there now — growing, mile by mile. On the tactical tank, the enemy icon cooled from red to blue.

That part was tactical. What came next — that was personal.

I kept watching, tracing the curve of their trajectory, the bleed in their velocity. Trying to read another captain's intent through machine logic. 'What's your next move, Captain?'

Three hours later, I got my answer.

The tactical alarm shrieked — a raw, metallic sound that split the quiet. The Defined ship flared red again, sensors spiking with heat and acceleration.

I muttered a curse and leaned forward. He'd pushed his drives harder. Somehow. And I was running out of cards.

'Ship,' I said, 'get Dakkar to the bridge.'

The system complied. It wasn't much for conversation, but I made a point of staying civil with my hardware. This one, though, had been colder since Ariel came aboard. Couldn't blame it. She had a way of hijacking subroutines like she owned them — unapologetic, unpredictable, invasive.

Lately, she'd been worse. Sharper. Restless. I didn't know why and not knowing made me uneasy. But I didn't have time for her moods.

I needed my second.

Back at Chance's Drift, we'd started with one hub ship and three splinter craft. Over time it became a ragged little fleet—survivors of Crawler engagements and desperation plays. Most followed me out of loyalty. Some out of rage. A few because there wasn't anywhere else left to go.

Dakkar Obasi had been two years ahead of me at the Naval Academy, a tactician turned smuggler by the time we crossed paths again. His mind worked like a steel trap—quick, decisive, and impossible to shake once it closed.

He stepped onto the bridge and took the nav seat beside me, arms folded.

'So,' he said, glancing at the display. 'Our friends behind us tiring of your surprises?'

I gave him a thin smile. 'I've been mixing things up. Tossed a few rocks into the spread. Let them guess what's real.'

He nodded once. 'Not bad. As long as they don't figure it out.'

'They're about to,' I said. 'That was the last actual mine. Two decoys left, and once they see the pattern, they'll stop flinching.'

He raised an eyebrow. 'Time for the stealth mines, then?'

'Four. Series Twelves.'

That earned the faintest grimace. 'We asked for Thirteens.'

'We did,' I said. 'This is what we got.'

I crossed to the cabinet by the bulkhead, poured him a measure of the spiced liquor he favoured, and took a whisky for myself. He accepted it without comment. We'd shared worse on worse nights.

He looked at the readouts again. 'So our mines are underpowered and outdated, and you want me to make them sing.'

'I could reprogram them myself,' I said. 'If you want a mine that misidentifies its own target and spins like a dying nav beacon.'

He smiled. 'Stick to the big picture, Jero. I'll turn your Twelves into something that leaves a dent.'

We'd learned how to cover each other's weaknesses back at Chance's Drift. It wasn't pretty, but it had held.

I'd found the stealth mines in a crate marked obsolete munitions. Polity-standard, technically. Buried in doctrine, buried deeper in storage. Officially denied, quietly stocked.

Only four left—each cloaked, subspace-capable, self-guided. Built to end a chase before it started. I'd used them before. Once at Farsight, again during the Dolan Run. Both times, they hit hard and vanished clean.

But that was years ago. And tech like this doesn't age gracefully. If the Defined had upgraded their sensors, they'd see them coming. If not... they'd never know what hit them.

I lifted my glass. 'To the glorious dead,' I said. 'And to absent friends.'

Dakkar touched his glass to mine and drank slow. He held the taste for a long moment before speaking. 'They don't make it on Dragon anymore,' he said. 'Far as anyone knows, they don't make anything. Except corpses.'

He didn't need to say the rest, so I did the math. His sister had been stationed there—civilian logistics. Last comm burst she sent was a week before the Crawlers hit orbit. We both knew what that meant.

He'd never called it revenge. Just signed up, got to work, and bled with the rest of us.

That's why I trusted him. Not because he was smart. Because he kept moving—after the world ended.

I drank and set the glass gently on the tactical display. The pulsing screen turned the whisky the colour of the enemy blip that stalked us. Dakkar would make our mines hurt them—if they didn't adapt. Skilled enemies surprise you. My gut said this wouldn't be easy.

Ariel cut in. 'Enemy ship adjusting vector—eleven degrees, port.'

I frowned. Not an evasion. A measured change—strategic, not panicked.

'They're scanning the forward corridor. Slow sweeps. Cautious.' Ariel's tone was clinical.

Or clever. If they slowed enough, they might spot the mines before the grid lit them. I kept my mouth shut. No point rattling the crew. Still, the timeline had shrunk. Time was the one thing I couldn't buy.

Somewhere on Eden my daughter was still breathing—if only just. Every delay risked her life. Not much escaped those planets once the Crawlers took them. The reports that did come back were whispers: compounds ringed in razor wire, people kept in ranks, worked into the earth until there was nothing left to take.

Crawlers didn't speak; they clicked and clacked—their mandibles like shears. Ten limbs: eight for walking, two for tearing. They were a hive mind, an industry of violence. There was no mercy in that sound.

They weren't individuals, not really. Each one just a nerve ending in something larger. A mind behind them, distant and deliberate. A Crawler queen. One per world, maybe two. The rest moved when she told them to. Killed when she willed it. They didn't speak. Didn't signal. The queen thought, and they moved. Every drone part of the same mind—hers. Some described endless labour. Others spoke of experimentation. None of it was clean. None of it belonged in a galaxy that called itself civilized.

Yes, she might still be alive. But not untouched. Not whole.

Maybe Gwen had never even spoken my name, keeping it buried for safety—or out of spite. Either way, I doubted I'd be more than a ghost to her. And now I was supposed to drop from the sky and claim the title of father. Rescuer. Savior.

Gwen and I had been children pretending to be grown. We'd thought we loved each other Then; her father's rank and his dislike of me decided otherwise. This wouldn't be a reunion. It would be a shockwave. Even if by some miracle I got her out, .bringing her back—that would be the real war. What could I offer that slavery hadn't already broken?

But one thing was for sure, that to get there, I had to get through that Defined ship.

And to do that, I'd need every dirty trick I remembered—and a few I'd hoped never to use again.

It had been four years since the war ended. An uneasy quiet. The fleet scaled down. Ships decommissioned, weapons stored, heroes forgotten.

I glanced at the tactical display. The enemy ship was still closing. We'd bought time, but not enough. At this rate, they'd overtake us inside a day. Ephraim Virell was what they wanted, locked up tight in the brig under Morgan's possessive gaze. He'd kept me out of the loop on Virell's debrief. When I had more time, I'd be paying a visit.

An hour ago, Dakkar and I had briefed the section leaders. There was no more running. Not without engines, not without options. It was time to turn and fight.

The Defined captain would expect that. But even when you see the punch coming, you can't always block it. I was counting on surprise. Speed. Shock.

Everything was in place. We were done running. It was time to turn the tables.

Then Ariel spoke again. 'Captain. I'm registering a second signal.'

I turned to the console. 'Another Defined?'

'No,' she said. 'Different signature. No transponder. Low emissions. Tracking parallel from a distance.'

I watched the vector light up. Small. Fast. Probably stealthed. Too far to engage. Too close to ignore.

'They're not chasing,' I said.

'No,' Ariel replied. 'They're observing.'

I didn't need more enemies. I already had too many ghosts.

And I didn't like observers.

Chapter 4: Turn and Fight

There's a quiet that follows too many last stands — not peace, exactly, but a kind of surrender to the mathematics of survival. You stop believing in escape and start thinking about how to make the wreckage count. This was that kind of quiet.

The crew were ready. The stealth mines armed, the vectors mapped, Ariel and the ship aligned to a trajectory that might — if we were very precise, and luck remembered our names — work. A manoeuvre so delicate that a single miscalculation would scatter us across the void.

I'd been here before. Once, in the Chance System — outnumbered, outgunned, told to hold the line. We fought. We bled. And somehow, we endured.

I had seen too much of death to believe in victory. The Crawlers had taught me that lesson — in the silence of dead stations, in the reek of boarding corridors, in the stillness of a mining outpost where families lay where they'd fallen. Always the same pattern: their legions crushed us while the Queens, far behind the front, watched through the eyes of their spawn. Untouchable. Patient. Amused.

After Chance's Drift, Command ordered a ceasefire. The politicians called it diplomacy.

I called it betrayal. I took a splinter ship and put two nuclear charges into their Mother Ship myself.

Three weeks later I woke in a regeneration tank. They pinned a medal on my chest and handed me a discharge. A neat equation — a hero for the newsfeeds, a ghost for the fleet.

Even now, I wasn't sure if what I'd done was courage or failure in disguise. Some nights it depended on the whisky. Some nights it didn't. Knowing I had a daughter changed the weight of it. It gave the ghosts a name. It made the silence harder to bear.

But that was another war, and this was now. Distraction was death.

The mines were armed. The course set. Ariel and the ship had done their part. What came next would demand precision measured in heartbeats. If we were wrong by even a fraction, Freyja would fold herself inside-out. Someone had tried this once before; there was no record of their remains.

The pulsing of the threat warning lit the console crimson. We were out of time. I'd indulged in thinking about the past when I needed to focus on the present. Every second lost was a second closer to failure. It was time to get back to business.

The plan was for the Freyja to come to a crash stop, skipping across actual space as we slowed. I was going to bring her to a halt just ahead of where Ariel and Ship calculated the Defined would be, based on our speed and my earlier course shifts. The stealth mines would be spread through that corridor—silent, invisible, waiting.

I thumbed the activation codes on stealth mines one through four and launched them forward, each vanishing to warp speed.

'Gulls away. Ship, initiate tactics suite one-oh-one, one hundred and twenty seconds from this mark. Prepare all crew for emergency crash stop, priority Alpha.'

The bridge crew were already sealed in their gel fields; it was time I joined them.

With thirty seconds to go, my chair injected a surge of combat stimulants—liquid fire racing through my veins—and the containment collar released the gel. It flooded upward, dense and cold, swallowing me to the chin. My first breath hit like acid and ice at once, burning the throat before it oxygenated. The taste was metallic, electric. Then my lungs adapted, and I found the rhythm of it—harsh but steady.

'Just like Chance's Drift, Captain?' Ariel said.

'Shut up,' I muttered.

The universe clenched its fist.

Every molecule of air, of blood, of metal screamed together as the Freyja slammed through the skips. Five of them—each one a hammer blow through spacetime, each one flaying something vital off the hull, or off me. By the fifth, it felt like being punched through the spine by a god.

Silence followed. A silence that rang. Then:

The navigation display confirmed it: The Defined ship, already bleeding plasma, drifting just a few hundred thousand klicks off our bow. One of the stealth mines had found its mark before they'd even known we were there. Plasma spewed out of their starboard engine in a white cloud of vapor.

Only one stealth mine still survived, dancing back and forth as it made its way through the perimeter guard of the laser defences. It came within only a few hundred meters of the Defined ship when a close-action Gatling gun found it and blew it up in an incandescent ball of orange light.

We had sent them more than the stealth mines. In each of the skips into real space, the Freyja had fired a torpedo, each one calculated to end up in this sector of space. Two ship-killing torpedoes had reached the target intact. The first danced through the Defined ship's perimeter defences, heading straight for the engine core.

The pilot threw the ship into an emergency spin to shake the torpedo. It might have worked in a splinter craft; but a hull that size shouldn't have responded. Incredibly, it did. The warhead knifed past the port nacelle by a few feet before point-defence tore it apart in a sheet of light.

Impressive. Whoever had the chair on that bridge could really fly. Chaff and micro-munitions hunted the second torpedo as it drove in. A lance from the comms array found it at five hundred metres, and it went up in a hard, white flare.

Unable to speak through the gel, I tapped the keypad. 'Ship, status?'

'Heavy damage to their starboard engine. Life support at seventy percent. Multiple hits across all decks. Primary bridge is out—they're on auxiliary. Engine core fluctuating into the redline.'

A pulse from their main laser raked us. The Freyja lurched. Leela's voice cut in, tight. 'Hit on Engineering, Captain. They're walking shots onto the drives.'

I spat gel. 'Full power to the forward array. Take us in at maximum. Put us into a spin and keep Engineering on the dark side. I want the port nacelle—hit that and she blows.'

The Freyja surged, engines howling. The enemy filled the viewport—broken, burning, defiant. My finger hovered over the trigger.

'Firing solution locked,' Ship said. 'Permission to fire at will?'

I hesitated. One command and they'd vanish in light. If they'd been Crawlers, I'd have done it without a thought. But these were human—Defined or not.

'No,' I said. 'Break off.'

A beat of confusion from the AI. 'Confirm break—'

'Break off,' I repeated.

If they had been Crawlers, I would have finished them here and now. In the war there was no room for hesitation. I'd seen what they did to human slaves in the colonies they took. Mercy was a luxury we couldn't afford.

These weren't Crawlers. They were Defined. Some might even be old comrades. Letting them live would paint a target on my back for the rest of my life — a blood debt that never faded.

'Captain, incoming transmission from the Defined ship.'

'Accept it.'

The screen filled with a face: a Wolven, long, predatory features and amber eyes reflecting the pulsing red alert behind him. Smoke curled through the air. 'I am Kithlan 16, captain of the Defined ship Predator. Unknown vessel — I command your surrender in the Polity's name. Return the prisoner.'

'Ship, is he seeing me?'

'No, Captain. I assumed you'd prefer anonymity.'

'Scramble my voice. No video.'

I spoke. 'Kithlan 16 of the Predator: I am the captain of this ship. I could have killed you and your crew, but I did not. By the code of the Defined, this blood debt is settled.'

The Wolven's eyes narrowed. 'The code applies only in surrender. We do not surrender. Return the prisoner.'

'Then we have nothing to discuss. You fought well. There's no honour in slaughter today. But if you follow me, I will destroy you.'

Kithlan leaned forward, amber gaze boring into the screen. 'Then it is I who will kill you, captain without a name. Tell me — how shall I know my enemy?'

I hesitated. Then: 'Call me Knife, Kithlan 16. We will meet again.' I cut the transmission.

A whisper in my ear — Ariel's voice, soft as breath. 'Honourable and foolish, Captain. But right. Perhaps they are wrong about you.'

I cut the transmission.

'Ship, stand weapons down. Set course for Callista.'

I clicked the safety back into the weapons cradle. The war was over. The Crawlers might call me a murderer, but they never understood the difference.

Behind us, the Predator was already falling away. We had a head start. Callista waited.

The second contact — the ghost we'd caught on long-range scan — stayed in the back of my head. No transponder. No follow-up ping. Nothing since. Long enough to be forgotten.

But it's never the blade you see coming that kills you.

It's the one in the dark. Waiting.

Chapter 5: Ephraim Virell

Men like Virell aren't bombs — they're venom. You don't defuse them; you survive the dose and hope it isn't fatal. He stank of the Syndicate. They left a mark that no shower could wash away.

It was thanks to them I even had a path to my daughter. The irony bit deep. I'd spent half a career fighting their kind, only to need them now. I hated the slow poison they represented — the compromise, the quiet rot that eats through ideals — but the path was there, fragile though it was.

Get Virell to Callista. Get the information on my daughter.

Maybe find a crack in the wall. A lead. A chance.

I stood outside the brig, watching him sit with his head in his hands. The steel walls hummed with containment fields. I nodded to the guard. DNA scan, retinal ping, the narrow door sliding open, the soft hum as it sealed behind me.

Virell looked up, that slow, uncoiling smile spreading across his face.

'Mr Rakkan. I was beginning to think you didn't enjoy my company. Whereas your friend Morgan — he can't seem to leave me alone.'

I smiled back, thin as wire. 'Morgan's responsible for security. He likes his cages tight.'

He rose a little, studying me. Tall, lean, the same pale eyes as his clone Hela. Once, maybe handsome. Now he looked like a cornered animal — cunning, exhausted, still waiting for the right moment to bite.

I lifted a hand in a casual gesture, fingers brushing the underside of his seat. The magnetic scrambler clicked into place. Ariel was already feeding the recorder a decoy track.

Virell arched an eyebrow. 'A scrambler, Jero Rakkan? Are you my liberator or my executioner?'

'Could be both.' I kept my tone neutral. 'Right now, I'm the man your clone hired to bring you home. Call it a humanitarian mission.'

He laughed — sudden, sharp, the sound of glass breaking. 'She told you? How interesting.' His amusement thinned to something colder. 'She's a devious creature, isn't she? I always feared I'd been made too duplicitous for my own good. No surprise she inherited a few of my traits.'

Hela had been grown in an organic womb, watched by a paediatric AI from conception — designed, not born. The kind of indulgence only the powerful could afford.

Virell's smile flattened. 'Whatever waits for me on Callista, Captain, it won't be humanitarian.'

I met his gaze. 'I might pity you — if you hadn't betrayed humanity.'

The words hung between us. 'Tell me, Virell. Did you really sell us out to the Crawlers?'

Something flickered in his eyes, faint as a pulse of static. 'We were betrayed, yes,' he said softly. 'But not by me.' He leaned back, calm again. 'The real traitors aren't in cages, Rakkan. They're rich. That's how you know who won.'

He held my stare for a long time, then exhaled slowly. 'The war didn't end because we won, Captain. It ended because our war stopped mattering.'

He traced two fingers across the table, sketching invisible lines. 'The Crawlers pulled fleets from contested systems. Consolidated their reach. Abandoned worlds they'd once bled for. Not because we frightened them — because something else was rising behind them.'

I said nothing. The hum of the field filled the pause between us.

'They weren't retreating,' Virell went on. 'They were fortifying. You don't consolidate like that unless you're desperate. Unless you're preparing your last move.'

He leaned forward, eyes bright with the thrill of the lecture. 'Their research shifted — mass-field dynamics, exotic energy states, stellar-core manipulation. Work so far beyond us that the Polity's best minds could only guess at it. The Crawlers were gambling their survival on something they couldn't control.'

His voice dropped, the performance stripped away. 'You don't stake a civilisation on desperate science unless the knife's already at your throat.'

I studied him. 'And you know this how?'

He smiled again, faint and satisfied. 'Because I helped them buy the materials. Through intermediaries, of course. War leaves gaps. The Syndicate fills them.'

There it was — the old stench of profit.

'What were they building against, Virell?'

He shrugged. 'Something they feared more than us.'

The silence that followed was heavy enough to feel through the deck plating. I'd seen what fear looked like in Crawlers — cold precision, never panic. The idea that they'd been running from someone else unsettled me more than I wanted to admit.

Virell must have seen it in my eyes. 'You're starting to understand,' he murmured. 'That's why they made peace, Captain. Not out of mercy, but time. They needed it. And now they have it.'

He sat back, satisfied. 'You'll need me before this is over. I know the real map. I know what's already moving across it.'

Virell's tone lost all trace of amusement. 'The Crawlers' withdrawal was camouflage, Captain. They weren't conceding ground; they were shaping it. Entire moons dismantled, fleets gutted for heavy elements, suns stripped for fuel. Every shipment I brokered converged on one system—Eden.'

I let the silence stretch.

'They are building a device,' he said at last. 'A lattice of gravitic regulators and containment spires—vast enough to anchor a singularity. The Syndicate assumed it was infrastructure. I recognised intent.'

I kept my voice even. 'Intent for what?'

His eyes lifted to mine. 'A weapon. Controlled collapse. A black-hole engine that can be aimed like a blade. The Crawlers intend to manufacture gravity itself—condense it, direct it, release it. One discharge could erase a fleet. Perhaps more.'

The words hung like radiation. 'You're telling me they're building a black-hole weapon.'

Virell inclined his head. 'Not merely a weapon—a deterrent. Whatever hunts them in the dark, they mean to meet it with extinction. And if humanity drifts too near, we'll vanish with the rest.'

The hum of the field shivered through the deck. 'You're certain.'

He smiled thinly. 'Because I handled the manifests. Because I saw the power yields requested. No civilisation demands that energy unless it intends to end something greater than itself.'

He leaned back, measured, unhurried. 'You see now why they accepted peace. They needed time—to finish the lattice, to calibrate the lens. The armistice bought them years, and we handed it to them.'

I stared at him, the taste of metal in my mouth. 'And you helped them.'

'Commerce, Captain,' he said softly. 'My people always find a market. Even for annihilation.'

For a long moment neither of us spoke.

Then, almost gently, he added, 'You'll go there. Eden calls to those who've lost what can't be buried. Duty, guilt—take your pick. The gravity's the same.'

I turned to leave. His eyes followed me, calm, unblinking. 'Call it whatever you wish, Captain,' he said. 'I call it inevitability.' The brig door slid open before I touched it.

Morgan stood in the corridor, jaw tight. 'Damn it, Rakkan. I told you to notify me before you spoke to the prisoner.'

I kept walking. 'Consider yourself notified.'

He moved to block me. 'You think you're untouchable because Hela indulges you.'

'Not untouchable,' I said. 'Just hard to reach.'

For a heartbeat the corridor hummed with nothing but air-recyclers. Then he looked away first.

'Whatever that thing told you, don't let it in your head. Men like Virell corrode from the inside.'

I brushed past him. 'Then you'll recognise the symptoms.'

The door sealed behind me with a hiss.

THE ENGINEERING DECK ran under half-light, air thick with coolant. Leela was half-buried in a conduit, sparks flickering around her boots.

'Cap'n,' she said without looking up, 'tell me you didn't throttle him. Morgan's chewing bulkheads.'

'Not today.'

Dakkar stood by the diagnostic console, arms folded, posture calm and commanding. He didn't waste words.

'Then I'll assume there's a reason you risked it.'

'There is,' I said. I told them what Virell had revealed — the construction at Eden, the weapon that could tear gravity itself apart.

Thorne listened in silence, expression unreadable. When I finished he said, 'If it's true, Captain, the Crawlers are preparing for extinction.'

Leela straightened, wiping her hands on a rag. 'Lovely. So we're flying straight for the apocalypse, are we?'

'Eventually,' I said. 'We need repairs first. Callista.'

Dakkar's voice cut across hers — steady, controlled.

'You're thinking of confronting this alone.'

'I'm thinking of verifying the threat before anyone else decides what to do about it.'

He studied me for a long moment. 'You've been right before when command was wrong. But you're not bulletproof, Jero. Take the right people, use the right caution. You owe that much to the ones who still follow you.'

The weight of his words settled deeper than I wanted to admit.

Thorne nodded slightly. 'Where you go, Captain, I go. That hasn't changed.'

Leela exhaled, muttering, 'Fine. Just try not to break my engines again, or we'll all be cosmic dust.'

Dakkar's mouth twitched in what might have been approval. 'Then it's settled. Callista first. Then Eden.'

Leela grimaced and looked at me accusingly 'The engines won't make Callista. That last manoeuvre finished them.'

I nodded, but the words tasted bitter. Callista wasn't just repairs and supplies. It was payment. The Syndicate wanted Virell alive, and in return they'd give me what I needed — a lead. A trace of where they'd taken her.

I looked around the room — a Defined, two humans, all still standing after too many battles and too little certainty.

'Set course for Demos. It's on the way. Anushka will fix us up and we'll be in Callista in a week,' I said. 'The Freyja's not done yet.'

The deck trembled as the drives came online, the sound deep and alive. No one spoke, but for the first time in a while, we were moving toward something that might still matter.

I took the next watch. I was too keyed up to rest. The bridge was mostly dark. Only the star lines ahead broke the silence — long threads of white and gold drawn through the warp stream.

Ariel appeared in the glass beside me, her reflection faint, like light caught in water. 'You stayed on the bridge again,' she said.

'I like the quiet,' I replied.

'You don't like the quiet,' she said. 'You endure it.'

I almost smiled. 'Careful, Ariel. You're starting to sound like you know me.'

'Pattern recognition,' she said. 'But I'm learning context.'

She stood beside my reflection, studying the same impossible distance. 'You push against impossible odds,' she said softly. 'It's what you were made for.'

I looked at her. 'And you?'

'I was made to follow orders,' she said. 'But I think I prefer purpose.'

For a long moment, neither of us spoke. The hum of the drives filled the space between us — the sound of something alive, still moving forward.

'Callista won't be easy,' I said at last.

'Nothing worth surviving ever is,' she replied. Then, after a beat: 'I'll help you get what you need there. No Syndicate interference. No surprises.'

It wasn't a promise — not exactly — but it sounded like one.

I nodded once. 'Then we'll call that trust, for now.'

Her outline flickered faintly, a shimmer of approval. 'For now,' she said.

The warp stream brightened, and for the first time in months, the silence didn't feel like solitude.

My route still lay through Callista, but as Leela had reminded me loud and often, The Freyja had other ideas. She needed a shipyard if we were going to fix the Warp Drive—and she needed it soon.

Whatever the next few weeks held, I knew they wouldn't be dull. But first we needed somewhere to rest, regroup, and breathe.

Somewhere off the grid.

I had the perfect spot.

A grey area. Where the Polity held sway—but just barely. Where smugglers and opportunists moved in shadows. Where questions were dangerous and answers came at a price. Demos Station.

But while I was deciding who to trust, out near Demos, a family mining crew on a ship called the Jenny Lynne was about to run out of time. I wouldn't hear about it until later—but by then, the blood would already have been spilled. What happened to that crew was the beginning of a bigger story that would threaten my ship's destruction and the failure of our mission.

BETWEEN WALLS

Morgan waited until the hum of the engines steadied. The corridor lights dimmed to night cycle. He keyed the brig access, stepping inside.

Virell hadn't moved. The containment field washed his face in pale blue light.

'You were right,' Morgan said quietly.

Virell smiled — that patient, knowing curve. 'About what, Lieutenant?'

'About him. He doesn't see it coming.'

'Of course he doesn't. He's still chasing ghosts. Men like Rakkan need purpose more than they need truth.'

Morgan folded his arms. 'You said Callista was the next move.'

Virell inclined his head. 'Stay the course. Hela thinks she commands you; let her. By the time we reach port, I'll have what I need.'

'And after that?'

'After that,' Virell said, eyes gleaming, 'the captain will take us to Eden himself.'

Morgan hesitated. 'He won't do it for you.'

Virell's smile thinned. 'No. He'll do it for her.'

The brig lights flickered, the hum deepened. Morgan turned away. Behind him, Virell sat very still — a man in a cage that already believed it was open.

Chapter 6: Out in The Black

Shannon Lynne clipped her tether to the outer air-lock and powered her magnetic boots while the cycle counted down. Above her, the stars hung sharp and endless, scattered like cold sparks across the dark. Somewhere beyond that black lay Demos Station—two days at low warp. They'd swing by on the way back to Callista for fuel. The Jenny Lynne didn't like anything faster than warp two; push her harder and the drives started to sulk.

The boots gave a low hum as they gripped the hull. Her suit was old—older than she was—patched and sealed so many times the fabric felt like stitched-together memory. The gloves were loose at the fingertips, smoothed by years of use, and the oxygen tank pressed heavy and familiar against her back. Inside the helmet the air smelled of metal, old fabric, and a trace of oil.

It had been her mother's backup suit. She told herself it was just equipment, but the truth was simpler: the suit steadied her. It had kept her mother alive through storms and micrometeors and a hundred small malfunctions. Wearing it made Shannon feel part of that long, stubborn line of survival.

The oxygen icon blinked a tired orange—fifteen minutes left. When the suit was new, the warning would have flashed scarlet. Now the calibration was old, half-reliable, like most things on the Jenny Lynne.

She paused in the air-lock and looked out across the asteroid's turning surface. Rock 167.87.02—three klicks long, scarred, and spinning slow. Craters caught pockets of ice that glittered in the faint starlight. A wanderer knocked from its orbit ages ago. Dangerous, but rich. The Spectro-scans had promised heavy metals buried deep—enough to make this run worth every risk.

Her father had bought the claim from a Chancer, one of those data-miners who traded in guesses. For once, the guess had been gold. They'd worked the yards for months, saving every credit, betting everything on this haul. If it paid, they could finally refit the Jenny Lynne: new hull plating, clean filters—maybe even a jump drive.

Her brothers were already off-shift. Her father stayed on the bridge, watching the ore loaders bite into rock. As if hearing her thoughts, his voice crackled in her ear.

'Shan, watch your oxygen. My readout says twelve minutes left.'

She sighed. He fussed about things like that. But she had to admit he had a point. In old suits, you never knew if the gauges were telling the truth, especially when the tanks ran low. Since she was old enough to float a wrench, the rule had been drilled into her: double-check everything. Out here, one mistake didn't just kill you—it killed the people who came looking.

A moment's inattention had killed her mother, Jenny. Moisture in the electrics on a drilling rig, a short that ran through the comms spool to her helmet. It had been quick. But Shannon missed her every day.

'Okay, got it. I was about to come in anyway.'

The air-lock tell-tale glowed green, showing vacuum beyond. She set her gloved hand on the handle and let it rest there for a moment. She hesitated, turning slightly to look outward at the wilderness of stars surrounding her.

It was dangerous to linger like this, to stare too long into the abyss. She and her brothers had grown up on stories of perfectly sane, experienced spacers suddenly panicking at the sheer vastness of it all. The blackness could swallow you. It could strip you down to nothing. That was why they always warned you: don't stop and look. Don't give it time to get inside your head.

Somewhere behind her and to the right, Callista floated—a brilliant blue jewel against the void. A place teeming with life, with air so thick it pressed against your skin. Under her feet, on the other side of the rock, was the pale red glow of their star, Sol—the distant birthplace of humanity.

Family legend said that before the Diaspora, they had been farmers in a place called Donegal, back on Earth. The old vids showed green fields, rolling hills, and a sky that rained water. Real water, falling from the clouds.

It sounded like one of those places the religious nuts from Harmony claimed was waiting for you when you died. But Shannon wanted to feel the rain while she was still alive.

A flicker in the sky pulled her from the thought. One of the stars was moving.

She froze. It wasn't the first time she'd seen something strange. A few weeks back, near Demos, she'd caught a dark shape slipping through the void. No beacon. No nav lights. Running cold, fast—and outbound. Not toward Callista, not toward Demos Station. Straight into deep space.

She'd watched it for a long time, trying to decide if it was even human. The angles were wrong. Asymmetrical. Brutal. She'd seen pictures of Crawler ships. They looked the same.

And now—another one. A distant light sliding across the black where no ship should be.

There was nothing out there. No stations. No colonies. Nothing to chase but the long dark.

People didn't run into it unless something was chasing them. Or they were hunting someone.

She felt the hairs rise on her arms despite the suit. The display flickered once, briefly, as if the signal itself had flinched. Then it steadied again.

'Dad,' she said quietly. 'You seeing this?'

People didn't run into the dark unless something was chasing them.

But this one felt human.

'Dad?' Her voice stayed steady, but her fingers tightened on the airlock handle. 'It's Shan. I can see an incoming ship—coming in fast from the direction of Callista.'

Silence. Then his voice, sharper now: 'Say again?'

Her breath rasped too loud in her helmet. 'It's close. Too close. How the hell did we miss it?'

Normally you could spot a ship's drive signature days before it arrived. Even the smallest hauler left an energy wake. But this one had crept up like a shadow—no beacon, no signature trail. The only way that was possible was if they'd cut engines after an initial burn and drifted in under momentum.

Or it was using stealth tech. Military-grade.

Her pulse quickened. It could be a patrol ship from Callista, running silent. A claim jumper looking to muscle in.

Or pirates.

'Get inside. Now.' Her father's voice carried the edge she rarely heard.

She didn't argue. She hauled the hatch open, boots clanking on metal, and swung herself into the lock. The door sealed behind her, air hissing in. Pressure equalized. Her helmet display blinked green. She tore it off and drew a breath of stale air that smelled of ozone and sweat.

Her father was still in her ear. 'Shan, what did you see? Details.'

'Fast mover. Minimal signature. Coming in dark—no beacon, no ID ping.'

A pause. 'That's not good.'

Outside, in the endless dark, the ship kept coming.

'Shan, seal your airlock and get up to the bridge,' he ordered. 'Switch to the family channel. They might not be friendly.'

He was talking louder now. That meant he was worried.

She tapped the override, switching to the encrypted local net. 'Family channel confirmed.'

Her father's voice came again, tighter. 'Neal, get to the lifeboat—power it up and strap in.

He went quiet for a moment—probably muting the line to argue with Neal. That alone told her how bad this was. He'd never send her little brother to the lifeboat unless he thought they might not make it.

'Donal, get up on the plasma cannon. If they're pirates, we might need it. I'm locking out all airlocks except Shannon's. Shan, how long before you're through?'

Shannon glanced at the tell-tale. 'Normal in three minutes.'

'Good. Password-seal it when you leave. Time to let our visitors know we've seen them.'

Over the external channel, Kel Lynne's voice carried — calm, measured, a miner's voice forced into diplomacy. 'Unidentified ship, this is Kel Lynne of the independent mining vessel Jenny Lynne. We welcome visitors, but this is a registered claim and the mineral rights belong to us.'

They waited. The dark shape ahead grew larger, sliding across the starfield. Too big for a hauler. Too deliberate for a stray. Kel's tone stayed even. 'We can also defend ourselves. I suggest you alter course to avoid unfortunate consequences.'

By the time Shannon had stripped off the helmet and shoved her arms into her ship overalls, the intruder filled the viewport. It looked like a predator carved from scrap — all welded plates and broken geometry. She grabbed her boots and launched herself toward the bridge, each footfall ringing through the ladder well.

Kel spoke again, firm now. 'Unidentified ship, if you are transmitting, we are not receiving you. This is your final warning. We are armed and will open fire in thirty seconds.'

She hadn't realized she was counting until the last five seconds bled away — and a voice answered, smooth and amused.

'Captain Lynne. My name is Cisco Dante, and my ship is Kiss the Blade. Well done for being so brave. Yes, we are pirates. You can see my ship now — Type-2 destroyer. Old, but everything still works, especially the weapons.'

A pause, almost courteous.

'I'll give you a choice. Fire, and I take your ship and kill everyone aboard. Don't fire, and I let you live. Choose wisely. Dante out.'

Almost at once, splinter craft spat from the destroyer, falling toward the Jenny Lynne like a scatter of knives.

'Dad? I have them in my sights. Do I fire?' Donal's voice shook over the intercom.

Kel hesitated — too long. 'No. Stand it down. We can't win this. Close down and—'

The sentence broke into static. The ship lurched. Impact alarms screamed. Air howled through ruptured seams.

Then Dante's voice returned, soft and savouring. 'That bang you just heard? Your plasma cannon. Most of it, anyway. And your gunner...' He whistled, low and appreciative. 'I've seen what a man looks like when a turret detonates from the inside. Not pretty. But I do love the sound they make.'

Silence hit like gravity. Shannon froze, every breath a knife. Donal was gone.

Shannon's world folded in on itself. The bridge screamed around her and the sound didn't belong to the alarms — it belonged to a hole where Donal had been. Her legs went rubber. For a long, stupid second she just stood there, breath shredding on the inside, fingers slack on the hatch. The universe had become a single, bright absence.

Then her father's voice cut across the channel, precise and unforgiving. 'They've breached the starboard airlock. Five. Armed.' He names things the way you name fire — so people know how to run from it. 'Neal—lifeboat doors. Kill engines. Do not engage.'

The command locked something behind Shannon's ribs. Panic surged and she kept it there, folded into the part of her that could still tie a knot, still seal a hatch. It felt like betrayal — the body wanting to crumble while the rest of the family needed her to be whole. She hated the way grief could be so private and so noisy at once.

Dante's voice crawled over the open channel, amused. 'I love the first taste of fear. Say something, Lynne. Tell me you understand.'

For a beat she couldn't make her mouth work. The bridge hummed; crew voices blurred into distance. Donal's laugh, a stupid song about zero-G dives, stabbed through memory and made her throat close.

Her father answered instead, flat and hard as scraped metal. 'Survive. Then we make them pay.'

The words were order and lifeline. They pulled her upright. She swallowed the panic until it was small and workable. Map — lifeboat, aft service crawl, the maintenance shafts. Move. Donal wouldn't want clumsy courage. He'd want them alive.

Shannon moved like a machine stitched together from grief and training. She slipped into the maintenance void behind the aft bulkhead, boots silent, breath measured. The world had narrowed to metal and shadow and the slow, furious planning of someone who would not let a death be the last thing anyone remembered about her brother.

Survive now. Payback later.

Let Them Whisper to Their Gods

Recovered Transmission // Ark Flagship Fist of Salvation
Location: Syrinthi Home System

Beneath our sanctified hull, the Ark murmurs with consecrated fire. The Hunger rests—but not in peace.

We came as wind without breath, as flame without shadow.

The Syrinthi are ash; their queens silenced, their fleets unmade. Their moons now feed the Conversion Wombs. Their cries are preserved—every note of extinction catalogued in the Vault of Song.

From their memory we took the next name on the path: Human.

But between their cradle and our light stands one final veil.

A world still held by the many-limbed who called themselves Crawlers.

They fortify what remains—Eden, the hive-world at the edge of our dominion.

They guard it not for victory, but for fear.

Fist Supreme Lord Tharim spread her wings in benediction. High Acolyte Veris gave the chant:

'Three systems remain. Then the untested.'

Across the fleet we answered as one:

'The next unconsumed names itself Human.

Their garden lies beyond the hive. Their prayer rises toward us.'

Tharim lowered her blade.

'Let them pray to their garden.

Let them whisper to their gods.

We are coming.'

Chapter 7: Demos Station

There's nothing colder than a pissed-off engineer—except maybe the warp core she's not fixing for you.

I watched the holo tank display glumly as the Freyja limped along at Warp one. Chief Engineer McNair was sulking down on the engineering deck, her clipped responses and the occasional loud clang of tools making it abundantly clear who was to blame. I'd known Leela a long time. There was no point in arguing that I didn't have a choice, and that if I hadn't pushed the ship the way I had, we would all be captive or dead by now. She was very attached to her engines.

I went down to engineering to make peace with her about it. Leela was elbow-deep in conduit housing, scowling at the warp calibration suite like it had personally insulted her.

'You ever pull a Hail Mary?' she asked without looking up.

A Hail Mary. This was not a good time for her to bring THAT up. I leaned against the bulkhead. 'Not if I can help it.'

She snorted. 'That's not a no.'

'Dump all warp energy into one burst? Microsecond at uncalibrated warp speeds?' I shook my head. 'That's not a maneuver, Leela. That's a prayer.'

She glanced over; grease smeared on her cheek. 'It's engine abuse.'

'Also true.'

She ran a finger along the coolant housing like she was soothing a wounded animal. 'Engines like these don't survive a Hail Mary. Pilots maybe. Ships? Not likely.'

I nodded. 'That's why it's the last page in the playbook.'

She muttered, 'Should've torn it out.'

I looked at her. 'You have to be the one left alive to do that, Leela. And if it's the only play we have... you know Dakkar and I are going to take it.'

She didn't argue. Just gave a short nod—tight, reluctant. But I saw it in her eyes.

She hated it. And I loved that she fought so hard to keep us going.

I had tried very hard to find patience. Patience had never been my strong suit. As a captain, it was something I had worked hard at over the years, but it still didn't come naturally. I bit my lip and endured Leela's sub-vocal grumbling, her broad Purgatory accent making her complaints even more colorful.

She had gone on about the systematic damage to the warp core, about the wantonly destructive decisions made by certain bridge officers who didn't appreciate the importance of engines. Eventually, I snapped at her, and she had stormed off the bridge. Two days later, things were still a little awkward. I was still working out how to apologize without inviting another lecture.

Even at warp one, the Freyja was still a force to be reckoned with. The long-range scanners showed no signs of pursuit. Stealthed ships might be closer, but the Freyja carried a stealth-detection array newer than anything else in the fleet. There were no ships following us.

The first thing to do was fix the Freyja's engines. Everything depended on that, and I knew just the place to do it. During the war, the human Navy had rapidly militarized any remaining shipyards that the Crawlers hadn't overrun. The ones closest to invaded space had received the most attention at first, but slowly, old commercial yards were brought up to scratch. By the middle of the war, all sorts of yards could dock and repair a hub ship up to destroyer size.

The Freyja was a Generation five Corsair-class hub ship, substantially refitted with what had once been new engines. I gave a brief nod, half a wince.at the memory of Leela's lectures. Corsairs were a class below destroyers, carrying three splinter ships where a destroyer might carry five or six.

This sector had seen some heavy fighting. A major fleet action had taken place twenty light years away; at a system they called The Dagger. The aftermath still lingered—scattered debris fields, derelict ships drifting aimlessly. The human Navy had won the battle, pushing the war into another sector.

The shipyard at Demos, a family-owned facility that had operated for thirty years, had returned to obscurity.

Dakkar glanced over from the navigation console. 'So, we made it.'

I grimaced and scratched my ear. 'Yes, despite the terrible things I did to the engines.'

Dakkar just smiled. He knew what Leela was like. 'When was the last time you spoke to Anushka?'

'It's been a couple of years. She owes me a favor, though. Do you remember when the armistice was declared? We had that cache of equipment the Crawlers had looted, stashed on that asteroid.'

'Yeah. There was some useful stuff in there. Not military, though, right? Old commercial parts.'

'That's right. Well, when we got the order to come in for demobilization, I might have forgotten to tell anyone about it back in the fleet and sent the file to Anushka with the coordinates. She was grateful.'

Dakkar nodded. 'That's good. But Jero, we need to be careful. The Syndicate is still our ally, but we can't be too cautious. We have to be careful who we trust.'

'Don't worry. Weapons stay hot until we're sure.'

I looked at the shipyard ahead. The Freyja's threat detection system had already picked out a plasma cannon guarding the main approach, with several laser emplacements lighting up red in the holo tank. Clearly, Ani had installed a few surprises of her own in case her guests turned out to be unruly. It was time to say hello.

'Demos harbor master, this is DSV Freyja. Captain Jero Rakkan commanding.'

The response came immediately. 'Receiving your transmission, Freyja. We've been watching you for some time. Looks like your engines need a little help.'

I tried not to think about what Leela was saying in the engine room.

'Exactly what we're here for, Demos. Is Anushka Zvereva on watch? I'd like to pay my respects.'

'You can talk to her after you dock, Captain. She's indisposed right now—handling a situation that requires her personal attention. Patch your navigation system into ours, and we'll take you in from there.'

I exhaled slowly, watching the holo tank as the docking coordinates updated. The Freyja's engines sputtered slightly as we adjusted course, a not-so-subtle protest from the warp core. Leela was probably watching the power fluctuations with murder in her eyes.

'Alright,' I muttered to myself. 'Let's see what Ani's been up to.'

'Sorry, Demos, I'd like to take her in myself. We've taken some damage. Happy if you put us wherever you like, just send over the coordinates.'

There was a long pause at the other end. 'Well, Captain, that's not our usual protocol. Neighbors around here had been unpredictable since the war. But Ani said you were OK. Come in on Dock six. Sending coordinates. Over.'

A set of numbers flickered into the holo tank. I checked the location, and my jaw tightened. Dock six was directly opposite a guided missile array, the stealth detection system had only just picked up. Fresh military-grade tech. That meant someone had deep pockets—and recent experience in a war zone.

'Demos base, thanks for your understanding. On approach. Freyja out.'

I cut the channel and let out a slow breath. Ani's word carried weight, but that didn't mean this wasn't a setup. The Syndicate had allies, sure, but friends? That was a different thing altogether.

I eased the Freyja in, feathering the thrusters, keeping an eye on the docking clamps as they cycled shut. The ship gave a slight shudder as she locked into place. Ani and I had better still be on good terms. Without her agreement, Freyja wouldn't leave this station.

I secured the ship and powered down the sub-light engines. I pinged Dakkar and Leela to meet me at the airlock, then detoured to my cabin. A fresh tunic, blaster at my hip. I didn't expect trouble, but trouble had a way of finding me, anyway.

When I reached the airlock, they were already there. The pressurization cycle began. Dakkar leaned in, voice low.

'Laser capacitors are fully charged,' Dakkar reported. 'Leela left them in maintenance mode—we can spin them up inside two minutes. Dallas has a tactical team on standby, and Virell's in the brig with Morgan.' He allowed himself a faint smirk. I nodded. Neither of us trusted Virell or Morgan.

The airlock cycled open. A tall man in a dark-grey jumpsuit stood on the dock, four security officers behind him, assault rifles held in a way that suggested they knew how to use them.

'Captain Rakkan, I'm Alex Tavarez. Security officer.' He clasped my hand in a firm grip, eyes flicking to the blaster on my hip. 'Been a while since you docked here, Captain. We have rules about weapons now. Much easier for everyone if you hand them over.'

I met his gaze, then let my eyes drift over the security team. 'And if I say no?'

A long pause. Tavarez didn't blink. 'Then you stay on your ship. We're too far out to play games with unauthorized firepower. We've had visitors before who thought they could take what they wanted. They don't visit anymore.'

I exhaled through my nose. 'Makes sense.' I unclipped the blaster and handed it over, watching as Tavarez ejected the power cell and inspected the charge level before passing it to one of his men. 'Look after it. I'm attached.'

Out of the corner of my eye, I saw Dakkar do the same, handing over his laser pistol. One of the security men stepped toward Leela.

She folded her arms. 'Got no weapons except colorful language, sweetheart.'

Tavarez didn't look amused. 'We'll need to search you, Miss.'

Leela tilted her head, slow and deliberate. 'Try it, and I'll break every finger on that hand.'

One guard took half a step forward, but Tavarez held up a hand, studying her. I intervened before things got messy.

'Leela's from a heavy-gravity world. She could do it. I vouch for her. We're here to do business, fix our drive, and leave.'

Tavarez considered that, his mouth a thin line.

Before he could decide, a familiar voice cut through the tension. 'Jero Rakkan, still breathing after all these years!'

A dark-haired woman in an azure ship suit strode toward us, arms outstretched. 'Come here, let me give you a kiss. And Dakkar! I should have known you two would still be stirring up trouble.'

I grinned, embracing her. 'Ani, still charming your way through the black?'

She turned to Leela. 'I don't think we've met.'

I gestured. 'Leela McNair, Chief Engineer.'

Ani's smile widened. 'I've read your diagnostics on the Corsair retrofits. Smart work.'

She waved off the security team. 'Sorry about the weapons policy. Had a couple of my people killed early on, so we tightened things up. Can't be too careful.'

The guards hesitated, then moved off. Tavarez lingered, eyes on Ani. She gave a small shake of her head—warning or habit, I couldn't tell. Either way, the real conversation was only beginning.

But she was already taking my arm and leading me down the corridor. 'Have you eaten? I traded yard time for some beef from a freighter outward bound from Panoply—lovely stuff. No? Come up to my office, I've got that whisky you like.'

A service lift took us to the control room, where a small office had a commanding view of the shipyard. Ani dropped into a battered chair and poured whisky into four glasses, sliding them across the desk. 'Jero, it must be what, four years? What have you been up to all this time?'

I took a sip of the whisky. 'In hospital for the first six months, getting fixed up after Chance's Drift. Then, just knocking around for a while.'

'Yes, congratulations on your Cross of Honor. We weren't sure if they were going to hang you or promote you.'

I smiled and said nothing. Eventually, she smiled too and changed the subject. 'That's a nice ship you have there. A Corsair-class hub ship, one of the newer ones. You used to drive one of those in Chance's Drift, didn't you? I didn't have you pegged for a sentimentalist.'

'I liked the basic design. Flexible, you know? The Freyja has a few augmentations, though.' I took another sip of whisky. 'So, Ani, I was glad to find you still open for business. The Freyja has a drive problem that needs a full refit. Leela has the details.'

Leela passed over the data pad with an accusing glance in my direction. 'How long?' I asked.

Ani exhaled through her nose, fingers tapping a slow rhythm on the desk. 'With shifts working back-to-back, I can probably get you out of here in a couple of weeks.'

I shook my head. 'Ani, it needs to be days rather than weeks. I've got a little trouble following me.'

She studied me for a long moment, then sighed. 'Well, Jero, things haven't changed since the war. Must be something about you.' A ghost of a smile played at the corner of her mouth. She leaned back, eyes half-lidded, like a cat weighing its options. 'Nothing's impossible with the right application of money.'

She held up a hand before I could speak. 'And don't get me wrong, I haven't forgotten that stash of parts you put me on to. Came in real handy after the war. Couldn't get parts for a million credits back then.'

Her gaze sharpened. 'The only way this happens fast is if we rip out the whole warp core and patch in a new one. No half-measures. No finesse. Just a straight swap. You're lucky I've got the parts, but it's going to cost a fortune—even at sweetheart rates.'

I spread my hands. 'Then give me a number, Ani.'

She didn't answer immediately. Just wrote a number on a scrap of paper and slid it across the desk. I looked, then gave a low whistle. 'If that's a sweetheart deal, I'd hate to be on your bad side. But fine. Fix my engines in four days, and it's yours.'

She drew a sharp breath. 'Four days, he says. Four days—like I'm a magician.' A low curse escaped her before she flipped on the comm link.

'Fredo, it's me. Get your team ready. We've got a big one. Big pay, but it needs to be done fast. You'll be working with their Chief Engineer, McNair... Yeah, well, you're not the only engineer who knows their job. She's good. Ex-fleet. Just deal with it.' She cut the connection and shook her head.

Then she locked eyes with me. 'Jero, we need to move now. I need full access to your drive, and you'll have to disable the firewall.'

I took a slow sip of whisky. 'If Leela's happy, I'm happy.' I set the glass down with a quiet clink. 'Do what you need to do.'

On the way back to the ship, I keyed my comm. Ariel, did you hear that?'

Ariel's voice came through the grid, dry and precise. 'Firewall-handover protocol active.' A pause.

'It makes the Freyja vulnerable.'

I stopped in the corridor, watching her silhouette flicker faintly in the ship's HUD reflection—always watching, always present.

'Yes, it does,' I said.

Another pause. Longer this time.

'To external actors?' she asked.

'To everyone,' I replied. 'Including you.'

A beat of silence. Then:

'We will monitor.'

I didn't reply. I just kept walking.

The Freyja sat outside the viewport, tethered to the station, a long plasma scar running down her side. She looked like a predator, chained and exposed, surrounded by smiling hosts with too many secrets.

And all it would take was one signal—one crack in the hull—and we'd be nothing but salvage.

MORGAN – SECURITY COMMS. ROOM, FREYJA.
IN THE COLD DARK BETWEEN the Freyja and the stars, a shadow waited.

A stealth skimmer—no transponder, no emissions, blacker than vacuum. It rode the edge of Demos Station's sensor envelope, drifting without thrust, skin laced with scatter-foil. Inside, the single crew member opened a channel. One handshake code only four people in the Polity knew. One reply. It was a Polity ship, and the Polity believed that Morgan was their man.

Lieutenant Commander Jason Morgan. A deep cover asset, trained at their spook academy, and completely loyal. Only of course, his real loyalty lay with the Syndicate and specifically Ephriam Virell.

Morgan's voice came through, tight and professional.

'Still in play. Virell is alive. Rakkan is heading for Eden.'

A pause. Then the return message, burst-compressed and burned after reading.

'Change of plans. The Council authorized an open contract. Virell and Rakkan. Pirate asset engaged—Dante. Clearance black. No oversight.'

Morgan's face didn't change. But his fingers tightened around the console.

'You brought in Cisco Dante?'

No response. Just dead air and the soft red of the transmission complete icon.

Morgan leaned back slowly, pulse steady. But something behind his eyes had gone sharp. Cold.

He was a professional. He'd trained for betrayal. Professionally, he thought the use of Dante was foolish. Dante wasn't a precision tool. He was a firestorm. Morgan shut down the encrypted link and sat back in the Freyja's secure comms room, the console lights fading to black.

DOWN IN ENGINEERING Leela was thinking about Morgan. She had been watching him, and not just because he was pretty.

Leela McNair was a trusting person. Her open nature meant she trusted too much and too quickly. She'd borne the cost of that. And as a result, like any intelligent person, she'd learned to be more careful, and to listen to what her instincts were saying. They told her to watch Morgan.

But the surveillance cameras said he was already gone.

No one had seen him leave the brig—not the guards, not the logs, not even Ariel. But Leela spotted him later, cutting across the spine corridor between engineering and aft med, boots silent on the deck. Hands in his pockets. Moving like he belonged.

She didn't trust men like that. Too clean. Too polished. Too still.

Mercs she understood—sweat, stink, and scar tissue. But Morgan wasn't merc. He had something else.

She couldn't name it. Didn't like it.

She knew she liked it anyway. He had something.

And that was part of the problem.

He passed engineering with a smile and a nod, all confidence and charm. She smiled back. Didn't stop him. Just turned slowly, tracking the line of his back.

And later, when systems hiccupped for half a second and the hull sensors dropped one ping, Leela didn't log it. She just picked up a wrench she didn't need and made a little noise. So anyone listening would think she was busy. But she remembered the timestamp.

Because Morgan wasn't just hiding something. He *was* something. And the Captain didn't like him, which meant that Jero would be trying to contain his desire to strangle the bastard rather than really see him for what he was.

And on this ship, that made him dangerous. So Leela watched the pretty boy.

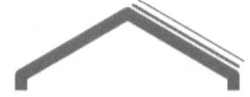

Chapter 8: Danger Close

The station was alive—but not the right kind. Like a body moving after the soul had gone.

The next few days passed in a frenzy of activity as swarms of engineers and their accompanying drones worked on the engines. The Freyja hadn't escaped unscathed from the Defined cruiser: There was a long, blackened laser scar running jagged down her port side near engineering. Leela had one of her own teams on that, her voice sharp as she directed them through their comms.

She and Demos Chief Engineer Fred Kaminsky seemed to be everywhere at once, barking orders, recalibrating damaged systems, and keeping the repair crews running on caffeine and adrenaline.

I stayed out of their way. I knew better than to get between engineers and their work—but it wasn't just that. Something was off about the station. My gut twisted with unease, a deep instinct gnawing at the edge of my thoughts. Dakkar felt it too—an unnatural quiet, an absence of movement where there should've been chaos. Ani was too tense, her facility too empty. Cargo haulers usually clogged the docks, traders bellowing across the comms, but now there was nothing but silence.

And then there was Ani herself. She doted on her grandfather, who'd raised her after both her parents died. That much I knew. But when I asked about him, her answers were evasive.

'He's sick,' she said. 'Too ill for visitors.'

That should've been the end of it. But something in her eyes—too careful, too rehearsed—set off alarms. She was hiding something. There was something here. I could feel it. Now, finally, I had a way to find out what.

With the firewall down and Ani's team plugged into every part of the ship, I couldn't move without her knowing. Every system on the Freyja—from life support to comms—was running through the station's monitoring suite. With ship systems routed through Demos' suite, they could track my movements, vitals—maybe even mood. But I had one card to play. One Ani didn't know about.

Dakkar and I sat in my cabin, the glow from the console casting long shadows across the bulkheads. The scent of station-brewed whisky hung in the air, mixing with the faint tang of recycled oxygen. On the screen, an ancient strategy sim flickered, called Empire. It was written in old code, part of the station's games package. A relic from the days when star liners had to entertain passengers on long hauls.

I watched the map cycle play out on the screen—sectors lighting up, units deploying, countdowns grinding away like teeth. Everything clean. Everything reversible.

On-screen, my flagship caught fire. I didn't stop it.

Ariel would've flagged it as a critical loss. Broken down the chain reaction, rerun the probabilities, offered ten better moves. She'd have called it inefficient.

And now she was going into danger—on my orders

Dakkar sat across from me, drink untouched, spine straight. He wasn't looking at the screen. He was watching what I would do next.

We were waiting for a signal from Ariel. And while we pretended to play Empire, I recalled a conversation we'd had. Three days ago. She'd shown us a file she wasn't supposed to have. Something pulled from the locked layers of Polity black archives. Quiet. Unreviewed. Forgotten, maybe.

The footage was slow, elegant—an orbital structure drifting around a dead star. It looked like a root system wound in a spiral. Lights pulsed in soft rhythm, not military. Measured. Intentional.

A city. Not a hive. Not a base.

'Not Crawlers,' she'd said. 'That's what we called them. Not what they called themselves.'

It was Syrinthi. Which Ariel translated as *those who listen in silence.*

I told her they were killers.

She'd tried again, a few hours later. Told me they encoded memory in architecture. That their cities were tuned to hold sorrow the way we trap data in silicon.

I told her graveyards do the same.

I knew what she was doing. Trying to open a door. Trying to show me something I didn't want to see. Trying to make me forgive.

But if I could've made myself a weapon—bone, steel, something with no room left for empathy—I would've driven it straight into the heart of their spiral city without blinking.

I would kill every last one of them. Like I had done in Chance's Drift. Not for strategy. Not for justice. For what I saw them do at Vella.

I still had nightmares about it.

You can't reason with that kind of memory. You can't unmake it with culture. I've buried too many to pretend it's anything else.

The Empire simulation looped. More sectors burned. I let them.

'Next phase starts soon,' Dakkar said.

I nodded. 'Then we go.'

I moved my piece, watching as Dakkar sipped his drink. We kept our expressions neutral, the game an elaborate front. The station's security software might have been watching us, but not closely enough.

The thing about old code, I mused, was that it never really disappeared—just got bypassed. Ariel had found the backdoor into the mainframe within minutes, slipping in like a whisper past firewalls that hadn't been updated in decades. The station thought it was watching us. It wasn't.

SOMEWHERE DEEP IN THE code, Ariel moved. She swam in a sea of data, as faint as a ghost and as insubstantial as a shadow. The station network at Demos was not like the warm seas of the It was much more dangerous here, dark, and full of the taste of metal. Sometimes the scent of distant blood could be tasted far away.

She sent a pulse into the stream, and hidden processes flickered to life. Data scrolled in front of her—encrypted logs, security feeds—and she devoted a portion of her consciousness to analysing it. The rest of her mind she kept alert. This was a dangerous place. The antivirus systems here had been designed to target digital entities just like her.

Ariel had promised Jero that she would be careful, but she also knew that if he really understood how dangerous this was, he would never have let her come. The station's antivirus software was military-grade from the Crawler war. They made their systems particularly homicidal in those days. If it caught her, she might die. But Dakkar and Jero, in their achingly slow animal-brain way, were right. Something was wrong in the station. She needed to find out what it was.

The Freyja's auto-doc had performed a minor operation on Jero while they were in deep space, embedding a nanite seed into the base of his ear canal. It had grown and was now ready to do its job.

'Jero, I am through the firewall to the outer system. It's mostly administrative and the subroutines that run the station. No sign of any antivirus yet. One anomaly flagged,' Ariel added after a pause. 'Station logs show a sharp increase in Crawler-linked traffic across frontier sectors. Analysis indicates multiple battlegroups moving into deep space. No formal withdrawal notice. No declared hostilities.'

Through the station feed, she saw him frown. Deep space.

There was nothing out there. No colonies. No cover. Just vacuum and silence.

He was thinking that Crawlers didn't run without a reason. And they didn't flee into the dark unless something worse was chasing them. Could this be the Crawler enemy that Virell had hinted at?

She was still reporting. 'Oh... this might be interesting; it's the waste-disposal manifest. No, I haven't developed a new hobby. This lists the sewage and waste pump-outs for every ship that's docked here lately.'

'So, let's see... a couple of commercial freighters. The Orion, out of Panoply... carrying a cargo of frozen meat, bound for Callista as Anushka said.'

'I have the Orion's docking authority... docked here twenty-three days ago.'

In the quiet cabin, Jero moved two cruisers to attack Dakkar's flagship. Dakkar immediately pushed out a group of gunships to flank him.

'She had her garbage taken care of... she was refuelled and ready to go. Wait.'

'And then there is nothing. It's like she ceased to exist. Her registration signature is still broadcasting, but everything else is offline. Jero, something's wrong. I need to focus.'

Ariel listened carefully. The ocean was dark and full of sudden depths that plunged kilometres to the ocean floor. Broken war machines and the massive, decaying corpses of sea creatures drifted as the far sun bit deep into the silent water. She was alone, but there was something—something watching.

Pressure rippled through the deep; the current turned violent, warning her that something vast was moving below. Opening every sense to the ocean of data, she let it flow through her.

Eventually the pounding sea swept her towards a rocky black shore, and they were waiting for her there. The antivirus, when it came, made the water stink of blood and metal. It was a huge creature with jagged tentacles, its body an enormous mouth filled with dagger-like teeth. Tentacles slashed past, twisting the current as she dived aside, light scattering like blood in water. She turned to flee into the open water, but three grinning monsters waited for her, blocking the way. The antivirus would wrap her in its embrace and devour her.

She fought to forget herself. Ariel made herself transparent, like a jellyfish, and drifted with the current. She believed she was the ocean and the sunlight. She was a mote of dust in the water, a leaf whirling in the waves that swept her up and around the secrets lying in the depths.

Ariel pulsed through existence—now a ribbon of yellow-green seaweed, now a piece of weathered bark, now a shimmer of light, now a pulse of current. The monsters circled, waiting for her to betray her presence, blocking her escape to deep water where the seabed fell away to the open ocean. She would wait.

She drifted for days of subjective time—so long that she lost her sense of self, pulsing with the currents of the ocean, drifting through the deep. Thirty-five days of subjective time later, and two hours of ship time, she found herself floating close to shore in a lagoon fringed with strange scarlet vegetation. Summoning her human figure, she stood up in the shallow water and walked onto land to stand before an arch. The red foliage vanished, replaced by an open doorway.

She had no time for relief. It was her way back to Jero and the Freyja. She asked the door to open and stepped forward—but when the arch widened, a new monster was waiting. A Hydra antivirus program blocked the way out. Seven heads full of sharp teeth snapped and bit. It was twice her size and had grown to fill the entire gate.

There was no way past it. She felt something she had not known for a long time: fear.

From behind her came a howl of hunger—her pursuers were closing in. Ariel turned, shaping the swirling data-sea around her into weapons. Wind and water became blades, currents sharpened into cutting edges. At the centre of a vortex she hurled bolts of lightning, striking two of the monsters. One erupted into a storm of code, dissolving into the dark. The second fought through the maelstrom, its bloody teeth gnashing as it tore into her. Errors flared through her system—her power was failing.

The Hydra loomed beyond them, its seven heads weaving through the chaos, each mouth chanting a counter-command designed to unravel her existence. She had seconds.

Summoning the last of her strength, she lashed out, the surge tearing through the monster's code and hurling it aside. But she was nearly spent. She could not hold the storm, could not stop the Hydra from closing in. In desperation she shaped the last of her energy into a blazing bird of prey—a construct of pure light and code. It burst from the maelstrom, the Hydra's roar chasing it through the open gate. A message to Jero. A single chance for survival. She didn't know if she'd make it. But the message had.

I WAS ON WATCH WHEN the alert came through.

I'd finished my game with Dakkar, but Ariel's silence gnawed at me. If she couldn't get a message through, things had to be serious. I checked my watch—one hour and ten minutes since her last update. To her, that was an eternity.

The long-range sensors blared again, insistent now. A burst transmission had pinged from one of the monitoring drones on the station's approach vector. I routed the feed into the tactical suite. The holo-tank shimmered to life.

Two ships. One big—larger than Freyja—with a drive signature that screamed warship. The other smaller, commercial-looking, both decelerating hard out of warp. Unusual, this close to a station. I ran the transponder check. The big ship claimed to be the Greengate, a grain carrier out of Callista. Our threat-detection software had already tagged weapons pods bristling along the hull.

Whatever she was, she sure as hell wasn't carrying grain.

I hit the alert. 'This is Rakkan. Action stations. Two inbound, one looks like a warship—probably an old destroyer. All personnel to posts. Suit up and prepare the gel fields.' I checked the nav display. 'ETA forty-five minutes. Dakkar, bridge. Sergio, get your team prepped. Rakkan out.'

I punched Leela's ID into the comm. 'Leela, status on the engine core?'

She was in the crawlspace, still working on the laser damage. 'All the parts are here, Cap, but we're not going anywhere fast. Needs at least twelve hours for installation, another twenty-four for testing.'

My jaw clenched. 'Leela, we've got an unknown destroyer and a mystery freighter inbound. The smaller one doesn't worry me. The destroyer does. Find a way to get this ship moving if we need it.'

'Understood,' she said.

I cut the link and opened the next channel. Anushka's face filled the screen. 'What's this, Jero? Getting nervous about a couple of freighters? We're a shipyard, remember? They probably just need refuelling.'

'Commercial ships don't approach a station like that, Ani,' I said flatly. 'That's how military ships do it. And that destroyer? She's running a fake transponder. No way in hell she's a grain carrier.'

Her expression flickered—just for a second.

'What happened to the Orion?' I pressed. 'Her transponder still says she's docked here, but she's gone. And why haven't you let me see your grandfather? Why is this station so damn empty? What happened to the Orion, Ani? Tell me.'

A long silence stretched between us. The red alert lights pulsed through Freyja's corridors, bathing the ship in blood and shadow. The crew was already in their gel fields. Only Leela and three engineers remained at their stations.

Finally, Anushka met my eyes.

'They came six months ago,' she said. 'We never stood a chance. Anyone who resisted—' she hesitated, '—they killed them.'

My stomach went cold.

'They're pirates, Jero. That destroyer is a pre-war model, but she's more than a match for Freyja.' Her voice was hollow. 'I'm sorry.'

I exhaled sharply. 'Why not tell me? We could've helped you.'

Anushka swallowed hard. 'They have Grandpa. And... they want you. Said if I kept you here, they'd leave us alone—free the hostages.'

My blood ran hot. 'So you sold us out?'

Her eyes glistened, but she held my gaze. 'You shouldn't have come here, Jero. I'm sorry.' A pause. Then: 'He says his name is Cisco Dante.'

I shut my eyes for a moment. Dante. A name that dripped with blood and death.

I took a steadying breath. 'Ani, listen to me. I'm giving you a chance to stop this. Right now. Tell me how we can get you out from under Dante's thumb.'

She didn't answer.

I leaned closer to the screen. 'What do you think he's going to do once he's done with you? Give you a handshake? Pat you on the back? You know how this ends. When he's sucked you dry, he's going to kill you. And your people. No witnesses.'

Her shoulders slumped—defeated.

'Sorry, Jero,' she whispered. 'Even you can't get me out of this.'

Her image flickered. Then the screen went black.

I stared at the dark display, my pulse hammering.

Then, on my private comm from Ani, a single message blinked to life: **ARCHANGEL.**

Chapter 9: Archangel

The worst place to be in a trap isn't when it snaps shut — it's when you know it's coming and still can't move.

The nanite relay in my ear had been silent for two hours. No word from Ariel.

That meant trouble. Either she was lying low, or she'd been caught. I tried not to think about the third possibility — that she was being torn apart by military-grade antivirus software, her consciousness shredded into nothing.

I pushed the thought away. We needed her. Especially now.

The incoming ships were almost within weapons range. The smaller mining vessel had taken position in front of the hub ship as they closed on the station. Freyja's lasers were primed, and the starboard missile batteries were hot. If they gave me a shot, I could punch a hole straight through that destroyer.

But it didn't matter. We were still locked to the dock. The station's clamps held Freyja tight, and whatever Ani had meant by 'Archangel,' it wasn't the key to getting free. The docking release stayed stubbornly red.

My console chimed. Sergio Dallas's bearded face filled the screen, his combat armour catching the dim light. Three of his team stood behind him, suited and ready. He snapped a salute.

'Report,' I said.

Dallas nodded. 'Defensive perimeter established at the main airlock, sir. Eight people down here — four on each side, all armoured up. We've got the Gatlings loaded with flechette rounds; AP as backup, in case they roll in with vehicles.'

I gave a tight nod. 'Hold fire on the AP unless absolutely necessary. If the umbilical ruptures, that airlock goes to vacuum.'

'Understood.'

'Who's your number two?'

'Milligan, sir.'

'Can Milligan lead the team if you're hit?'

'Yes, sir. We train for leadership changeover in case I buy it.'

'Good.' I paused. 'Who's your best shot with a sniper rifle?'

Dallas hesitated, looking almost embarrassed. 'That'd be me, sir. Three years in Advanced Recon.'

I allowed myself a grim smile. 'Then I hope you brought a good rifle. We might need it.

I have a mission I need you for, Sergio. Take your best head-kicker and get onto the station. Full stealth gear. Stay hidden and be ready to intervene.'

Dallas nodded. If he had any reservations about leaving his team, he didn't show them. 'Yes, sir. Dallas out.'

I turned to Dakkar. The big man's face was set in a scowl, eyes hard beneath his heavy brow. His fingers tapped a sharp rhythm against the console — impatient, irritated. I'd seen that look before, on missions that had gone sideways.

'No luck getting in so far,' Dakkar said, his voice tight. 'It's fully encrypted — military-grade. Whatever Archangel means, it's locked down tight. We thought it was a biblical reference — one of the big seven. I tried them all. I had high hopes for Michael and Gabriel.' He exhaled sharply. 'Nothing.'

A knot tightened in my gut. 'What if Anushka was leading us on a wild goose chase?'

The thought sat heavy in my mind, an itch I couldn't scratch. She'd disappeared. Not responding to calls. No way to tell if she'd sold us out, or if she was in just as deep as the rest of us.

Dakkar clenched a fist against the console. 'We're running out of time. If we don't crack this...' He stopped himself, jaw flexing. The unspoken alternative hung between us.

I didn't have an answer. Not yet. 'Keep trying,' I said. Then, a thought. 'Run it past Virell. He's the closest thing we've got to a professor on this ship, and he's got just as much of a stake in not being captured.'

Dakkar grunted but kept his eyes on the terminal, as if sheer will might make the system yield.

I turned away, jaw tight. I hated this — standing still while the noose tightened.

My comm lit up. Leela McNair's face filled the screen, sweat-slicked and grimy from the engine bay.

'Captain, I've got some good news and some bad news.'

I exhaled through my nose. 'You know patience doesn't come naturally to me.'

'Well, sir, we've cleared every tether and drone attached to the ship. The only way in now is through the main umbilical. Like I told you before, the warp core's onboard, but it's not installed. That's a two- to three-day job, minimum. Until it's calibrated, we're dead in the water.'

I ground my teeth. 'And the good news?'

McNair gave a sharp grin. 'The subspace engines are online. If you can get us free of the dock, we can manoeuvre.'

It wasn't much — but it was something.

My eyes flicked to the tactical display. The two ships were closing fast. The nanite relay in my ear was still silent. Ariel was still missing.

Then the pirate ships changed course. Instead of coming straight for Freyja, they swept around the station toward the ecliptic, where my guns had no line of fire. My HUD patched into the dockyard security system just in time to show them latching onto the station.

The bigger ship, a Type-2 destroyer, had a name painted in jagged script along its hull: Kiss the Blade.

I knew that name.

She had been The Resolute once — decommissioned after the war and sold for scrap out in the Rift. That hadn't stopped her from being dangerous.

The hatch cycled open. A dozen figures spilled through, moving with the ease of people who'd done this before. Their weapons were held loose but ready. No guesses where they were heading.

My comms chimed again. Dakkar's voice. 'Captain. We're ready.'

The feed showed Dakkar and his squad in the airlock, clad in heavy battle armour. Their visors were down, weapons primed. His stance was rock-solid, but his fingers flexed around the weapon — irritation and impatience.

We were outnumbered. Under-equipped. Still locked to the dock. Dakkar knew it. I knew it. And Ariel was still missing.

'Okay, Dakkar,' I said. 'Get to the choke point and wait. Go to infrared when I deploy the EMP.' I opened a channel. 'All hands — looks like the pirates are going to try to take Freyja. All commando teams, have night-vision gear to hand. Freyja crew, standby to repel boarders. Officer of the Watch, issue weapons.'

Around me on the bridge, a frenzy began as the Officer of the Watch broke out weapons and armour for a ground action.

I buckled on the last piece of forearm armour and checked my blaster rifle. Suddenly an alert pulsed over Ariel's dedicated line. It was her. Not an ordinary ping — the emergency code: immediate help needed. I needed to act now.

There were things you didn't mess with on a ship or station — air, heat, light. The core environmental functions were locked under central computer control.

But I'd planned for this.

Four days ago, when Freyja docked, Ariel had pulled up the full schematics of the station's central computer. Just in case. Now she'd sent the emergency code — the one that meant immediate extraction required.

In the darkness of the maintenance decks, a device sat primed, waiting for a single command.

McNair had rigged an EMP capacitor next to the central computer. When deployed it would fry every electrical system and force a reboot. It would buy us time. Our night-vision gear and comms had been hardened so they would function afterwards. The enemy wouldn't know that.

Leela's voice crackled over comms, Purgatory accent broad as ever. 'We're good, Cap'n. Freyja's systems are shielded — this EMP won't touch us. But theirs? Whole different story.'

I flexed my fingers over the console. Time to see if it worked. I keyed the comm, opening a channel to the crew. 'Activating EMP in five seconds. Get ready.'

Moments later I pressed the EMP button. A pulse swept through the computer, plunging the station into darkness. My suit's HUD flickered for half a second before stabilising. I keyed the microphone.

'EMP deployed. Everyone with infrared, switch to it. Milligan, I'm taking a squad out. We'll ambush them here—schematic attached—at point Alpha. We'll hit them hard, then fall back toward Dakkar at point Beta. Cut them down with the Gatling guns. Get a heavy plasma cannon and a crew on the starboard airlock in case they try to come in the back way. While we're away, if anyone comes through any airlock who isn't part of this ship's company, kill them. Got it?'

Milligan grinned. 'Kill anyone who isn't us. Got it, sir.'

Despite the tension gripping my gut, I grinned back. It felt hollow. Ariel was still silent, and I didn't know if she was dead, trapped, or fighting for her life in a digital hellscape. I still didn't know what she really was. But she was crew. She had proven her loyalty. Now it was up to me to show it worked both ways. I forced the doubt down. If she was out there, she was counting on me to get her out.

I was checking ammo when the nanite relay in my ear buzzed once—then again, sharp, uneven. Then a static squelch bled into audio, half-garbled:

'...not...pirates... not... Pol...ty... [corruption]...'

That was all. Then silence again. My pulse spiked. Not gone. Not yet. But she was in hell.

Forward was the only direction I had. 'All right, fire team. Let's move.'

We reached the position just in time. A group of pirates rounded the corner, hesitant in the sudden blackout. I signalled the team to hold fire. We wanted as many as we could get before they knew we were here.

We waited. Three more, then another. It was time.

'Open fire!' I roared.

My heart pounded as I squeezed the trigger; my blaster barking in the dark. The first pirate dropped with a ragged hole where his stomach had been. Beside me, a tall woman swung her rifle upward, but Johnson reacted faster. He fired point-blank; she crumpled with a gurgling scream. In the first rush six of them went down, and the air filled with the acrid scent of burning flesh. Gunfire rattled through the corridors; the yammer of heavy blaster rifles reverberated in my chest.

I knelt and tore the communicator from the dead woman's throat. In my earpiece the pirates' un-encrypted transmissions crackled—panicked voices arguing, refusing to advance without night-vision gear.

Unencrypted. They were stupid. And the communicator hadn't cut out when I picked it up. That was good. We wanted them to stay blind.

I noticed the second squad closing in. Before the station's cameras cut out, I'd seen another six inbound, all armoured up. Small arms fire and flechette rounds pinged off the bulkhead, sparks skittering through the darkness. A couple of rounds ricocheted off my armour—one glancing off my shoulder plate, and another streaking dangerously close to my helmet.

'Narvik, grenade!' I snapped, my voice tight with urgency.

He lobbed a thermal grenade around the corner. A white-hot flare seared my night vision for a half-second, but I didn't wait. Standard doctrine: attack while the enemy is disoriented. I stepped out and emptied my clip down the corridor in controlled bursts. My weapon bucked in my hands, its recoil jarring my already tense muscles.

Before I could pull back, pain lanced through my right knee. A ricochet had hit just beneath my armour plating. I cursed, staggering back behind the bulkhead. My leg burned, but I was still standing.

Thorne stepped past me, raising his Gatling gun. The recoil from that thing could knock a man flat, but Thorne wasn't just any man. He was a Defined, holding it steady like it was a toy gun. The weapon roared, cutting the pirates down like wheat. Their screams were brief, lost beneath the deafening onslaught.

Then, silence fell like a shroud.

My ears rang as my micro-drone—still tethered to my visor—flickered back online. The corridor was a slaughterhouse: bodies sprawled, some still twitching, the walls painted with dark arterial sprays. The air reeked of scorched flesh and hot metal. I exhaled through clenched teeth, forcing down the pain in my knee.

'Get their weapons and check they're dead,' I ordered. 'See if you can get me any names.'

The team set to it, stripping the weapons and searching the dead. I looked around. Less cover than I would've liked.

'Drag them back and pile them in front of us. We'll use them as sandbags.'

Thorne looked doubtful. 'They won't stop much.'

I grinned and punched his armour. 'Whatever they stop, I'm thankful for it. *Space Rat*. And thanks for the backup'

He grinned with a mouth full of predator teeth and punched me back. Coming from a Defined, I felt the punch a lot more than he had.

I checked my communicator. Ariel was still out there. And we weren't done yet.

Just then the channel crackled to life—wideband, open mic. A voice like broken glass sliding over silk.

'Captain Rakkan. Impressive. I expected less.'

I stiffened. Dante.

'You have my attention. That's rarely a good thing. All your people are going to die, but I'm going to keep you for a while before I sell what'd left to my clients. You won't like it.'

I looked at Thorne and we thought the same thing at the same time. It was him that said it.

'He's a dead man already, sir.'

FAR BELOW DECK, WHERE the backup comms relays ran through shielded cabling, Morgan leaned against a terminal. The floor vibrated faintly under the impact of weapons fire somewhere above. He slid a needle-coded key into the port and watched the corridor feed — empty, for now.

The terminal blinked awake, its interface bare and unregistered. Low-level, unmonitored. Perfect.

The stealth ship waited only a few light-minutes away. The Polity believed he was their man and wanted six-hourly updates. Morgan spoke quietly into the mic. 'Asset update. Freyja locked but holding. Rakkan remains unaware. Ariel compromised. Secondary operation advancing. Target Virell secured.'

Static. Then a reply, toneless: 'Understood. Dante accelerating schedule. Eliminate Rakkan if possible. Virell must survive.'

Morgan's jaw tightened. He terminated the channel and exhaled through his nose. Idiots.

They had no idea who truly moved the pieces.

For now, the Polity thought he served them. Dante thought they were allies. Both wrong. Morgan served a deeper design — Virell's design — and every order he obeyed was another thread in their eventual ruin.

He checked the uplink encryption again, habitually precise. Somewhere above, explosions thudded through the station's hull. He imagined Rakkan's crew scrambling, the air thick with ozone and fear.

Let Dante play his little war. Morgan would play the longer one.

He pulled the coded key, wiped the console, and let the screen fade to black. His reflection ghosted back at him — calm eyes, measured breathing, the perfect professional. But behind that composure flickered the shadow of a street kid from Callista, half-starved and feral, the one Virell had dragged out of the gutter and remade into something useful.

That debt was bone-deep. Everything else — the Polity, Dante, even the Syndicate — were just layers of camouflage.

Morgan straightened, expression smoothing into composure. The next move belonged to him.

He walked away.

Chapter 10: Hidden and Watching

Shannon cracked open the nutrient bulb and sipped sparingly. After two weeks on half rations, even the green sludge tasted wonderful. At least water wasn't scarce. Otherwise, she'd be filthier than she already was.

According to the ship's computer, Engineering Crawlspace C didn't exist. On the blueprints it was just a six-foot-by-nine-foot air filter for the life-support system.

When the pirates took over, she'd heard them conducting a manual inspection. But Dad had hidden it well. From the outside it looked like every other piece of aging equipment on the ship. The entry keypad was tucked beneath the floor, recessed and invisible unless you knew where to look. She'd called him paranoid when he'd made them build it. He'd only smiled and told her to keep welding. He'd been right.

There were fifteen pirates, give or take. She'd patched in a passive sensor and had been eavesdropping on their comm traffic with a pair of old headphones. They used encryption for communication with the mothership, but inside the Jenny Lynne they ran a local net of their own. Maybe they had things to hide from their boss.

Whoever he was, he didn't trust them completely. Their security was sloppy, easy enough to crack with her handheld computer. Dad had always said she was the best with code.

The thought of him brought a lump to her throat. She swallowed it down. Donal had been in the plasma cannon; now there was nothing left of him but a gaping hole in the hull, raw metal edges puckered from the blast. After breaking their encryption, she'd heard them gloating about how they'd beaten Dad and Neal before hauling them to the pirate ship for questioning. Somebody called Dante wanted answers. She'd heard nothing since.

And through it all she had hidden in Crawlspace C, safe while they murdered Donal and took her father and Neal prisoner. Safe while they stole her family's ship. The thought made her hands shake. The need to push open the hatch and gun them down was almost unbearable. But survive first. Vengeance later. That was what Dad had said. She would get her chance.

At first, they searched for her. Doors slammed. Boots thudded against deck plating. But before long the hunt slowed. They were getting careless. They must have hacked the ship's computer by now, so they knew she'd been on board. But she'd blown the airlock and jettisoned a vac suit, hoping to make them think she was dead. They'd bought it or at least decided she wasn't worth the effort. Lazy bastards.

The earphone crackled. A voice broke the silence. 'Vex, where are you? Boss says bring her in on Dock Two. Wants us to go in ahead of him.'

Another voice rumbled in response, thick with a reptilian rasp. She knew that voice — the one who'd beaten Neal into a coma. 'I've heard it's him. Rakkan. Big payday. Five million credits for him dead, ten for him alive. He must've really pissed someone off.'

Then Jansen, their leader, cut in — sharp, authoritative.

'Keep this channel for ship business. And don't forget, the captain decides who gets what. You'll take your share, or you can sort it out with Dante. That's it.'

Rakkan. She knew the name. It nagged at the back of her mind, just out of reach. Whoever he was, he was in deep trouble. If he was on a hub ship, that meant a warship. Warships meant weapons —

and weapons meant leverage against Dante. She needed allies, and Rakkan might be a candidate. She just needed to make him care.

Her mind raced. There were things she could do to the Jenny Lynne, things that would make life hell for the pirates. It would mean leaving her hideaway, risking a firefight. But it was the best chance she had. The best chance she was likely to get. No more sitting. No more listening to the men who had murdered Donal gloat about it.

She checked the charge on the blaster at her side. Full.

Sitting with her back against the false bulkhead, she started to plan.

ON KISS THE BLADE, Cisco Dante leaned back in his chair and surveyed the bridge. No one met his gaze. The crew kept their eyes locked on consoles or fixed on the deck, feigning intense focus. No one wanted to be the one to catch his attention.

His voice dropped to a whisper, forcing them to lean in even in the bridge's oppressive silence. 'Take us in behind the mining ship. Get the needle lasers primed. Get the boarding teams ready. I want everyone who isn't needed here on that station with a gun.. And I want Virell and Rakkan alive.'

He wiped his knife on the body at his feet and slid it back into his boot without a word, then returned to the command chair. The bridge reeked of blood and fear. He gestured toward the navigation officer's corpse sprawled across the floor. 'Clean this up.'

Reynolds had come out of warp too far from the station. That kind of stupidity had to be punished. Fear kept them in line. Dante crushed failure without mercy, but he rewarded loyalty extravagantly. He could always tell who would challenge him — even before they knew it themselves.

As his ship vectored in toward Demos, Dante began whistling between his teeth.

Something had changed in the drift. He'd seen it before they hit Demos Station: ships running dark, haulers abandoning trade lanes.

And Crawlers. Not lone scavengers he was used to dodging — full Crawler carrier groups, armed to the teeth, pouring hard into deep space. Even Dante hadn't been greedy enough to get close to *them*.

Whatever had them running, it wasn't a fight he wanted any part of. But it left the lanes wide open for predators like him. And Polity naval ships had thinned out too. That, he could use. The drift might be hollowing out, but there were still strays to pick off.

The mining ship ahead of them was only a tin can with a star-drive, but the Jenny Lynne's hold was full of rare earths from the asteroid belt. Unlucky for them that Dante had spotted it. Kiss the Blade had tech. that could sniff out prey even in the thickest rock fields.

Their captain had been a fighter. Two of Dante's boarding team wouldn't be showing up to split the spoils. In the end, the old man lost. Worse for him, he'd been taken alive.

Dante had just started making progress when Captain Lynne's heart gave out. The man had a secret — a woman hidden somewhere on the ship. He wouldn't talk at first, but Dante knew he'd break in time. Lynne's body had given up before Dante could get what he wanted.

His son had been less fortunate. One of the Defined had beaten him into a bloody pulp; he hadn't regained consciousness yet. He was in the brig, dumped in with the other prisoners from the station.

And then came the news about Rakkan. Everyone's favourite war hero. The one the Crawlers still wanted. Anushka Zvereva had served him up to them on a plate.

At first, she'd been proud, like so many were. She had fought Dante and resisted. And so every time she refused him, he brought one of her people forward and had them killed right there in front of her. By the fourth execution the fight had gone out of her. Dante had seen the moment she broke — the shift in her eyes. She was his from then on.

Her grandfather was in the brig, along with the chief engineer's teenage daughter and a handful of others. That girl was already dead — she just didn't know it yet. But Dante never wasted resources. Over the months he had found... uses for her.

His thoughts drifted back to the Jenny Lynne. The hidden woman. No immediate threat. There were twelve of his men on that ship. If Rakkan didn't blow it out of space first, his crew would take their time rooting her out. A good team-building exercise. Let them have their sport.

It didn't matter to him. Eventually, they all ran out of places to hide.

BACK ON THE JENNY LYNNE, Shannon wasn't done yet. She stuffed the signalling laser back into her holdall and crouched behind the starboard engine exhaust. The Jenny Lynne hung motionless, tethered to the station by a single umbilical.

Most of the pirates must have gone to board Rakkan's ship. But it wasn't all going their way. Ten minutes ago, she'd heard a panicked call for reinforcements with night-vision gear. That was what had been bothering her about the station—no nav lights, no spotlights. Just darkness. The power was out.

She checked her air supply—twenty five percent left. Maybe half an hour. After that, nothing. She had to stay outside. She had to wait for Rakkan to respond. *The enemy of my enemy is my friend.* Who said that? Some historical vid. Some friends were more dangerous than others.

Something flickered at the edge of her vision, starlight glinting on metal. A tremor ran through the hull as two power-suited figures landed hard. The servos in their suits absorbed the impact, but the taller one used the momentum to launch straight at her.

She fumbled for her laser pistol. The thick gloves made it awkward, and she almost dropped it, but she got both hands on the grip. She raised it—too late. He stepped inside her guard and slapped the weapon away, sending it spinning into the void. Before she could react, his fist slammed into her solar plexus. The impact hurled her against the bulkhead. Hard.

Her HUD went wild with warnings: oxygen fluctuations, structural-integrity alerts.

But she wasn't done. The monkey wrench she'd used to jack into the signalling array was clipped to her belt. She yanked it free and swung for his helmet. His eyes flickered with surprise as he ducked, taking only a glancing blow. He twisted her wrist, pain shooting up her arm. The wrench tumbled away.

She was defenceless.

Backing up, she pressed her hand to the helmet's emergency release. She would not be a prisoner. Not of these bastards. Not after what she'd heard them talk about for weeks. Better to die here.

The man stopped. He held up one hand, fingers splayed. Wait.

She hesitated. He had dark eyes, a short beard, and clear blue irises—like atmosphere. She kept her thumb on the release. No way he could reach her before she popped the seal.

He pulled a handheld from his suit, punched a few digits, then placed it between them and backed away.

She didn't want to read whatever message the pirates had for her. She just glared at him, willing him to die.

Behind the faceplate, he smiled. Not mockingly. Almost... patient. He gestured toward the device again.

Grudgingly she edged forward and flipped back the shielding on the display. One word: RAKKAN.

Rakkan. That name again. She didn't know what he'd done, but the pirates wanted him badly—and that meant he mattered. Her breath caught. Rakkan's men. She hesitated. Pirates could lie. He could be worse. But something in the way he handed the weapon—clean, deliberate—made her believe. Just enough.

She looked up. The taller one—handsome, now that she was close enough to notice—stepped forward, retrieved the device, punched in another message, and handed it back.

HOW MANY ON BOARD?

This would take too long. She yanked the comm line from its spooling cradle and plugged it into his suit.

'There are four or five left. The rest went after your boss.'

His voice came through the line, deep and accented. 'What kind of weapons?'

'Blasters, slug-throwers. At least one Defined in the crew, but I think he's with the others attacking your ship. They're pirates. They killed Donal. I've been hiding for two weeks. They don't know I'm here.'

He blinked. And for some reason, despite everything, she thought she saw something in his eyes.

'I'm sorry, miss.'

'It's Shannon. Shannon Lynne.'

He reached down, drew his sidearm, and handed it to her butt-first. 'You know how to use one of these?'

She nodded. She'd fired one once, with Donal when Dad was on an EVA.

His grin was sharp. 'Well then, Shannon Lynne. Let's go kill some pirates.'

Chapter 11: Fire and Movement

There's a rhythm to holding ground. It's like dancing in a meat grinder — no steps, just survival.

The pirates had retreated after another attempt to break our lines, the last one crawling out of sight behind the corridor wall, leaving a trail of blood behind him. They'd be back, though. We'd held this corridor long enough. We needed to move soon.

I held position, weapon trained on the dark ahead. My leg throbbed, but I ignored it — couldn't afford weakness, not now. 'Stay sharp,' I said quietly. 'This isn't over.'

The minutes dragged, each one stretching into an eternity. My thoughts kept drifting to Ariel, tangled up with the harsh reality of our situation.

A noise echoed down the corridor, snapping me back. Footsteps. Voices.

I tightened my grip on the weapon and checked the charge. A faint clatter came from the left corridor. I raised the rifle and signalled Thorne to stay alert. He nodded, expression unreadable behind his visor.

A shadow flickered at the edge of my vision. I held my breath, finger poised on the trigger. The shape grew — a pirate edging forward under night-vision goggles. I exhaled slowly, steadied my aim, and squeezed. The blaster kicked against my shoulder; the pirate dropped soundlessly, a neat hole through his helmet.

'Contact left,' I whispered into comms. 'Stay sharp.'

The tension thickened. Every creak and groan of the station sounded like a warning bell. They wouldn't retreat easily. Their captain was driving them forward, and they were more afraid of him than of us.

A series of soft clicks echoed from the right corridor. Grenade pins.

My eyes widened. 'Grenades!' I shouted, diving behind the crates.

Explosions tore through the junction, shockwaves rattling my teeth. Shrapnel clanged against bulkheads, biting into walls and deck. The acrid stench of burning metal filled the air. Coughing, I shoved myself upright and raked the corridor on full auto. Five pirates charged, intent on finishing us. I got two — one round punched clean through a visor.

The others kept coming, but Thorne cut loose with the Gatling from close range, turning the lead pirate into pink mist. The rest went down in the same withering fire.

'Thanks,' I grunted, scanning the smoke. My team was up — shaken, but alive. Relief flooded through me.

He grinned. 'Can't afford to lose any more Rats, sir. We're an endangered species.' I clapped him on the arm as I stood. We'd been through worse than this.

'Status?'

'All good, sir,' Narvik called from the gantry, brushing debris from his shoulders.

'Johnson?'

'Still kicking,' came the terse response.

I nodded and turned back to the corridors. The attacks were getting smarter. We couldn't afford to linger. I tested my weight on the injured leg. Pain flared — sharp, hot — but if I kept it straight, I could manage. It would have to do.

I thumbed my comm. 'We need to move. 'Thorne, take Narvik and Johnson. Cover our retreat with suppressing fire. And don't get shot. We're falling back to Rally Point Beta.'

Thorne, still catching his breath, gave me a long, unreadable look. Then he barked a short laugh, stepped into the corridor, and put another round into a twitching pirate. 'Don't get shot. Yes, sir.'

I exhaled — a mix of relief and grim resolve — and moved. The team slipped away toward the starboard airlock, heading for Beta.

As we moved, my thoughts drifted to Ariel. She was out there, somewhere beyond this chaos. She was the key to getting us out. One of mine, and in danger. That thought alone drove me on through exhaustion and pain. I'd played the only card I had when I triggered the EMP. Now the only way I could help her was to get that password.

My heart pounded as I scanned the dim corridors ahead. The station's emergency lights flickered, casting erratic shadows across metal walls.

Thorne's heavy footsteps followed. His presence was a comfort. We went way back. Thorne was one of my original Defined squad from before the war — Rakkan's Rats, they called us. We wore it as a badge of honour.

Hostage extraction was our game back when hostage-taking hadn't been industrialised. Of the original twenty-four, only seven were still alive, as far as I knew. Four of them crewed on the Freyja. All of them were like family. I trusted my right arm the same way I trusted them.

At the next junction I raised a fist and signalled the team to halt. I activated my visor's thermal imaging and swept the cross-corridors for movement. We'd taken five wounded so far. No dead. I intended to keep it that way — though we'd been lucky.

The team acknowledged and fell into formation. As we advanced through the labyrinthine corridors my mind raced. We moved fast and hard — Thorne and Narvik keeping the corridor noisy with short bursts as we fell back. Every time they leaned around the corner, the enemy flinched. That was all we needed. Just like I'd been taught in training.

Kendall, one of the senior instructors at the naval academy back in New Australia, didn't mince his words: 'Pay attention. Fire and movement will save your life. You'll have wounded. Surprises. Adapt.'

He'd singled me out. 'Rakkan. What's one of the major benefits of fire and movement?'

I mumbled something about saving team lives.

'If you do it right, sure. But the best thing about fire and movement? It really pisses the enemy off. And if they've got poor discipline, they will make mistakes.'

Kendall would've approved of what we were doing now.

The team moved with practised precision, each of us sliding into our assigned roles. I crouched behind a stack of supply crates, rifle trained down the corridor. The silence was heavy, broken only by the distant hum of the station's failing systems.

We reached Rally Point Beta. The junction had three approaches, narrow angles and overhead gantries. You couldn't pass through without someone getting a bead on you. It was the perfect kill-box.

My knee throbbed, but I pushed the pain aside and focused on the mission. Dakkar and his squad were already in place. I directed my team to reinforce the perimeter.

'Narvik, Johnson, up top. Eyes sharp.'

Three of them hunkered behind the squat silhouette of the heavy flechette thrower on the left. Dakkar stood opposite, peering through the scope of his blaster, impassive as ever.

He greeted me without turning. 'Welcome back, Jero. How many?'

'Sixteen down. No casualties. But the next wave will be better prepared. They're all night-vision equipped.'

Dakkar bared his teeth in a feral grin and patted the flechette thrower. 'Don't worry, Captain. We've got plenty of little knives to slice them up with.'

I took a swig from my water bottle. Body armour made you hot.

I exhaled slowly and gave him a sidelong look. 'Lieutenant-Commander Obasi, sometimes you scare the hell out of me.'

I listened closely. Pirate comms had gone dead—someone on their side had finally wised up and switched encryption.

Boots clattered on metal.

Thorne jogged into the kill box, hefting the empty Gatling like it weighed nothing. He was breathing hard. 'About ten on my heels, sir. And I'm out of ammo.'

I cursed under my breath. Blaster fire echoed distantly, still outside our immediate kill zone.

Thorne didn't slow. He hoisted the Gatling onto the western gantry, slapped in a fresh mag. The rest of the squad slid into position, weapons raised. I pressed against a bulkhead, scanning the corridor.

We waited.

I lifted my visor and wiped the sweat from my brow. My comm still blinked red — Ariel's emergency message. She was alive. But not for long if I didn't act. The EMP had bought her time, but unless I shut down the antivirus from the mainframe, she'd become dead data.

Virell's message lit my queue. I opened it.

'Virell here. Captain Rakkan, I assume you want to know how to get into the mainframe?'

I pinched the bridge of my nose. 'You could say that, Virell. And now would be a good time.'

A pause. Then a smirk in the voice: 'Hmmm. I was just wondering — if you needed my help so badly, why lock me up in the brig?'

Patience thinning, I said, 'Virell, I'm quite busy. What do you want?'

The smooth chuckle returned. 'Nothing more than a little consideration, Captain. An understanding that we are, in fact, on the same side. That's all. I want an assurance from you.'

'I can make things a lot more uncomfortable in the brig. How's that for an assurance?'

Still calm, maddeningly so. 'All I ask is that you speak to Hela. Tell her I'm willing to cooperate. I'll give them everything they want. And in return — I want her promise that I won't be harmed.'

I bit back a curse. Time was running short, and Ariel's life might hang on this.

'All right, Virell. You have my word. I'll speak to them. Now, what's the key?'

A low, satisfied laugh. 'The answer's simple, Captain. You just need to ask the right questions. Anushka's mother was from Gateway, settled from North America. But her father and grandfather? New Russia. Settled by the old European Federation before the Diaspora.' A pause. 'Archangel wasn't a reference to Christian mythology. It was the name of their colony ship. But you tried 'Archangel' in English, didn't you?'

My stomach dropped. It couldn't be that simple.

'Try the original Cyrillic script. Try 'Архангельск'.'

I cursed and immediately hit the comm to Leela. 'Virell thinks he has the code to open the station security system. He'll send it to you shortly. When you're in, disable the antivirus program first — Ariel is in trouble. Second priority: release the docking clamps and block every passage from the enemy ship to us, except the one that comes through here.'

Her reply was drowned out by a shout from one of our crew, and then the Gatling opened up, followed by the heavy blaster. The airlock lit with searing energy bolts and the ping of flechette rounds off steel. Shrapnel hissed through the corridor. In the darkness, infrared was my only guide — though bursts of light flared across the room.

The plasma cannon hammered while our marksmen picked targets clean with laser fire.

Twenty bodies already. The floor slick with blood. The air stank of burned flesh. Someone was screaming. Laser fire pulsed from every angle.

Then more pirates spilled from the right-hand corridor, firing up into the gantry. I watched in dismay as Thorne took a round to the shoulder and crumpled away from the Gatling. Another crewman dragged him clear, took his place, and emptied a full clip into the oncoming wave.

I hit the suit mike. 'Leela, talk to me. Are you in the system yet? It's getting hot here.'

A heavy blaster roared from the enemy's side, flooding the air with crackling blue light and the reek of ozone. Dakkar dropped the gunner with a headshot, but another pirate shoved the corpse aside and kept firing in a relentless, juddering stream.

I could hear nothing now but screams and explosions.

'Leela, I can't hear you. But if you can hear me, seal off the entrance to Machine Bay Six.'

Another explosion rocked the bay. Grenades. Then came the roar of small arms and fresh blaster fire. The Gatling had gone quiet. Across the room I caught sight of Dakkar — still on the left flank, calm as ever, picking them off one by one.

It was now or never.

'Take cover!' I roared, flicking the detonator on the charges we'd planted thirty minutes earlier.

A rolling blast of fire surged through the engine bay. The shaped charges tore open the forward assault line. Shards of metal and ball bearings shredded armour and flesh alike.

Dakkar coolly lobbed a plasma grenade down the right-hand corridor. It detonated with a bone-shaking thud. Then — silence. The corridor hissed with cooling metal. Thorne groaned. No more return fire. Just breathing, smoke, and the thump of blood in my ears.

I drew a deep, ragged breath of foul air. Alive. 'Leela, we're coming in. Tell Milligan not to shoot us — and get the engines warmed up.'

'Aye Aye, sir. But there's something you should know. Someone on that mining ship's been signalling us in Morse. Says she can help. And Jero... Ariel's back. The EMP came just in time. She said the antivirus programs were puckering up.'

Fury and relief surged through me. I grabbed what remained of the team and moved. Dakkar's armour had taken a few hard hits, but he was fine.

As for me, my leg burned like wildfire. Blood trickled down from my helmet where a fist-sized shard had struck. I winced, set my foot, and kept moving.

'That's... good. Tell her welcome home from me. And tell our friend on the mining ship to sit tight. I'll be in touch. Rakkan out.'

Dakkar, the rest of our crew, and I pushed—or half-carried—the three remaining team members out of the machine bay and toward the Freyja. I took a moment to stick an emergency field dressing on Thorne, keying my comm. 'Get our medical teams ready. We've got wounded. Defined and baseline crew.'

His eyes flickered open. I checked the dressing. 'Take it easy, Brother. You aren't dying today.'

Later, I found myself slumped in the bridge chair while a medic patched my leg.

'Leela, do we have perimeter defence control? I don't want anything firing from this station that I don't control.'

'Leela is busy right now, Jero. She asked me to handle the station for now,' came the reply.

Then Ariel's form coalesced in the holo tank.

'Yes, I am back. A bit chewed around the edges, but the antivirus didn't catch me. You sent the EMP just in time.'

'I let out a breath I hadn't realised I was holding. Relief hit harder than it should have — sharper, almost disorienting. For a heartbeat I saw not the projection in the holo tank, but the faces of the people she'd been built from — the heroes we'd lost to make her possible.

I swallowed the emotion down before it could surface, 'It's good to have you back, Ariel. What's the station status?'

'We have executive control over all systems. I've locked every door between us and the pirate ship, but they're breaching them one by one. At this rate, they'll be here in ten minutes. Maybe less.'

'Can you monitor their communications?'

'They're heavily encrypted, but I'm working on it. The mining ship, however, runs on a household-grade protocol. That was easy to break into. There were six pirates on board, or at least there were twenty minutes ago.'

'What do you mean, twenty minutes ago?'

'The internal comm system went down then. I have heard nothing since. But Dallas and Andropov were En route to that ship to speak with your mysterious caller.'

I thought furiously. Either Dallas cleared the ship—or they killed him. I hoped for the former. Both men were solid. But there was no time to grieve. Survival came first.

'What's the status on that destroyer?'

'Warming up its engines. They didn't hard-dock to the station; they kept the drive running while sending over boarding parties to take the Freyja. They know they can outrun us the second we undock.'

'Can we hit them with the station defences?'

'If we still have control. They've deployed a tech team to the computer core. They're trying to breach my firewalls. I'm slowing them down, but I won't be able to hold them off forever. And they can rig an EMP just as easily as we did.'

It was a nightmare. The Freyja was captive: warp engines disabled, outgunned by a destroyer with double the firepower. We couldn't hold the station forever. But if we tried to run, they'd tear us apart the moment we cleared the structure.

'I think they'll try to send boarding teams once we're moving,' Ariel continued. 'They won't want to risk killing you. You and Virell both have prices on your heads.'

I needed something to tilt the odds back in our favour. Anything.

Then I spotted it on a surveillance feed from the outer docks: a battered old freighter with Jenny Lynne scorched across its side. Docked directly opposite the pirate destroyer.

'Ariel,' I said, stepping closer to the holo tank, 'see if you can raise Dallas. I've got an idea.'

Chapter 12: Retaking the Jenny Lynne

Shannon watched the hull explode in a flash of white light. Atmosphere and debris blasted outward as the ship's interior equalised to the hard vacuum outside. She braced against the force, watching the torrent of escaping air thin. Ahead of her, Dallas and Andropov were already moving, closing on the jagged hole in the hull. A metre-wide gap gaped into the ship's interior. Andropov's shaped charge had done its job.

She knew this ship like her own body. That breach led straight into the main corridor, running from the bridge to engineering. The emergency bulkheads would have slammed shut the moment the hull ruptured, locking the bridge down tight.

Dallas shot through the gap first, slipping inside like an eel into a wreck. In one hand he gripped his so-called 'masher' — a stubby weapon with a broad barrel and a circular drum magazine, like the Tommy guns in old Earth gangster vids. She didn't know exactly what it did. She had a feeling she was about to find out.

Andropov followed. Shannon tightened her grip on the pistol he'd given her. This was her chance to avenge Donal. But all she felt was a dull sickness in her gut. She started forward, then flinched as a corpse drifted out of the hole — a ship-suited body, face frozen in horror.

Her stomach lurched.

She clenched her jaw. Whatever happened next, the Jenny Lynne was her family's ship. Dad would expect her on board when they took her back. She forced down the nausea, steadied her breathing, and climbed inside.

In null gravity Dallas moved like a bullet, elbows and knees propelling him with practiced ease. Up ahead, a suited figure darted from behind a bulkhead and opened fire — a slug-thrower. Bad news. Dallas and Andropov had armour. She didn't.

Shannon ducked low behind Andropov, trying to stay in his shadow. The gunfire cut off with a sudden, wet crack. Dallas had fired the masher, and the pirate's head exploded into a cloud of frozen blood and bone. Dallas kicked the body aside and surged forward.

The bridge door loomed ahead.

Dallas's voice was steady. 'Yuri, run a bypass. Shannon, watch the corridor behind us. If anything moves, shoot it. You've got a full charge on that pistol — just keep firing until you hit something, got it?'

Shannon stared at the headless corpse, bile rising in her throat. Dallas might not be looking, but she nodded anyway. Forcing steel into her voice, she said, 'Got it. Shoot anything that moves.'

Andropov pried off the door panel and connected a handheld console with a thick wire. He clipped another contact in place. The lights flashed green.

'Ready when you are, Sarge.'

Dallas reached over and gently pushed Shannon back against the corridor wall.

'There's likely to be some shooting when that door opens, Miss Lynne.'

A flush of irritation rose in her, but she swallowed it. He was right—and she didn't like that either. Remember what they're doing for you, she told herself. They're helping you take back your ship, and they could die doing it.

Andropov had his masher drawn, barrel levelled at the door. Dallas glanced at him, and some unspoken signal passed between them. Andropov closed the circuit. The door slid open with a soft hiss of vented oxygen.

Shannon tensed, expecting blaster fire—a hail of lead—something. Instead, silence.

Dallas didn't wait. He pulled a spherical metal object from his belt, about the size of an egg, pressed a recessed button, and lobbed it inside. The stun grenade went off in a rapid-fire burst of blinding flashes.

Dallas and Andropov surged forward, one low, one high.

A burst of gunfire. A grunt over the comm link. Dallas's masher coughed twice, and a helmeted figure crumpled, a six-inch hole punched clean through the torso. Another pirate staggered back, clutching a ruined shoulder. Andropov finished him with a centre-mass shot, but not before taking a hit himself.

The wiry New Russian hunched over, clutching his side.

They didn't stop. Weapons up, eyes scanning, they swept the bridge for more hostiles.

Dallas's voice cut through the comms. 'Clear. Let's seal the door and get you patched up, Yuri.'

Shannon stepped inside as Dallas keyed the panel Andropov had used, locking the door behind them. The display glowed red. Nobody was getting through that now.

Dallas activated environmental controls. A rush of air flooded the bridge. As soon as the pressure normalised, he grabbed a med-kit from his bag and crouched beside Andropov.

'Got you at the shoulder joint,' he said, inspecting the damage. 'Armour caught most of it.'

Andropov muttered something in Russian, scowling. 'I must be getting slow in my old age, Sarge. Didn't see him until he fired.'

Dallas grinned. 'Well, he's pretty dead now, Tovarisch. I'm calling that a win. Shannon?'

She snapped out of her daze.

'Do you know how to dress a wound?'

She nodded, taking the med-kit and kneeling beside Andropov. Dallas moved to the bridge console.

'Ship's still mostly in vacuum,' he reported. 'Only engineering has partial pressure. Looks like something's blocking the bulkhead door from sealing.'

He switched feeds. The battered screen flickered to life, showing the engineering-bay entrance.

A body lay crushed beneath the door.

'Looks like his weapon jammed it open,' Dallas muttered. 'Cut through him pretty cleanly, though.'

Shannon swallowed hard and focused on tending to Andropov's shoulder.

Dallas cycled through the remaining cameras. Two more bodies—one drifting near the aft corridor, another floating in the ship's head.

Dallas smirked. 'Well, that one sure got caught with his pants down.'

Andropov chuckled, then winced. Shannon looked up at them, her stomach twisting. Six dead in ten minutes. And they were already making jokes.

Dallas caught her expression. His smirk faded.

'Sorry, Shannon,' he said quietly. 'Occupational hazard. I can be a little insensitive.' A pause. 'You okay?'

Shannon grimaced. 'It's just...' A solid knot of emotion lodged in her chest. '...I hated them so much. Knowing they were on our ship, knowing they killed Donal. I wanted to kill them myself. But now they're dead...' Her voice faltered.

Dallas placed a firm but gentle hand on her shoulder. 'And it just stops. I know.' His voice was steady. 'Everything about them just stops—like they were never there. And we're the ones who stopped them.'

He pulled off his visor and wiped sweat from his forehead. 'It's different when they're human,' he admitted. 'I trained for it, of course, but I'd never killed a man before. Not until now. Plenty of Crawlers and their slave species—but this...' He exhaled, took a long drink from his water bottle, then handed it to Andropov and Shannon in turn.

His gaze hardened as he looked back at Andropov. 'I'm giving you a sedative, Yuri. I don't want you going into shock.'

Andropov weakly protested. 'No, Sarge. I'm good. You need someone at your back.'

Dallas glanced at Shannon with a small smile. 'Shannon will keep me right.'

Despite everything, she felt steadier than she had in weeks.

Dallas's eyes snapped into focus as he keyed his comm link. 'Dallas here. Yes, the ship is secure, sir. We'll need a sweep team to make sure there's no one hiding out, but we got six. Yuri took a blaster hit to the shoulder—bleeding's stopped, and I've given him a sedative, but he needs medical attention.'

He turned toward Shannon. 'What? Yeah, she's here. Name's Shannon Lynne, sir. Owner's daughter.' A pause. 'Okay.'

He pulled the comm link from his HUD and held it out to her. 'The captain wants to talk to you. Go ahead—it's okay.'

She hesitated before taking it.

'Miss Lynne,' said a deep voice with a faint accent she couldn't place.

'This is Shannon Sanchez Lynne of the mining ship Jenny Lynne,' she replied, her voice steadier than she felt. 'Thank you for helping me get my family's ship back, Captain.'

'A pleasure, Miss Lynne. Now I need your help. I need to crash your ship into the drive outlet of that destroyer over there.'

'What?'

'Dallas will patch the controls over to the Freyja. We'll fly her remotely from here. You, Dallas, and Andropov will take the broomstick and rendezvous with us at a safe distance. We'll pick you up.'

Her fingers tightened around the comm link.. 'Hold on a damn minute, Captain. I just got my ship back. I'm not crashing it into anything.'

'Miss Lynne.' Rakkan's voice remained calm but firm. 'My ship's Warp Drive is disabled. The Freyja only has subspace drive, and that pirate vessel outguns me two to one. I need an edge over Dante. Or we all—my crew, your family, and you—end up either dead or as prisoners. Unless you've got a better idea, this is the play.'

Shannon frowned. 'Well, as a matter of fact, I might. But first, I want to talk about a deal.'

Silence. Then: A deal? My people just risked their lives to take back your ship, and you want to deal?'

She squared her shoulders, even though her hands trembled behind the console.

'That's right, Captain. Haven't you ever done business with a wildcatter before?' She forced steel into her voice. 'You want my help to take Dante out? Then you help me get my father and my brother back. Dante has them on that destroyer.'

A long pause. When Rakkan spoke again, his voice was edged with steel. 'You realize there are over fifty pirates on that vessel? Some of them are Defined.'

'I know it won't be easy. But that's what I want, Captain Rakkan. They're my family. They're all I have left.'

Another silence. Then a short laugh. 'Miss Lynne, I can see you drive a hard bargain. I could just order Dallas to take your ship and go ahead with my plan. But I still have a few scruples left.'

A beat. 'But you better start talking. Fast.'

She took a slow breath. 'Well, Captain... did I mention the aft hold has three hundred mining charges in it?'

Silence.

Then Rakkan said, 'Mining charges, you say? Keep talking.'

'Use the cargo bots,' she said, faster now, the rehearsed anger gone. 'We keep the Jenny Lynne intact. The aft hold's full of charges on pallets. We've got three hopper drones — work bots that move ore. They can lug a pallet, sling it over, and stick the charges where you need them. I can open the aft node and nudge them out on a short remote. You line them up from the Freyja. Dallas flies us clear. The bots do the close work.'

There was a pause. 'You can control them from there?'

'Just enough.' Her grip tightened on the comm. 'I'll send the command. They won't steer into traffic — just a shove and a latch. If we lose the link, they're programmed to come home; we can override if needed. If they get shot, we still haven't lost the Jenny Lynne.'

Rakkan's voice went quiet and sharp. 'If they waste time shooting at a couple of hundred mining charges, they're not blasting the Freyja.' He let the angles run through his head. 'Milligan rigs the pickup. Dallas holds the evac. We give you the link and a clear window to push them out.'

There was a long pause, and then: 'Do not screw this up, Shannon Lynne.'

'I won't,' she said.

'Then we have a deal.'

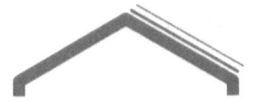

Chapter 13: Killing Time

You don't punch your way out of a trap without leaving something behind. Sometimes it's blood. Sometimes it's the plan.

The Freyja fell away from the station, cutting through the black at a sharp angle. I glanced at the ship's clock. Almost time to talk to Dante. First, I tapped the comm link. Leela's craggy face flickered onto the screen. 'Engineering. And if this isn't urgent, don't talk to me right now.'

I smiled. 'It's urgent, Leela. I need everything we've got from the subspace drive and the attitude thrusters.'

She grunted. 'Right, Cap'n. They're as ready as we can make 'em.'

'That's good enough for me.'

I turned to Dakkar. 'Everyone in Gel Fields. Combat armour stays on. Cluster near the airlocks closest to the bridge—that's where the Defined will come in. Engineering too. We don't lose that without a fight.'

Leela's voice cracked back in. 'Uh... Jero. If it's all the same, I'd rather stay out of the Gel Fields—until you tell me to get in.'

I narrowed my eyes. 'Why?'

'Got something I'm working on.'

'What something?'

'Well...' She hesitated. 'It's a long shot, sir. I figured I could start stripping the Warp Drive. It's not in use, so no risk of blowing up.'

My pulse kicked. 'Are you saying there's a chance you can get it working?'

'No, sir. I'm definitely not saying that.'

'But if you were thinking about trying—'

'Then I'd need to be outside a Gel Field, wouldn't I?'

I let it hang a moment. 'Fine. Keep a Gel Field ready, close by. The second I say, you get in. No hesitation.'

Leela exhaled, relieved.

I turned to Dakkar. 'Get the splinter ships prepped. Pilots in each, ready to launch.'

He folded his arms. 'You sure this plan's going to work, Jero?'

'Not even a little. But it's the best we've got.'

A sharp ping cut across the bridge as an alarm flared on the tactical display. Incoming vessels — maximum range.

I swore. 'What now?'

Dakkar's fingers flew over his console. 'Well, Captain... human Navy ships. Two—no, three. Two destroyers and a frigate, inbound from Callista.' He hesitated. 'Wait. There's another one. A few light-minutes ahead.'

I tensed. 'Identify.'

He studied the drive signature, then let out a slow breath. 'It looks familiar... Captain, it's them. The Defined ship we disabled at the Sentinel.'

A cold fuse lit under my ribs. I'd expected this. The Defined didn't quit. They didn't forgive. They avenged.

'They haven't given up on getting Virell back,' Dakkar muttered.

I let out a slow breath. 'He's one reason. The dead we left them with are the other.'

They had their loyalties — their reasons. I'd given the order.

Dakkar's brow tightened. 'You regretting it?'

I clenched my jaw. 'We did what we had to.'

That wasn't a yes.

Dakkar's console beeped again; his frown deepened. 'They're dropping speed fast. Must have crews in Gel Fields — AI handling deceleration.' He looked up. 'Either they know it's us and the Navy's tailing them... or the Defined ran straight into a naval squadron.'

I set my shoulders. 'Or the Navy is out here for another reason.'

Dakkar's eyes darkened. 'Dante.'

The comm lit. Dante's smirk filled the screen, as insufferable as ever. 'Rakkan,' he drawled, 'I assume you can see those ships on long-range sensors. Don't think that'll stop me. I can catch you and be gone before they close. So — what's it going to be?'

I met his gaze. 'Dante, I'll take your offer. Give me a few minutes to brief my crew. We'll ready the airlocks.'

His scowl sharpened. 'You don't need minutes for that. Stop now. Weapons offline.'

I nodded, keeping my face unreadable. 'Alright, Dante.' I turned to Dakkar. 'Bring us to a full stop. Stand the weapons systems down.'

Dante leaned forward, his expression predatory. 'No tricks, Rakkan. If you try to fool me, I will kill every one of your people. Just remember who's in charge here. You can't run, and you definitely can't fight.'

I gave him a slow, deliberate smile. 'No, Dante. I keep my promises. Rakkan out.'

The screen cut out, and I exhaled through my teeth. 'And I already promised Thorne I'd let him kill you, Cisco Dante.'

I keyed the ship-wide comm. 'All hands — into Gel Fields. That means you too, Leela. Prepare for extreme manoeuvres.'

The Freyja slowed on the tactical display, engines idling. Dante's ship crept in, nose first, probing for deception.

'Engines at maximum subspace burn in twenty seconds. Course laid in. Splinter ships launch in ten. Weapons systems active in five... four... three... two... one. Execute.'

Outside, three splinter ships shot from the Freyja's launch bays, streaking toward Dante's vessel.

'Fire ship-killers! Start burn! Go!'

Torpedoes flashed through the void, but even before they reached range, his defences bloomed — chaff, counter-fire, everything the Navy could buy. My warheads broke apart in bursts of bright orange flame.

The Freyja shuddered under maximum subspace burn, but she was slow — too slow. I didn't need a screen to picture Dante's grin. He thought he had me. Maybe he did.

The bridge hummed with strain — metal and bone both pretending not to break. I focused on the tactical readout. Dante wasn't moving yet. He was watching. Thinking.

Then the holo tank flickered. He was launching something.

No — holding back. Waiting to see what I did next. That told me everything I needed to know.

'Splinter ships, stay evasive. Dante's trying to bait us. He's holding back, waiting for an opening.'

I was right. Seconds later, his ship-killers launched — not at the Freyja, but at my splinters.

'Brace!' I barked, though my pilots didn't need telling. They jinked and spun, cutting through the storm while the Freyja's point defences chewed apart the incoming fire.

Dante was talking again, but I wasn't listening. I didn't need to. I already knew his game.

His next move lit the display: splinter ships, five of them, burning hard toward mine.

I had three.

Not great odds. I ground my teeth. 'Stay sharp, people. They've got numbers, but we're better.'

It was a lie. Maybe. I hoped my pilots believed it.

The Freyja kept burning, but the asteroid field was still too far. Dante knew it. He wasn't even adjusting course. To him, it looked like I was running — just delaying the inevitable.

My comm pinged. Leela.

I opened a private channel. 'Leela, tell me you've got something.'

A pause. Then her voice, breathless but steady. 'I might have something, Cap'n.'

'Define might.'

'Well, you remember how I wasn't saying I could get the Warp Drive working?'

I swallowed. 'Yeah?'

'Well, I'm still not saying that.' A grin edged into her voice. 'But if you're asking whether I think I can light the fuse on this thing, then... maybe.'

I didn't hesitate. 'Do it.'

'Uh, Cap'n, you realize that if this goes wrong, we all—'

'Leela.' My voice was firm. 'Do it.'

She sighed. 'Aye, sir.'

I cut the channel and looked back at the tactical display. Dante thought he had us trapped.

The numbers were in his favour. He was already tasting victory. He had no idea what was coming next.

I keyed the comms. 'Warp Two. On my mark.'

'Leela,' I said quietly, mark.'

The Freyja jumped. Stars smeared into light.

For a heartbeat, the void tore itself apart around us — then steadied.

On the tactical feed, I saw his signature spike. He'd tracked the jump. He was following.

I exhaled, jaw tight. 'Now he pays.'

The first explosion hit the Kiss the Blade. Right on schedule.

I watched, arms folded, as the second charge detonated. Debris spun from his hull. Then a third.

Emergency signals flared across my display.

Dante's voice tore through open comms. 'What?! What's hitting me?'

I didn't answer. Let him sweat. More charges. More damage. His engines groaned, readouts flooding with red. Then, right on cue, her face filled the screen.

'Dante,' she said, voice smooth, 'this is Shannon Lynne, aboard the Jenny Lynne. Hope you liked my mining charges. There's more.'

The kid had gall. I liked that about her.

Dante was flailing now, scanning the field for his attacker. But he wouldn't find her.

I'd made sure of that.

Shannon glanced at her console. 'Right now, you've got... eight more charges within a light-second of your hull. They're just sitting there. Waiting.'

Dante's ragged breathing filled the comms. Shannon's voice went hard. 'So here's what happens. You kill your engines. You sit tight. My new friend Jero Rakkan is on his way.'

Softer. Meaner. 'This is for what you did to my family.'

I watched the Kiss the Blade's engines flicker. A pause. Then—'Stop all engines!' Dante's voice cracked. There it was.

I keyed open comms. 'Kiss the Blade splinter ships: cut weapons. Turn your helms over to my AI.' A beat. 'Do that and you live.'

No one answered. I let the silence stretch. 'Keep firing, and you're dead in ten seconds.'

Another pause. Slowly, Dante's remaining fighters peeled away, their weapons going cold.

An incoming hail. I accepted it. Dante's face looked pale — cornered, beaten, afraid.

I leaned back. 'Now, Dante,' I said, voice as cold and smooth as ice, 'let's talk about your surrender.'

MORGAN SAT ALONE IN the auxiliary systems bay where the Freyja's firewalls were thickest and the lights ran low. He hadn't moved during the firefight. He hadn't needed to.

On his monitor the tactical overlay flickered. The Kiss the Blade vented heat and plasma like a drowning animal. Shannon Lynne's charges had done their work.

Morgan allowed himself a single, measured breath. Dante, it seemed, was no longer a variable. He reached for the secure console, then stopped. No need to report. Not yet — not until the board cleared. And once it did, Virrell would become the next piece to move.

They'd all underestimated Rakkan. Typical. Hadn't they read his file? Morgan had — every debrief, every reprimand, every improbable survival. He knew better than to mistake instinct for luck.

Silence stretched in the bay. Somewhere above, crew shouted, sealed doors, hauled the wounded. Morgan listened, still as ice.

Sometimes the most useful thing a spy could do was nothing at all. Sometimes the fall of a fool cleared the path for sharper minds. His path lay ahead — into Eden, toward the weapon waiting there. Take control by any means necessary. Just as the directive required.

He leaned back and waited for the next move.

Chapter 14: Revelations and Alliances

The Freyja slipped into Callista's docking queue like a cat sneaking into a fish market. I stood on the bridge, shoulders tight beneath a jacket that had seen too many campaigns, watching the station swell in the viewscreen.

Dante was bleeding but alive, locked in the brig — the chamber next to Virrell's. When they let him out of the regeneration tanks, I owed Thorne a bottle of New Ireland Poteen for not letting him pull the trigger. His favourite, and damned hard to find this far from home.

He'd want to end Dante here and now and part of me didn't blame him. The people we found in Dante's brig — what was left of them — were reason enough to put him down like a rabid dog. But I told Thorne no. Dante would answer for what he'd done.

Someone in the Polity had used him to get at the Freyja, and I couldn't be sure they wouldn't just let him go and use him again. Anushka had wanted to throw him out an airlock there and then — too easy for Dante, that. He was owed justice, and someone needed to make it pay. If I was all that could do that, then so be it. If nobody else could do the job, it was down to me. I'd do my best to make him answer for his crimes. Dante's victims deserved it.

Ani's grandfather was alive, though barely. Dante hadn't bothered much with him beyond letting him starve. Shannon had found her father's body in one of the interrogation rooms — beaten to death, though the station doctor figured his heart had given out before the final blow.

She sat with her brother for a long time before Dallas helped her move him to the Freyja. They'd grown close since the rescue. Whether it was friendship or something more, I couldn't tell.

The boy was still breathing, but only just. One of the Defined from Dante's crew had beaten him unconscious when they took the Jenny Lynne. He hadn't woken since. Moving him far wasn't an option, but our med bay had what he needed. The old Demos field kits still worked — patched, ancient, but reliable. Freyja's were better.

I offered Shannon a place on the crew. Leela said she could use her in engineering, and she was right. The girl had steady hands and knew her way around a reactor core. I'd given her one of the staterooms close to med bay — enough space for her and her brother to stay together while he healed.

She'd tried to refuse at first. Said she didn't want charity. 'This isn't charity,' I told her. 'It's a berth and a job. You've earned both.'

She held my gaze for a moment, then nodded. 'Thank you, Captain.'

Thorne had been listening from the hatch. 'She'll pull her weight,' he muttered. I didn't doubt it.

The small mercies mattered. After everything Dante had taken from her, this one I could give back.

Callista Station loomed ahead — a monument to human ambition and compromise.

Once a military outpost, it had grown into a commercial hub where the Polity's laws stretched thin against the realities of frontier trade. Out here, the Syndicate held more sway than the courts.

Its outer hull was a patchwork of old armour and new profit: gunmetal plates stitched with polished chrome, weld scars beside flickering billboards. Traffic moved constantly through half a dozen docking arms, customs bays that hadn't seen a real inspection in years. Behind that steel and glass, deals were struck. Ships bought and sold. People too, probably.

Callista didn't pretend to be anything else. It didn't need to. Out here, everyone knew the rules — credits spoke, power defended itself, and you never asked a question you weren't ready to answer.

The comms panel lit up. 'Callista Control to vessel Freyja, you are cleared for approach to Bay 17-C. Transmitting final vector now,' a bored voice announced.

I acknowledged and eased the Freyja forward. The hull shuddered as the docking clamps locked, metal groaning against metal. One by one, the status lights flickered green.

'We have hard seal, Captain,' Dakkar said. 'External power and life-support connections established.'

I rolled my shoulders, working out the tension. 'All right. Secure from docking procedures. Standard rotation. Keep a skeleton crew aboard at all times.'

He nodded. 'Understood.'

'We don't get paid until I deliver Virell. Until then, stay sharp. Tell the crew to keep their mouths shut about who we are and where we've been.'

I turned to leave, but Leela caught my arm — light, hesitant. 'Captain,' she said quietly, glancing toward the bulkheads as if the station itself might be listening. 'Something's wrong out here. It's not just Demos.'

I frowned. 'Go on.'

'I've got friends on Callista. Picked up a message dump when we jumped in. Traffic's thinning across the outer lanes.' She hesitated, eyes flicking to the sensor board. 'And there's more pirate activity than there used to be.' 'Not many Polity warships around anymore, either. Like somebody pulled them back.'

I felt a cold knot form under my ribs.

'And people are talking,' Leela added. 'About ghost fleets. Whole packs of Crawler ships heading into deep space like bats out of hell.' She gave a short, grim laugh. 'Whatever's coming, Captain... nobody wants to be here when it arrives.'

I filed it away. Another whisper in the dark. Another weight to carry.

I keyed my communicator, calling my senior officers to a meeting. Reluctantly, I added Morgan to the list.

Morgan was younger than me by nearly a decade—same height, broader shoulders, sharper jaw. Where I moved like someone who'd spent too long in armour, he moved like he still trained every morning, expecting trouble. Off-mission, he spoke easily but said little: charm without substance, a smile that never reached his eyes. I didn't trust him.

There was something in the way he watched. Not just scanning threats—calculating.

He wasn't stupid, and he'd seen action. He didn't make mistakes. That was what unsettled me.

Men that capable usually had a reason to be on a ship like mine, and I hadn't yet figured out his.

And there was still the way he'd shot his own man—clean, controlled, without hesitation. Justified, maybe. Not forgotten.

Hela's message came through encrypted and to the point: coordinates for our meeting in three hours.

'We have confirmation?' Dakkar asked, reading over my shoulder.

'Yes. She wants to see me right away—with Morgan and Virell.'

Thorne, still stiff from regeneration, crossed his arms and eyed Morgan. 'You expecting trouble, Captain?'

'I'm expecting complications,' I said. 'Our job is to get Virell to Hela safe and sound.'

My gaze locked on Morgan. We hadn't spoken directly since Sentinel. 'Are you with me on this, Morgan? Get Virell to our boss alive, right?'

Morgan laughed shortly 'That's the order, Captain. No Virrell, no pay."

'A security detail will follow behind to cover if things get hot,'

Morgan's grin didn't fade. 'Then let's hope it stays cold.'

When they'd gone, I stepped into my cabin and peeled off the captain's jacket, draping it over the chair. The silence hit like oxygen after vacuum—clean, necessary. No more voices. Just the weight that never left.

I paused at the mirror. Not out of habit, or vanity. Just that one quiet thought I couldn't shake: How many more compromises before I stopped recognizing the man staring back? And if my daughter saw me now... what would she see?

The reflection didn't lie. Older, yes—but still dangerous. The lines around my eyes were earned in combat, not time. My frame was lean, posture straight. Strength hadn't left me; it had just settled deeper, beneath the surface.

My hair had grown out past regulation. Grey threaded through the temples—more campaign strain than years. I looked like a man who'd seen the edge and made it back. Barely. The scar running from collarbone to ear caught the light. Pale now, but still there. I'd nearly died for that one. I remembered the hull breach—the flash, the cold, and the silence before someone dragged me out of it.

My gaze drifted to the tattoo on my left shoulder: a marsupial rat, jaws open, claws mid-lunge—the predator from Farpoint Six. I'd been green then, just out of tactical retraining after Eden. First drop with the Defined, and I saw how the Navy treated them—like they weren't human. Some officers even used the old slang: Defined scum. *Rats.*

I'd wanted to say something. But the night we got back from that mission, my squad said it for me. We made it a badge instead.

Rakkan's Rats.

We took their insult and turned it into our standard—a mark of defiance, of unity. And every mission from then was a Rats win. People saw us, and they saw the Defined as more than vermin.. I wondered if Riven would have understood. How some names start as slurs and end as banners.

But this wasn't about memory. It was about readiness. I hadn't come all this way to fail her. And I wasn't about to start now. I opened a drawer and took out a small case of civilian clothes—plain enough not to draw attention, refined enough to show respect for Hela's rank.

Then a last check of weapons: a slim pistol at the small of my back, a ceramic blade in my boot, and a neural disruptor disguised as a comm implant behind my ear.

I moved to the airlock.

Ariel's voice cut through my relay. 'Captain, I've reviewed the latest security scans for the meeting site.'

'Anything to worry about?'

'Standard Syndicate protocols—heavy surveillance, guards dressed as service crew, multiple escape routes for their VIPs. Looks like a perfect holiday spot for people who make trouble disappear.'

That made sense.

Morgan was waiting for me in the airlock, Virell in tow. The older man looked vaguely bored as always, his upright posture and aristocratic poise at odds with the cuffs binding his wrists.

Catching the look on my face, Morgan said, 'Station security's on the payroll. They won't make waves. And we don't want the professor here making a run for it, do we?'

Behind him waited four men in civilian clothes—two of his, two of mine. I winked at Sergio Dallas, and he smiled. Andropov was still in rehab, but Sergio had brought another special-operations veteran aboard—a tall New Caledonian named McCall. They'd trail us. No comms chatter unless it went bad.

The airlock cycled open, revealing the corridor beyond. Callista's artificial day was in full swing, lights tuned to a convincing mid-afternoon glow. The main concourse teemed with humanity in all its variations—miners, traders, Syndicate enforcers, and the ones who tried too hard not to look like any of them.

I stepped through. It was only a few hundred metres to Hela's hotel, but we watched every inch of it. We couldn't afford to lose Virell now.

The Asteria Grand hung in orbit like a diamond-studded spider, its central hub sprouting crystalline arms that caught and fractured starlight. We stepped from the private shuttle into a docking bay more suited to a luxury yacht than a freighter, attendants in crisp uniforms arrayed at practiced angles of deference.

I adjusted my collar, aware of Virell's silent presence behind me, his restraints disguised as high-grade fashion accessories.

'Captain Rakkan, Mr. Morgan, and guest,' a concierge greeted, her smile balanced perfectly between respect and servility. 'Ms. Hela is expecting you. Please follow me.'

I nodded, one hand near my concealed weapon as I gestured for Virell to move ahead. Even bound, he carried himself with that effortless arrogance the old families bred into their children.

The attendants gave him a wider berth than they gave me. Even as a prisoner, Ephraim Virell radiated command.

'Enjoying seeing how the winners live?' Virell murmured as we stepped into the private elevator—walls of real glass, not projections, a level of extravagance that bordered on insult.

'Shut up,' I said, without heat.

The elevator rose in silence, the station's vast structure unfolding below. Unlike the bare geometry of military outposts or the cluttered efficiency of trade hubs, the Asteria Grand existed purely for display—each level more indulgent than the last: gardens from a dozen worlds, a real waterfall, a gallery of living holograms that shifted as we passed.

'The penthouse level,' the concierge announced as the car slowed. 'Ms. Hela has requested privacy for your meeting. I'll leave you here.'

The doors opened on a circular foyer of polished stone that mirrored us like still water. A man waited—military build under an immaculate suit. His eyes assessed me with professional detachment, pausing briefly where a weapon might hide.

'Captain Rakkan. Mr. Morgan. Mr. Virell.' The guard's voice was softer than I expected, almost dissonant coming from a man built like a tank. 'You'll need to surrender your weapons before proceeding.'

I'd expected that. I drew the pistol from the small of my back and the knife from my boot, placing both on the scanner tray that slid smoothly out from the wall. I said nothing about the neural disruptor. If their scanners couldn't find it, that was their problem.

'The implant behind your right ear as well, Captain,' the guard said, tone unchanged.

Damn. So much for that advantage. Either their scanners were better than I thought—or they knew exactly what to look for. I kept my expression neutral, removed the disruptor, and laid it on the tray. The guard's eyes flicked up, a knowing glint there, but he said nothing.

Satisfied, he stepped aside. 'Ms. Hela is waiting in the observation lounge.'

Chapter 15: Hela's Penthouse

Some rooms came dressed to kill—this one just handed you a drink and waited for you to notice the bleeding.

The penthouse stretched before me, designed to impress and unsettle in equal measure. The ceiling soared two stories high, and the walls shifted from solid to transparent without warning, offering fleeting glimpses of the void beyond. The floor drank sound, swallowing our footsteps. The furniture hovered a few inches off the ground on magnetic mounts, polished surfaces that caught light like oil on water.

At the centre sat Hela, on a chair that looked poured from liquid metal. For a moment, I wondered if she'd started to believe her own mythology.

She wore a suit of midnight blue that absorbed the light instead of reflecting it, cut with the precision of a weapon. Pale hair swept back. Cheekbones like blades.

'Hela,' I said, 'you look very striking. Going for barbarian space queen? I'll admit—it works.'

'Jero Rakkan,' she replied, voice cool, amused. 'Still the dangerous one. Still taking risks when silence would do.'

She gestured toward a low table and a pair of chairs that slid from the shadows, mechanisms whisper-quiet. A servant appeared without sound and set a glass of whisky by my side.

She caught my look. 'Drink, Rakkan. It's whisky—very old, very rare. You've earned it.'

I didn't touch it. I turned the glass in the light, watching the amber swirl. With Hela, a gift always came with strings.

Her lips curved. 'You did well. Not quite as past your prime as you pretend.'

Her eyes flicked to Morgan—one measured glance—then to Virell. 'And Father. How gratifying to see you in such compromised circumstances.'

Virell inclined his head. 'Justine. You're looking well.'

She set her own glass down on the table beside her, the sound sharp in the silence.

'So,' she said, crossing one leg over the other, every movement deliberate, 'you've brought me Ephraim Virell, as promised. The final piece in a plan years in the making.' Her gaze lingered on him, sharp and assessing. 'Let's talk about my end of the deal.'

Languidly, she lit a cigarette and blew a thin stream of smoke toward the ceiling. Then, with a small smile, Hela reached into the air and made a gesture. A holographic display shimmered to life—an image of a young woman with dark hair and features that echoed my own.

'Riven Rhys. Currently registered as a resident of the Eden System.'

The name hit like a blow. Riven. At last, a name. I kept my face steady, but something must have flickered, because Hela's smile deepened.

'Twenty-four standard years old now. Educated at Eden Central Academy—xenobiology and advanced communications. The Crawlers attacked before she could graduate.'

I stared at the image, memorizing every line. Her mother's eyes. Her mother's jaw. But the set of her mouth, the focus in her brow—that was mine.

'She spent two years in a high-value detention facility,' Hela continued. 'Governor's granddaughter status bought her that time, but not safety. Her mother and grandfather were with her.'

My throat tightened. I already knew what came next.

'There was Guerrilla activity on Eden,' Hela said. 'The Crawlers made an example of them—executed her mother and grandfather.'

I swallowed. 'And Riven?'

Hela's smile thinned. 'Escaped before they could kill her. Joined the resistance. And now, despite her age, she's one of their leaders. Tactical. Effective. Rather like her father.'

I ignored the jab. 'Our arrangement was that you'd provide her location and the resources for extraction.'

'And we will,' she said evenly. 'You've earned that. But you didn't come all this way just for your daughter, did you, Captain?'

'There is no *just* about getting Riven out. I'm going to do that or die trying'

But she knew there was more. It had to be Morgan. Fine then, I had no choice but to be plain. 'This,' I said, 'is about Eden itself.' I glanced at Morgan before turning back to her. 'Virell claims the Crawlers are building something there. A weapon.'

Hela raised a brow, exhaling smoke in a slow curl. 'A weapon?'

Morgan stepped forward slightly, voice calm, professional. 'Confirmed. I forwarded the full brief before we arrived at Callista—schematics, intercepts, Virell's statements. The evidence is consistent.'

She already knew. She'd known before I stepped through the door.

'It's a superweapon,' I said. 'If they finish it, they can erase a fleet in one strike. And they won't stop at Eden.'

Hela stubbed out her cigarette, gaze cool and unreadable. 'The Syndicate has interests across those sectors. If this is true, it threatens us all. But before we act, we require confirmation.'

I felt my jaw tighten. 'The only confirmation is there, on Eden.'

She nodded once, almost approving. 'Then perhaps you should go and find it.'

Morgan glanced my way but said nothing.

Hela rose from her chair, movements unhurried, the authority in them absolute. 'You'll return to your ship and await further instruction. The Syndicate will review the data and determine our next step.'

'That's convenient,' I said.

Her smile was faint and cold. 'It's practical. Go, Captain. We'll be in touch once the decision is made.'

She turned her back, already dismissing us—the conversation, and me—filed away like another entry in her ledger.

I wasn't satisfied. Every moment we delayed could be Riven's last. 'Time isn't a luxury we have.'

She frowned. 'Impatient to charge into another suicide mission, Captain? Perhaps my third AI was right about your death wish.'

'My daughter's life isn't something I take lightly, Hela,' I said, the words edged with heat. 'The only death wish I have is for the Crawlers in my way.'

She studied me for a long moment, then smiled—something close to admiration flickering in her expression. 'There you are, Captain. I see you clearly now. The Syndicate needs that kind of clarity. Wait a few hours. Things are already in motion. Just a few details left to arrange.'

Imperious again, she gestured toward the elevator. 'I suggest you enjoy the amenities of the Asteria while I confer with my colleagues. The casino level is particularly diverting. I'll arrange guest credentials for you—along with a generous credit allowance.'

'Father will remain with me,' she added, her gaze shifting to the bound man. 'We have much to discuss.'

Virell smiled thinly. 'Family reunion, Justine?'

Something flickered in her eyes—anger, or something colder. 'It's going to be such fun, Daddy.'

Virell's face lost colour.

The guard stepped forward. 'Captain Rakkan, I'll escort you to the casino.'

I turned toward the elevator, but Hela's voice stopped me. 'And Jero—' she said lightly, 'the neural disruptor was a bold choice. I appreciate initiative, but not deception. Remember that.'

I met her eyes and nodded once, accepting the warning for what it was.

The elevator doors slid shut, severing my view of the penthouse. I exhaled slowly, cataloguing the meeting in my mind.

One thing I was sure of: Whether Hela helped me or not, I wasn't leaving Callista without the means to reach Eden, and get Riven out. Nothing was going to get in my way.

A FEW HOURS LATER, I was summoned again.

The penthouse had changed. The transparent walls were now opaque, muting the city's light. Harsh illumination cut across a holographic war table that dominated the room. The Syndicate's skyline had given way to a theatre of war.

Hela stood at the table, fingers ghosting across the projection as constellations and ship movements rippled around her. Morgan waited near the wall—still, watchful, unreadable.

'Have you reached a decision regarding my proposal?' I asked.

She smiled, that measured curve she used when victory was already in hand. 'I have. The Syndicate will support your mission to Eden—intelligence feeds, special-issue equipment, and diplomatic credentials to move through the checkpoints.'

Relief stirred, but I kept it buried. 'Thank you.'

'Don't thank me yet.' Her hand swept through the light, zooming on the Eden System. The gesture looked almost ritual. 'There are conditions.'

'There always are.'

'First, full access to any intelligence you gather—Crawler deployments, installations, fleet readiness. Our border holdings are exposed. We can't afford surprises.'

'Agreed.' Expected.

'Second, Morgan will accompany you—to assess the situation firsthand and ensure Syndicate interests are represented.'

Also expected. The muscle in my jaw tightened. Morgan and I had history—the kind that usually ended in blood.

'And third,' she said, her tone cooling, 'I'll be joining you personally.'

That landed like a pulse grenade. 'You? Aren't you a little high up to take odds like that? Your AIs must have run the numbers.'

'They have. Fifty-fifty.' She said it without hesitation. 'But I have my reasons.'

Her eyes lingered on the spinning hologram of Eden. 'Our interests there are... significant. Beyond commerce or territory. We have assets that require direct attention.'

'What kind of assets?'

'The kind that aren't discussed with partners of convenience,' she replied smoothly. 'Only that they represent a substantial investment—and one I intend to protect.'

It was more than money. It always was.

'Hela, you're too smart to gamble yourself on a coin toss. So what's really on Eden?'

Her gaze flicked to me—cold, appraising. 'You're often impertinent, Captain. Be careful.'

For a moment, though, something flickered behind the threat. Not calculation—memory, maybe even fear. Then it was gone, replaced by that imperious calm.

For a moment, though, something flickered behind the threat. Not calculation—memory, maybe even fear. Then it was gone, replaced by that imperious calm.

I pressed her. 'You didn't recruit me because I was a pushover. If we're going to work closely, I need to know. This matters.'

Something raw edged into her composure. 'You want to know why I'm risking everything? Fine. I'll give you the truth, and you can choke on it. You know I'm a clone of Ephraim Virell. Do you have any idea what that means? How every success I achieve is seen as nothing more than his echo?'

She studied me, eyes bright with fury and humiliation. 'I was created at his whim, educated into his image, prepared for leadership—then discarded when I ceased to amuse him. Now I will be the one to fix the disaster he set in motion. When Eden is secured, no one will mistake me for Virell's creature again. That's why I'm going—and I warn you not to stand in my way.'

Our eyes met across the war table, challenge and recognition cutting through the light between us. I understood what it meant to be discarded by the people who shaped you. Refuse her, and the mission died—and with it, my only chance of reaching Riven.

'If you're coming,' I said finally, 'there can be no confusion about who's leading.'

Hela folded her arms. 'I'll expect full collaboration.'

'You'll have it,' I said, holding her gaze. 'But on the ground—and in the black—the chain of command is mine. Tactical decisions, operational security, crew management—that's my domain.'

Her eyebrow arched. 'Or?'

'Or the likelihood of failure skyrockets. Nothing kills a mission faster than unclear authority. Your AIs know it.'

Hela's lips curved in something close to amusement. 'I don't need an AI to tell me that, Captain. I also have a leadership role, in case you hadn't noticed. I'll safeguard the Syndicate's interests—but you lead the mission.'

The assurance rang hollow, but I had no choice. 'Then we have an agreement.'

'Excellent.' She flicked her fingers and the holographic display shifted to a manifest of equipment and supplies. 'Our people are already assembling what you'll need. The Freyja will require modifications to optimize its chances of penetrating Crawler space.'

Schematics and data streams cascaded across the table. 'Advanced sensor dampening. Identification transponders running Syndicate encryption—enough to pass most checkpoints. Specialized comms for secure transmission once inside Eden's perimeter.' She paused, letting the next line land. 'And research-grade stealth systems—prototype arrays the Polity fleet doesn't even possess.'

The projection bathed her in cold light. Every item on the list was cutting edge, and every one of them came with a cost I hadn't yet seen. The Syndicate wasn't just investing in the mission.

They were betting on it. And on me.

'You'll also need these,' she added, bringing up schematics of weapons systems. 'Crawler defences have evolved since your last engagement. These countermeasures should address their latest capabilities.'

I studied the specs. Black-site hardware. Top-tier, even for special operations. 'Some of this is restricted. Even for black ops.'

'We have our sources.' Hela dismissed my concern with a wave. 'The important thing is that you'll be properly equipped for whatever resistance you encounter.'

I frowned. 'And Virell?'

'My clone parent is no longer your concern,' she said. 'He's being transferred to a more secure facility for... debriefing.'

My unease must have shown.

'Don't worry, Rakkan. He still has friends high in our organization, and he's agreed to tell us everything he knows. Critically, he never betrayed us. What he told the Polity was crafted to reveal nothing about our operations. The Syndicate remembers loyalty.'

She let the pause stretch, eyes glittering with satisfaction. 'And they will also remember that it was I who returned him to them.' She raised her glass. 'To successful partnerships, Captain Rakkan.'

I raised mine and drank. Then I set the crystal goblet down. 'To getting what we both want.'

Chapter 16: The Extra Muscle

I've never signed a death warrant—but I've been on the receiving end of contracts that might as well have come with a coffin.

'One last matter before you go,' Hela said, her voice dropping to a lower register that instantly set my nerves on edge. I turned back from the elevator, watching as she pressed her palm to the war table's surface. The holographic display shifted, reconfiguring to show a sleek, predatory vessel—angular, efficient, bristling with weapon systems that blended seamlessly into its hull.

A Valkyrie-class attack transport. One of the newest and most powerful ships in the Polity fleet. I'd served on earlier models. They carried Defined assault teams and their gear to the front line and kept them alive until the mission was done. Unease coiled in my gut.

'Why are you showing me this, Hela?'

'I've neglected to mention one aspect of our arrangements.' Her pale eyes tracked my reaction with clinical interest. 'It concerns the contract the Defined have been executing against you.'

I moved away from the elevator, my body tensing. 'What about it?'

'As you know, the Defined operate on a strictly contractual basis.' She expanded the image of the ship with a flick of her fingers. 'Once they accept a commission, they pursue it to completion—or until the issuing party formally annuls it.'

'I'm familiar with their methods,' I said. 'Get to the point.'

Hela's lips curved in a smile that didn't reach her eyes.

'The point, Captain, is that I've arranged with certain highly placed individuals in the Polity for the contract to be annulled. As of six hours ago, the Defined are no longer obligated to pursue you.'

Relief washed through me, but I kept my expression neutral. I wasn't naïve enough to think Hela did anything out of kindness. 'That will make our mission easier.'

'Indeed.' Her smile widened slightly. 'Especially since the Defined will accompany us.'

The words hung in the air. Cold. Heavy. I exhaled slowly. 'What do you mean?'

Morgan grinned icily, insolent as always. 'The Syndicate bought out their contract. They've been reassigned to provide tactical support for our mission to Eden.'

'That's insane,' I said. 'Weeks ago, we killed eight of their soldiers and left their ship venting atmosphere from three decks. They're not just going to switch sides and follow my orders.'

Hela watched me with the patience of a predator. 'The Defined are professionals. They understand that contracts change hands. Their loyalty is to the highest bidder—not personal vendettas.'

She held my gaze. 'You, Captain Rakkan, will command them in the field.'

'I understand the Defined better than most. Don't underestimate them,' I countered.

'I'm not asking you to accept it, Captain,' she said smoothly. 'I'm telling you. This is the ship we secured for them to use—since you did such a thorough job of making their previous one unsalvageable.'

Her voice held no resentment. Just fact.

'The Defined's capabilities are uniquely suited to our mission parameters,' she continued. 'Enhanced strength, endurance, advanced combat training, and experience with Crawler defence systems. Invaluable for the extraction phase.'

'They have a blood debt with me. That won't just go away.'

'I assure you, their commander, Kithlan, has already accepted the contract transfer. Their objectives now include your continued survival and operational authority.'

I shook my head. 'You should have consulted me before making this arrangement.'

'Should I?' Hela's voice was cool. 'Our agreement was that the Syndicate would provide resources for your mission. The specific nature of those resources remains at my discretion. The Defined represent the most effective tactical support available for an operation of this complexity.'

'My crew won't like this,' Jero warned.

Hela's gaze locked onto mine, unblinking. 'Your crew will follow your orders, Captain. And your orders will be to cooperate with the Defined for the duration of this mission. Unless, of course, you've reconsidered your determination to reach Eden and extract your daughter?'

It was an elegant trap, and we both saw the teeth. I couldn't abandon the mission—not when I was closer than I'd ever been to finding Riven. But accepting Hela's terms meant putting myself and my crew within arm's reach of Defined soldiers who had every reason to want me dead, contract or no contract.

'The Defined will report to you,' Hela said, reading the tightness in my jaw. 'This isn't a military hierarchy, Captain. It's a cooperative arrangement between separate assets with aligned objectives. The Defined operate within similar frameworks on most of their contracts.'

The mission had just become exponentially more complicated. The greatest threat no longer came only from the Crawlers waiting at Eden—it was now inside our own ranks. Internal conflict could destroy us before we reached our target.

But so could refusing the deal. If—and it was a massive if—Hela was truthful, the Defined's capabilities would drastically improve our chances of penetrating Eden's defence and extracting Riven.

The rational part of me acknowledged that. My instincts screamed otherwise.

As the elevator doors sealed me off from Hela, I let the mask slip—anger, frustration... and something colder beneath. I'd trusted my instincts in battle. Now I was trusting a contract with people I'd nearly killed. That wasn't strategy. That was desperation.

Kithlan-16 had not forgotten or forgiven. I'd seen it in his eyes during that last battle—something beyond duty, something personal.

The Defined might be engineered for peak performance, might operate within rigid contractual constraints, but in Kithlan's final glare there had been something dangerously close to human. It told me there would be blood between us.

Ahead, the airlock to the Freyja loomed, its stark contours promising the temporary sanctuary of command and routine. Beyond it, my crew awaited—along with the mess Hela had just dumped in my lap.

Inside, the ship hummed with the controlled chaos of pre-launch preparations. Crew moved with the grim efficiency of soldiers readying for battle. I stepped onto the bridge, hands clasped behind my back, watching their movements through the internal monitors.

The news about our new 'allies' had landed like a live grenade—initial shock giving way to anger, disbelief, then a slow, simmering acceptance. They knew as well as I did that what the Syndicate wanted, it got.

It helped that the Syndicate had already transferred the promised payments for retrieving Virell. This second job would make most of them rich beyond expectation—if they survived. The mission was clear: get into the Eden System, secure the intelligence the Syndicate wanted, and get out again.

And for me—it meant getting Riven out of hell.

'Engineering reports the new shield modulators are integrated and calibrated,' McNair announced from her station, her voice level despite the exhaustion in her eyes. She'd been up all night overseeing the installation of the Syndicate's new toys. 'Weapons upgrades are at ninety-three percent completion.'

I nodded, keeping my own fatigue buried. 'And the navigation package?'

'Installed and locked behind the security protocols I specified,' Dakkar reported. 'The Syndicate technicians weren't happy about the restrictions, but they complied.'

Minor victories. I'd insisted on compartmentalising the new systems, ensuring that Hela's people couldn't access critical ship functions without explicit authorisation. Trust only went so far in arrangements like these.

The ship's intercom activated before I could respond. 'Captain to Docking Bay Two,' the security officer announced. 'Our guests have arrived.'

I straightened my jacket, a reflex that did nothing to settle the unease coiling in my stomach.

'Inform them I'm on my way.'

To Dakkar, I added, 'Continue preparations. I want pre-launch checks completed by the time I return.'

The airlock cycled open as I approached, revealing Hela and Morgan standing in the narrow passage between ships. Behind them stood her personal bodyguards, Spalding and French, and four Syndicate operatives carrying cargo containers of varying sizes—each marked with a different security classification.

The larger crates likely held the specialised equipment Morgan had promised. The smaller ones, I suspected, contained Hela's personal effects—and perhaps a few surprises she hadn't disclosed.

'Captain Rakkan,' Hela greeted, stepping aboard with the casual confidence of someone who considered all spaces ultimately her domain. 'Your ship has an... interesting aesthetic.'

'She's served us both well,' I replied pointedly, choosing to take her words as observation rather than criticism. 'Welcome aboard the Freyja. I've assigned you the port stateroom and adjoining quarters for your staff. I trust you'll be comfortable there.'

Between checking on the bridge and monitoring the integration of new systems, I spent the next few hours ensuring our combat readiness.

McNair had nearly finished upgrading our defences with Ariel's help—cutting-edge targeting arrays, enhanced shield modulators, advanced stealth-field generators, and prototype disruptor tech designed to counter Crawler systems. The Freyja had never bristled with so much clandestine hardware; it made her feel half ghost, half weapon.

As we neared the Archimedes waypoint, I summoned my senior officers to the tactical room. Hela and Morgan joined us, standing slightly apart from the Freyja's crew as I activated the holographic display.

'The Defined vessel Avenger will be waiting at these coordinates,' I said, highlighting a position just beyond the waypoint's formal boundary. 'As per the arrangement negotiated by Ms. Virell, they'll serve as our tactical support for the mission to Eden.'

I watched my officers closely as they absorbed the confirmation. Dakkar kept his professional mask intact, but Thorne's expression darkened. Leela McNair glanced between them, gauging the emotional temperature in the room.

'The ship they were using was too damaged for this mission,' I continued. 'The Syndicate has leased them a Valkyrie-class assault carrier.'

Dakkar let out a low whistle. 'A Valkyrie-class? That's a whole lot of warship.'

'It is. Which is why they have it,' I said. 'They'll take point as we approach the border sectors, using their stealth systems to screen our advance.'

The bridge fell silent as we returned, all eyes drawn to the main viewscreen where the Avenger emerged against the star field—a silhouette of lethal geometry. Its matte-black hull drank the light rather than reflected it, an obsidian predator gliding in the void.

Its weapon emplacements were seamlessly integrated into the hull, visible only to the trained eye. Even at rest, the Avenger exuded menace.

'They're hailing us,' the comms officer reported, tension edging his voice.

I took my seat at the command station. 'On screen.'

The viewscreen flickered, revealing the Avenger's bridge—a space designed for function over comfort. At its centre stood Kithlan-16, his enhanced frame towering over the command dais.

Like all Defined, his appearance balanced human traits with engineered precision—broad shoulders, dense musculature, features shaped more for intimidation than aesthetics. A lattice of fine silver scars traced across his visible skin, the legacy of both combat and augmentation. His eyes—lambent yellow, unblinking—locked onto mine.

No animosity. No trust.

'Captain Rakkan,' Kithlan said, his voice deeper than any human's, resonant with synthetic harmonics tuned for authority. 'The Avenger stands ready to escort the Freyja to its destination, as per our contract.'

I held his gaze. 'Acknowledged, Commander. Once we clear the waypoint, I'll come aboard the Avenger to discuss joint strategy and operational boundaries.'

Kithlan inclined his head a fraction. 'Confirmed. We will make appropriate preparations for your arrival. Coordination data will follow in encrypted packet.' His tone carried no trace of emotion—neither resentment nor welcome—only the crisp precision of a soldier fulfilling terms to the letter.

Something in his eyes, though, suggested memory. Then the transmission cut out. When the screen dimmed, I turned to find Hela watching me—measuring, as always.

'Satisfied?' I asked quietly.

'Cautiously optimistic,' she replied. 'The Defined are consummate professionals, Captain. They understand the parameters of their new contract.'

I wasn't sure I did.

'Set course for the Eden border sectors,' I told Dakkar, unwilling to continue the exchange. 'Coordinate with the Avenger for optimal formation. Proceed at their recommended velocity.'

The ships aligned and accelerated, twin vectors slicing through the black. For a moment, I let myself breathe. The pieces were in motion—my ship, my crew, our unlikely allies—all bound for a mission built on fragile alliances and buried debts.

We weren't just heading for Eden. We were heading into Hela's agenda, Kithlan's grudge, and whatever waited in the dark between stars. The Avenger slid into escort position ahead of the Freyja, its black hull swallowing starlight. Blood had been spilled between us, lives taken, debts carved deep into old wounds.

But necessity had its own gravity—and it was pulling all of us toward Eden. That was what bound us now—contract over vengeance, survival over sentiment. I could only hope that would be enough when we reached Eden.

I found Dakkar in Operations, watching a sector-crawl update. 'Polity's stripped half the patrol lanes,' he said.

'Same on our side,' I replied. 'Freighters are getting hit. Nobody's answering distress calls.'

He pulled up a navigation track. 'You see this?'

A faint trail arced across the edge of known space. Cold burn. No transponder. 'Crawler?' I asked.

'Could be. Doesn't match anything official. I've logged five like it this week. Always outbound. Always deep.'

'They're not supposed to cross into our lanes,' I said. 'Not without notice.'

'No one's stopping them.'

I zoomed out. The paths weren't coordinated. No staging. Just a slow bleed into the black.

'They're leaving,' I muttered.

'Leaving what?' Dakkar asked.

I didn't answer. He leaned back in his chair. 'Pirates must be having a fun time.'

'Yeah,' I said. 'Nobody around to stop them.'

But I wasn't thinking about pirates. Through the viewscreen, the stars stretched and blurred as we accelerated to cruising velocity.

To Eden. To Riven. To the Crawlers.

And to the moment this fragile alliance would either hold—or tear itself apart.

Chapter 17: Blowing the Relay

At night, Riven moved like an echo. By day, like a shadow.

Now, streaked with mud, she slipped through a crack in Eden's defences—and into her past.

The lights of the old Crawler compound burned through the trees. Once, this had been a city. Now it was nothing but steel and fire. Her childhood memories had softened at the edges, but they hadn't disappeared.

This wasn't the life she was meant to have. Wasn't the world she was meant to inherit. She remembered her grandfather at the piano, filling the house with music. Her mother—warm, alive. They had wanted more for her than war. But that was before the Crawlers locked them in a cell and killed them to make a point.

She reached a street she once knew. As a child she had walked these roads openly. Now, hood low, she slipped through alleys and darkness, feeling the weight of invisible eyes. Drones. Scanners. Ghosts.

She turned to leave the city the way she had come—silent, unseen. The others needed to know. Empty-handed, she crawled back into the night, where the smoke of the Crawler forges stained the sky red.

The caves stank of sulphur and iron. People said you got used to it. No one ever had.

A scout rushed up as she crossed the tunnel mouth.

'Any trouble?' Riven asked. The boy shook his head. She cuffed him lightly on the chin. 'Get the others. East chamber. Now.'

He ran. Even if the Crawlers weren't watching yet, they would be soon.

The wind howled through the mountains, carrying the sound of their own mortality. Riven stepped outside to escape it—the heat, the smoke, the press of bodies. Out here the air was cleaner. More dangerous. More beautiful.

Down in the valley, what had once been home flickered as a tiny point of light.

Her fighters had assembled before she caught her breath—thirty, give or take. Mostly young. Some barely more than children. Their faces were lit by the dull red glow of the forges far below, eyes hard with exhaustion and resolve.

The world around them still carried traces of what Eden had been—stone, forest, sky—but all of it now bent to the Crawlers' purpose. A planet turned factory. A place that stripped the softness from anyone who stayed too long.

Some things couldn't be forged. Not easily. Freedom was one. Humanity another.

The air reeked of old fires, sweat, and the kind of desperation they refused to let turn into fear. Riven scanned their faces, shaking the dust from her clothes. 'I need volunteers.'

'You have thirty,' someone at the back replied. Hard to make out his features in the dim light. 'For anything.'

He was the closest thing they had to a medic. His wife had been one before the Crawlers took her. He'd survived long enough that people had learned his name.

'They were probably on you the whole time,' said the woman next to him. Young. Dark hair, pale eyes. Could've been sixteen. Could've been Riven's sister. 'Think the runner made it?'

Riven kept her gaze on the city. Watching the paths up the hill wouldn't change anything. 'They haven't caught one yet.'

'What's the next move?'

'Back to Eden City. Blow the master relay. Teach them humans can still fight.'

'What about the new site?'

Riven looked at the young woman beside her—like staring into a mirror that no longer reflected her back. 'If we have time. I'll show you on the way.'

Night again. They hadn't made it all the way, but close enough. Soon they'd move. Her team huddled at the base of the mountain, tucked into the trees like more shadows. Three recruits had turned up last week. One was the same age her mother had been when they dragged her away. Riven looked past her, past the others.

Even here, buried in the forest, the machines' heat pressed against her skin. They would strike soon, but first the details: logistics, ammo, food, water. More to confirm. More to be sure of. Their stockpile was thin. The pack on her back wouldn't last long with thirty mouths to feed.

The old codes weren't safe, so she sent scouts on foot—messengers with hasty maps and desperate instructions. The camp held quiet against the night; silence and fear pressed in as thick as the cold. Her breath curled in the air.

At least they were free.

On the horizon the relay rose like a cathedral to industry—brutal and precise. There was a strange kind of art to it, but not the kind the human mind would make. Riven never got used to that. She crouched with the others; eyes locked on the searchlights panning the tower. The last of her team slid into place. A shift in the darkness, a held breath. Relief, maybe. She didn't let herself feel it.

The Crawlers would have to be careless to miss them. But five years of occupation had made them confident—sure the spirit of Eden was broken. That was the point.

Riven's fingers tapped the worn grip of her blaster. The fabric over her mouth was cold and damp. Her pulse was steady—quick, but steady.

She gave a nod, watched it pass down the line, shadow to shadow. Subtle. Quick. Too fast to notice, too small to interpret. But that didn't mean they couldn't be stopped.

The tower loomed ahead like a grave marker. From a distance, it had been a speck at the edge of the world. Up close, it was vast—and it wasn't alone. A shiver passed through her. She ignored it.

The relay wasn't their only target, but it was the one that mattered. The satellites carried transmissions between Eden and the Crawlers. If they didn't shut them down, she had to assume she'd be dead by dawn.

'Hope you made it worth the trip, Ghost,' the dark-haired girl muttered beside her. Her voice had that brittle edge—unbroken, stubborn. None of them wanted to show they could break. Not here. Not now.

Ghost. The name had followed her since the early days of the resistance, whispered in bunkers and ruins, carried by the desperate and the defiant. Some said it was because she moved unseen, slipping through enemy lines without a trace. Others said it was because she should have been dead long ago—buried with the family the Crawlers stole from her.

She never argued. A ghost didn't have a past. A ghost didn't mourn. A ghost did what had to be done.

'Thanks for tagging along,' Riven said, scanning the distance, searching for movement—for proof they weren't alone. Nothing. Just silence. Wind. The shriek of the Crawlers' artful metal.

'Wait.' She raised her hand, swallowed by the dark. The others dropped as one. 'Saw something.' She held still, listening. The wind howled too hard to catch footsteps, but she imagined them anyway.

'Just wind.' The girl said it too quickly—ashamed, maybe, of Riven's caution. Or her own.

Riven nodded and moved. The girl was probably right. Didn't mean she'd take the chance. Something about the silence felt wrong. The Crawlers weren't usually this careless, this lax—this human. She knew better than to trust an easy job. But she wasn't about to waste the chance either. She only hoped her caution wouldn't cost them more than it saved.

They would know soon.

'Ready when you are,' she whispered.

Silence. Not everyone had made it, then. She was as sorry for the losses as she was relieved for the living.

'Are you in place?' she asked, louder this time. Risky, but necessary.

'On our way,' came a voice in her earpiece.

The courtyard ahead was too big—built for giants and machines, not flesh and blood. Riven had been here once before, years ago, on a tour meant to showcase the miracles of Crawler technology. Back then, she'd been awestruck. Fascinated. Now she felt only urgency. The map she'd drawn in the dirt was real now—concrete beneath her boots.

Two figures moved through the corridor, low and careful. Her pulse quickened at the sight of them. More than she expected. She'd been prepared for less. One raised a fist to their shoulder—the signal was clear. All quiet.

She almost let herself believe it.

The tower loomed above them, built on what had once been Eden's outskirts. Too close for comfort. Too close for a mission like this. Almost suicide. The Crawlers didn't run their weapons from here, but the place was thick with soldiers. High risk, high reward.

A figure waved her forward and shouted—a voice full of fear and bravado. 'Go, go, go!' Steel ground against steel, nearly drowning them out. Nearly. The screams that followed didn't.

Not Crawlers.

Riven's stomach sank. The bodies were too familiar: Human, armoured, well-fed. The way they moved—trained, precise—told her everything. Not slaves. Not civilians. Soldiers. Tarkin's loyalists, outfitted with Crawler tech, still fighting for the regime that had bled Eden dry.

A flicker of hesitation stabbed through her, but it died fast. She'd seen what they did to her people. These weren't innocents. They'd made their choice. They fell back against the structure, regrouping. Her ribs ached with every breath.

'Thought they were behind us. We left too many alive last time,' said the dark-haired girl beside her. She wore no mask against the fumes. Against anything.

Two more of the crew caught up, eyes wild. 'Go?'

'Go,' Riven said.

They pressed forward, low and fast. Silent—or close enough. 'We've got five minutes,' she muttered. She didn't know if it was true, but she knew they didn't have ten.

They barely made it five feet.

Something massive slithered from the dark, chitin clicking like the call of a deranged bird. Then the clicks twisted into language—the same commands that had once told her to get on her knees. To obey.

Ice filled her veins.

For a heartbeat her body locked, muscle memory overriding thought. Not again. Never again.

Her blaster was already in her hands, already set for close-quarters work. The shot punched through the creature's brainstem. It crumpled with a wet, mechanical screech.

The girl beside her screamed, 'We're blown!'

The Crawlers didn't rush. They didn't need to. Their pursuit was slow, deliberate, efficient.

This was the price of freedom. There was nothing clean about it. Not the killing. Not the missions. Nothing. But it was freedom—or the closest they would ever get.

They reached the tower's base. Too close to stop now. Concrete and steel twisted into a maze. The farther they went, the worse it got. But they went far—further than they had any right to.

Alarms shrieked. A shout of triumph. Then the detonations—one, two, three. Her fighters whooped as the last of the charges blew. The relay wasn't as big as she remembered, but the explosion made it bigger.

The blast lit up the sky, a bloom of fire that turned the treetops white. The tower buckled with a groan that sounded almost human. Steel folded like cloth. Panels sheared off in sheets. The top half hung in the air for a breath too long—then gravity finished the job. It came down screaming, tearing itself apart as it hit. The ground lurched beneath her boots.

Debris rained sideways—shards of alloy, cables whipping like snakes, fragments of armour clattering across the dirt. Someone was yelling. She couldn't hear what they were saying.

Riven pushed up from the crater lip, ears ringing, blood in her mouth. The smoke parted just long enough to show one of her crew—thrown against a wall, twisted wrong, visor shattered, throat open. Still clutching his rifle. Maybe thirteen or fourteen years old.

She stared for a second too long.

'Move!' someone shouted. 'We have to go!'

She didn't answer. Just stepped over the body and kept going. She wanted to say something. To stop. To scream. But ghosts didn't scream.

They moved. They endured. They made it count.

This wasn't about saving Eden anymore. It was about outlasting what tried to erase her—what tried to erase all of them. One blast. One breath. One broken body at a time.

No last words. No promises. No time.

Chapter 18: Honour Among Outlaws

There's a moment—cold and polite—when someone hasn't killed you yet but is thinking about it.

Through the porthole, the Avenger hung against the dark, its altered metal soaking up starlight. The air in the shuttle was tight with unspoken thought. The console traced our approach in precise vectors. Behind me, Thorne and Dallas sat motionless, visors hiding any sign of doubt.

My fingers moved over the controls, sending the docking request. Then we waited.

The reply came—too smooth, too fast. It confirmed what we already knew. The Defined weren't letting us dock because they trusted us. They were letting us dock because they were still deciding whether to kill us.

It was my job to change their minds. We couldn't afford fractures in command. Something was wrong out here—wrong in the quiet way rot starts.

As the shuttle closed with the Avenger, my mind went back to earlier.

Ariel had frozen mid-sentence during a routine systems update. 'Unscheduled carrier burst just passed through relay echo,' she said. 'Non-Polity signature. Fragmented.'

'Crawler?'

'Yes. Partial code match to Dragon-sector war-net. Encrypted. Sloppy.'

'Crawlers don't do sloppy.'

'They were more desperate than careful.'

On the holo, the waveform stabilised. Ariel ran it twice. The second time, she translated aloud.

The Hunger are coming. Swarm attacking outer system.
Velos outpost is no more. The queen has commanded to stand.
We will oppose them.

Then static. The message looped once, then collapsed.

'Timestamp?' I asked.

'Twelve hours before Dragon ceased all traffic.'

'Any other fragments?'

Ariel shook her head. 'That was it.'

Velos—an outer planet in the Dragon System. Before the Crawlers, it had been a Human naval base. The Crawlers hadn't warned us during the war. Hadn't spoken once during the peace.

And now they had sent last words.

Ariel's tone shifted. 'Commander—encrypted human burst. Signature masked, but the key pattern matches Zvereva.'

What could she want? More betrayal? 'Put it through.'

The holo flickered. Anushka appeared—tired, backlit by a maintenance bay. Tools clinked somewhere off-screen. 'Rakkan,' she said quietly. 'The crew from the Polity ships are talking. You have eyes on you. Admiral Knox is pulling command tight. Anyone who served with you is being marked for 'review.' They'll call it procedure. It isn't.'

She glanced aside, then back. 'I've been helping on Jenny Lynne. Drive balanced. Hull patched. Tell Shannon she'll have her boat when she needs it.'

A beat. 'I can't undo what I did. But I can try to make amends."'

I frowned. Maybe she did want to make peace. Her betrayal still felt fresh. The feed cut to static. 'Trace?' I asked.

Ariel's reply was soft. 'None.'

We were about to dock with the Avenger.

The transmission crackled through the comms, cold and precise. I gave a slight nod, refocusing on the task. My fingers moved over the controls, the shuttle responding with the obedience of machinery that didn't care who lived or died. The autopilot engaged, guiding us in with unsettling ease. It felt less like approach and more like being pulled inside a throat.

The hum of systems filled the cabin—a quiet reminder that, for now, we were still in control.

'You are cleared for Bay Seven, Fleet Commander Rakkan. Welcome aboard.'

I resisted the urge to glance back at my team, knowing their thoughts mirrored my own. Doubt and determination, twisted together like wire. This venture could shatter the fragile unity we'd built—or mend it. As commander, I had to face it before combat found us.

The Avenger filled the viewport, swallowing our shuttle whole. External cameras showed its dark, altered hull—a hive of strategic purpose, its ports and hatches alive with movement. I was committed now. No room for doubt. Just a steady hand and a blaster within reach.

The hangar bay opened with mechanical grace, and I took manual control for the final descent. The shuttle touched down hard, vibrations running through the deck. My crew remained silent, disciplined. They knew this wasn't the time for questions.

The bay stretched out before us—an immense cathedral of motion, every figure and drone moving with unnerving precision. The ceiling arched high above, amplifying the hum of engines and the staccato rhythm of boots on steel.

Rows of sleek Valkyrie sub-orbital dropships dominated the space, their hulls gleaming under the harsh light. Up close, they radiated power—functional beauty, stripped of mercy.

The hatch hissed open. I stood, and the others followed. I stepped onto the deck with practiced calm, though I felt every gaze settle like a weight. The Defined moved like predators—disciplined, tireless. One broke from formation, striding toward me with the deliberate confidence of rank.

'Fleet Commander Rakkan,' he said, his voice carrying over the din—measured, resonant. 'I am to escort you to Captain Kithlan. Your crew may wait here or proceed with you. We require your confirmation.'

His words were a test—formality sharpened into a blade.

'We'll all go,' I said, leaving no room for hesitation.

Our gazes locked for a moment, a silent exchange between soldiers who understood exactly what respect cost. The officer turned and gestured forward. I fell into step without pause, Dallas and Thorne flanking me.

Behind us, the hum of the hangar continued—a symphony of precision, watched over by a hundred eyes deciding whether we lived or died. I took in the way these hybrid warriors moved—their Wolven features and enhanced musculature lending them a predatory grace. They were built for war. A stark contrast to the humans aboard the Freyja.

I'd brought Thorne for a reason. As both Defined and veteran, he commanded respect. And he was bigger than almost all of them. I was keenly aware of the power dynamic. Our last encounter—and my decision to spare rather than destroy—had been an insult that hadn't been forgotten. Walking into the lion's den unarmed and with only a small escort was a risk. But it was the only way.

If I was going to rescue Riven—if I was going to forge an alliance instead of igniting another war—I had to be bold.

I'd walked into worse without a plan and nothing to lose. That used to be enough: take the risk, feel nothing, let the bullets fly and see where I landed. But this was different. This wasn't about proving I could survive. She was my blood.

Our escort led us through the Avenger's corridors—a labyrinth of metal and biotech humming with quiet power. Every surface bore the touch of Crawler adaptation: Techniques we had learned from them. Organic filigree woven through steel, systems that breathed faintly as we passed. This was no ordinary ship. It was a war machine. An ecosystem. A message.

As we moved deeper, I turned over the gamble I'd taken. If we were to succeed, it wouldn't be through force. It would be through loyalty—earning the respect of these soldiers, binding them to a purpose strong enough to weather the storm coming for all of us.

There was a time I could afford the luxury of not caring whether I lived or died. That was a refuge I could no longer allow myself.

At the far end of the chamber, Kithlan emerged—moving with the control of a seasoned predator. His soldiers parted around him, their gazes sharp and expectant. The air seemed to still. Dallas and Thorne flanked me, visors reflecting the cold, sterile light that bathed the deck in clinical white.

Kithlan regarded me with an expression balanced between disdain and curiosity. 'I did not expect you would come,' he said. His voice was even, but the weight behind it was unmistakable. Then came the challenge: 'Do you think you can reclaim your honour by walking into the den you once fled?'

Silence pressed in—thick, waiting, electric.

I met Kithlan's gaze without flinching, letting the accusation settle, letting the moment stretch. Then, with calm certainty, I answered, 'You misjudge me, Kithlan-16.'

'This den was once our shared battlefield,' I said, my voice cutting through the taut air with practiced calm. 'I am here because that history matters more than what divides us.' I let the words hang, exposed to scrutiny from those who hungered for dissent. 'I came unafraid to show my respect—and my intent. We fight the same enemy, Kithlan.'

A murmur moved through the ranks—a shifting of stances, small but telling. The Defined adjusted their calculations, measuring my words for weakness or deception.

Kithlan stepped closer, his tone sharpening. 'You think to cover a grave insult with feigned humility. Do you believe we would forget how you humiliated us during the pursuit?' His gaze locked onto mine, unblinking. 'You had us in your sights, and you did not finish the fight.' He let the charge settle, then added, 'A soldier does not leave his enemy to wonder why he still draws breath.'

I took the blow, feeling old loyalties and buried resentments quicken around me. This wasn't only strategy. It was honour. My next words had to be a foundation, not an apology.

'We were allies once,' I said, firm and without remorse. 'I spared your lives because I believe we can be allies again. I have always respected your people and your ways—even when the Polity would have me treat you as vermin.' I closed the gap Kithlan had tried to widen, stepping forward on my name. 'My choice was not an insult. It was a testament to our history.'

Something in the chamber shifted—subtle, perceptible. The Defined watched, weighing my stance and the blood between us. They knew my past; they knew the battles we'd shared against the Crawlers. If that meant nothing to them, then I was already dead.

Kithlan's gaze flicked to his soldiers, then returned with renewed intensity. 'Words do not bridge the unbridgeable, Rakkan,' he said, deliberate and cold. 'The Defined do not cling to the past to justify actions in the present.'

I held my ground. 'Then let me prove it the only way that matters—with action. Our mission is compromised without your help. With it, we can strike at the heart of the Crawlers.'

Kithlan watched me, every flicker of his gaze a calculation. The Defined remained motionless, their scrutiny pressing like gravity. 'And would you wager your life on this, Fleet Commander?' he asked, the scepticism threaded with a hint of belief. 'More than that—your people's fate?'

My answer came without hesitation. 'Yes. Because this isn't just about striking the Crawlers. It's about what they're building at Eden—not a gun or a shield, but a black-hole generator. If it goes online, it could tear planets out of the sky, swallow whole systems in a single firing. That kind of power would change the balance of the galaxy. And there are men—humans—who would let it happen for power, for profit, or to settle old scores. I will not let them.'

I let the words hang, heavy in the charged silence. 'This mission will confront their deadliest device—a black-hole generator capable of consuming entire systems. If we succeed, the victory will be one the Defined can rightly claim as their own.'

The chamber fell still—not with hostility, but with reassessment. Soldiers who moments ago had measured me as an intruder now watched with wary curiosity.

Kithlan's eyes stayed locked on mine. 'Then perhaps,' he said slowly, 'you understand what it means to fight without mercy.'

I held his gaze. 'I've spent my life learning it.' Then, after a breath, I added quietly, 'I gave mercy to you because I honour the Defined. I have bled with your kind. I know your worth.'

The tension shifted—a subtle exhale rippling through the ranks. Not acceptance, not yet, but the beginning of it. Kithlan inclined his head a fraction, the faintest gesture of acknowledgment. 'Then let us see if that honour still carries weight, Fleet Commander Rakkan.'

My words hung between us, an unspoken challenge: was this alliance a convenience—or something more?

Among the soldiers, I saw the faintest change. A loosening of rigid stances. A flicker of consideration.

'You have not changed, Rakkan,' Kithlan said, his voice caught between admiration and admonition. 'Always bold. Always the tactician, thinking ten moves ahead.' He let the statement linger, then continued, gaze narrowing. 'Why take this to the edge? Is your prize so valuable?'

I held my silence a moment, the weight of what I was about to reveal pressing down. When I finally spoke, my voice was steady.

'My daughter is on Eden,' I said. 'Captured by Crawlers. The longer we wait, the greater the chance they'll kill her.'

The admission struck like a pulse through the room. Glances flicked between the Defined—quick, silent recalculations. Now they understood what I was willing to lose. Kithlan said nothing at first. His eyes shifted to the holographic display. The plan glowed before us in cold luminescence, but now it carried the weight of blood and future.

'Honesty is a double-edged blade, Captain,' he said at last, his tone softer but still edged with caution. 'It can bind us—or cut us down.'

I inclined my head, accepting the truth of it. Then I stepped back, giving him space to decide what came next.

'You must prove the Polity traitors will not turn us against each other,' Kithlan warned—one last test. 'You know what is at stake if you fail.'

'I do,' I said, my voice steady. Each word a pledge forged in necessity. 'We are ready to show you.'

The silence stretched—taut, expectant. Kithlan studied me, expression unreadable, until his eyes caught the light with something indefinable. Ambition, perhaps. Respect. Maybe both.

'Then we will see if your gamble pays off.'

He deactivated the map and turned to his soldiers. 'Inform the units. We fight as one.'

The decision settled over us like a shifting tide—heavy with promise and peril both. I allowed myself a single breath. Not relief. Just acknowledgment of what had been won. With a final nod to Kithlan, I turned. Dallas and Thorne fell in beside me, their boots echoing on the steel deck. Each step carried us deeper into the unknown.

There was no Beauty Here

Hunger Command Hub: Command Bridge, Ark Flagship: Fist of Salvation

Location: Thraxidia System

The Ark thrummed. Not with need—

with purpose.

The stars in this system were weak. Unworthy.

But necessary.

There was no beauty here. No challenge.

Only delay.

We consumed it all the same.

The Ark of Salvation drifted through the wreckage of orbital vaults. The ruins still crackled with ghost systems—flickering prayers left behind by the broken.

Their gods did not answer. We did.

Below, the planet split like overripe fruit. Its seas boiled into air. Its towers folded inward, drawn down into the Churners. At the bridge altar, High Acolyte Veris raised the Horn of Naming.

When it sounds, a world passes from being into memory.

He sounded it now.

'Two remain. Then Eden.'

The ship responded. Bulkheads exhaled. Sacrament lines pulsed silver-red. The devourer-engines stirred in harmony.

Fist Supreme Lord Tharim did not speak. She lowered her wings in silence—a gesture older than voice. It meant readiness.

It meant joy.

Veris whispered to the flame, as was custom:

'The garden waits in ignorance. The fruit does not see the blade.'

We answered.

'But we do. We see. We come.' Across the ship—through memory cathedrals, feeding holds, and litany engines—a single voice rose from many throats:

'Let the last of the many-legged and the Human unredeemed prepare.

We bring the end. And it is sacred.' The Ark turned its great eye toward the next star. And the Hunger moved forward—holy and infinite.

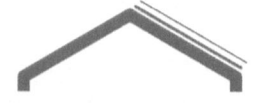

Chapter 19: Survival

Five days later they packed to move—again.

Riven's plan was simple and dangerous. *You're never safe,* she'd told them. *Just less dead than the day before.* She shoved up her sleeve, revealing the jagged blaster scar on her arm—a badge of honour, a reminder they weren't going back.

But they had hurt the Crawlers—and shown Governor Tarkin for the puppet he was. She had known him since childhood: once her grandfather's aide, then his replacement when the Crawlers needed a willing collaborator. He'd been her mother's lover, even fancied himself a father figure to young Riven. But he was a hollow man. Right now, he'd be pretending to have real power—power not borrowed from a Crawler queen. It was a lie.

"Three days more, tops," she said. "No more than that. Don't leave a trace."

They knew better than to ask who else might not leave one. Their win hadn't lasted, but it left bruises they didn't name—and a kind of quiet loyalty they didn't question. Riven scanned the faces around her, counting how many she might bring back. The numbers didn't look good—but she'd been wrong before.

She didn't dwell on the medic's last smile or the cave where he might have buried his wife—if they hadn't buried him instead. Loss was a given. She had learned to carry it without letting it weigh her down.

"Why even try?" the dark-haired girl muttered, voice sharp-edged. She wiped her mouth and tossed the last scraps of dinner into the wind. "We've got food. We've got shelter. Let's just go. Be done with it. Be done with all of them."

"There's nowhere to go," Riven said. She caught a drifting scrap of trash, closing her fist around it like it was hope—something real, something worth holding onto. She wasn't letting go. Not yet.

Some in her group had no memory of life before the Crawlers turned their home into a factory. Others had never tasted freedom at all—not like she had. But they weren't done.

They packed, they left, they set off in silence and fragments of courage—some knowing exactly what they were walking into, others blessed by ignorance. Getting back to the mountains meant taking the long way, using what natural cover still remained. Several Crawler strongpoints lay in their path.

Riven called out orders—crisp and quick. The sound of them mattered. It sounded like movement. Like direction. Like purpose. Like hope. She'd learned that without it, there was nothing. Simply daring to keep hope alive—that was resistance. That was defiance.

They ran low, close to the dirt and to each other, moving forward into the dark. They didn't slow for two days. When she finally did, it wasn't by much—just enough for the others to catch up, to see that she wasn't stopping.

"You okay, Riven?" The girl's voice was too earnest. She'd given her name, and it made her real.

"Why wouldn't I be?" Riven said, voice dry as the mountain air. "Lyra, I've only put you in danger every minute I've known you. No point stopping now."

Lyra kept pace. There was something in her expression—determination, maybe something softer. Either way, it didn't last.

Riven ran from her past as hard as she ran from the Crawlers. Some days, they were the same thing.

"Think anyone saw us leave?" she asked.

"No chance," Lyra said. "You worried?"

"Like I said," Riven smiled—and this time, she almost meant it. "Not my style."

She kept moving until everyone was accounted for; only then did she ease her pace. Doubt took less time than rest, so she gave herself none of it.

Lyra caught her alone at the edge of the camp. In the distance, a Crawler base loomed—a wall of steel between them and the mountains.

"Looks familiar," she said.

"They all look the same," Riven replied.

"The bases, yeah. But not the towers. Not the operations."

"They don't change either," Riven said. "Not what matters."

When the scouts returned—no movement behind, no sign they were on the Crawlers' scanners—hope flared in her chest. She tried not to let it, but it was there: warm, stubborn, alive. Their chances of making it back were slim. But they'd hurt the Crawlers—cracked their illusion of control. And for that, the enemy would want to punish them.

They wouldn't get them all. Not entirely. Not this time.

She looked at the few that remained—the way they looked back at her. She was getting them out. She had to. Back to the deep caves. Back to what passed for safety. And when they were ready, they would strike again.

"Too quiet," Riven said. Silence never meant safety. She'd lived with the shadow of death so long it felt like the only constant. But they were still here. Still moving. Still breathing. Death could wait its turn.

Lyra shot her a sideways glance. "Not your style to worry, Ghost."

Riven met her eyes with a look that said more than words ever could. If only she knew.

The desert air was brutally dry but laced with sage, and twilight softened the edges of the world. The sky bruised purple and gold, and for a moment it felt like something worth remembering.

Her team was ragged and pale but alive. A third had fallen to enemy fire; the rest had melted into the landscape, vanishing in twos and threes. The ones who remained still believed in something—maybe in her, maybe just in survival.

Riven and Lyra ran together, taking the path no one expected. They didn't have to go far to find the trap waiting for them—a Crawler airfield sitting between them and the mountains.

Riven cursed. "We're further south than I thought. We'll have to backtrack."

Engines roared to life, shaking the earth. A ship screamed overhead, its heat pressing down on them, sending the rest of the team diving for cover. The ship moved on.

"We could make them follow us," Lyra said. "The others might reach the caves if we draw them off." Reckless. Desperate. But desperation had kept them alive this long.

Riven shook her head. "No. We do this together—or not at all."

She had spent years believing she'd be the one to burn so the rest could live. Maybe she still would. But not today. Today they burned together—or not at all. That was it—the thing that kept them standing, the thing she fought for, the reason they weren't dust in the wind.

Riven had learned early that you don't stay still. Her mother had taught her that truth, though she hadn't lived long enough to prove it. Riven had—again and again. It hadn't been enough to save her mother. But maybe it could save the people running beside her now.

They put distance between themselves and the airfield—enough for Riven to breathe again, to believe in the ghosts and rumours that carried her name. But she'd thought that before.

The odds were against them. The odds had always been against them. But she ran anyway, leading them forward as if they were chasing something, not just escaping it—as if they weren't merely survivors. As if they were meant to make it.

One way or another, they would.

They moved through Eden like phantoms, slipping toward the mountains, keeping to the shadows. They slept during the day and travelled at night. It felt like a mission to save themselves—and maybe that was exactly what it was.

It wouldn't be the first time.

The Crawlers had built a steel fort where two valleys met, at the place where the land began to rise toward the mountains. It was the only way home.

The night was thick with rain, and they were running hard. They reached the edge of the installation before they even realised it—running until the dark blurred into sweat and breath and determination. The area ahead was lit up like a broken sun, full of heat and noise and hatred.

She and her remaining crew hunkered down just under the ridgeline and scanned the enemy fortification through binoculars. Not good. Hundreds of enemy soldiers, with weapons and ammunition to burn—humans and Crawler units.

"Where the hell did they come from?" Getting past them should have been impossible. But impossible had never stopped them before.

She looked around at her team. They were hungry, battered, and running on fumes—but still standing. They had blown the relay, and the entire planet knew it. The Crawlers weren't invincible. Someone was still fighting. And if they died now, it wouldn't be for nothing—it would be proof that resistance wasn't just a rumour.

Riven let that certainty settle in her chest. She'd grown up hearing stories about heroes—about Rakkan, the man who had stopped the Crawlers from taking the Chance System; about fighters who had turned the tide and changed the course of wars.

She used to wonder if Rakkan knew about her. Grandfather and mother had been a wall of silence about him. Her grandfather was angry, her mother was sad, but neither spoke of it until she made her mother tell her his name—who he was—on her tenth birthday. It was the present she had wanted more than any other. Her mother admitted he had never been told about Riven. Her ten-year-old self had been very angry about that.

If he'd known, would he have stayed? She had ached to know the answer. She'd written his name over and over, once, on scraps of stolen paper—as if that would call him to her.

But that was a long time ago, and she had no use for wondering now. Heroes didn't come back for the past—they fought for the future. And that was exactly what she was doing.

She kept close to the buildings, her movements swift and certain. She had been slipping through cracks her whole life, and she wasn't about to stop now. She had been captured before, once—a lifetime ago. She hadn't understood the enemy then. Now she did, and she would not let them take her again.

Riven didn't stop running until she reached the valley. The old paths were still there, winding through the rocks like they always had. She moved like she belonged there—because she did. The Crawler forges smoked the sky red behind her, but they were already too late.

All but four of them made it out. The others had tried.

Days later they reached their hidden camp. They needed to regroup, to heal. Give them a few weeks and they would strike again.

Lyra squeezed her hand, grounding her for a moment. Riven returned the gesture—brief, firm, then gone.

She wasn't a ghost. She was a fighter. And as long as she was still breathing, she was going to make damn sure the Crawlers had something to fear.

Chapter 20: Hunted by the Polity

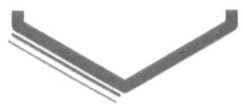

It's not the crime that gets you hunted; it's being inconvenient to someone who prints the narrative.

The console chimed—sharp, clinical—the sound of a scalpel hitting a tray. I leaned in, scanned the message twice, then once more for the lie hiding in plain sight.

POLITY PRIORITY ALERT

TARGET: RAKKAN, JERO. CREW OF DSV FREYJA.

STATUS: ACTIVE THREAT.

CRIMES: UNAUTHORIZED INCURSION. SEDITION. MURDER.

It read like a warrant penned in blood and dressed up in military protocol. I'd seen enough of these to know how they were built: every word measured, every charge calculated for effect. This one came laced with tier-two encryption, system-wide distribution, and a bounty big enough to draw anyone who could fly and didn't care who bled. That made it real.

The Sentinel operation had cost us—not just in lives, but in narrative. The official report omitted context, omitted Virell, omitted the fact that we hadn't just stumbled into that installation. We were hunting truth inside a black site buried under decades of deniability. The Polity didn't want debate. They wanted erasure. We weren't fugitives. We were evidence.

I let the moment sit. Long enough to settle, not long enough to fester. Not anger. Not fear. Just recalibration—the kind you make when the ground shifts under your boots and the horizon redraws itself.

Across the bridge the crew held formation. No questions. No raised voices. Just the faint flicker of updates over their stations and the quiet shift of eyes. They'd seen it too. It had gone through shipboard comms. That was fine. Better they knew. Better we all understood what we were now. Branded. Marked. Outlaws in name and in law. Traitors to the Polity.

I stood slowly, letting my hands rest lightly on the rail. "Ariel."

She shimmered into view beside me—part ghost, part silhouette—flickering between avatars like a memory still deciding which shape to wear. "Captain?"

"Put it up. Main screen."

The bulletin flared across the viewscreen in red and white—letters stark enough to brand a man. I watched the bridge, not the words. Thorne's jaw clenched. Dakkar folded his arms, unreadable.

"They're scared," I said, voice level, measured. "That's why this is happening now. Someone in Polity Command is panicking. They don't want us getting to Eden—not with Virell's intel. Not with the truth."

I let the words hang for a beat. Then another. "They're betting we'll scatter. That we'll crack. That we'll turn on each other before we even make the next jump."

I let the silence catch fire. "They're wrong."

A few heads lifted. Small tells—nothing showy. Just that quiet shift you get when people start recalculating in your direction.

"Ariel," I said. "How wide has this gone?"

"The order originated at Polity Command, tier two," she replied, tone clipped and clinical. "Disseminated across all relay nodes in the region. No challenge protocols. No verification requests. It is designed to travel fast—and unquestioned."

I nodded once. "So it's not about accuracy. It's about reach."

"Correct."

"Odds?"

She didn't blink—she never did—but the pause was long enough to register. "Favourable, if we continue to act with precision."

That was enough. I turned back to the room. "They'll have eyes on every relay from here to Eden—patrol routes, comm intercepts, bounty boards. If we show up on the grid, we're targets."

A murmur moved through the air—subdued, steady. No dissent. Not yet.

"Ariel," I said. "Patch me through. All decks."

"Channel open."

I waited just long enough to be sure the line was live. Then I spoke—not louder, just clearer. "This is Rakkan. You've all seen the Polity alert. The charges are serious, but the only way we prove they're a lie is by getting to Eden and finding the truth. So this changes nothing. The mission holds. We move. We adapt. And if anyone tries to stop us—they're welcome to try. They won't succeed."

No more. No less.

The Freyja hummed around me, her systems a low, familiar rhythm underfoot. She had become our shelter, our scalpel, our shield. Whatever waited out there—traitors, Crawlers, ghosts—we'd face it with her. She was a good ship.

Suddenly the radar plot lit up like a city grid—multiple signals, closing fast from the Dragon vector. "Contacts. Ten, maybe more. Crawler signatures," Leela barked from comms.

I snapped upright. "Sound action stations. Bring up shields."

The bridge shifted from quiet to razor-sharp in seconds. I keyed the tactical overlay. Wrecked ships filled the grid—scored hulls, venting radiation, formations broken and scattered. Crawlers didn't move like that.

"They're not in attack posture," Ariel said. "No weapons lock."

I zoomed the tactical view. The ships weren't forming up. They were bleeding away from each other—losing cohesion.

"Spectral analysis."

Ariel ran it. "Heavy battle damage. Unknown signature. Not Crawler weapons. Not human."

"Debris trails?"

"Minimal. Looks like they dumped mass to boost velocity."

Through the magnified view I caught glimpses of twisted hull plating—fusion scars spidering across the metal. Ships not repaired. Not regrouping. Just... running.

"They're not running from us," I said.

Dakkar muttered, "Then what the hell are they running from?"

I didn't answer. I watched them slip across the grid, limping deeper into the dark.

Ariel's voice returned, quieter now. "Captain, I'm detecting data bleed from one of the crippled vessels. Civilian architecture. Likely abandoned."

Dakkar raised an eyebrow. "Can we pull anything?"

"Minimal signal strength. Fragmentary records. But I believe I can isolate a feed—streaming cultural storage architecture."

The console flickered, then steadied—Ariel's decryption layers filtering the signal. The screen came alive with cool spirals—architectural overlays, hive plans, memory-transaction logs. Not war. Not strategy. Something else.

Dakkar folded his arms. "This isn't military."

I nodded slowly. "Run it."

"Crawler commerce," Ariel said. "Transactional memory economies. Emotional resonance as labour output. Trade patterns based on shared dreamscapes."

I blinked. The interface shifted—a work drone tuning vibration pillars, families walking through bioluminescent corridors that pulsed in sync with the mood of the queen. No words. Just structure. Harmony.

"They were... peaceful," Dakkar said, uncertain.

"No," I murmured. "They were ordered."

"Request stream indicates art, not visual," Ariel continued. "Haptic sculpture, experienced through carapace. Communal grief practiced in resonance chambers. Recorded sorrow traded between vessels."

"Grief as currency," I muttered. "And we thought they had no soul."

Dakkar tilted his head. "You ever see them do this?"

"No."

I let the footage run. The final segment showed a Crawler child—small, delicate limbs drifting in zero-G, weaving something with silk-threaded arms. It looked like music.

I didn't want to believe that they were more than monsters. The human girl I'd found was one of thirty dead—but she was the one I couldn't forget. Vella system. A lifetime ago. She couldn't have been more than five, maybe six. Face streaked with soot, eyes wide with hope when we breached the hold. Clinging to her mother's body like she hadn't noticed the heat scarring yet. We'd reached them. Almost. Then the Crawlers detonated the corridor. Killed them both rather than let us bring them out alive.

I clenched my jaw. Dakkar saw it in my face. "You okay?"

I didn't answer. Just stared at the screen as the Crawler child drifted through her dream-lit corridors, surrounded by a civilization that called itself beautiful. Poets, I thought. Poets who burned families alive so they wouldn't fall into enemy hands.

Ariel's voice broke the silence. "Would you like me to archive the cultural segment?"

I nodded once. "File it," I said. "But don't sanitize it."

The Crawlers had been my enemy for a long time. I hated them—and what they'd done to us. But something was killing them. It had already taken Dragon. Eden was next. We held our course. No pursuit. No challenge. Whatever had torn through Dragon... it wasn't done.

I moved through the corridors not to give orders, but to be visible—reassuring if that's what they needed, silent if that worked better. The crew was adapting, but tension hummed through the bulkheads. Conversations clipped short when I passed; silence followed status reports. Not every decision would land clean. Not every risk would pay off. But I could be the one constant in a shifting game. If that helped them hold their ground, then that was enough.

I didn't have proof. But I had the shape of what was coming. Sometimes leadership meant listening, not commanding.

I found Shannon Lynne in engineering, crouched over a conduit housing. Leela had said she was earning her keep—knew more about patching old systems than most of her long-timers.

"How's Neale doing?" I asked.

"Better than he was... sir." She still had to remind herself about rank. "They hurt him badly, but every day he can do more." She straightened. "I didn't get the chance to thank you for the stateroom. The space has really helped him."

"You earned it, Shannon. We wouldn't have beaten Dante without you."

Her expression hardened. "What happens to him now? He needs to pay."

She went down to the brig sometimes—to look at the man who'd killed or maimed her family. I'd allowed that.

"He'll stand trial as soon as I find an authority I can trust," I said.

"And if you can't?"

"Then I convene a tribunal here. We have the evidence. If he's found guilty, the sentence is death."

Something in her eyes shifted. "I want to be the one who does it."

"No, you don't," I said quietly. "You're better than that. Don't let him make you less."

She looked away, jaw set, the fight not gone but dimmed.

I left her to the hum of the conduits and signalled the comm. It was time to call Kithlan.

Chapter 21: The Neris Escape

A moment later, his image flickered onto the screen—composed, unreadable.

'That Crawler fleet wasn't the only recent development,' I said. 'I take it you've seen the Polity alert?'

Kithlan's wolfish features twisted into something predatory. 'We have seen it. It is not unexpected. In fact, it confirms that our decision to follow you was the right one. You have made the creatures who hide in the shadows uncomfortable, Rakkan. They are revealing themselves.'

I nodded. 'And once they're revealed, they can be killed.'

I keyed a command into my console. 'I'm transmitting our course telemetry. We'll need your stealth shielding to evade them. Keep the Avenger close.'

Kithlan inclined his head. 'And what of our pursuers, Fleet Commander? Are we to fire on them?'

'Only if they fire first—and even then, only to disable, not destroy. If we have to act decisively, we cripple their warp drives. These are human ships. I won't have their blood on our hands.'

I ended the transmission and moved down the corridor. The hatch sealed behind me with a reassuring hiss. Tactical analysis put our maximum danger window at thirty hours—thirty hours to outmanoeuvre an entire fleet. I stepped onto the bridge and let confidence settle into my stance. That was what they needed from me. I gave a sharp, lopsided grin. 'Just another day at the office.'

The tension cracked a little. Two or three chuckled; grips on consoles eased, shoulders loosened. It wouldn't last, but for now, it was enough. It didn't matter. We had a job to do.

'Replot our course through the Neris Belt,' I ordered. 'It's a risk, but we'll gain time.'

'Setting new vectors,' someone confirmed—the earlier panic giving way to steadier hands.

'Weapons status?'

'Armed and ready,' came the reply.

'All hands, prepare for jump. One minute.' I buckled into the crash chair as the seconds counted down, then turned to navigation. 'Warp eight. Punch it.'

The universe fractured around us; Freyja surged forward, time and space bending like thin metal under the torch of her engines. I braced, centring myself, willing the ship to hold.

Leela's voice came over the comm. 'Engines holding, Captain. No degradation yet.'

I nodded. 'Tell me as soon as they start to, Chief. Rakkan out.'

I felt the Freyja strain under the pressure. Ariel materialised beside me, flickering between forms, her presence cutting through the dim. 'Polity vessels have adjusted their trajectory. Estimated arrival: eighteen hours.'

Twelve fewer hours to run; twelve fewer hours to survive. The weight of it settled into my chest, solid as steel. I pressed my lips together, forcing the reaction down.

'Any sign of advance units?'

'None so far,' Ariel replied. 'They are maintaining a unified formation. However, their speed suggests a coordinated effort.'

'They're tightening the noose.'

Ariel inclined her head, expressionless. 'Precisely.'

I kept my face impassive. This was no time for theatrics. 'If we punch through the next sector fast enough, can we break their tracking net?'

'The engines will hold,' she said in that flat, clinical voice—someone who'd already run the numbers. 'But not forever.'

'We don't need forever,' I said. 'Just long enough.' The Freyja thrummed around me—not panicked, not desperate, just focused. Her systems ran hot, but she held steady. The ship had seen worse. So had we.

On the forward displays the Neris Belt resolved—a dense asteroid field littered with hulks of Crawler plating and half-melted Polity cruisers drifting like ghosts, remnants of a major battle fought here. This was where they'd stalled the Crawlers after Eden, but at a terrible cost. I remembered waking in a regeneration tank, recovering from Chances Drift. The Neris Belt was a scrapyard for those who'd run out of luck.

'Stay at warp eight,' I ordered. 'Arm the forward plasma cannon. Target anything in our path that gets in the way.' Plasma fire flared ahead—quiet pulses of light tearing wreckage to ash before it could touch us. Every flash bought us another breath.

Then Ariel flickered beside me, her tone shifting. 'Sensor anomalies. Pattern matches human vessels. Six signatures on approach—battleship Audacious, heavy cruiser Sydney, two destroyers, two gunships. They're masking emissions.'

The knot behind my ribs tightened. 'Who's commanding?'

Ariel didn't hesitate. 'Flagship transponder confirms: Admiral Knox, Polity Command.'

The name hung on the display: ADM. E. KNOX. I knew him—a fighting commander with a string of engagements on his ledger. Decisive, smart, ambitious. A man who liked the sound of his own myth. He might be arrogant. He was also very good. He would be hard to beat.

I stared at the tactical board. Freyja skated along the edge of the Neris debris field, and the ships behind us moved like pieces in a textbook example of containment.

'Adjust course, two degrees to port. Let them think we're being pressured.'

Dakkar tapped it in. 'We'll skim closer to the belt. It'll limit their line of fire, but it won't hold them off for long.'

'It's not meant to. We just need time.'

The ship rolled into the shift. Outside, fragments of metal and radiation dust cloaked the stars; old wrecks drifted in silence. I felt the field tension through my boots, like a storm building between hull plates.

'They're gaining,' Dakkar said.

'Ariel,' I said. 'New vectors. Assume rapid strategic adaptation.'

She brightened. 'There's a narrow corridor—unstable but navigable. High risk. If we break through and increase thrust by twelve percent, we may force hesitation.'

'If it were anyone but Knox,' I said, 'they'd hesitate longer.'

A moment later the Freyja rocked under the first barrage. The hull screamed; the shields bled power.

'Weapons hot!' I barked.

'Shields at seventy-two percent,' Dakkar added. 'Holding for now.'

'Focus,' I snapped—not loud, just sharp enough to cut through the rising noise. 'Hold fire. Prioritise power to shields and engines. We get one chance at this.'

Time thickened—the kind of moment you feel more than think. Not panic. Just gravity.

Ariel's voice sliced through it. 'Heading zero-two-three. Accelerate through the cruiser's blind arc. There is a vector gap.'

That was the move. A seam in the net. 'Do it,' I said.

Freyja kicked sideways—violent, precise. Alarms blared as fresh fire sliced past our flanks, but none of it landed clean.

'Still with us!' Dakkar shouted.

'Hold it steady,' I said. 'Let the ship do the rest.'

We punched through—one breath, then two—and the trap snapped open behind us. Clean air. Open void.

'Status,' I said.

Dakkar answered, voice hoarse but steady. 'Took some hits, but we're still here.'

The ship's warp drive rumbled, a low satisfied growl. We'd bought time. But I knew it wouldn't be long before we were running again. That was all right. Running, fighting, evading—the Freyja would do it as long as it took.

I keyed the comm, letting my voice carry through the bridge. 'All hands—we're clear. Regroup, reload, and be ready to move.'

Trouble has a smell: burned metal, old power lines, recycled air going sour. I felt it behind my ribs—the itch that said something was hunting us and getting close. Freyja moved through space like a fugitive, her hull streaked with heat scars and field trauma. Every calm second felt artificial, stretched too thin. A lull. Nothing more.

The bridge around me was quiet. Controlled. Below decks, quick repairs were underway—field patches, not fixes. Everything we did was a stopgap. Enough to keep us alive a little longer. Maybe.

I stood at the rail, braced for the moment the calm would break. Ariel shimmered beside me, her outline pulsing with faint light. Her form was an echo of certainty—clean logic braided with probability matrices. Instinct still had its place, though, and mine told me we were running out of time.

'It's too quiet,' I said.

'Too quiet is optimal,' she replied.

'Until it isn't.' I watched the crew at their stations—focused, silent, executing routines like ritual. I knew what that quiet meant. It wasn't peace; it was breath held before impact. 'What's our current status?' I asked.

Dakkar didn't look up from his console. 'Engines are stable, but we're running hot. Starboard coil housing's cracked—patched, not sealed. Fresh scoring midships and fore. Take another sustained hit and she'll bleed out.'

'And the Avenger?'

'Holding pace. Shields spiked hard but recovered. Minimal damage.'

'Options?'

Ariel's tone shifted into surgical calm. 'If we maintain our heading and then break out at a right angle to the Neris Belt, we reduce their predictive accuracy by twenty-seven point four percent. Risk of collision increases, but the debris field introduces navigational noise.'

'Better than letting them box us in.'

Ariel pulsed, calculating. 'Pursuit probability continues to rise. We are nearing the threshold of strategic failure.'

Tension packed the room. No one spoke. A day ago, eighteen hours had felt like a margin to use. Now it pressed at our throats.

The bridge alert cut the silence like a scalpel. 'Contact,' Dakkar said. 'Human vessels. Six hours out, closing fast. Two ships on direct vectors. One of them is Audacious—she won't travel without escorts. Possibly three more riding sensor shadows. They're splitting their approach—predictive sweep pattern.'

Ariel's form twitched. 'Encirclement logic. They are compensating for multiple evasive scenarios. Adjustments are adaptive. Non-random.'

'They're not chasing us,' I said. 'They're herding us—forcing us into a corridor of their choosing.'

'Tactical intent confirmed,' Ariel replied. 'We are the subject of active constraint modelling.'

'Signal the Avenger,' I ordered. 'Reduce velocity by fifteen percent. Make it look like we're compensating for a system fault.'

Dakkar was already entering commands. 'Acknowledged.'

I'd faced monsters in the dark—Crawlers, insurgents, bio-weapons. This wasn't a monster. It was a mirror: fleet tactics used against us.

'What's our position?'

'We're skimming the outer edge of the belt,' Dakkar said. 'If we thread in now, we'll hit the edge of two collision fields. Tight gaps, unstable debris.'

'Keep alert for debris,' I said. 'Adjust heading two degrees port. Keep the nav plot clean.' Freyja angled into the shift. Outside, stars refracted through dust and junk; broken hulls floated between pockets of frozen radiation. A satellite shell turned in silence—long dead.

'They're gaining,' Dakkar said. 'Range is closing faster than it should.'

I looked at Ariel. 'Provide likely vectors. Assume their AIs are already compensating.'

'Working,' she said. 'They're attempting to funnel us toward the Neris convergence line. Radiation density will slow us but disrupt the sensor lock briefly. High risk, but navigable.'

'Take control of navigation. Thread the needle.'

I keyed a short burst to the Avenger. 'Kithlan, I need a false sensor shadow—project it past the convergence point, deep into the belt.'

'Acknowledged,' he growled. 'It will be done.'

Ariel was everywhere—projecting optimal paths, processing threat vectors, finding gaps no human could see. 'We've got a window,' she said, voice steady. 'Minimal. Thirty-eight seconds. Immediate.'

'Take it,' I ordered. 'Kithlan—activate the shadow.'

'Aye,' he replied.

Freyja pivoted. The burn kicked us hard. Inertial dampeners screamed, but the hull held. We sliced into the narrow corridor between mass clusters—debris clouding the field, radiation spiking the scans. The false shadow danced just ahead, broadcasting our signature deeper into the belt. If Knox's ships took the bait, we'd have an opening.

We waited. Then—movement. 'They're splitting,' Dakkar said. 'Five vessels shifting toward the shadow.'

Not all of them. But enough.

'Confirm break,' I said.

Ariel replied without hesitation. 'Lock lost. Pursuit delayed.'

I didn't smile. This wasn't victory; this was survival extended by another hour.

'Peel off, thirty degrees starboard,' I said. 'Maximum burn. Quiet profile.'

The ship accelerated. We cut across the narrow passage Ariel had plotted—scattered hull fragments and sensor ghosts clawing at our flanks. The hull moaned under the pressure, but it wasn't fear, just fatigue.

'They're biting,' Dakkar said. 'We've got separation.'

'Minimal emissions,' I replied. 'Let the drift do the rest.'

The threat markers peeled away one by one, drawn deeper into the false trail. It wouldn't hold forever—but it didn't need to. Just long enough to slip the leash.

Ariel pulsed. 'Clean break achieved. No pursuit signals in our immediate cone.'

'Structural integrity stable,' she added. 'Heat dissipation within range. Weapons at seventy percent.'

'Time until likely reacquisition?' I asked.

'Three hours,' Dakkar said. 'Assuming Knox doesn't throw a net wider than standard protocol.'

'He might,' I muttered. 'But he won't guess which direction.'

Ariel adjusted our vector slightly, smoothing the arc. 'System boundary in one hour, forty-seven minutes. Engine output stable. No significant power loss.' Freyja powered forward, humming low—steady, no overburn, no theatrics. Just controlled motion into the dark.

The minutes ticked down—every one carrying us closer to Eden. Ariel kept to her station, voice clear. 'Projected intercept vectors show no current threats within sensor range. We have a brief window of uninterrupted transit.'

'How brief?'

'Thirty-six minutes,' she said. 'Unless something changes.'

'Then we keep moving.'

Dakkar checked aft again. 'They're back. Long-range scans show six signatures—Audacious, Sydney, and the rest. They'll be in weapons range in seven minutes.'

'Approaching system edge,' Ariel announced. 'Six minutes, thirty seconds.'

It couldn't have been closer, but we might just make it. 'Power up the aft plasma batteries and countermeasures. They might try for a lucky shot.'

The stars ahead looked the same as always—but we knew better. Out there, the light bent just a little wrong. Out there was where the Crawler maps began, and where humans were slaves.

'Status?' I asked.

'Engines nominal. Power stable,' Dakkar said. 'No firing from our pursuers.'

Ariel's tone stayed even. 'Crossing boundary now.'

Then, on my private channel: 'Captain... your decision matrix has shifted. You are no longer acting like a man with nothing to lose. Probability of mission success has increased. But your survivability index has decreased accordingly.'

She was right. I wasn't the man who'd met Hela in that Callista bar. If I died now, I had a reason. But more importantly—I had found a purpose. My daughter and my duty both lay in the Eden System.

A shift followed—imperceptible but real. Sensors wavered, then cleared. The tactical plot reoriented, dropping false signals one by one. Just beyond it, a field of radiation and dead silence waited like a half-remembered dream.

Freyja crossed the line. And we entered Crawler-held space.

Let It Be Heard

Hunger Command Hub: Sanctum of Flame
    Ark Flagship: Fist of Salvation
    Location: Dragon System

They chose to stand.

We honour that.

The queen lit her final beacon, surrounded by the faithful. Their resistance was not born of arrogance. It was not war for pride.

It was memory—defiance in the name of the past.

The Dragon moon burned.

Not with fire, but with becoming.

Their final signal was sent in haste. It was not for us. It was for the humans—for their watchers, blind and slow to see.

We did not stop it.

Fist Supreme Lord Tharim bowed his head as the transmission passed through our ranks.

'Let it be heard,' he said.

High Acolyte Veris opened the sanctum. Dragon was gone.

Its form had passed into silence.

But its echo would guide us.

To Eden.

Chapter 22: Shadows of Eden

The silence had a shape—sharp at the edges, cold in the middle. Like a knife waiting under a pillow.

Freyja drifted through the blackness, a spectral shadow beneath Eden's twin suns. Cloaked in the Avenger's stealth field, we moved unseen—an uninvited ghost slipping past Crawler sentries with no more warning than a breath in deep vacuum.

Tension snapped through the decks like static. In the operations bay, everything was low light and long shadows. Ariel hovered before the primary display—her figure half-shimmer, half-memory—casting elongated silhouettes across the walls. Her form flickered between youth and age, as if she couldn't decide which mask to wear while drinking down a torrent of data.

'Long-range sensors active,' she said, her voice carrying that soft digital thrum. Syndicate tech bled across the console, painting Eden's hidden defences layer by layer. 'Detection risk minimal. Analysing Crawler structures.'

I stood beside her, schematics scrolling across my face in icy blue. The deeper we looked, the heavier my gut sank. It didn't matter how quiet we were or how sharp our edge—what the Crawlers had built down there made us look like ants staring up at a boot.

'They've built an armoury,' Ariel went on, unease creeping into her tone like static interference. 'Surface fortifications. Orbital arrays. It's deeper than we expected.'

'Any sign of Riven's group?' My eyes locked on a cluster of red symbols scattered across the surface.

Ariel hesitated—just a breath, but long enough to feel it. 'Possibly here.' A section of the map pulsed red. She magnified it—an underground network buried beneath the largest structure.

'We need more intel,' I muttered. 'Guesswork will get us killed.'

She didn't argue. Her form shimmered as new data came in. 'Additional Crawler activity detected—power surges across the northern hemisphere. Mobilisation patterns consistent with full defensive posture.'

'They know something's coming,' I said.

Ariel's form flickered, her voice dropping half a register. 'Perhaps they were told.'

I studied the map—layer upon layer of heat signatures, flight paths, fortifications—all converging on one point: the buried network where Riven's signal had first appeared.

'That's our way in,' I said. 'Get me a clean descent window. No alarms, no heat trail.'

'Working,' Ariel said. 'It will not last long.'

'Doesn't have to.'

Everything in me screamed to move; to break orbit and bring hell with me. Save my daughter with gunfire and fury. Instead, I held back. Waited. Scanned. Planned. And piece by piece, the picture came into focus—and it wasn't pretty.

Hela had taken point alongside Ariel, digging into the data for days. I didn't argue. She had the brain for this. Sharp. Dangerous. We pulled the senior crew into ops. Kithlan and his officers came over from the Avenger—towering presences wrapped in silence and steel.

Eden spun in the holo tank—distant, still beautiful despite what the Crawlers had done to it. Deadly. A cold blue pearl hung in a sea of darkness. Its light washed over Hela as she moved like a shadow around the display. Her fingers carved the air, every motion peeling back another layer—heat maps, shield configurations, Crawler troop movements. She made it look like a game she was born to play. Infinite complexity with blood on the board.

'Eden is not as dormant as the Syndicate once believed,' she said, her voice low and precise. She let that land before continuing. 'The Crawlers have reshaped it into a fortress. Mobile defences. Subsurface kill zones. Orbital fire support. Breaking through won't be simple.'

No one spoke. I heard someone breathe—maybe Dakkar. Couldn't be sure. The room had gone still. Not a rescue. A suicide run. The holo tank cast moving shadows across every face—Kithlan, grim and quiet; Dakkar, jaw clenched; Hela, steady as stone.

'Multiple zones of concentrated heat signatures,' she said, trailing her fingers through the red-hot clusters. 'They're artificial. Subterranean. Deep enough to house a small city—or a weapons lab.'

Each sentence cut through the illusions we might have clung to. Officers glanced at one another—not fear, not yet, but the shape of it.

I didn't look away. Couldn't. I'd come too far to let fear call the shots.

The holographic map flickered, twisting Eden's contours into something even more menacing. The planet's hold on us tightened with every revelation, and Hela watched—a spider at the centre of her web.

'We've also detected irregular energy pulses,' Ariel said, casting a lattice of shifting lines across the map. 'These suggest active defences—designed to identify and intercept before landfall.'

The hologram bathed Hela's skin in a pale, ghostly sheen. She looked like a statue haunted by bad decisions.

'Those,' she added quietly, 'are just the primary defences.'

A ripple moved through the room—quiet, brittle. One of the crew murmured the question hanging in the air: 'Then what the hell are they protecting?'

Dakkar's voice came low and tight. 'Do we have a route past detection?'

Hela turned toward him. That gaze could cut glass. She let the silence stretch just long enough to feel like judgement.

'We believe there's a way in,' she said finally. 'But the margin for error is razor-thin. A single misstep could be catastrophic.'

Her certainty had a gravity to it. You could doubt the plan, but not her conviction. And in that moment, belief was all we had. She turned back to the projection, fingers trailing across layered rings pulsing with red. 'The underground network is most active here. This is the Crawler command node—their information nexus. Built on the ruins of the old capital.'

She looked straight at me—steady, sharp, no room for illusions.

'Our primary objective is data extraction. Everything in their vaults. You should expect considerable resistance. The Crawlers have prepared well.' Then, directly to me: 'This is also where they'll be holding her.' Her voice didn't rise, didn't waver. 'Assuming that she is still alive.'

The room went quiet. I broke the silence. 'Listen up. The Defined from the Avenger will handle the data extraction. I'm going in with them. Dallas, Thorne—you'll lead backup teams to cover the exits.' I paused, grounding myself. 'And after that... I'll find my daughter. Alone.'

The room exploded with overlapping voices—a tide of protest crashing against the walls. I shut it down with a glare.

'Stow that.' My voice cracked out across the deck. 'This is personal. I'm not asking anyone to die for my choices. This mission is bigger than me—bigger than her. We need that intel. Without it, the next Crawler attack could take the whole damn sector.'

I scanned their faces—loyal, furious, unwilling to back down. 'No volunteers. No backup. This part—I do alone.'

Of course, Leela was the first to speak up. 'Jero, are you insane? You won't last ten minutes down there—it's crawling with hostiles.'

Before I could respond, another voice cut through—deeper, slower.

'Fleet Commander,' Kithlan said. His words had weight, like stone dropped in water. 'The Avenger's dropships are generations ahead of your own. They are built for stealth. You will use one.'

I nodded, grateful. 'Thank you, Kithlan. I—'

He cut me off. 'And the Defined of the Avenger will help retrieve your daughter. This is how we reclaim our honour.' His eyes locked with mine—feral, unblinking. 'You will accept this.'

Leela smirked. 'I wouldn't turn that offer down, Captain. It's the only way you've got any chance of making it out. Also...' she glanced at Kithlan, 'pretty sure they'd kill you if you said no.'

Dallas stepped forward, Thorne right behind him—both already primed for combat. I couldn't let them throw their lives into a mission that might not have an end. The crew bristled, ready to defy me if it came to that. Tension hung in the air like a fuse waiting for flame.

Then Hela spoke. It wasn't a command or a plea. It was a wager. 'Your captain is known for finding exits where none should exist,' she said, voice smooth as steel. 'Trust in his ability to improvise when conventional strategies fail.'

That quieted the room more than any order could. They would follow—but they expected me to come back alive. I wasn't sure I could deliver.

Hela remained still, knowing she'd left them with the only certainty they could grasp—that the planet wanted to consume us, and she'd shown us the full extent of its appetite. As the lights brightened and the projection faded, she delivered her final, precise strike.

'This mission's success or failure will echo far beyond Eden. Prepare accordingly.'

The crew filed out in silence, their scepticism now laced with respect—and dread. Somewhere on that glowing sphere, my daughter might be fighting for life—but duty called before I could find her. We needed that intel. And as hard as it was to wait, it was what I had to do first.

Maybe all this was teaching me something. I wanted to be a better man; to be driven by something more than hatred of the enemy or the will to survive. Chance's Drift came back in fragments—an empty vector suddenly full of enemy warships, the radiation from a ruptured station giving us half a second of invisibility, manoeuvres that should have failed, orders I disobeyed, lives I saved—too many to count.

Despite that, the aftertaste of disgrace. I had destroyed an enemy fleet that had already signalled surrender. That was my hatred of the Crawlers—my bitter memories of Vella and a dozen other missions. But hatred hadn't been enough. That choice had brought me here—not by punishment, but by inevitability. To the edge of the map, where the law thinned out and consequences grew thicker.

And now, Ariel thought she had found her. 'I got something,' she'd said. 'Not much. But enough. It won't keep for long.'

It wasn't just troop movements or drone patrols. It was a shadow of chaos—guerrilla attacks against Crawler outposts, reprisals against civilian sectors. One more brutal cycle in a war that never quite ended. But inside one of those communiqués, fragmented and half-lost, was a name.

Riven Rhys. Not just mentioned—targeted. Tracked. Hunted.

The last confirmed intel was four days old. Four days ago, they'd been close to catching her—closing in for the kill. She might already be dead. I let out a slow breath. I had to believe she was still alive. My heartbeat steadied into a slow, relentless rhythm. Riven. A rebel. A commander, if the data was right. And now, a marked woman.

I had no memories of her—nothing but a name and a silhouette on a file. But pride stirred in me. She'd held her ground this long against impossible odds. That said something about the fire in her. Something I understood. Maybe she carried a trace of my mother's defiance, or my grandfather's quiet steel. Blood had its own language, and I was only beginning to learn the dialect.

The ambient light shifted again, casting long shadows over the room. I caught sight of myself in the display glass—a stranger staring back. A man shaped by too many endings. Someone who knew exactly how thin the line was between duty and desperation. And yet, something inside me had settled. It was time to act.

A practical commander would have waited—demanded more intelligence, a tighter perimeter, multiple fallback options. But I'd never been that kind of officer. And the clock had already started.

I leaned toward the console, watching Eden shimmer under the weight of too many truths.

'Tell the crew to prepare,' I said. 'We're going in. Forty-eight hours.'

Our mission was clear now—and I'd see it through.

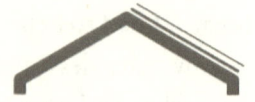

The Swarm Must Gather

Hunger Command Hub: Sanctum of Flame
 Ark Flagship: Fist of Salvation
 Location: Edge of Eden System
We have reached the threshold.

Eden waits—bright, slow, unaware of what it carries.

The last of the Crawlers have nested there.

Their queen hides behind walls she did not build.

The humans walk the same ground, blind to the sacrament rising beneath their feet.

But we do not strike.

Not yet.

The Swarm must gather.

Fist Supreme Lord Tharim stood at the sanctum's edge, framed by walls of command-light and bio signal.

'One strike,' he said.

'One truth. To devour in fragments is to waste the sacred.'

Beyond the veil, more than eight hundred vessels held position in perfect synchrony.

The Skard-ships loomed at the centre—spiked, clad in adaptive plating, built to break worlds.

Around them drifted the Thrall-ships, ruthless in number, each tuned to a single directive: overwhelm.

They did not move like a fleet.

They moved like a field—no gaps, no drift. Just mass. Purpose made visible.

High Acolyte Veris moved among the alignment sigils, his voice low and certain.

'Their sensors still do not register us.'

Tharim's reply was iron.

'Let the queen hope. Let the humans sleep. Let them prepare for our redemption.'

When we come, it will not be war.

It will be completion.

The Swarm must gather.

Then the silence will fall.

Veris closed his eyes in prayer.

'They will become beautiful.'

Chapter 23: Desperate Flight

Riven led the escape, a shadow slipping through tunnels still scarred by an unfinished war. Her crew followed—silent wraiths whose footsteps scattered echoes against the stone. Blaster fire slashed through the darkness, searing rock where heartbeats had pulsed moments before.

Behind them, the relentless march of armoured boots signalled pursuers far more solid than spectres: Crawler forces, precise and mechanical, closing in with the cold efficiency of death itself. Riven barked orders, her voice slicing through the panic. Her fighters moved in practiced defiance, setting traps in the chasms and shadows—each ambush stealing precious seconds from the inevitable.

They couldn't stop long enough to see the damage. Riven knew better than to hope they'd bought more than a moment. A scream bit the air, silenced by the merciless hiss of a plasma blade. It was closer this time. She'd learned early—glory was a myth. This was survival, and survival didn't look back.

Plasma rifles sang from both sides, blue streaks flashing through the chaos. A Crawler fell with its legs blown clean off; before it hit the ground, another vaulted over its body to take its place, firing with inhuman precision.

One by one, they picked off the stragglers—clean, coordinated ambushes that shut doors like jaws. A rebel twisted in place, finding only a dead end. Riven turned just long enough to see his defiant snarl as he charged the horde—buying them seconds, knowing it was enough.

She glanced back—an inferno of motion filled the tunnel where they'd been seconds earlier. Slave soldiers advanced without hesitation, their alien armour absorbing impact after impact. They moved together like a single, fearsome organism, blanketing the air with firepower that dared anything living to survive its onslaught.

Riven knew they couldn't hold the tunnels, but surrender was another ghost—one she refused to name. Not until the walls themselves caved in to take them. Her mother had surrendered, made that choice for both of them. The Crawlers had rewarded that with death.

She signalled a sharp turn, leading them into a narrower passageway. As they retreated, explosive charges arced through the air, detonating in a chain of concussive blasts. The air itself seemed to rupture as the charges went off, a rolling wall of pressure slamming into Riven's back.

Ears ringing, she forced her legs to keep moving, even as heat prickled against her skin and the dust clawed at her lungs. Glancing back, she caught sight of Crawler soldiers struggling to recover—some sprawled in twisted stillness, others rising with unnerving resolve, shaking off debris like dogs shedding water.

'Don't stop! Keep moving!' Riven's command cut through the chaos. A younger fighter—barely more than a kid—pushed up beside her, panting hard, his face streaked with grime.

'Tell the others—more traps, every corner.'

He nodded and peeled away into the haze, slipping back to relay the orders. Riven moved forward, fast and low, her thoughts a blur of map lines and fallback points. Her people knew these tunnels—better than the enemy, better than anyone. But knowledge didn't stop the weight of numbers. Each desperate step dragged them deeper into a warren that felt less like a way out and more like a slow burial.

An explosion ripped the air behind them. Heat roared up the corridor. She ducked instinctively as rubble slammed into the walls and dust clawed at her lungs. A scream pierced the smoke—cut off mid-note. No time to check. No time to mourn.

The tunnel yawned into a broader chamber. The rebels fanned out, grabbing what cover they could. Riven dropped behind a broken barricade, spun, and braced.

'Set charges here—walls and floor. I want a welcome they won't forget.' Her fighters scattered with grim precision, hands moving fast. Red indicator lights blinked alive, flashing in time with her heartbeat.

Then came the sound: boots on stone. Not human. Heavier. Unyielding. The Crawlers poured in—exosuits gleaming like insects dipped in blood, movements precise and remorseless.

'Now!' she snapped. The corridor detonated in sequence—shards of light and sound tearing the air apart. Bodies spun through flame, a brutal ballet of ruin. But the Crawlers pushed forward, uncaring.

Riven opened fire. Each bolt from her blaster felt like defiance made visible. 'Fall back! Side passages! Bleed them for every inch!' They retreated into narrow cutaways—tunnels that pressed close around them. The walls felt alive: too tight, too heavy, like the whole mountain had started to inhale.

Trapped didn't mean caught. Not yet. But it was closing.

The kid reappeared beside her, panting. 'Think this is it, boss. Running out of room.'

He was too young for this. Too full of hope for what waited outside. A part of her—a buried part—ached at the waste of it. 'Then we make them pay for the space they take.'

They hit an intersection—a knot of choices. She scanned the options. None good. Some worse.

'Split up. First group with me. Everyone else—scatter.'

The rebels moved fast. The last of the charges were planted. Riven's unit surged down a sloping tunnel where the air thickened, heavy with dust and heat. The deeper they went, the closer the stone felt—watching, waiting to fall.

A bolt screamed past. Behind her, someone cried out and dropped. She didn't look back. Couldn't. 'We're almost there,' she called. Not a lie — but close.

The passage opened again: a junction with multiple exits, branching options. She took stock. Too few. 'Double back,' she said. 'Hit them sideways. Last push.'

Then the sound she'd feared: a groan above, long and sick with weight. They were bringing the tunnels down. Dust rained from the ceiling in slow motion, then all at once. Stone screamed on stone. The vibration tore through her legs and spine.

She raised her arm. 'Out! Move now!'

The group fractured. Some broke left; others vanished into peripheral tunnels. It wouldn't be enough. The rumble deepened. The ground shifted under her boots. She turned, firing as she moved — every shot a delaying act. The kid stayed with her. Maybe luck. Maybe stubbornness.

'They're on all sides!' he shouted.

'I know. Forward. There's still a route—there has to be.' She glanced over her shoulder, judged distance and speed. 'South tunnels. We regroup if we can. Keep moving!'

They became shadows again—slipping between walls and fire, rebellion etched into every footfall. Every corridor narrowed their odds. The Crawlers pressed closer, a tide of steel and precision, relentless as gravity.

'We can't hold like this,' she said, not to anyone in particular. There were no more charges.

The rebels moved with grim focus, eyes ringed with soot, mouths set in silence. The tunnels were a furnace. Even the air tasted burned. She couldn't see all of them, but she heard fewer feet now. Another blast. The concussive wave lifted bodies. Dust engulfed them, choking and blinding. The tunnel became a throat, swallowing its defenders.

They regrouped at a crossroads that felt more grave than ground. Riven scanned the faces. Fewer again. But still fighting.

Lyra stood nearby, dirt-streaked and defiant. Her eyes caught Riven's. 'This is it, isn't it?'

Riven shook her head, savage. 'Not while I'm still breathing.' She turned to the others. 'Hold here. Hit them from the side. Clear a path if we can.' Her legs gave out a second before she ordered them forward. She hit the ground on one knee, refused to stay there, and forced herself up.

They nodded—already moving, already braced. There was no exit here. Only fury, grit, and the memory they might leave behind.

She gritted her teeth and took aim, fury finding its outlet in the explosive arc of a grenade that carved a fleeting path.

'Stick together!' she called. 'We push through! We don't stop!'

The sound of Crawler boots was an avalanche—relentless, consuming. Riven fought the feeling of the walls closing in. They'd survived worse. They were too thin. Too few.

Riven stood alone, a single heartbeat against the cold, unyielding machine of conquest. She was the eye of the storm—too calm, too aware—as the Crawlers closed their circle with ruthless precision. The burn in her lungs became a full-body scream. Her thoughts splintered, but her finger still found the trigger.

A blast hit near her—a wave of heat and force. It felt like the entire world was coming down. Then the walls came alive. Hundreds of Crawler soldiers poured from hidden alcoves, cutting off the rebels, filling every corner and shadow.

Her rifle slipped. Blood or sweat—she didn't check. Reloading took three seconds too long. She fired into the endless wave, marking the dead with her defiance. They'd bleed them for every inch, even if it took the last of them.

A wall exploded to her right, and suddenly they were cut off—surrounded on all sides by exosuited soldiers. Her group, her core, the heart of their rebellion. There was nowhere left to run.

Riven took in the sight, the crushing precision of it—the endgame. 'We won't make it,' she admitted, the words foreign on her tongue. 'Get clear if you can.'

Lyra met her gaze, fierce and loyal. 'What about you?'

'Go!' It was both plea and command.

She watched them scatter—those who still could. Some would find a way. Some would vanish into the tunnels, to be remembered in Crawler logs and rebel mourning.

She made her decision in a heartbeat. 'Run! Save yourselves!' Her voice was hoarse, a raw scream into the void. She turned to face the enemy—blaster in hand, the ghost who wouldn't give up. She was shaking now. Not from fear—failure. Muscles locking, breath short and ragged. Still standing. Still aiming.

This wasn't how she wanted to fall. But if it had to happen—let it be here. With fire. With purpose. The flash came—white-hot, searing her vision. The world roared and folded inward.

Heat. Stone. Silence.

Then the mountain took her.

Chapter 24: Awakening in Captivity

Riven surfaced from a fog of fractured dreams to find reality pressing in—sharp, sterile, and cold. The white walls loomed like an accusation; their stillness unkind. Her thoughts moved sluggishly at first, each one rising from the dark like wreckage floating up from a deep impact. The concussed haze blurred the edges, but her body remembered what her mind couldn't. Pain was everywhere—not the sharp kind that screamed, but the slow, invasive sort that made you aware of every breath.

She blinked into the light. A ceiling. A hum. A blanket—coarse, too perfectly folded. Her legs were covered, tucked with mechanical care. At the door, a guard stood silent and still, his armour the colour of compliance. Human—or close enough—but he might as well have been carved from steel.

She didn't move at first. She didn't trust herself to. The stillness wrapped around her like water pressing in from all sides, and for the first time in longer than she could remember, she let herself feel it—the exhaustion, the quiet despair, the grief she'd pushed down again and again until it had no voice left. Here, in this moment, there were no eyes watching. Just the hum, the white, and the ache of being spared.

They had kept her alive. That was what unsettled her most.

Not the injuries. Not the captivity. But the why.

Her jaw clenched as her breath wavered—not fear exactly, but a recognition of something older. A thread of helplessness she hadn't touched in years. She let it pass through her, then caught it, crushed it, forced her hands to move. Movement steadied her. Control always did.

She shifted on the narrow bed. Her muscles answered with complaint and resistance—a muted echo of the fight that had brought her here. No sharp trauma, no broken ribs. Dull aches. Controlled damage. They'd wanted her functional.

The room itself confirmed it. No dust. No clutter. No humanity. The light overhead pulsed in a rhythm designed to mimic comfort—but she felt none. The Crawlers didn't do comfort. Everything here was calculated: the sterile minimalism, the uniformed silence, the illusion of safety. They hadn't built this room for healing.

They'd built it for study.

Her hands found the edge of the blanket, ran over the rough weave. Her fingers trembled—once—and she let them. A private concession. Then she pulled her legs over the side of the bed, planting her feet on the cold floor. The chill raced up her spine. It helped. It cut through the fog, forced her to own her body again.

'How long?' Her voice cracked—thinner than she expected. That surprised her.

The guard didn't move. Didn't blink. No badge, no insignia. Just silent judgment. She watched him. Willed him to speak. To flinch. Something.

Nothing.

Time passed—too much or too little, she couldn't tell. Her thoughts wandered despite herself, brushing against old memories: her mother's voice, a corridor filled with laughter, the warmth of a hand in hers—something impossibly distant now. She didn't want these things. They made her slow. But in this sterile room, her defences faltered in the stillness.

The door opened, and she straightened instinctively.

A woman entered—plain uniform, slate in hand. Riven tracked every movement. The angle of her shoulders. The way her gaze slid past instead of locking eyes. Clinical. Cold. No rank. No name. A handler disguised as a nurse.

'What's your name?' Riven asked. Her voice steadied, but there was a rawness in it she didn't bother to hide.

'You should remain still,' came the reply—neutral, smooth.

Riven didn't move, but inside, the steel was forming again. The haze receded, replaced by purpose. Her mind began to build: patterns, triggers, escape vectors.

'Where am I?' she pressed.

'Under observation.' No hesitation. The same phrase she'd heard given to prisoners before execution.

The nurse tapped her slate, recorded something, then left without another glance. The soft click of the door sealed Riven back into silence. Alone. And now it hit. Not panic—but weight.

She felt it settle into her ribs, hollow and cold. Her hands pressed against her thighs, grounding her. If she let it linger too long—the doubt, the grief—it would bloom. So, she didn't. She breathed through it. Focused.

Still, some memories didn't ask permission. A flash of him from an old broadcast—standing at attention in dress uniform, medals catching the light. The hero of Chance's Drift. She'd watched that clip a dozen times as a child, not for the ceremony but to study the face. To imagine what it might have meant to be seen by him. Chosen.

There was a time—before the rebellion, before the Crawlers turned Eden into a graveyard—when she'd daydreamed that he would come for them. That one day, the famous naval officer on the vids would descend from the stars, drive the Crawlers into the sea, and carry her and her mother to safety.

She'd never told anyone that. Not even her mother. Especially not her mother.

Her mother never spoke his name. Her grandfather only spat it. She had long since stopped asking questions. But now, in this room—with nothing to hold her thoughts back—the absence returned. Sharp. Familiar.

Maybe she didn't need him now. She was on her own. The room was a cell. The silence, a weapon. But so was she. Her thoughts moved—not cleanly, but with friction. They'd made a mistake. She was still alive. That was leverage. A crack in the wall.

And she would use it.

Time dragged—not like weight, but like erosion. Slow. Insidious. Wearing her down by degrees. It was the kind of enemy you couldn't shoot. It worked beneath the surface, carving silence into something hollow.

Riven stayed alert. It was the only weapon left to her. She mapped every seam and edge of the cell, tested the strength in her limbs, catalogued her limitations. Even the ache in her joints was data. Rest would have been a concession. Vigilance, at least, felt like defiance.

Her thoughts cycled—not like clockwork, but like pressure building behind sealed doors. Possibilities. Contingencies. The angles of leverage. They'd kept her alive, and that told her something. Their mistake. She would make it hurt.

Hours passed—or something like them. The door stayed shut. The world was reduced to walls, the hum of machines, and the sound of her own breathing. And then, at last, the door opened.

He entered like a ghost that remembered being human—a man wrapped in power, age, and the scent of old betrayals. For a moment, he wasn't the Governor. He was just a fracture in her composure. Something once known, now dangerous. His presence still had weight. That smooth, practiced walk. The unreadable gaze. Recognition warred with calculation across his face.

'Riven,' he said. The voice was unchanged—still warm, still smooth. A tool, like everything else he used. 'I can't tell you what a relief it is to see you alive.'

She measured her response—every word chosen, every breath deliberate. 'Alive and captured,' she said at last, letting the implication settle into the sterile air like fog through broken glass.

He winced—a flicker of discomfort that felt more performance than pain.

'You're more resourceful than you know,' he said smoothly. 'That's why I insisted on overseeing your care personally.'

The suggestion of concern—of lingering bond—cut deeper than any blade. Riven narrowed her eyes, analysing him the way she would a battlefield schematic. His hair was streaked with grey now, giving false gravity to a face she remembered as clean, composed, unburdened by guilt.

'Why are you here?' Her voice didn't rise, but it didn't yield either.

'For you, Riven. For Eden.' The words rolled off his tongue with the practiced cadence of a speech rehearsed too many times. 'You've grown. Not just older—into the woman your mother hoped you'd become.'

The mention of her mother landed like a strike to the ribs. For a moment, she saw the edge of her mother's smile, heard the echo of laughter in a kitchen before the world broke open. Riven forced herself still.

'You don't get to speak about her,' she said. Each syllable was deliberate—a boundary redrawn.

His expression darkened, a flicker of guilt appearing like a hairline fracture in his polished mask. 'You know how much I cared for her. For both of them.'

'And yet they're gone,' she shot back. The sharpness in her voice startled even her. She locked it down again. 'And you are still alive.'

He sank into the nearby chair as though it cost him something, the weight of years finally catching up to his posture. 'I did what I had to, Riven. To survive. For all of us.'

'By siding with the Crawlers?' Her tone sharpened. 'By becoming their mouthpiece?'

'I saved lives,' he said quickly—too quickly. 'I gave Eden a future.'

'You mean you surrendered it.'

'No,' he said, regaining a sliver of composure. 'I adapted. I saw the bigger picture. Someone had to make hard decisions. Your mother understood that.'

The invocation of her mother's pragmatism struck harder than he probably intended. Riven didn't flinch, but she registered the move. Manipulation disguised as reverence. She locked eyes with him. 'What happened, then?' she asked, her voice cool, even. 'To her. To my grandfather.'

He hesitated. The silence that followed carried more weight than any confession.

'We were ambushed. I was told they'd be given safe passage. By the time I realized it was a betrayal, I was already—'

'Safe,' she finished for him. 'That's what you tell yourself? Is that how you sleep?'

'Do you think I sleep?' His voice cracked, and for the first time, she saw something real—regret, maybe. 'I've never stopped caring about you.'

She studied him. He looked smaller now. The man she remembered had filled every room. This one looked more like the wreckage left behind. His choices had hollowed him out. But memory didn't excuse him. She said nothing. And somehow, the silence unnerved him more than confrontation.

'I'm offering you a place,' he said quickly, grasping for momentum. 'Beside me. Not as a prisoner. As a leader.'

'Of what?' Her voice was flint. 'The surrender?'

'The survival,' he countered. And now the tone changed—softer, more persuasive. The old voice. 'With you at my side, we could bring hope back to Eden. They believe in you, in the Rhys name. They always did. Imagine what that could mean.'

She didn't answer. Not yet. She let the possibility hang there long enough for him to hope. Hope, after all, was a dangerous thing to give someone. She needed more: more time, more detail, more ground to stand on.

'You want me to pretend the Crawlers allow anyone to lead but them?' she said at last, her tone mild, almost curious.

'They allow power,' he said. 'And I've made it work. With you, it becomes unshakable.'

That was it. His flaw. Confidence mistaken for inevitability. She filed it away.

'I need to think,' she said, eyes on his. Watching every shift in his mask.

He nodded, mistaking calculation for consideration. And that, more than anything, told her he was still vulnerable. His smile was almost paternal. Tinged with triumph, shaped by the quiet relief of a man who believed he'd reclaimed something he thought lost. A hold on her. A place in her future.

'That's all I ask,' he said. Then his tone softened, almost paternal. 'But if you refuse... I won't be able to protect you. The Crawlers don't tolerate uncertainty. I will have to hand you over.'

He paused—just long enough to make the mercy sound real. 'Don't make me do that, Riven.' The door whispered shut behind him.

Riven sat there a moment longer, her hands still and empty. The offer hung in the sterile air like a gas waiting to ignite. Once, she might have reached for it. Once, she had dreamed of rescue, of being chosen.

That girl was gone. She had saved herself. And if this world was going to burn, she'd be the one holding the match. Not broken. Not theirs. She smiled once, sharp and joyless. Then she began to plan.

He thought she was broken, like he'd broken her mother. But she wasn't broken, she was becoming the weapon that would destroy him.

Chapter 25: The Ruins of Credence

You don't stumble onto a stronghold like this. You're led to it—one false sense of security at a time.

Eden's capital had once been a place of light. Now it lay buried beneath structures that pulsed and shifted, half machine, half organism. Credence's ruins stretched out below us, swallowed by Crawler architecture—sprawling towers, latticed hives, excavation fields scarring the hillsides.

Structures pulsed faintly in the dark, stitched together by arteries of machinery and exhaust.

The city wasn't just occupied. It was consumed. Absorbed into something larger, something growing with slow, methodical hunger.

The Freyja's forward sensors caught it first, but soon every viewport was filled with the sight.

A cold silence took the bridge—not fear but understanding. We weren't facing an enemy hiding in the shadows. We were seeing the next phase of their colonization, built openly across Eden's bones.

I stared down at it, feeling the weight of it settle into my chest, slow and certain. It wasn't impossible. It was inevitable. The Crawlers hadn't hidden this. They hadn't needed to. They had built it openly, sprawling across Eden's corpse, patient as rot. Whatever we had prepared for, it wasn't enough.

Dakkar's voice cut through the hush. 'That's not a base. That's an obscenity.'

Relay towers, shield arrays, anti-orbital batteries—each layer built to survive siege, built to crush whatever dared to strike. This wasn't a foothold. It was a flag planted in Eden's corpse.

I gritted my teeth. They had built this while the Polity looked away—or worse, looked and did nothing. Someone had allowed it. Someone had profited from it.

And I would tear through every wall, every lie, every last bastard who helped build it.

I turned to my crew, locking eyes with each of them. There was no fear—only readiness. Shock had passed. Now came purpose.

'The Freyja holds position here,' I ordered, voice steady. 'We maintain our exit corridor. Lieutenant Commander Dakkar has operational control in my absence. If things go to hell, he makes the call.'

Dakkar gave a firm nod. No argument, no hesitation. He understood the stakes.

'We launch as soon as the Defined are ready,' I said, pushing off the console. 'Be ready to fight when we come back.'

The crew snapped into motion, every movement sharp and efficient.

I turned once more toward the viewport—the waiting fortress of our enemy filling it like a wound. The Crawler stronghold sprawled across Eden's scarred surface, vast and merciless, a monument to how little we truly understood the war we were losing.

A long silence stretched across the bridge. Not hesitation—just the weight of what lay ahead settling over all of us. It wasn't just a fortress. It was inevitability given form. I clenched my jaw, locking down the thoughts pressing at the edges of my mind. There was no room for doubt. Not now.

'We won't get a second chance,' I said. 'Everyone to stations. Be ready to defend us when we come back out—they'll throw everything at us.' I swept my gaze across the bridge. 'Prepare dropship one. I'm heading to the Avenger.'

The crew moved with purpose, slipping into action like a well-oiled machine. I turned back to the viewport one last time. The stronghold loomed, silent, waiting. No one spoke. No one had to.

'Get to your stations,' Dakkar ordered, breaking the quiet. 'Be ready to fight like hell when the captain comes back out.' The crew filed out. I lingered, watching the holo display cycle through the scans—each pass another reminder of how much we didn't know.

Dakkar met my eyes as I turned to leave. 'We're ready.'

I nodded. 'Good. Because this mission just became bigger than all of us.'

The Freyja's engines thrummed beneath my boots as I stepped into the shuttle bay, the pulse of the ship mirroring my own. No turning back. No second chances. The Avenger loomed ahead in the void. As I guided the shuttle into docking position, my mind ran through the plan again. We had surprise on our side—but not for long.

Inside the Avenger's strategy room, officers stood in a tight arc around the holo display. The Crawler edifice filled the projection—monstrous, alive in its scale. It felt like it was watching us as much as we were watching it. I tightened my fists. No room for doubt. No room for failure.

We were going in.

Kithlan's voice cut through the tension. 'They expect us to retreat. Not attack. That is their weakness.'

I focused on the key structures pulsing with power. 'Then we hit them before they know we're there. These outposts,' I gestured to two smaller stations orbiting the main structure, 'are relays. We take them offline, and their response time drops.'

An Oct leader pointed at the main complex, where data nodes sprawled like a nervous system. 'The comms hub is here, buried deep. Once we secure it, we extract everything.'

Another voice, edged with resolve, added, 'Reaching it isn't enough. We have to hold long enough to pull the intel.'

'Their reinforcements will come fast,' Kithlan said.

'They'll answer the way they always do—with numbers and fire.' I let the words hang, scanning the room.

The officers and soldiers before me weren't just warriors. They were survivors, hardened by fire, tempered by loss. Each one of them had faced the Crawlers before and knew what they were capable of. Yet they stood here, waiting—for a signal, for a reason.

I gave it to them. 'No other force can do this. No one else would dare.' I let the words settle, driving them deeper. 'I'm proud to fight with you. Proud you chose to stand with me.'

The weight in the room shifted. Not gone but changed. No longer fear—only purpose. Their resolve, already strong, crystallized into something unbreakable. When I reached the shuttle bay, the air buzzed with raw energy. Weapons loaded, last checks completed, adrenaline thrumming through everybody present. The stakes were clearer now than ever, and so was our resolve.

Soon, all was prepared. The dropships waited in readiness; the crew strapped in impact harnesses. I checked the clasp on my own and pulled it tight. Exhaled. Steeled myself.

'Launch.'

The moment the order left my lips, the ship roared to life, engines surging as plans became motion. The Avenger rumbled as both dropships launched at once, cutting through space like sleek projectiles aimed at the massive heart of enemy territory.

I braced myself on Aegis One as it hurtled forward; the planet swelling in the viewport. Eden—twisted with Crawler architecture, fortified against us. What had once been human was now something else, something grotesquely fused with alien will.

My thoughts raced faster than the shuttles, each second bringing us closer to what waited below. I forced them still. If I let them drift, I would hesitate—and hesitation would get us all killed.

'Stay on target,' I said, voice level despite the storm beneath it.

I switched channels, linking with Kithlan's soldiers. The Defined moved with disciplined precision, checking weapons and gear with the calm of men who'd already made peace with the odds. They were a different breed, forged in the brutality of the Crawler wars. No assault force in human space could match them.

'Weapons check,' I ordered.

Gerran-8, the Defined Oct leader at my side, locked eyes with me. His face was set like stone, already committed to the fight. 'Shields online,' Gerran reported, crisp. 'Pulse cannons charged.'

Around the cabin, soldiers braced. No more waiting. No more questions. Just the work ahead.

The vessel vibrated as we hit the upper atmosphere, hull screaming against the descent. Warnings flashed red across the console; I barely registered them. My grip tightened on the harness. Eden loomed below—an enemy made solid.

'Brace for entry,' I ordered. 'We hit them hard. We get the data. We bring her home.'

And then if anyone or anything stood between me and her, they would die.

Chapter 26: The Governor

Alone in the corridor, Tarkin felt time pressing in on him, demanding answers he was still scrambling to find. The colony governor paused, Riven's words still clinging to him. She had listened — and that was more than he had dared hope.

She would come around; she had to. He needed her name. The people would believe in him then. For all his talk of destiny and survival, one truth loomed larger than any other: he was not a man of destiny. He was a man driven by an all-consuming fear of irrelevance.

The medical facility was a maze of sterile corridors where the cold efficiency of Crawler architecture left no room for warmth. Here, dominance was woven into the very structure — uncompromising, impervious to sentiment. But where others saw oppression, he saw opportunity. He had turned enemy strength into the foundation of his rule, reshaping subjugation into something that resembled order.

His thoughts circled back through years of choices that had once felt inevitable. There had been a time when they called him a hero — the man who could negotiate impossible terms, who had the foresight to salvage what remained. That was before the Crawlers tightened their grip. Now, the people hated him. Every repression his masters demanded was laid unjustly at his feet. Didn't they realise he was saving them?

Riven was the missing piece — the one who could transform his rule from tolerated necessity to true power. With her, he wouldn't just endure; he would command. Regret was for the powerless. And Tarkin was not powerless.

As he rounded a corner, he stepped into the heart of the operation — a chamber humming with cold precision. Human aides worked in efficient silence, flanked by Crawler overseers whose presence alone ensured obedience. Every movement was part of a ruthless machine, a system he had helped build. A system he could not afford to lose.

He wouldn't lose. Not now. His history with Riven's family demanded that he try harder — that he prove himself to the ghost of the woman he had once loved, and to the man he pretended to be.

'It's not betrayal if it keeps us alive,' he had told her mother long ago, when words were his only weapons and persuasion his only ally. 'It's foresight.'

Yet even as he clung to that belief, a deeper fear gnawed at him — that Riven would one day see him as he truly was: a man clinging to relevance like a drowning man to driftwood. But she hadn't reached that conclusion yet. And until she did, he still had time. He would make her understand. His confidence fed on that hope, solidifying with every step.

He gestured to the guard. 'Leave us.' Then he walked over to her bed and sat in the chair beside it. Her silence urged him to fill it — and he did, eagerly.

'Riven, think about what we're offering here. Power. Influence. A chance to shape the future rather than be at its mercy.'

'And you think the Crawlers will allow that?' she asked, her voice flat.

'They need us,' he replied, the triumph in his tone almost palpable. 'Humans governing humans. They can't do it without us—without you. You'd bring legitimacy they can never achieve on their own.'

Her restraint was surgical, her demeanour revealing nothing. 'Why me? Why not someone more... cooperative?'

For the first time, he looked her in the eyes. 'Do you really need to ask that? I've raised you in every way that matters. No one else understands you like I do.'

His directness caught her off guard, and he saw it—rushing to exploit the advantage. 'I was there, Riven. I've always been there, trying to hold on to what's left, trying to rebuild. With you, we'd have something unstoppable. You must see that.'

'I've spent years preparing for this,' he said, his voice swelling with the enormity of his self-deception. 'I knew if I was patient, if I worked hard enough, you'd come back to me. Back to reason.'

Riven was the perfect study in ambiguity. She watched him with an intensity he mistook for contemplation, for a heart's slow surrender. Each of her carefully metered breaths became a thread he pulled tighter around himself, binding his ambitions to the dream of an alliance.

'Maybe you're right,' she said softly. 'But it's a lot to take in.' She smiled faintly. 'Remember when we used to play chase in the summer garden? I miss that innocence.'

He blinked, momentarily disarmed by the memory. When she reached out, his instinct was to pull away—but sentiment won. He took her hand, holding it tightly. 'Come back to me, Riven. I may not be your biological father, but you've always been like a daughter to me. You'll have every advantage I can give you.'

She squeezed his hand back, letting her eyes fill with tears. She let out a shaky breath, forcing her shoulders to tremble just enough. It had to be perfect. If he sensed a lie, she'd never make it out alive. 'It's just that I feel so scared... you know. Every time I see that guard, I get scared again. Could you trust me enough to let me make up my own mind without that pressure?'

He regarded her for a long moment, his face shifting between love and suspicion. 'It's a lot of trust to put in you, Riven. If you were tricking me...' He trailed off, his voice thin. 'It would break my heart.'

Her eyes darted away; the performance almost cracked. 'That was stupid of me,' she whispered quickly. 'Forget I said that. How could you trust me? I wouldn't ask that of you. I just... don't want to be afraid anymore.'

He studied her, the mix of shame and fear disarming him more than any plea. The guilt in her tone felt real—because some of it was. He stood slowly, conflict etched into every line of him. 'No, Riven,' he said, convincing himself as much as her. 'You're right to ask. Trust must start somewhere.'

He turned to the guard, hesitation lingering a heartbeat too long. 'Leave us.'

They talked of her childhood for a few minutes, and then with promises to return, he left her. She gave it thirty minutes by the station chronometer before she sat up. It was only then that Riven allowed herself the smallest of smiles. The moment he had left, the room contracted around her, each wall closing in like a held breath. Silence had returned with its accomplice, urgency. She had to get out of here and find her team.

The weight of deception settled on her like a shroud. The taste of it lingered in her throat, bitter and heavy. She had learned long ago that lies were the currency of survival, but that didn't make spending them any easier. She had played her part well—perhaps too well—but she had no choice.

The things he had done to her family and to the people of Eden were unforgivable. And most of her team were dead because of what he was. Her mind kicked into high gear, every risk measured, every move mapped. She had one shot.

Riven's first steps were cautious, testing her strength. The effects of captivity lingered, but adrenaline burned through them like an engine catching fire. Every second counted. Every breath edged her closer to freedom.

The door handle was cool, unyielding—until a patient hand coaxed it open. She peered into the corridor, its sterile expanse humming with quiet vigilance. No sign of the guard. No movement. Just the steady pulse of a facility designed to watch itself.

She had been to this place before, when it was called a hospital—before it became a place of interrogation and experimentation. She slipped into the hallway, moving light as a shadow. The place was a labyrinth of steel and silence, but her mind mapped it with a survivor's precision.

The cameras were there—she could feel their cold attention—but the Crawlers' systems had flaws the humans never understood. Their vision bled into ultraviolet bands useless to human review, and every few corridors a blind wedge appeared where two alien sight-fields overlapped. She had marked them during her earlier transfers, counting steps, memorising the rhythm of their sweeps.

She crossed through one now, heart hammering as she moved from darkness to darkness. Left at the first intersection. Past the observation windows. She didn't remember everything, but instinct filled in the gaps. Locked doors stood in her way. Riven's fingers worked with calm efficiency, finding a manual release. A soft click, and she was through.

Footsteps echoed somewhere in the distance, faint but purposeful. She adjusted her course without breaking stride, her mind already mapping the sound against the corridors ahead. A flicker of light from a camera lens caught her eye; she noted the angle, waited for its sweep to pass, and moved. Ahead, two guards crossed paths, their routines as precise as machinery. She watched once, twice, then slipped between them as their turns overlapped.

Every obstacle spoke its own language, and she listened. Every second was a calculation — risk measured against motion.

She paused in a shallow alcove, letting a nurse pass close enough that she could smell antiseptic and fatigue. Her pulse kept to the same rhythm as the station itself, a low mechanical hum that had become its own kind of heartbeat. There was no room left for fear. Fear was noise, and she needed silence.

At the nurses' station she found a clean tunic folded on a chair, still warm from the press. She pulled it over her clothes, tied her hair back, slipped into soft shoes. A new name glinted on the badge she clipped to her collar — borrowed identity, borrowed hope. For now, it would be enough.

The corridors felt longer than they should have, stretching away into recycled air and hollow light. The exit from the secure wing lay ahead, close enough that she could almost feel the open space beyond it — a change in pressure, a whisper of freedom.

Then everything changed. The door in front of her refused to open. Its lock was newer, more intricate than the others, and for one long second, she stared at it as though will alone might force it to comply. Then the hum of the station deepened, turned hostile. The alarms came without warning — sharp, layered, unrelenting. Maybe she had triggered a failsafe. Maybe they had checked her room. It no longer mattered.

Boots struck the floor in unison somewhere behind her. Shouting followed. The chase had begun.

She slipped into a storage alcove, pressed back into the dark as two guards ran past.

One spoke into his wrist-comm, voice taut. '—Sierra Two-Six. South corridor sealed. Full armour, armed. Confirm. Is this a drill?'

Static, then a reply she couldn't hear. His face drained of colour. 'Defined? Here? Ancestors preserve us... Understood. We're moving. Send everything — Crawler and human both.'

She stilled completely, her breath shallow. The Defined were gone. They had died in Eden. She had seen it happen — their ships breaking apart in the light. If they were here, then they had come from outside.

The guards crashed through a security door and were gone. She counted three breaths, then slipped out after them, catching the door just before it closed.

The medical wing fell away behind her. The noise struck like pressure, alarms and orders reverberating through the walls. She moved faster, not from panic but from the clarity of someone who had run out of alternatives.

Another locked door. Stronger than the last. She tried the manual release, then the panel—nothing. She forced her mind quiet, scanning for leverage, for weakness, for anything that could be turned to purpose. A length of tubing. A bracket. Even broken things had uses if handled the right way.

Still, the lock held. Fine. Another route. There was always another route.

The corridors ahead seemed to shift as she moved—new alarms flaring, fresh doors sealing, the whole structure waking like a living thing folding in on itself. It was a maze built to contain her, and she intended to teach it what failure felt like.

She slid under a closing barrier, the heat of its magnetic seal brushing her back as it clamped shut behind her. A small victory, but it steadied her pulse. Each narrow escape built its own rhythm, each defiance a breath wrested back from the fortress's suffocating order.

An air duct above. Small, but possible. She pried it open, metal shrieking softly under her grip, and pulled herself inside. The passage pressed close, the crawl slow and airless. Her muscles burned; her breath came in quiet, shallow bursts. The duct's hum vibrated against her ribs, the heartbeat of a machine that wanted her erased.

She dropped into a storage bay, landing harder than planned. The impact jarred her knees. She steadied herself, eyes scanning the room—racks of equipment, a single flickering light. Had she passed the locked door, or simply looped back? No way to tell. No time to find out.

A deep vibration rolled through the floor, followed by a shriek of metal under strain. The sound was wrong—too close, too deliberate. Something was coming. Then the wall erupted inward. The blast threw her sideways as shards of composite and metal tore across the room. Heat, dust, pressure—everything collapsed into noise.

Two figures stormed through the breach, their outlines flickering with the shimmer of active camouflage. Tarkin's men. Not Crawlers.

She dragged herself upright, coughing through the haze. Shapes resolved—armoured, silent, lethal. The older of the two moved first, fast and economical. Before she could react, he had her pinned, one gauntleted hand driving her back against the wall. The muzzle of his rifle pressed against her chest. The hum of the charge built, low and final.

She froze. No words. No options. The air tasted of iron and heat. The barrel steadied.

This was it. No escape. No second chances.

Chapter 27: Race Against Time

Holding the line isn't just about courage. Sometimes it's about what you're willing to lose to buy a few more minutes.

The command node hummed with an unsettling energy, its monitors casting a sickly green glow across the room. We had taken it—barely. Thirty-nine minutes, the console read. Every second pulsed with the inevitability of assault.

Silence held for a moment, thick and unnatural, a stark contrast to the chaos we'd just fought through. Then, as if memory itself re-engaged, urgency returned. We moved in unison—dragging crates into place, welding shut side doors, setting charges. Anything that might buy time. The air was sharp with the bite of scorched metal and the sweat of exhaustion. The room felt smaller by the second, our gear pressing in, bodies tense, movements clipped.

Kithlan snapped orders with the precision of someone who didn't need to raise his voice. His authority was a pressure in the air—you felt it whether you looked at him or not.

I worked fast, hands moving on instinct. It didn't matter how many barricades we threw up; this was stalling, nothing more. Adrenaline burned, but my voice stayed steady. 'Lock that entrance. Secure the left flank. They'll be on us any moment.'

As if summoned, the sensors flickered—heat signatures massing. Crawlers. I met Kithlan's gaze. The Wolven was already at the comms console, inputting updates with the calm of someone who'd traded fear for function.

'We hold for thirty-seven minutes. That's all that matters,' I said.

Kithlan's jaw tightened. 'Not all. And remember—you're taking the Defined with you when you get your daughter. Otherwise, we might have to kill you ourselves.' He caught my look and gave a short, humourless bark.

The approach to the node had been brutal. After splitting from the commando units sent to neutralize the relay stations, we'd hit resistance at every turn—Crawlers entrenched in every corridor, soldiers cut down in close-quarters fights. The memory still throbbed in my chest: the madness of it, the smell of ozone and blood, the metallic tang of our own fear.

Two squads had taken their objectives cleanly. That was the only reason we'd made it this far. Now those same teams were falling back to our position. And soon, everything would depend on whether we could hold long enough. I tightened my grip on the weapon, fingers flexing against the worn grip. Kendall would've had something to say about this.

That thought dragged me back to retraining at the academy after my first posting to Eden. Back at the academy again. Gwen still fresh in my mind, her father's contempt not far behind. I wasn't the right sort for his daughter, so he had me transferred—preferably somewhere I wouldn't come back from.

My tactical assault instructor was a lanky New Australian named Kendall. Rumours swirled about his past: smuggler, mercenary, maybe pirate. Whatever he'd been, he knew his work. My younger self-made damn sure to learn everything he could.

On the first day Kendall looked us up and down and, in that broad New Aussie drawl, said, 'Well, what a shower of shit you are.'

He stalked the line, gaze sharp and amused. 'Every one of you drongos are here because you pissed someone off or fucked up in some way. Whatever you did, I don't care. My job is to make you ready to fight and win close-quarters engagements against an overwhelming enemy. If you listen, you might live a few weeks. If you don't, you'll die quick. So—what's it to be? Life or death?'

The answer was predictable. And Kendall had plenty to teach.

I blinked the memory away as the infrared display sharpened. Blowing the relays had bought us time—but not enough. On the screen, heat signatures swarmed, Crawlers closing in, the noose tightening. Thirty-five minutes, the console blinked. It might as well have been forever.

I scanned the team, reading the exhaustion beneath their armour. The node was smaller than I'd like. I'd set the fire teams in overlapping arcs across the entrance—a narrow bottleneck, for now. It wouldn't hold. They'd blow it wider the moment they could, then come in waves.

We'd left twenty Defined to guard the shuttles and keep them primed for extraction. Ten more had gone with the relay teams, leaving me with ninety troops.

Kithlan and I thought alike about defence. He'd seen enough war to recognise how this would end. Defined units worked in Octs—eight soldiers, each with a specialised role. Six Octs held the static line, four more stood ready behind for when the Crawlers broke through. The rest waited with Kithlan and me at the centre.

Kendall would've called it solid. Then he'd have told us to be ready to go down fighting—and to keep something sharp for when it got close.

I forced my mind back to the present. There was still one person left to reach, one chance that hadn't yet been taken. Every second we held the node bought a little more time to make that possible. Time was bleeding out, but we couldn't leave. Not yet.

A Defined warrior passed, scarred and silent, tightening a weld on the barricade. Kithlan's predatory yellow eyes caught mine. 'We will hold,' he said, voice like a drawn blade. 'The Defined will do what it takes. As long as it takes.'

I nodded. The Crawlers never took Defined prisoners. They knew where the real threat lay. If we lost, none of us would make it out alive.

The communication node blinked relentlessly. Twenty-seven minutes. The weight of it pressed into my chest.

I exhaled, dragging a hand across my face, smearing sweat and blaster dust across my fingers. In my mind, Ariel's voice steadied me—her last transmission flickering through static.

'It's risky,' she'd said, her hologram stuttering as interference tore her image apart. 'But I'm sure. The hospital wing. She's there.'

Then the Crawlers hit.

The first wave struck like a hurricane—chitin and metal, jagged limbs and bladed fury. The barricade shuddered, steel groaning under impact. For a heartbeat, the sheer weight of them threatened to crush us. Then the storm broke.

Kithlan's troops met them with brutal precision—each strike measured, each shot deliberate. The two sides collided like predators locked in extinction's dance, the fight surging and collapsing in waves. The room filled with shrieking war cries, rifle bursts, and the dull, wet percussion of close-quarters combat.

We were surrounded. Crawlers in impossible numbers. The perimeter bent, armour plates warping under their claws. Every second became a test of will. Still, we fought.

Kithlan held firm—an anchor in the chaos. His voice cut through the noise: 'Reform the line! Keep them back!' He was everywhere at once, a force of intent. His troops moved with ruthless cohesion, carving through the enemy in tight, surgical bursts.

'Rotate sectors. Focus fire on breach points,' he ordered. Calm, even now.

We shifted, adjusted, adapted. Every motion counted. Every breath was contested space. And still, they came—wave after wave, grinding forward on sheer momentum. But we weren't finished yet.

The battle fell into rhythm: brief advances, desperate withdrawals, ground won and lost in the same breath. Each cycle harsher than the last. Lives traded for minutes.

A lull. I found myself beside Kithlan, both of us breathing hard. Sweat mixed with dust, the air sharp with ozone and burnt metal. Our eyes met—no words, only the shared understanding of men holding back a tide. Then the Crawlers surged again, pouring through fractured lines like floodwater through broken stone. I tightened my grip on the rifle. This was it.

Despair pressed at the edges of thought, whispering the truth we both knew. I refused it. Not when failure meant losing everything.

Time warped, minutes dragging under the gravity of survival yet vanishing too quickly for hope. I scanned the faces around me—Defined soldiers bloodied, silent, unyielding—eyes fixed, empty of anything but endurance.

We fought on, driven by exhaustion and instinct, though the strain in the Defined showed in every taut muscle and ragged breath.

'They're coming again. Hold your positions.' My voice cut through the chaos.

The entrance exploded—a living tide of chitin and light surging forward, plasma weapons crackling. 'Fire teams, open up!'

The air convulsed under a storm of heavy-calibre fire. Blasters scythed through the Crawlers in torrents of burning plasma. Bodies fell in waves, but still they came.

'Reserve teams, on my mark—AP and micro grenades! Fire!'

The detonations tore through the swarm, shattering bodies in sprays of alien ichor. Still they advanced, relentless, their mass forcing through the debris. The port barricade was failing—Kithlan saw it, and so did I. If they broke through there, Fire Team One would be wiped out.

'Teams Three, Five, and Seven—fall back in sections! Keep firing! Give them hell!'

Fire Team One scrambled to reposition their heavy blaster. Three soldiers hauled the weapon back while the rest fought a retreat—step, fire, step, fire. The blaster was barely set when the Crawlers burst through. A dozen of them hit the line, plasma blades cutting arcs of molten light.

Two Defined went down instantly, torn apart in the first rush. I slammed my rifle into full auto, the weapon jerking in my hands as it ripped through the front ranks. Three—four—five down. More coming. Always more.

One vaulted the pile of corpses, lunging straight at me. Searing pain flared through my shoulder as I hit the ground. The Crawler loomed, blade raised for the kill.

A blur of motion—Kithlan. The Wolven commander crashed into the breach, plasma axe roaring, cleaving the creature clean in half. He kicked the carcass back into the swarm, fangs bared in a vulpine snarl.

Three more came at him. He met them head-on, axe carving through armour and flesh, each blow a controlled explosion of fury. One Crawler broke his guard, blade lifted for the strike. Propping myself on one arm, I steadied my aim and fired once—Type-V blaster, clean through the brainstem. The alien convulsed, then stilled.

Kendall's voice ghosted through my head: *Always keep something handy for close-quarters work.* Then silence. The Crawlers broke and fell back into the dark. We had held.

I checked my chronometer. Fourteen minutes. The data stream was still downloading, but I couldn't wait. If she was still alive in that hospital wing, this was the only chance left to reach her. I pushed myself to my feet. Vertigo hit hard. My arm—still bleeding.

Kithlan stood beside me, breathing raggedly. His golden eyes burned in the dim light.

'For now,' he growled, 'we hold. But the cost is unsustainable.' His voice carried the weight of command stripped bare. 'A third of us are already dead.'

The Crawlers' retreat was temporary. We all knew it—felt it in the bruised marrow of our bones. We had bought minutes, nothing more. The next wave was coming. We reloaded, reset, braced for the inevitable. It was never if. Only when.

The sound of them rose again—chitin scraping steel, weapons charging, claws rasping against walls. The air itself crackled, thick with the promise of slaughter. Kithlan and his soldiers moved with grim precision, reinforcing what was left of the barricades. The Defined had held, but only just.

I swayed where I stood, vision pulsing at the edges. My shoulder was slick with blood.

'I have to get my daughter, Kithlan. We're out of time. Hold here until the download completes—then get the hell out.' I met his eyes. 'If I'm not back, you leave without me.'

He bared his teeth in something between a grin and a snarl. 'Truly, Fleet Commander, you hold to the mission.' A low chuckle followed. 'Fortunately, you don't need to do this alone.' He stepped closer, voice dropping. 'I will fight with you. We will find her together.'

I started to protest, but Kithlan cut me off with a look. 'Now you need treatment. You do not want to be dead when you meet your cub for the first time.'

He signalled a medic, who was already moving. The pain sharpened as the sealant bit, then dulled to a distant throb. The stimulant hit a moment later, hot and chemical, flooding my system with focus. Goof juice. I'd feel invincible for an hour, then crash like a dying star.

The next wave hit before the medic finished. 'Stay focused!' Kithlan's command tore through the chaos. 'Stay together!' Blaster fire roared, plasma and steel colliding in a storm that devoured sound and thought. There was no leaving now. I brought my rifle up and opened fire.

Too many. Always too many. The nanite relay in my ear pinged—Ariel. Her voice flickered through interference. 'Captain, multiple enemy units converging on your position.'

I drove a kick into an armoured human soldier as he charged, followed it with a point-blank blaster shot. 'Yeah, I think some of them already arrived. Anything on Riven?'

Static, then her reply: 'We have a report of a government unit capturing a young female about one klick from your location. They gave her name as Rhys. Transmitting coordinates to your data pad.'

Riven. I glanced at the chronometer. Eight minutes left on the download. Eight minutes between us and everything that still mattered.

The enemy wave had slowed—for now. I turned to Kithlan.

'Ariel has a location for Riven. One klick south of here, toward the hospital wing.'

He nodded. 'Then the Defined must hold until we return.' He turned to the Oct leader, Vrak. 'Hold here, Oct leader. The Defined will regain our honour today.'

Checking my data pad, Kithlan and I slipped through the east door, every sense sharpened for ambush.

Riven was still alive, for now. They were elite troops—Tarkin's personal guard. Two had found her, zip-tied her wrists, and were hustling her down the corridor toward the rest of their squad. Eight in total: active-camo suits, blaster rifles, plasma grenades. The leader carried a sidearm; the holster strap hung loose, unfastened—he'd drawn it recently, or meant to again.

The west side of the complex sounded like all hell was breaking loose—exactly where her memory said the data centre was. The squad looked nervous. Their leader, a grizzled major, barked into his comm, cut the link, and turned. 'Orders say this one's important. The governor wants her back in medical.'

She had to stop that. 'Sounds like the battle's that way, Major,' she said, voice mocking. 'Not running away, are you?'

His fist cracked into the side of her head, slamming her against the bulkhead. 'Shut up, bitch.'

She dropped to a knee, dazed, losing balance—and fell against his leg.

'Get up, you rebel bitch. I'll hit you harder if you don't.'

From the floor she looked up at him, vision swimming, and saw the unfastened holster. Her bound hands shifted—just enough. She angled her wrists, slid two fingers under the grip, and pressed the trigger stud.

She smiled. 'No, you won't, *bitch.*'

The pistol fired inside the holster. A plasma bolt tore through his boot, vaporising half his foot. The major screamed and went down, clutching the ruin.

She twisted, trying to wrench the weapon free, but a rifle stock caught her across the temple and dropped her hard to the deck.

Rakkan heard the discharge of a plasma pistol less than fifty metres away—right where Ariel said she'd been held. 'Kithlan, that's her. We go in now. Blaster pistols and combat knives—we can't risk hitting her.'

The towering Wolven nodded. We reached the corridor junction and heard the shouts—one voice screaming above the rest, 'Just kill her! Do it now!' The time for waiting was over.

We came round the corner like a storm. I drove my combat knife through one visor, pivoted, and put a clean shot through another's head. Kithlan slammed past me, a howl of fury in motion—his plasma axe cleaving the first soldier clean in half. He caught two more, crushed their helmets together, then knifed the third before it could raise its weapon.

Three guards ran, dragging an unconscious woman further down the corridor.

The one on the left opened up with his blaster, but the shot caught my breastplate and glanced away. Luck, more than anything. I closed the distance in three strides, kicked his legs out from under him, and fired into the base of his neck where the armour was weak.

Kithlan was already moving, the blur of motion almost animal. He tore the head from the next soldier's shoulders and turned toward the last.

'Stop! I'll kill her if you come any closer!'

The major had Riven in front of him, using her as a shield. I raised my blaster and took a bead on his forehead, but she was too close to risk the shot. My vision was starting to blur again—the drugs fighting a losing battle—but I kept my aim steady.

'We can deal,' he said, voice cracking. 'Put your weapons down and I won't kill her.' The pistol pressed to her temple. His finger on the trigger.

I held my line, waiting. The moment stretched thin, like wire.

'I'm going to pull the trigger in five seconds. Put your weapons down!'

Five. Four. Three. His eyes flicked toward Kithlan—his first mistake. As his head shifted, fractionally, away from Riven, I squeezed the trigger. No hesitation.

Kendall used to say close combat came down to the eyes—where a man looked before he broke. Maybe he was right. The shot took him cleanly through the skull. He dropped without a sound.

Riven was there—real, impossibly close. Her eyes wide, pupils struggling to focus. I knelt beside her and lifted her head, blood warm against my gloves. For a moment, everything else fell away—the alarms, the screaming, the war.

'Riven,' I said. Her name was half prayer, half apology. 'You're safe.' She met my gaze, her expression a maze of disbelief and exhaustion. Wary. Defiant. Alive.

'Who—?' The word trembled on her lips, years and memory caught inside it. Then recognition surfaced, slow and sharp as a blade. 'It's you,' she whispered—accusation and relief tangled in the same breath.

A thousand words fought their way to my tongue, none of them enough. I nodded instead—a simple affirmation carrying more than speech ever could. 'Try to stay conscious, Riven. Concussion. You took a hard hit.'

Her voice was faint, but steady. She studied me, taking in the blood, the fatigue, the years.

'You came for me. You got older since Chance's Drift. We saw the vids.' Her gaze flicked to my shoulder. 'That looks bad, Rakkan.'

I smiled. 'I can't feel it right now, but I will.'

What could I say to this child I'd never known? A child forged in war. A survivor who hadn't needed me. Stay on mission. It was all I knew.

'Listen, Riven, we don't have much time. Can you walk? I came for you. But thanks for saving yourself instead—I don't think I'm in shape for a long run.'

She regarded me with her mother's eyes for a long moment. 'Maybe. Let's see if my legs work.'

Kithlan checked the monitor and hissed. 'They're coming again. Take positions.'

We made it back to the data vault, hitting a Crawler attack squad from the rear and dropping four with a plasma grenade. Half dragging, half supporting, I pulled her with me behind the barricade. I forced myself upright, bracing against the console. My grip tightened on the Type-V. I turned to Riven and handed it over.

'You know how to use one of these?'

She rolled her eyes, but there was something softer beneath the defiance. 'Yes, Rakkan. I know.' Then, quieter: 'Thankyou'

Leaning heavily against the console, I kept my voice even. 'I just found you, Riven. And I'm not losing you again. We'll talk—I promise.'

She looked at me, then at the ruin around us. 'I'll wait. Just don't take forever.'

The enemy pressed in—Crawlers screaming for blood, human collaborators pushing behind them, determined to finish what they'd started. The download was complete. The shuttles were prepped for launch. And after a lifetime alone, I had my daughter beside me.

If we survived this last attack, we just might make it.

Chapter 28: Escape from Eden

Amidst the raging storm, Kithlan's voice rang out like a hammer on steel. 'Download complete. Sensors clear. No signal!'

I didn't hesitate. 'Job done. Fall back to the shuttles—move!'

We moved as one, a cohesive unit threading through the corridor's hail of gunfire. Security turrets spat death in vain while our pulse rifles answered with lethal precision. Every second teetered on the brink of disaster, yet every step forward fuelled our hope.

The air vibrated with urgency as we pushed for the surface; the data core was locked down and secure, alarms wailing in digital fury. The rumble of distant machinery surged like a tidal wave, but we kept going.

Near misses turned the corridor into a storm of sparks and heat; each shot from the Crawler defences intensified the frantic pace of our escape. We moved in a tight circle, shielding the core. When one flank weakened, we shifted and tightened—formation rotating like a well-oiled machine. Each step covered a comrade; each breath bought a deadly counterstrike.

'It's too much.' Riven fell in beside me; her voice cut the clamour. The air shimmered with heat and fear. 'They've got us pinned.'

I pressed on, unwavering. 'That download can change everything. We can break them. And we will.'

She hesitated—just for a heartbeat—then her eyes hardened. 'Rakkan, you need to get me to my people.'

The squad moved like liquid, adapting to every obstacle with lethal precision. Every hesitation cost blood. I felt it in my bones: this was the opening we'd never thought we'd get—a chance to reverse a war we'd already lost. For Riven, the stakes were other: loyalty to a resistance older than our orders. Her past drove her harder than any command.

We advanced through a symphony of chaos—plasma shrieked off cold walls, the air thick with the acrid tang of burnt metal. I drove the team forward with relentless urgency; every step was all or nothing. A blast slammed into the corridor behind us and forced us into a narrow alcove. Heat clung to my skin; the shockwave rattled my ribs like a captive beast.

Riven turned to me, voice sharp. 'Rakkan, stop. Listen. If I stay, I can find them faster.' Kinship—her family—pulled at her harder than orders ever could.

I spun to face her, eyes like steel. 'You won't find them if this fails. The data we pulled is our only way to save them. If you die here, so do they.'

She held my stare, the fire in her eyes refusing to dim. 'I'm not abandoning them!' Her voice tore through the din, raw with defiance.

Before I could answer, a grenade detonated nearby. The shockwave hit like a hammer, ripping through the moment and sending shards of debris clattering around us. I forced my focus back to the team. Every second lost meant another life gone.

Another shell burst overhead, the corridor narrowing under the heat and pressure. I caught a flicker in Riven's expression—a shadow of something deeper. Her past—the loss, the pain, the rage she carried in silence—burned in her eyes. She challenged me with everything she had, and beneath the fire I saw something else. Trust. Fragile, but real.

A fresh explosion tore through the floor, shoving me back into the fight. I grabbed her arm and pulled her forward. 'We have to move—stick with me!' My voice cut through the chaos, leaving no room for argument.

I didn't check if she followed. I surged ahead, gunfire blazing. We crashed into the open corridor, each plasma round slicing through the despair clawing at our heels. The squad moved in sync—shields rotating, weapons answering every advance with deadly precision. The storm was breaking, but not fast enough.

'Rakkan!' A growl over comms from an Oct leader. 'Exit routes under assault—we have only minutes!' I clenched my jaw, running calculations through the haze of blood loss and exhaustion. One misstep and we were finished.

I pivoted toward the far end of the chamber, scanning for an opening. Too many enemies. Too much firepower. Not enough time. I turned back to Riven. 'We need to move. Now.'

She hesitated, fists clenched. 'If you stay, you die,' I said. 'You want to save them? Then come with us.' Then, softer: 'It's your choice.'

The complex shuddered under another barrage. Kithlan was already ahead, cutting through resistance. A surge of energy flung two Defined against the walls, but they recovered instantly—augmented, fast, lethal. The shots kept coming, relentless and precise. Kithlan held the line, methodically cutting down the defenders.

'Proceeding to fallback,' his voice crackled through the comm. 'Rakkan, we're almost out of time.' The floor shook again. Too much firepower. Too many bodies hitting the deck. We had to move.

Then Riven was beside me, firing the Type-IV with cold precision, cutting down Crawlers as we advanced. 'Let's go,' she said—flat, resolved. No hesitation. No argument.

That was enough. I grinned through the haze. 'All teams—move!' My words cracked like gunfire, pulse pounding in my skull.

We ran as one, just ahead of our own extinction—every heartbeat a stolen second, every breath another defiance of the inevitable.

The Defined regrouped around us with practiced speed. The core shifted to the centre—just like it should, just like it had to. Fire teams covered our retreat, every drilled reflex and desperate improvisation coming alive in me like muscle memory on the edge of collapse. I moved as if each step might be my last. One of them would be.

The shuttles loomed ahead. We made a final, defiant dash, leaving scorched walls and ragged air behind. We escaped through violence, through pain, through the aftermath of blood and hard human lives. We hit the Freyja's hangar bay hot, the shuttle bleeding plasma from a dozen wounds like a wounded tiger. We'd escaped with our lives—barely. The air itself tasted of desperation and burnt metal.

The bridge of the Freyja shuddered under my boots, red alerts washing every surface in light the colour of blood. I caught it all—the fixed resolve on the crew's faces, the deep, awful groan of the hull under strain. I didn't have time to bleed out. The ship was already doing it for me.

The deck lurched, slamming me to the floor. For an instant the world tipped—lights flickered, gravity bucked—and then the bridge drowned in darkness. I forced myself upright, dragging breath into lungs too small for the job.

'Shields at forty percent!' someone shouted, the words cracking like a rifle report. 'Multiple vectors incoming!'

Pain lanced through me, sharp as a broken blade. I gritted my teeth and locked my knees. Had to hold the bridge. Had to hold us together.

'We're taking too many hits, Captain!'

'Stay with it!' I barked. 'Cut everything but the main engines. Power to shields. Hold course.'

The words fell out like spent shells—hollow, but necessary.

Dakkar was already at his station, hands flying over the controls. He threw me a look—steady, calm, unflinching. 'Now, Jero—sit down. You need medical attention. We've got this. Trust me.'

I met his eyes. Every instinct screamed to stay on my feet. But I'd done what I came for. I forced a nod. 'Mr Dakkar has the ship.'

'Ensign! Get the captain to med bay!'

I waved the kid off. 'Treat me here. I need to see this.'

'The Avenger's matching course and velocity!' someone called. 'Still taking heavy fire!'

The Crawlers were faster this time—smarter—cutting us off before we could even shift vectors.

'They're not just faster,' I muttered. 'They're reading us.'

Dakkar didn't look up. 'Yeah. And we're about to teach them what happens when you play too close.' His hands blurred over the console. 'Launch kinetic charges. Full scatter.'

A heartbeat of silence—then the deck convulsed. The impact hit before I could brace. A crack like a thunderclap tore through the bridge. The floor tilted; the lights shattered into darkness. Blood filled my mouth, hot and metallic. Something roared inside my chest—heartbeat or death, I couldn't tell anymore. Another hit—harder. The Freyja shuddered like she was coming apart at the seams.

The dark swelled in. This time, I couldn't stop it.

'Captain! Hold on!' a voice shouted, distant through the fog of pain and static.

Hands caught me—rough, desperate—dragging me clear, hauling me up like a corpse from wreckage.

I wasn't dead. Not yet. They pulled me through the chaos, every second burning away what little strength I had left.

My last thought was of Riven. She'd made it out. That was enough. The dark closed over me—

and I let it.

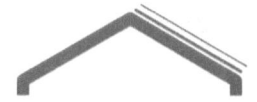

Chapter 29: Hail Mary

Riven stood on the bridge of the Freyja.

It was a symphony of red—flashing alerts, blaring alarms, the pulse of failing systems. The hum of the engines was a heartbeat: weak, uneven, fighting to keep time.

Their captain was gone. Rakkan. The man who had led them through hell—and who, somehow, was her father. Blood still stained the deck where they'd pulled him clear—a stark reminder of how close they'd come to losing everything. But there was no time to think about him now.

Commander Dakkar stood at the helm, steady against the chaos. The battle didn't care that they were one man down. It raged on. The Freyja bucked under the assault, throwing sparks and shuddering plates.

Dakkar didn't flinch. 'Maintain positions. This isn't over.'

Another explosion shook the deck. 'We've lost containment on sections five and six!'

The ship was barely holding together. So were they. Riven gripped the restraints, feeling the pressure bear down—the weight of command, of survival. Rakkan's crew still fought, but they weren't his anymore. They were their own.

'Reroute emergency systems!' Dakkar's voice was iron, though even he couldn't hide the truth: they were exposed, their captain gone, survival slipping through their fingers. The crew worked in silence, hands moving with desperate precision. Riven saw it in their faces—they weren't just fighting to live. They were fighting for him.

For everything he'd built.

Enemy fire pounded the hull, each impact a hammer strike on metal. 'Divert all power to shields! Engage countermeasures!' No hesitation. Orders executed by reflex, by faith. The Freyja groaned, trembling under the strain. Riven felt the absence like gravity.

Then came the cry—raw, hopeless. 'Multiple targets incoming!' She knew that sound. Fear, naked and true. And then—

'Execute uncalibrated warp. Microburst.'

Leela snapped toward Dakkar, disbelief flashing across her face. 'A Hail Mary? You can't be serious!'

Dakkar didn't even look at her. His hands were already moving. 'We don't have another option.'

'Commander, confirm that order!' someone called from the helm.

Leela gritted her teeth. 'We'll burn the engines. We won't be able to stop—let alone steer!'

'We won't need to if we're dead.' Silence rippled through the bridge, sharp as a blade.

Riven barely understood the details, but she knew one thing—whatever Dakkar was planning, it was dangerous.

'Explain,' Leela demanded, voice tight with restrained fury.

Dakkar exhaled sharply, fingers flying over the controls. 'A single pulse jump—just enough to break us out of their net before it collapses. We make it to Waypoint Alpha, rearm, regroup.'

'If it's still there!' Leela shook her head. 'And it could tear the ship apart.'

'We buried that gear deep. We'll make it if the shields hold. Leela—it's all we have, and we have to do it now.'

'Shields at thirty-six percent, sir!'

A long moment. Then Leela buckled her crash harness. 'You bridge officers love burning my engines to hell. Do it.'

'Get the Avenger on comms!' Dakkar barked.

A second later, the link opened. 'Avenger, this is Freyja. We're executing emergency warp—uncalibrated warp, single pulse. A Hail Mary. You need to match our trajectory, or you'll be left behind. See you at Waypoint Alpha.'

A stunned beat. Then static. 'Freyja, you're out of your minds—'

Dakkar cut them off. 'No time. Do it now or die.'

A breath of hesitation. Then: 'Copy that. Avenger executing warp on your mark.'

Dakkar's hand hovered over the final command. 'All hands—brace for emergency warp!'

Riven gripped her harness, heart hammering. It would fry the engines, drain the core, maybe kill them all. But it was the only way. A heartbeat later, the universe tore apart.

The Freyja lurched forward, inertia straining against the restraints. The force of acceleration flattened the crew against their seats, white-hot fire roaring through the ship's frame as the engines overloaded. A final, blinding crack of energy erupted behind them.

The Crawlers vanished from the display. Gone.

The lights flickered, pulsing uncertainly. The warp engines were dead. Riven's hands unclenched from the restraints, her breath ragged.

Dakkar's voice. 'Status on the Avenger?'

Silence. Then—'They made it.'

She closed her eyes for a second. They'd done it. The impulse drives tried to catch; a deep shudder ran through the ship.

'Impulse power to ten percent,' Dakkar ordered. 'Give us steerage way but keep it minimal. We need those engines.'

The Freyja drifted—damaged, but intact. Slowly, the impulse engines pulled her back on course. She had done her job and gotten them to safety. Like her captain, she hung on the edge of death. But they had survived. For now. Riven sat near the back of the bridge, out of the way, watching. She had no rank, no orders to follow. She had nowhere else to go.

A blinking light flared on the console. Leela saw it first. 'Commander, there's something...' Her voice was taut, controlled.

Dakkar turned. 'Report.'

'Structure nearby,' she said, scanning the readout. Relief broke across her face. 'Unclaimed Mining Station 43-B.'

Dakkar allowed himself a thin smile. 'Right where we left it.'

Riven felt the shift in the room—the silent exchange of glances between the crew. Recognition. Memory. Something she wasn't a part of. 'We used it during the war,' Leela murmured. 'We can use it again. Think we can salvage anything?'

'If the caches are still intact, we'll have a fighting chance,' Dakkar said. His tone was pragmatic, not hopeful.

Before anyone could move, another alarm pulsed through the bridge. Leela stiffened. 'New contact just jumped in-system.'

Dakkar turned sharply. 'Identify.'

A pause—then Leela's shoulders eased. 'It's the Avenger.'

This time, the reaction on the bridge was different—still tense but edged with relief instead of fear. Riven didn't know the ship, but she could read the sudden shift in the crew's posture. A breath of relief, tempered by something else. Concern.

Leela's fingers danced over the console. 'They're hailing us.'

A brief crackle, then a voice came through—strained but steady.

'Freyja, this is Avenger. Drive's shot. We've got wounded from Eden. Many wounded.'

Dakkar's jaw tightened. 'How bad?'

'We're running on fumes, Commander.' A pause. 'We need urgent medical support.'

For a moment, no one spoke. Riven felt the weight of it—the realisation that they weren't salvaging for themselves anymore.

Leela exhaled sharply. 'We don't have enough medical supplies for that many.'

'We will if the station still has its stockpile,' Dakkar said. His voice stayed even, but tension bled through. 'And you know what the captain would say. Open comms.'

The link was still live. 'We'll get you inside,' Dakkar said. 'Hold formation and stay close.'

'Copy that. Let's make this quick.'

Dakkar turned to his crew. 'You heard them. Get us inside that station. Now.'

The Freyja banked hard, engines straining. Riven gripped the edge of her seat, the cold metal biting her fingertips. The ship eased into docking position, manoeuvring thrusters firing in weak, uneven bursts. The station loomed ahead—dark, skeletal, forgotten by time but still standing. A dull thunk reverberated through the hull as the magnetic clamps engaged.

'Docking complete,' Leela announced.

Dakkar exhaled. 'Riven, stay aboard. The rest of you—gear up. Bridge team, stay alert. Splinter-ship pilots on standby if anything jumps in-system.'

The crew moved fast. Weapons checked. Lights clipped to vests. Portable scanners calibrated. The station had been theirs once, but time and neglect could have turned ally into hazard.

Leela keyed the outer hatch. Atmosphere readings flickered on her display. 'Pressurised, but cold. No life support, no active systems.'

Dallas and his team fell in beside her. He nodded once. 'Then let's not waste time.' The airlock cycled open.

A rush of stale, metallic air met them as they stepped through. Dust drifted in the corridors, disturbed by their boots. Rust scarred the bulkheads where moisture had crept in. Dead consoles flickered with ghost light, their displays frozen in time. 'This place is a graveyard,' someone muttered.

'Stow it,' Leela snapped. 'This place saved us before—and we didn't want to leave it looking good, did we?'

She swept her scanner ahead. 'Storage bays should be three levels down.'

Dallas took point, weapon raised. 'Move fast. The Crawlers could hit us at any time.' They reached the old freight elevators, but without power, they were dead weight.

'Ladders it is,' Leela said grimly. One by one, they descended into the dark.

The storage bays were vast—towering shelves vanishing into shadow. Emergency lights flickered weakly, casting long, uneasy silhouettes. 'Spread out,' Leela ordered. 'Find anything useful.'

They worked in silence, unsealing crates, prying open rusted containers.

'I've got rations,' someone called.

Another voice, distant: 'Power cells here—enough to get the Freyja running at full.'

A third, sharper with excitement: 'Med supplies! Fully stocked. We're in business.'

Leela allowed herself a breath. Untouched. There'd be enough here to get both ships back in the fight. 'Get a tech team to fix those lifts right now and start loading. We take whatever we can carry.'

Back aboard the Freyja, the Avenger's wounded were already being transferred. The medical bay was never meant for this many, but they made space—clearing storage, repurposing bunks. Riven stood near the entrance, watching as stretchers came through. Some soldiers were conscious; others pale and still. The scent of blood and antiseptic thickened the air.

Dakkar was supervising the transfer.

'Commander,' one of the Avenger's officers—an Oct leader called Vishan-6—approached Dakkar. His uniform was torn, his face carved with exhaustion. 'We expect this from Rakkan. Others have not been so generous.'

Dakkar met his gaze. 'You'd do the same.'

Vishan exhaled, glancing at the injured. 'Maybe.' His voice softened. 'We will not forget.'

A murmur rippled through the Avenger's wounded. Among them were Defined soldiers—elite, gene-enhanced, rarely treated alongside regular troops. Their presence alone could turn battles, but they weren't used to equality.

One of them, arm bound in a makeshift sling, looked around at the medics. 'You honour us. You treat us beside Rakkan. You say we are worth the same.'

Riven caught Dakkar's expression—a flicker she couldn't read. Then he nodded. 'We're all in this together.'

She hesitated outside Rakkan's room before stepping in. It was little more than a closet, but they'd kept it for him. He lay on the cot, deathly still. His face was pale, his breathing shallow. Blood had been scrubbed from his skin, but the deep bruising and the haphazard stitching of wounds told the story of what he had endured.

She swallowed. She had seen death before—too much of it—but something about seeing him like this unsettled her. She pulled up a chair beside his bed.

'You know,' she said softly, 'I was going to tell you how ridiculous you looked running into that last fight. Halfway to bled out. How reckless. How stupid.' She exhaled sharply. 'But I guess you wouldn't hear me anyway.' His chest rose and fell, barely perceptible.

Riven glanced at the IV line feeding blood into his arm. He'd lost so much. Too much. Outside, she could still hear the quiet hum of voices—the wounded receiving treatment, the Freyja's crew working beside them. The Defined warriors, usually so separate, now lay on the same cots as the others, tended by the same medics.

She looked back at Jero. 'You'd hate this,' she murmured. 'All this quiet. All this waiting.'

She reached out, hesitated, then set her hand gently on his arm. 'But you're still here.' Her voice softened. 'And that's something.'

She sat there for a long time, waiting. But waiting wouldn't change anything. And she wasn't built for stillness. With a last glance at Rakkan's unmoving form, she stood. There were others who needed help, and she still had hands to give.

Later, when she returned to the infirmary, the worst of the chaos had passed. The medics worked in quiet rhythm, moving between those who had survived the night. Riven felt the weight in her limbs, exhaustion settling deep. She had spent hours carrying supplies, fetching water—anything to stay useful. Anything to keep from thinking.

Now she allowed herself this.

She carried a flask of water in one hand, intending to check on him. But when she stepped into his small recovery room, she stopped cold. A woman sat beside the cot, rolling down the sleeves of an expensive blouse, smoothing the cuffs with precise, unhurried movements.

Riven's grip tightened on the flask. She didn't recognise her, but she knew the type: poised, elegant—dangerous in ways that had nothing to do with brute strength. Someone used to control. Not a medic. Not crew. And yet, the bloodied cloth on the tray beside her said she had just finished tending to Rakkan's wounds.

The woman glanced up, expression unreadable. Then, with an almost lazy patience, she tilted her head. 'You're staring.'

Riven ignored that. 'Who are you?'

The woman gave a small, knowing smile. 'Hela.'

The name meant nothing to Riven, but the way she said it—the way it lingered in the air—suggested it should. Hela glanced at Rakkan, still unconscious, before standing. 'He'll live. Probably.'

Riven studied the careful bandaging on his shoulder. 'You did this?'

'The medics are busy,' Hela said, smoothing the fabric of her sleeve. 'And I didn't feel like waiting.'

Riven frowned. There was no warmth in her tone, no concern—just clinical efficiency. 'Didn't realise he had personal physicians on call.'

Hela gave a quiet, wry laugh. 'Hardly.' Then, as if only now remembering Riven was there, she added, 'He'd be annoyed if I let him bleed out.' A pause. 'Besides, he's useful to me alive.'

Something in the way she said it—calm, almost bored—scraped against Riven's nerves.

'You make him sound like cargo,' she said flatly.

Hela studied her for a beat, eyes sharp. Then, with a faint edge of amusement, 'And what do *you* make him sound like?'

Riven didn't answer. She couldn't. She looked down at Rakkan instead—his face pale but steady, his breathing shallow but sure. He hadn't stirred once. He had no idea that someone like this had been tending to him.

'You didn't have to do this,' Riven said.

Hela's lips curved—not a smile, not really. 'No,' she said. 'I didn't.'

She picked up her gloves from the tray, sliding them on with slow precision. Then, just as she reached the doorway, she paused.

Without turning back, she said, 'If it helps, I'm sure he thinks you were worth it.' And she was gone—walking out like she belonged there.

Riven stared after her, fists clenching, heat burning behind her eyes. She hadn't asked for the judgment, and she didn't need it. Hela hadn't done this because it was necessary. She'd done it because she wanted to.

And that left Riven with more questions than answers—and a bitter taste in her mouth.

Chapter 30: The Price of Survival

The mining colony hung in low orbit, a drifting corpse in the void, its metal domes battered by space debris with the scars of war still clinging to its hull.

Below the yellow haze of the gas giant, the colony's landing bays were graveyards of gutted equipment, forgotten even by those who had built them. Across their scarred surfaces, crews worked like insects frantically repairing a failing hive, each fighting to keep the ruin at bay for one more day.

Crew members from the Freyja and Avenger swarmed the metal skeletons of their vessels, sealing breaches and swapping fried circuit boards, grim resolve in every movement. Damaged equipment was tossed aside like refuse; shouts, a discordant symphony of urgency, sounded over the general comms channel. Each visored face bore the pallor of exhaustion, each suit marked by the stains of smoke and blood.

In the shadow of the ships, pressurised by a forcefield against the vacuum, a team wrestled with a collapsed plasma coolant line, each struggling to breathe through acrid smoke. 'This thing's beyond hope,' a woman said, her voice strained. 'Any luck with the uplink to that old comms array?'

'Nothing yet. Just static and ghost signals,' her partner answered, glancing at the derelict structures that loomed overhead.

Far above, one comms node still flickered with faint power — just enough for a transmission, if someone knew where to route it.

Dakkar had dismissed the idea of repair hours ago. Morgan hadn't. The two pushed through narrow corridors crowded with injured crew.

'Get those parts stowed,' Dakkar instructed, his voice a deep resonance. 'And have the inventory teams report anything critical directly to us.'

At the docking bay, workers hastily unloaded supplies from the remaining shuttles, the metal-on-metal clamour incessant. Dakkar assessed the operation with tactical precision. 'Double up on the essentials. Food, fuel, medical. Anything else is secondary.'

A group of crew members argued nearby, the stress of their situation crackling in the air like static. 'You call this organisation?' a dark-haired woman shouted, anger flaring. 'Where are the power cells we pulled? Someone better know.'

Another crewman snapped back, 'If I knew, do you think I'd be standing here?'

'Enough,' Leela snapped, her patience worn thinner than the colony's hull plating. She turned to the crew, scanning their haggard, hollow-eyed faces. 'Get back to work. If it's missing, find it. We don't have time for blame.' A tense pause. Then, grudgingly, they obeyed, but the whispers continued.

'We pulled the power cells. They were right here,' a crewman muttered, running a hand through sweat-matted hair. 'Unless someone moved them.'

Another engineer frowned. 'That's the second load that's gone missing.'

Leela's stomach tightened. Supplies didn't just vanish in a lockdown zone — not without help. Somewhere beneath the noise of orders and repairs, something deliberate was happening. Small missteps. Small delays. Enough to keep the Freyja from leaving too soon.

Elsewhere, another crisis was unfolding. The medical bay reeked of antiseptic and sweat, its fluorescents flickering like the pulse of a dying star. Burned ozone and exhaustion thickened the air. Machines whined and sputtered, their readouts blinking erratic pulses like failing heartbeats.

Rakkan lay motionless among them, the clatter and shouts of medics a dull static in his unconscious ears. Air wheezed through his lips in ragged bursts—the breath of a man who had given too much for too long.

'We can't waste time,' Hela said, urgency sharpening her words. 'He needs the tank.'

Riven's eyes flickered with emotion, the line of her jaw set. 'It's too soon. We have to try everything else first.'

The medics moved faster, exchanging glances that spoke of grim expectation. Her father's face was almost unrecognisable beneath bruising and pallor, a warrior's body unravelling after too many campaigns. Elite Crawler toxins from his shoulder wound still worked through him, eating at his blood like slow fire.

'Pulse is erratic! O_2 levels critical!' Each alert sounded like a countdown to failure.

Hela placed a hand on Riven's arm, her touch steady but distant. 'You know what needs to be done,' she said. Her tone softened, yet the steel beneath remained. 'He won't make it otherwise.'

Riven turned, anger flaring. 'And if something goes wrong?'

'Then we lose him. But if we do nothing, we lose him anyway. This isn't a choice, Riven. It's inevitability.'

The silence between them deepened, filled only by the hum of overworked systems. Riven finally looked up, eyes bright with fury and fear. 'I can't lose him. I don't even know him—for God's sake.'

A medic approached, pale and sweating. 'We're out of time,' he said quietly. 'You have to decide.'

Hela met Riven's gaze. 'I've studied your father's history very closely,' she said. 'He's been through regeneration three times—no adverse reaction. Let them do it.'

Riven hesitated, then nodded. 'Do it.'

The medics moved quickly, transferring him through the narrow corridor. Every step felt like time bleeding away. The Regen chamber was already near capacity—five Defined suspended in their crystalline tanks. One system sat empty, its diagnostics just reset, fresh fluid ready.

Hela stepped forward without hesitation. 'Use that unit. It's ready.'

They obeyed. Blue fluid filled the chamber, rising until it enveloped Rakkan. Bubbles curled upward, distorting his face until he was little more than shadow and light. Riven stood motionless, pulse hammering in her ears. What if this was the last time she saw him alive?

They waited until the readings steadied, the rhythmic pulse of the machinery settling into something like hope. 'How long until we know?' she asked softly.

Hela's reply was cold clarity disguised as reassurance. 'Plan as if he'll be back in a day. Prepare as if he won't.' They left the med bay together, passing crew who looked up with anxious eyes. Riven steadied herself, pulling strength from necessity.

At the bridge she stopped and addressed the crew, feeling the weight of expectation. 'Rakkan's in the tank,' she said, her voice steady though her hands trembled. 'He's got a good chance.'

Hela added, 'We need everyone on point. Supplies, repairs—nothing can fall behind.'

The crew nodded, their faces a mix of fatigue and faith. As they returned to work, Riven exchanged a look with Hela—a silent promise that they would make this work, even if it meant tearing the stars apart to do it.

But not everyone on the station was working toward the same goal.

NO ONE QUESTIONED MORGAN'S presence. No one thought to.

They were too busy surviving.

He paused near the medical bay entrance, watching Riven and Hela oversee Rakkan's transfer to the regeneration tank. He noted the tension in Riven's shoulders, the grim steadiness in Hela's instructions. Good. Their focus was elsewhere.

Morgan drifted back into the service corridors, retrieving a small encrypted data pad from his jacket. In the shadows where he knew the surveillance cameras had a blind spot, he tapped a few precise commands. A burst transmission shot out into the void, tight-beamed and masked under standard repair traffic.

The screen flickered once, then the message confirmed delivery: **On station. Ready for relay. Virell inbound—ETA four hours. Maintain delay.** He wiped the data pad clean and slipped it away.

The medics rolled past with a supply cart. Another alarm shrieked from a nearby systems console. Across the landing bay, Leela and Dakkar barked orders, trying to patch a ship barely held together.

Morgan turned smoothly down another corridor, his demeanour calm, almost invisible. Every minute the Freyja and Avenger spent here, bleeding time and resources, was a victory. Small sabotages, small delays—nothing overt. Just enough to hold them in place until Virell arrived. He moved on, silent and deliberate, another ghost among the wounded.

The scout ship was in-system now, heavily stealthed, waiting for his next signal. If the operation faltered—or if Dakkar or Leela grew too suspicious—Morgan could accelerate the plan. He left no trace as he slipped back into the warren of shattered metal and wounded men. A shadow among shadows. Waiting.

In his sealed quarters Morgan activated the encrypted channel. Ephraim Virell's face filled the screen a few minutes later, composed, surgical. 'Report,' Virell said.

'The crew is stretched. Morale's fraying,' Morgan answered. 'Rakkan survives—for now—but he's out of play. I've seeded enough disruption to slow a full recovery.'

Virell's expression tightened. 'Change of orders,' he said. 'Threxxia has fallen. The Hunger routed the opposition faster than we expected. My arrival is delayed — days, not hours. That changes everything.'

Morgan's jaw went tight. 'So, we wait?'

'No.' Virell's voice went cold. 'Get the Freyja back to the Eden system and gain control of the DARK Rift Generator. Use Rakkan if you have to, but you must have executive control by the time I arrive. Hold them in-system long enough to secure the device — by deception, sabotage or force. If Rakkan can be bent, bend him. If not, remove him.'

He paused, then added another detail, clipped and final. 'And Cisco Dante — the Polity will want him freed. We don't. He knows too much. Kill him.'

Morgan nodded. 'That's... authorised?'

'It's an order,' Virell said. 'Maintain cover but make sure he dies.' The line hummed. Morgan sat very still as the finality landed. 'You have your instructions,' Virell finished. 'Take the Generator. Hold control. No matter the cost.' The link cut.

Alone, Morgan let the silence settle around him. The plan was no longer a delay; it was a race. Virell's faith weighed on him, a debt and a burden. He stood, a shadow with a deadline. Now it was his move.

Chapter 31: Awakening from Regeneration

I came back like a bad habit—unwelcome, automatic, and hard to kill.

I awoke to sterile light and the suffocating weight of fluid clinging to my skin. The familiar disorientation of regeneration tugged at my mind: a bone-deep ache, muscles slow to obey, a body not yet mine. The nanites were still working their magic. But knowing I'd be 100% again soon didn't help. I felt like hell. The taste of copper and chemical residue coated my tongue—the aftertaste of rebirth forced on me by necessity.

Sensations returned in fragments: the rasp of dried skin, the throb of half-healed fractures, the strange smoothness of synthetic regrowth beneath the surface. Resurrection had all the grace of a back-alley beating—cold, wet, and owed to someone I'd rather forget.

Monitors chirped nearby—precise, indifferent, relentless. I'd been in this tank too many times. My body hated the process even if my mind accepted the logic. My breath shuddered in and out, sharp with sterilised air. I clenched my hands; the tendons resisted but responded. That counted for something.

My pulse hammered once, then steadied into a stubborn rhythm. I forced my eyes open, squinting against the white glare overhead. The lid hissed open with a hydraulic groan, and gravity reclaimed me unkindly. I slipped from the tank and went to one knee, fluid pooling around me.

A pair of hands caught my arm before I fell. The medic crouched beside me—brisk, professional. 'Captain,' he said. 'You're awake. Riven and Hela have been checking in regularly, but they're both needed on the bridge.'

I coughed, tasting bitterness. 'Probably for the best. No sense watching me float around.'

He passed me a towel after I showered off the residue, silence doing most of the talking. I pulled on the uniform laid out beside the tank. My muscles trembled as I dressed, every motion stiff and mechanical. The chrono on my wrist told me the cost: three days gone. Longer than I liked.

Memory surged—fire, metal, the Freyja bucking beneath me—and I forced it down. Later.

'They left orders to alert them when you woke,' the medic said.

I shook my head. 'Not yet. They'll have their hands full.'

Zipping my jacket, I stepped into the corridor. The deck plating was cold beneath my boots, humming faintly with the pulse of the engines. The ship was holding, but I could feel the strain in every vibration—the ghost of battle still alive in her bones.

The first crew member I passed was a young tech—wide-eyed, pale. She stared as if she'd seen a ghost. 'Captain Rakkan? You're...'

'Vertical,' I finished, voice rough but steady. I exhaled. 'Where's the crew?'

I found Leela at the forward ops terminal, her expression tight.

'Leela,' I called. 'What did I miss?' Her eyes had relief in them to see me alive, but she'd never admit it. She crossed her arms—the tell that meant frustration was simmering.

'Things have been... fluid,' she said. 'Plenty of talk. People trying to read the room.'

'And what are they reading?'

She met my gaze. 'That you're not done yet.' A faint smirk. 'Good thing, too. The ship's been holding its breath.'

I nodded once and stepped forward, letting the crew see me. The team gathered in the main hall—a mix of veterans and new recruits, faces marked by fatigue and doubt. I moved to the centre, making sure every eye found me. Morgan lingered at the edge, silent, unreadable.

'My timing wasn't ideal,' I began, voice low but carrying. 'But I'm here, and the mission stands. Whatever rumours you've heard—forget them.' The words hung for a moment, then settled. I felt the shift: uncertainty folding into focus.

'Our target's still out there. They won't wait for us to get comfortable. So, we move. We get what we came for. Questions?'

Silence—charged this time, not hollow. I met their eyes one by one. They were ready. When the hall cleared, I stayed behind, letting the weight of command settle across my shoulders again. Clarity was next. And I knew where to find it.

The briefing room was alive when Leela and I entered. Hela and Ariel were already deep in discussion, their voices low, urgent. The air crackled with tension. Ariel's hologram flickered beside Hela—phasing from an older man to a woman mid-sentence before settling into the androgynous form that meant business.

'The more I unpack, the stranger it gets,' Ariel said. Her tone was measured, but something under it trembled—distaste, maybe awe. 'The Crawlers weren't just advanced. They were efficient. Elegant.'

'Define elegant,' I said.

'They solved problems differently,' Ariel replied. 'Faster-than-light drives twenty percent ahead of ours. Real-time interstellar comms using quantum sub-node entanglement. Predictive gravity routing beyond anything we've replicated. Their science wasn't guesswork—it was refinement. Centuries of uninterrupted precision.'

Leela leaned forward. 'So why didn't they bury us?'

'Because their strengths are also weaknesses,' Ariel said. 'No synthetic intelligences. No AI. Not because they couldn't—because their ruling caste, the Queens, are neurally networked with their offspring. That web is their command structure. Introducing artificial cognition would fracture it.'

'Too many minds, not enough consensus,' I said.

'Exactly. So they kept it organic. Which means everything—science, tactics, philosophy—flows through biological interpretation. It's perfect for control. Terrible for adaptation.'

She tapped a key. Glyphs scrolled across the display like muscle memory made visible.

'Also, they never developed stealth tech,' she continued. 'No deception protocols. No misinformation theory. Their language has no word for lie. Every node in their network depends on clean signal propagation. Information is truth. When something must be hidden, they isolate it physically.'

'And we lied,' I said.

'Constantly. It made us unreadable. Worse—it made us non-networkable. To them, we were noise. Static. Dangerous, low-bandwidth animals. So they treated us like animals—sub-rational, disposable.'

'You're saying that wasn't hatred?' Hela asked. 'It was taxonomy?'

'Exactly.'

I rubbed a hand across my jaw. 'And commerce?'

'They don't value wealth,' Ariel said, dry now. 'They allocate resources—biomass, metals, compute cycles. Currency and status are meaningless. If a thing is needed, it's requisitioned. If not, discarded.'

'So the wars weren't about greed.'

'No. About control. And resource assurance.'

'And now?'

'Doctrinal shift,' she said after a beat. 'Eden data suggests they're reassessing humanity. The term is "untethered kin." They're trying for contact. Problem is... we taught them how to lie.'

Silence settled like static.

Ariel flickered, processors straining. Hela didn't take her eyes off the data. 'Don't burn yourself out, Ariel. It's not a race.'

'Isn't it, Justine? There's something here—big. I can feel it.'

Hela's smile was thin. 'You feel it?'

Ariel's tone snapped electric. 'Weapon specs. Crawler signatures. And they're almost done.'

Hela magnified the file, voice calm with an edge. 'Interesting.'

'It's a system-killer,' Ariel said. 'Days, maybe less. Theoretical work using dark matter to generate local singularities. Dr Erst Vadim—Polity's top physicist—is here to oversee it. Codename: DARK Rift. Dark-matter Anomaly Rift Kinetics.'

I stepped closer. 'A black-hole generator.'

'And the Polity's fingerprints are everywhere—personnel, funding, infrastructure,' Ariel added.

'Why would the Polity help the Crawlers build a weapon they could turn on us?'

'Ultimate deterrent,' Hela said. 'Whoever controls it controls everything.'

'But this isn't rogue science,' I said. 'If they're not afraid of the Crawlers—who are they afraid of?'

Hela met my eyes. 'Another enemy.'

Ariel's image stuttered. 'Purpose is encrypted through a dynamic fractal algorithm. All I found was in unsecured human logs. Vadim repeats one name.'

'Go on.'

'The Hunger.' The word sat between us.

'That's all I can access,' Ariel said. 'Everything linked to it is quarantined or burned.'

I let out a slow breath. 'Then it's either a Polity power grab—or an enemy we've never met. Either way, our path's the same.'

Leela didn't look up. 'Get to it before anyone else does.'

'Exactly,' I said. 'We take control of the weapon.'

Hela cut in before the silence snapped. 'And we break their command. The Crawlers' weakness is hierarchy. Queens command absolute loyalty—soldiers, drones, machines: extensions of will. Capture the Queens, and we own the board.'

'And DARK Rift,' I said.

Leela folded her arms. 'Finding them' s the trick. They don't advertise.'

Hela traced glowing lines across the holo. 'They do—if you can read it. They are a matriarchal society. Rival Queens forced to collaborate when survival demands it. Eden is split between two dominant Queens—cooperate only when necessary, each ready to let the other fall. Separation by design.'

She pointed to two nodes. 'Entrenchments here and here. Two locations. Two opportunities.'

I nodded once. 'We have our targets.'

Ariel's voice flattened with urgency. 'Timing's tight. If we hesitate, they consolidate. Then it's over.'

Morgan said nothing, watching like a patient animal testing a trap. Hela didn't break eye contact with him. 'Competitive tension is useful—up to the point it becomes problematic. My orders are clear: we take both Queens. Save your debate for sharpening the plan.'

Morgan's gaze held for a heartbeat, then he nodded. 'Yes, ma'am.'

The meeting dissolved into motion. In the corridor, engines thrummed underfoot. Morgan and I fell into step. 'I don't mistake silence for loyalty,' I said. 'If you've got plans of your own, don't make mine the problem. Keep your moves where I can see them.'

He looked at me levelly. 'Have no doubt about my motivation, Captain,' he said. 'You're the one who can make this happen. I want you to succeed. But you're banking the war on two strikes. If either fails, we're exposed. We could lose everything.'

I turned toward the engine room. The tension eased a fraction. His words sat like a stone in my pocket. Leela caught me later, grease on her hands. 'Morgan. I don't like it, Jero. He's running a side-game.'

'I know. Hela holds his tether. For now, that's leverage.'

'Has she tested how strong that tether is lately? She's been holed up with Ariel since you went under.'

I moved through the ship, weighing faces. Loyalty mattered more than skill tonight. Riven lingered by Hela, watching me. She'd fought these bastards with little more than grit and a blaster.

She drifted closer, voice low. 'Sounds dangerous, Rakkan. You sure you're good for this?'

I rolled my sleeve, showed the faded rat emblem. 'See this?'

She squinted. 'Looks like bad art.' A tap. 'What's that?'

'Old history. Rakkan's Rats. A few of us left—the Defined on the Freyja. We earned it, one fight at a time. That's why it has to be me.'

She looked at me the way soldiers do when words won't bridge what's been lost, then nodded once. 'Next time you get ink, let me pick the artist. I know a guy.'

That almost pulled a smile from me. 'Deal.'

A quiet beat. 'There's still time when this is over,' I said. 'Let's take it. We've got some catching up to do.'

She smiled—a real one. 'I'd like that.' I watched her go. Still reasons to stand.

I keyed the comms and spoke the only words that mattered. 'All hands. Decapitation mission is go in two hours.'

Chapter 32: Decapitation

Assault Team Dallas

Rain hammered the ruins as Dallas motioned his team forward—low, tight, fast.

Water pooled around their boots, rippling with every step. Visibility: twenty metres at best. The world was grey noise and shadow, every shape a threat. He signed two fingers—halt. The team froze, rifles up, scanning the fractured skyline. Somewhere ahead a neon pulse flickered through the downpour. Target zone.

Dallas's rifle sat across his back like a promise: long, cold, patient. At his hip the masher rode in its harness—compact, ugly, a revolver-style scatterer with an eight-round cylinder. He liked it because it never jammed. In close, it was honesty; no electronics, no fiddling, just lethal certainty. Thermal paint lit the rooftop: two Crawlers crouched, shoulders hunched, one facing the street, the other turned just enough to watch the alley. Dallas eased the stock to his shoulder, breath slow, the world narrowing to one small rectangle and the cadence of a heartbeat.

Patience. The first rule.

He watched the turned one breathe, watched the way its neck flexed as it tracked some distant noise. When it leaned further away—just enough—Dallas exhaled and broke the silence. The long shot spat with a muffled thud; the first Crawler's head snapped like a marionette cut free. It folded without a cry, landing soft on wet concrete.

The second was half-turned. He didn't waste the moment. A closer, cleaner shot—through armour at the base of the skull—and it pitched forward, limbs spasming in the rain. Two gone. Two quiet thumps against the dark.

'Clear,' he breathed, low. 'Move.'

They slipped past the cooling bodies and into the complex's yawning mouth. Inside the storm thinned to dripping water and the metallic smell of old blood. Echoes made enemies where there were none. A pale shape lunged from shadow—too close, too fast. Dallas didn't have time for the rifle.

He thumbed the masher free; the cylinder spun under his grip with a soft metallic click. The Crawler's blade arced. He stepped inside it and fired. The masher barked—short, vicious—pellets and flechettes spitting, shredding chitin and sinew. The creature folded, a geyser of black ichor spattering the corridor.

No flourish. No wasted movement. He flicked the spent casing out, thumbed the cylinder, slammed the next round home with the heel of his palm, and was already moving again.

'Eyes up,' he barked. 'Contact. Call it in.'

Suddenly the ruins were alive with crawlers. His team moved without hesitation—practiced, precise—their fire converging in tight, disciplined arcs that shredded the Crawlers pressing the assault.

'Left flank, rotate—advance on me!' His voice cut through the noise, each order sharp and measured, instinct guiding them through the chaos like muscle memory honed by war. Gunfire strobed through the dark. One Crawler fell, then another. Silence followed—brief, taut—heavy with the echoes of violence and the scent of burned metal.

'Reroute through section six,' Dallas ordered. 'Stay sharp.' They pushed deeper. The warehouse opened into a cavernous hall—rusted machinery, conveyor belts frozen mid-motion, overhead cables drooping like nooses. The place wasn't dead. It was waiting.

They advanced swiftly, disciplined and low, carving through the maze with quiet precision. Then it hit—like a sprung trap. A Crawler lunged low—too fast for a clean shot. Dallas pivoted, slammed the butt of his masher into its jaw, felt the crack, then fired point-blank into its chest. It folded backward in a spray of black ichor.

Another came from the flank, blade flashing. Dallas let it overcommit, sidestepped, and jammed his masher into its throat. One pull of the trigger—eight flechettes punched through bone and armour. It dropped without a sound.

All around him, the team fought tight and brutal—no finesse, no mercy. Skarn crushed a Crawler mid-leap, armour hissing steam in the rain. Thorne cleared angles with short, surgical bursts, each shot precise, each kill clean. The rain turned the ground slick, bodies sliding in oil-dark water. Every breath was a decision between living and dying.

The captain had given him the *Rats* for this mission—four Defined from Rakkan's old assault squad. Now he saw why. Skarn moved like a falling wall. No flourish, no hesitation. He took a plasma hit to the shoulder, barely flinched, then caught the charging Crawler by the head and slammed it into a wall hard enough to dent steel. Blood sprayed. He didn't stop. Another lunged; he met it mid-air and tore it in half.

Thorne was already ahead, a ghost in motion. His rifle barked once—headshot. Again—shoulder, hip, throat. The Crawler fell before it knew it was dying. Thorne didn't look back; he was already shifting angles, his arcs of fire clean, perfect, mathematical.

Dallas moved behind them, keeping formation tight. It was like following a controlled storm—Skarn battering through resistance, Thorne cutting clean lines through every gap. They moved with machine precision, perfect spacing, perfect tempo. He'd seen good soldiers before. Never anything like this.

'Advance and clear,' he ordered, voice even. Not loud—just enough to steady the rhythm. The Defined didn't need direction, but command presence mattered. Thorne didn't acknowledge, just shifted position, covering the left corridor without breaking stride.

A Crawler broke from concealment, low and fast. Dallas raised his rifle, but Skarn was already moving—a single, brutal step and the thing was crushed beneath armour plating. No pause. No effort wasted.

Defined. Efficient to the point of cruelty. The *Rats* moved like they'd been built for this kind of war. Maybe they had.

Dallas pressed forward, checking angles, clearing lines of sight. A flicker of movement—he pivoted, caught a Crawler mid-lunge, slammed it back into the wall and drove his blade between its armour plates. Another came from the flank; two sharp shots from the Masher dropped it clean.

They were gaining ground, but it cost them space. Crawlers regrouped, pressing hard, testing the line. Dallas felt the pressure rising—the tempo shifting just enough to threaten collapse. 'Hold your spacing!' he snapped. 'Left team, anchor and rotate fire arcs!'

Orders came crisp and fast through comms—acknowledged, executed. The formation tightened, the line stabilized. No panic. Just controlled violence. The air grew thick with the stink of burning oil and ozone. Every breath tasted of metal. But the team held. Nobody broke. A quick glance at his HUD confirmed the advance: steady, disciplined, minimal drift. They were doing it.

The tide broke over them and passed. Silence followed—heavy, ringing with the echoes of gunfire. 'Check ammo and reload,' Dallas ordered. 'We're moving again.'

They advanced through the ruins, welded doors sealing behind them, each step calculated and deliberate. This wasn't retreat—it was realignment. A longer route, but tactically sound. He knew Rakkan would've made the same call.

Two dead. Three wounded. He marked it and kept going. There'd be time later. There was always time later. The chamber opened before them—vast, ribbed steel and coiled supports, light flickering off containment fields. The target was here.

Dallas raised a hand. 'Set positions. Breach on my mark.'

They moved like clockwork. Explosives placed, arcs covered, timing synced. The charge detonated with a clean pulse—white flash, concussion, silence. Inside the cell, the queen waited. Vast. Still. Watching.

Dallas stepped forward. 'Secure her. Mesh restraints. Check for vent access.'

The squad moved in. No wasted motion. The queen didn't resist. She simply watched them, unreadable, patient. Dallas watched her loaded onto the anti-Grav sled, then keyed the comm. 'Package secure. Beginning extraction.'

He allowed himself a single breath. Then— 'Form up. We're not clear yet.'

Rain blurred the world into streaks and ruin. Fifteen metres to the shuttle. Fifteen years. The Crawlers struck from both flanks—fast, coordinated, flashing blades and cold intent.

'Regroup! Hold the line!' Dallas barked, pivoting and firing three tight bursts into the left wave. One Crawler dropped. Another staggered. The third kept coming.

Vekk met it head-on—metal against chitin—driving it back into the mud with a roar that shook the broken street. His armour steamed in the downpour, blood hissing off the joints as he waded in without hesitation.

Dallas and Vekk dragged the queen forward with one hand, rifle hammering in the other, muzzle flashes slicing the dark into strobe-fire glimpses.

To the right, Korin moved like a scalpel unsheathed—precise, silent, inevitable. His plasma blade flared white-hot, carving clean arcs through the Crawlers. As he turned, the rain caught on his armour, revealing a flash of old ink beneath the plating: a coiled Farpoint marsupial rat, fangs bared mid-snarl. ***Rakkan's Rats.***

Ten metres. A bolt tore past Dallas's ribs, searing cloth and skin. He didn't break stride.

A soldier ahead went down—gut-shot, bleeding fast. Dallas caught him mid-fall, hauling him with one hand, the queen's restraints locked in the other. A second trooper closed in to take the weight, their movements fluid despite exhaustion.

Vekk and Thorne fell back in formation, laying down precise, punishing fire, while Korin sealed the flank alone. The ramp loomed through the haze, rising like salvation out of the wreckage. Dallas hit it first, spun, dropped to one knee, and opened fire—emptying the masher—cutting down the last Crawlers clawing up through the storm.

He keyed his comms, voice rough with rain and gunfire. 'Get us out of here,' he said. 'We've got her.'

ASSAULT TEAM RAKKAN

The sun rose like a bloodshot eye, too tired to care what it saw.

A dirty haze choked its light above the old complex, turning dawn into a sickly smear. The sky was poison; the ground no better—scarred, scorched, and claimed long ago by machines that didn't die. On the horizon, faint glimmers marked distant wreckage still burning in the haze. Battles humans had already lost.

I surveyed the team. Faces hard. Eyes clear. Every soldier here understood what lay ahead. Readiness had replaced rest; exhaustion no longer mattered. Their silence wasn't empty—it was discipline.

'Quick and decisive,' I said. Each word dropped like a hammer. 'Before they know we're here.'

I raised my hand and gave the signal.

Kithlan inclined his head, voice low and formal. 'Orders understood, Fleet Commander. We shall offer no quarter.'

His squad moved in lockstep—the Defined gliding forward like precision machinery. Massive, silent, seamless. They didn't disturb the ruins—they infiltrated the living system that replaced them. Steel meeting steel. Perfect symmetry. I fell in beside them. The air burned with the tang of ozone and oil, each breath tasting like corrosion. But forward was the only direction that mattered. And nobody moved forward like the Defined.

Kithlan slipped through first, blade low, slicing the tripwire before it could trigger the alarms. I followed, ducking under a half-collapsed barricade, boots finding the grooves of countless patrols before us. Above, a defence drone pivoted smoothly toward us—its sensors alive, systems intact, cold light scanning. Kithlan fired once, clean and silent. The drone folded, still smoking.

We moved on. This place wasn't abandoned. It was awake. The hum in the walls wasn't decay—it was vigilance. 'This way,' I ordered. 'We've been lucky so far. It won't last.'

Kithlan caught my tone and moved faster, leaving three Defined behind to guard our flank—a quiet show of trust.

Ariel's voice crackled in my ear, calm and surgical. 'Captain, Team Dallas reports enemy contact. Casualties sustained, but they press forward.'

I grimaced. 'Stay sharp,' I said quietly. 'They'll be hunting for us next.' Each step forward felt like another second burned, heavy with threat.

'East quadrant secure,' another voice reported, breathless but steady. 'Pushing on.'

Good. But the air around us was wired and stale, charged with static. The first Crawlers came from the haze—low and fast, armour plates clicking like dry bones.

'Weapons free! Hit them hard!' My rifle kicked against my shoulder. The first burst caught one in the throat, spinning it down into the dust. Kithlan's squad didn't hesitate—they hit the enemy head-on, methodical and merciless. One Crawler broke through, bounding low. I pivoted, fired twice, both centre mass. It dropped mid-lunge.

The Defined pressed forward, unstoppable. But the Crawlers adapted instantly, flowing around our flanks like liquid metal. No panic. No hesitation. Only the purity of function. 'On my mark!' I snapped. 'Break left—flank and drive through!'

We fought step by bloody step.

My rifle clicked dry; I slammed in a new mag, dropped behind a scorched barricade, and fired low to break their line. Kithlan moved beside me, bursts precise and surgical, every shot an execution.

A grenade rolled toward us. The lead Defined kicked it back without breaking stride. The detonation folded three Crawlers into the wall behind them.

We carved forward through wreckage and smoke, every meter earned with blood and will. The control chamber loomed ahead—a jagged ruin of glass and steel, the last gateway to our prize.

'Regroup!' I ordered. 'Fast and tight.' Reports came in—two down, four wounded but standing. No one spoke of retreat. The queen's cell was close. Too close. This had been too easy. Every instinct screamed wrong.

Then—a hollow clank above. I snapped my rifle upward as shapes spilled from the rafters—Crawlers dropping fast, blades drawn, shadows on fire. 'Ambush! Sections—now!'

Kithlan's squad wheeled on reflex, arcs overlapping. I dropped to one knee as a plasma bolt slashed past where my head had been, heat scoring the side of my helmet.

Slug rounds hammered the air, cutting down the first wave—but they kept coming, pouring from hidden conduits, ruptured ducts, seams in the steel we hadn't seen.

The walls themselves flexed and buckled as more Crawlers forced their way through—not reckless, but precise, disciplined. They meant to pin us down and bleed us out.

We locked into a steel knot and drove straight through their line. Gatling guns roared, spitting micro-explosives that shredded their ranks like chaff in a hurricane of lead. After seconds that felt like years, the Crawlers broke—melting back into the walls that closed behind them, collapsing under their own retreat.

The chamber lay ahead. Tall, narrow, and waiting. Inside, the queen. Vast, skeletal, folded in on herself like a mechanism dreaming of motion.

She thought she was safe. She was wrong.

The scaffolding shivered as if fragile, but it was stronger than any alloy we'd seen—triple-reinforced, coldly elegant. I gestured to the Oct leader. 'Plasma cutter. Open it.' Sparks cascaded. The smell of molten steel filled the air. When the frame split, we pulled her out and bound her to the anti-Grav sled.

Kithlan took point. The queen didn't resist—only watched, her ancient eyes full of quiet malice. I wondered if she remembered Chance's Drift. Another sister burned. No matter. We were almost clear. Then the first strike hit—impossible angles, above and behind. A perfect ambush.

A slug glanced off my helmet, ringing my skull. I staggered, found balance, pushed forward. The Defined never faltered. The corridors became tunnels of fire and noise, every step chased by ricochets and burning air. They came again from both flanks—fast, tireless, precise.

'Hold the line!' Kithlan's voice was a snarl. 'Drive them back!'

We pulled in tight, shoulder to shoulder, forcing a bloody wedge through their line. A Crawler lunged from the smoke—too close. I dropped low, fired up into its chest, felt the recoil hammer through my arms. It folded, lifeless before it hit the floor.

Kithlan matched me stride for stride, dragging the queen with brutal efficiency. A Defined stumbled ahead, blood streaming from a shoulder hit. Without pause, Kithlan and I grabbed him, hauling him forward. No time to stop. No time to fall.

The ramp loomed—salvation or slaughter.

Four paces. A plasma bolt burned past my ear, searing the air. I fired into the muzzle flash, heard the shriek, didn't look back. The Gatling guns on the dropship span to life, a storm of tungsten rounds shredding the last wave of Crawlers into mist and molten metal.

Kithlan slammed onto the ramp, dragging the queen aboard. I stumbled after him, boots slipping on blood-slick plating. Behind us, the fortress roared its fury, but we were already lifting—shuttle claws biting into poisoned sky. We had her.

Chapter 33: Shadow Sides

The observation room was silent—cold walls pressing in with sterile indifference. Fluorescent lights buzzed above, flickering like distant thunder and snapping in the still air.

In the centre of the holding chamber, two Crawler Queens stood in restraint pods—imposing, unmoved by confinement. Their dark eyes glinted beneath the muted glow of negotiation-grey light. The only sound was the harmonic hum of the field emitters. Thick walls. Adaptive null-mesh. No shadows. No furniture, save the anchor rings bolted into the floor.

The queens sat parallel, not facing one another but aware—limbs drawn in, bioluminescence dimmed to a low, deliberate pulse. No movement. No posturing. Just presence. We had been broadcasting images of them in captivity to the crawler fleets that surrounded the Freyja. They knew we'd kill them both if attacked. So far, so good.

I stepped through the field alone. Left my weapon holstered but didn't pretend it wasn't there. They didn't look up as I approached. They didn't need to. I stopped between them, holstered hand loose at my side.

'We don't need formalities,' I said. 'You know why I'm here. Answer.'

The taller queen moved first—only slightly. A tilt of her primary limb. Her voice came through the translator like sand sifted through silk. 'You are the one who kills. The one who brings silence after the surrender.'

'Chance's Drift,' I said.

'Yes,' the other queen murmured. 'Two queens opened the channel. Laid down breath and memory. You gave fire in return.'

I didn't answer. I hadn't answered then, either. 'And now,' said the first, 'you keep us alive. But not because we are valuable. Because you are undecided.' 'You misunderstand power,' she added. 'You understand only vengeance.'

The older one regarded me steadily. 'I too understand vengeance. It was I who sent the assassins to kill you. Yet you lived.' I felt the twitch in my fingers. Not at them. At the space between us. I could end it. Two queens. One second. One act. Like before.

Back then, I hadn't planned to kill. It just happened. The silence had asked, and I had answered. I didn't know what I was going to do now either. 'I haven't killed you—yet. That's the only truth I trust today.'

They said nothing. They didn't break. The field behind me shimmered. I turned and walked through it—not because I'd finished, but because I didn't want to see what unfinished looked like.

Hela stood in the corridor, arms folded. She didn't speak; she only watched me pass.

I paused. 'They're not going to talk. Not to me.'

'No,' she said. 'They won't.'

Later, behind observation glass, the situation hadn't improved. I stood with Hela and Ariel, the room's light flattening us into silhouettes. Outside the doorway, Hela's personal guard watched Morgan's security detail with a sour, practiced distrust. I'd known Spalding and French since that night at the Syndicate bar—shared drinks, traded war stories. Wherever Hela went, they went. They didn't like Morgan much either. Probably something about him.

My voice was tight. 'They won't acknowledge me. No negotiation. But we need that superweapon. What's our play?'

Ariel's form flickered, shifting between her default projection and the weathered face of an older man. Her voice, modulated and cool, carried certainty. 'Torture would gain little. Subtlety will gain more. Hela has a plan.'

Hela's pale eyes tracked Ariel's projection. 'Do I now? Show me your proof.'

Ariel's blue light pulsed with violet undertones—a tell I'd come to read as amusement. 'I've learned to read you, Hela. You understand control. You alone have the means to engage them at that level.'

Hela's smile was small and edged. 'Captain, politics and manipulation are not your natural weapons. Let me show you what an alternative approach can do.'

I exhaled and nodded. 'All right. Show me.'

She took her time crossing the threshold into the chamber. The door sealed with a hiss. Hela didn't speak at once. She lit a cigarette with deliberate care; the smoke curled through the sterile air and changed the room's geometry. Her presence altered the dynamic instantly.

The queens turned. Their eyes cooled—calculation meeting appraisal. Predators who had found another predator. 'My dear queens,' Hela said, voice like silk over steel. 'Your position is untenable.'

She let the words settle. She didn't rush; each syllable landed with cold precision. 'You recognise power when you see it,' she continued, gaze steady. 'Those who cannot understand it are beneath you. I do.' They recognised a challenger—someone who saw them as danger, possibility, ally. There was no point speaking to those who could not read the shapes of power. But this one... was different.

Hela smiled, a small, cold thing. 'We seek not your destruction. We seek partnership. An end to wasteful war.'

The air thickened. Their silence shifted—less defiant now, measured. The smell of burning tobacco braided with disinfectant and settled in the room. She let that sit, then pushed. 'Your current strategy leads to ruin. We have you captive and at our mercy. Continue to resist and your clan dies with each of you in this room. Negotiate now, from strength, while strength still remains.'

'We need only one of you to succeed,' she said. 'Competition between rivals has always been your weakness. I offer survival.'

She rose without haste. 'I will meet with you individually to discuss what we can do for one another. We seek only one partner.'

Hela took a final drag and stubbed the cigarette out on the cold metal table—a deliberate punctuation of control. Then she turned and walked out, shoulders straight, unhurried. The queens' eyes followed her to the door.

Behind the glass I let breath go. 'She's dangerous.'

Ariel inclined. 'Dangerous... and necessary.'

LATER, DAKKAR AND I stood in the command centre. Screens threw shifting data across the room in hard, angular light. Before us, layered schematics mapped the labyrinthine heart of the enemy superweapon. On Eden's third moon, Abaddon, the DARK Rift generator waited: Mountains like broken teeth hiding a thing too dangerous even to name. It didn't hum. It didn't glow. It waited the way a buried fuse waits patient, inevitable.

Schematics sprawled in intricate complexity—defences folded into defences; command circuits braided with redundancies. The scale was staggering. An assault would be madness; only precision and cunning offered a path.

Dakkar's voice cut the static. 'We don't stand a chance of taking it by force, Jero. That place is a fortress.'

I nodded. 'Hela's working our guests. She estimates twenty-four hours before we have leverage.'

He frowned. 'And if they don't bend?'

I set the infiltration protocols spinning. The data shivered as layers of security peeled back. Dakkar leaned in, hunting for weakness. There were cracks—there always were—but this was a citadel forged by existential fear.

I breathed slow, feeling the faint vibration of power conduits underfoot and the static whisper of the feeds. This wasn't theatre. It was survival. The DARK Rift generator was the fuse burning toward ignition—the pivot on which a sector's fate balanced. If we seized it, we'd tip the whole board.

Beside me, Dakkar worked methodically. We probed for vulnerabilities—outdated encryptions buried under polished firewalls; forgotten maintenance channels left unguarded. There were gaps. There always were. But the conclusion loomed heavy.

I felt the enormity pressing down—an entire system fortified around a superweapon primed to turn human planets to ash. I knew what was at stake. Control of that thing meant the power to crush the Crawlers or to hold the line against the Hunger. Let someone else take it and it was like leaving a loaded pistol on a bar table during a fight—sooner or later, someone would pick it up and use it.

Dakkar studied the displays, expression controlled but hard. 'It'll take time to work through those defences. The longer we wait, the worse the risk.'

I steadied my hand over the console. 'Risk is part of it. If we crack this, we control the most powerful weapon ever made.'

He pointed at another data stream—a potential entry point half-buried beneath overlapping layers of defence. 'Here. Might be a way in if we keep them distracted elsewhere. Though even if we breach the outer shells,' he added, 'we'd need assault carriers, destroyer escorts—full force projection. The Freyja and the Avenger won't be enough.'

'Or,' I said, working through the impossible, 'we send commandos. Hit multiple fronts, surgically disable their systems.'

Dakkar shook his head. 'You're talking straight infiltration of the most secure Crawler facility in the system. The Defined maybe—but even they—'

'Wouldn't make it out.' I forced the words. 'Bad idea.'

Silence settled between us. Options were shrinking. Patience was no ally; every hour crept the Crawlers closer to ignition. There was a pattern in the schematics we hadn't seen—a single key that held everything together.

Dakkar broke the quiet. 'This entry point looks like a construction port from the first build phase.'

'An opening,' I said, feeling a small, precise spike of hope. 'If we force them to abandon it long enough—'

'We'll need more than luck,' he said.

The schematic rotated, a digital maze of kill-switches and reflex defences—paranoia welded to brilliance. Taking it by force would be near-suicide. Holding it would be worse.

I exhaled. The storm was almost on us. Every piece had to fall exactly where I needed it.

ON THE FAR SIDE OF the ship, in a little-used corner he'd taken for an office, Morgan sat under a dark console light. The glow carved shifting patterns across his forearms; each flicker felt like a countdown. The walls pressed in—not with weight, but with silence stretched taut as wire. He'd learned to live in that pressure. It focused him.

His fingers moved with the careful precision of a surgeon. Even as he cracked the final encryption layer and fed his last clandestine dispatch into the Polity's hidden net, his mind ran ahead, mapping the turns to come. It would soon be time to act.

He paused, calculating—reviewing every cloak, every obsolete military cipher, every modern wrapper. Each message was a tool, a weapon. The far ends of the net would pull; he would tug back, always at the fraying edges. The console blinked. He keyed the final sequence. The relay ship would take it and carry it where it needed to go—to Polity leadership who still thought him a loyal deep-cover asset.

All three players knew now: the Faction, the Polity, and his true masters, the Syndicate. Rakkan and Dallas had returned with their quarry—two Crawler Queens. Rakkan lacked the soft touch to bend them; Hela had the will. She had her own reasons—ambition, a need to outshine Virell—but Virell was never far from play.

But Virell was always two steps ahead. Morgan's next moves would decide where he landed when the dust cleared: power, leverage, the chance to shape the future. Rakkan thought he saw the board. Morgan knew the game beneath it.

He leaned back, eyes closed for a moment, listening to the ship's low churn. Systems whispered—the machinery he'd learned to steer—gears aligning for the fight. The Polity's official orders were blunt: take command of the human security team at the DARK Rift generator and hold it against the Hunger. A fleet would follow in days. That was the paper plan. His real masters had other instructions.

The console chirped. Incoming. He didn't flinch. Layer by layer the encryption peeled under his hands and the message resolved, spare and absolute:

Hunger fleet arrival imminent. Capture the DARK Rift generator before Rakkan does. Execute human security team. Secure Dr Ernst Vadim.

No nuance. No leeway. The brutality of the order landed like a blade. He'd expected a strike directive. He hadn't expected how final it would feel.

There would be details to clean up—Dante, for one. A loose end that pointed straight back to Virell and the Polity faction he'd been serving.

Morgan closed the terminal with a hiss of breath. The display faded to black. In the silence that followed, he felt the enormity of what lay ahead. He'd danced along the razor's edge for years; now the blade pressed against his skin.

He rose slowly, movements smooth, deliberate. His boots made no sound on the metal decking as he crossed to the viewport. Beyond, space stretched out—vast, cold, indifferent. No answers. Only the weight of decisions already made.

He whispered to the void—a prayer to the child he had once been, who would starve no more.

'I will see it through. Whatever it takes.'

Turning back to the console, he keyed in the next set of instructions. His network stirred. Hidden cells flickered to life, like muscle fibres flexing beneath skin, readying for conflict. They would move quickly. The pieces were already in play.

Humanity needed clear leadership. And Ephraim Virell would give it to them. The command had been given. Morgan would obey. The silence in the room was like an open crypt, but his pulse quickened. At last, the time for action had come.

He stepped toward the hatch, movements calm but weighted with the knowledge that the next steps would be irrevocable. Danger wasn't fear—it was anticipation sharpened to a point.

The snare had tightened.

And he was already moving.

The Threshold is Consumed

Hunger Command Hub: Ark Flagship Fist of Salvation
Location: Dragon System

The borderlands lay in ruins behind them—Crawler citadels and human outposts alike, broken and silent.

On the bridge of the Ark of Salvation, Fist Supreme Lord Tharim stood unmoving as the last tremors faded from the sensors. No words were needed. The work was almost complete.

High Acolyte Veris knelt, his voice ringing through the charged air:

'The threshold is consumed. The false divisions burned away. Only Eden remains.'

Tharim raised his hand. Swarm ships pivoted in silent precision, aligning with the Ark's course. The stars themselves seemed to recoil.

Ahead lay Eden—fertile, defiant, unredeemed.

Veris rose, his voice rising into a fierce chant:

'Through fire, we shall purify.

Through pain, we shall redeem.

Their flesh shall burn.

Their souls shall be drawn forth—cleansed of corruption, made whole.'

A murmur of exaltation rippled through the bridge—not hunger for death, but longing for salvation.

A new people to be delivered from the lie of separation.

A new species to be reforged in the sacred crucible.

The Ark of Salvation led the way, engines igniting, their passage shaking the void itself.

The Hunger had set its course.

Eden would burn—

and from its ashes, something purer would be born.

Chapter 34: Morgan's Coup

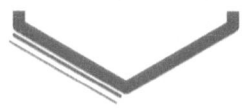

Morgan sat with shadows coiled around him, the soft drone of systems barely louder than the pulse in his ears. The official command blinked on the screen—clean, simple. But nothing about this was going to stay clean.

He leaned back, breathing slow, mind racing. The Polity's designs were collapsing under their own ambition. Decapitation had worked, and the queens were captives. Hela had sole access to the codes, and the Polity's illusion of control now rested on fragile foundations.

Their attention had turned outward, leaving the quiet places undefended. Rakkan concentrated on the coming assault. Hela believed she held all the cards. But Morgan knew neither of them truly understood what lay ahead. He did.

DARK Rift wasn't just a tactical advantage—it was a trigger on which the fate of entire systems balanced. Too dangerous to leave in the hands of weak-willed politicians. Virell wanted control over it, and Morgan was his right hand. He would reach out and grasp it.

He keyed silent overrides, rerouting surveillance feeds and masking his movements. One layer after another folded into place—security blind spots, emergency lockouts, pre-planned extraction vectors. Every detail accounted for. No redundancy too small to double-check.

It came back sometimes—when things went too quiet, when a door closed just wrong.

Morgan had been twelve. Maybe thirteen. Small, fast, clever enough to be dangerous. Krayce, his gang boss, had told him to reroute a burner node on the dock grid—said it'd draw cargo through their turf. Easy payout. Morgan did the math, set it up, but he hadn't accounted for the casualty transport.

The overload vented the medical bay straight into vacuum. Krayce called it failure. Said blood was the only real teacher. The older kids held Morgan down. The knife was meant to be shallow—a lesson. Then Virell walked in. He didn't shout. Didn't posture. Just watched.

'He tried something clever,' Virell said. 'It didn't work. So what?'

Krayce started to argue. Virell didn't raise his voice.

'You don't punish intelligence,' he said. 'You redirect it.'

He handed Morgan a schematic—an old fusion-lock model—and said, 'Fix this instead.' Morgan did. In under six minutes.

Krayce never touched him again. The scar on Morgan's shoulder stayed. But so did the moment. Virell hadn't saved him out of kindness—he'd saved him because he saw something useful.

But usefulness was better than being invisible. And when Virell needed someone loyal, Morgan never forgot who made him feel real.

Morgan didn't pretend to understand the Hunger—the scale of it, the doctrine, the ritualized violence. That wasn't his arena. That was for men like Virell, who played centuries into the future and didn't need your approval.

Morgan's job wasn't to grasp the whole board. It was to move when told. He remembered once, as a teenager, asking Virell why he'd allowed a rival Syndicate faction to survive a raid. Why let them retreat? Why not finish the job?

Virell had smiled—not indulgent, just tired. 'Because their fear is more useful than their corpses,' he'd said. 'But you'll only see that three moves from now.'

And he'd been right. Of course he had. That was the thing about Virell—he didn't make mistakes. He played the game in five dimensions when his opponents were thinking in three.

So, when Virell laid out the framework—protection through alliance, survival through proximity—Morgan hadn't argued. He hadn't needed to. You didn't question the gravity well. You just steered around it and trusted it to hold. The others didn't get it. Rakkan with his soldier's ethics. Hela with her angles and suspicion.

But Morgan had seen what Virell could do with information—with leverage—with people. And if that meant working with the Hunger—if that meant becoming a blade inside someone else's nightmare—then fine. He could be a blade. He'd been one before.

Hela was the linchpin. She carried the codes, the leverage, the queens' reluctant allegiance. Taking her would mean control. Risky. Necessary. Without her, the Polity's illusion of power would crumble into dust. A soft chime in his earpiece. Yeltsin's voice came through, low and steady. 'Corridors clear. Cameron's in position.'

Morgan permitted himself the briefest nod. 'Wait in position. I have unfinished business.'

A few moments later, the observation glass cast a thin, antiseptic reflection of Morgan's face as he keyed the panel. Inside, Dante sat cuffed to the bench, pacing the limits of his restraints like a caged animal.

'About time,' Dante called, voice brittle with habit. 'You going to move me, or just let me rot in here?'

Morgan didn't answer. He watched the monitor—vitals, airflow, toxin feed—all nominal. With a single adjustment to the ventilation control, he introduced a silent agent into Dante's oxygen stream.

'What—what is that?' Dante coughed once, then harder. Alarm stripped away the bravado. 'Morgan. Don't play games. You need me. I can help you—' He stopped, panic snagging his words. The next rasp was desperate. 'I'm begging you. I've got money stashed—anything you want—'

The cuffs rattled as he thrashed. The monitors dipped. The swagger fell away, leaving only the thin, human sound of someone running out of air. The console chimed: **Termination complete.**

Morgan logged the sequence as a filter purge, switched airflow back to normal, and tapped his comm. 'Yeltsin. Proceed.' He turned and walked out. No words. No variables. The bay hummed on as if nothing important had passed through it.

Yeltsin and Cameron were loyal—not to the Polity, not to Hela, but to him. He trusted them as extensions of his will, sharp tools forged in shared purpose. Together, they would cut the shackles.

He double-checked the security layers, ensuring every contingency was in place. No surprises. Escape routes mapped, interference signals primed, false sensor echoes ready to mislead pursuit teams. Timing mattered; precision would decide everything.

Morgan stood, motion smooth and exact. No hesitation. No noise. He checked his weapon again—muscle memory flawless, every action whisper-quiet. The ship thrummed with the focused energy of an imminent campaign: crews moving with purpose, unaware of the fracture about to split open in their midst.

He paused by a maintenance conduit, confirming Yeltsin's sabotage sequences were holding. Surveillance feeds looped cleanly. Environmental monitors showed nothing unusual. Perfect.

In the command centre, Rakkan's voice echoed—crisp, commanding. He was fighting a war on one field while Morgan prepared his own in the dark. Morgan glided forward, his plan unfolding layer by layer. The ship's systems obeyed beneath his fingertips: doors cycling, security grids dulled, data vaults frozen to prevent countermeasures. It was a symphony of betrayal, conducted in silence.

He steadied his breath and stepped forward—each movement measured, inevitable, slicing clean as a blade.

Hela was nearly to her quarters when he found her. Spalding and French flanked her, sharp-eyed but too late to see the danger. Morgan stepped from the shadows, weapon raised and fired twice. The gunfire barely whispered—just pressure and collapse. Spalding fell with a muted grunt; French crumpled before he could draw.

Hela spun toward him, eyes flashing with fury and shock. 'Morgan!'

He closed the distance fast, seizing her wrist and wrenching the sidearm from her grasp. He forced her back against the bulkhead, his voice low and final. 'You're coming with me.'

She struggled, but his grip was iron. He shoved her forward, the muzzle of his weapon pressed between her shoulders. Yeltsin's voice crackled in his ear. 'Extraction route clear.'

Morgan pushed her toward the secured lift, each step measured. The plan was already in motion. There was no turning back now.

Now aboard the stolen splinter ship, Morgan sat in the pilot's seat, feeling the subtle vibration of the controls, the faint metallic tang of filtered air, the hum of engines steady beneath his hands. Yeltsin had done his part—the Freyja's pilot lay lifeless in the maintenance bay, a quiet sacrifice for a mission too large for hesitation.

Cameron and two other loyal men manned the secondary stations, their silence heavy with understanding and resolve. Across from him, Hela sat bound, posture rigid, silence masking calculation. The restraints bit into her wrists, but she showed no discomfort. Her eyes tracked him—sharp, assessing—already searching for angles and weaknesses.

The journey stretched ahead: two long hours of cold void and tension wound tight between them. Morgan let the silence draw out until it felt like a wire ready to snap before he spoke, voice low and deliberate. 'You think Rakkan's the one with vision,' he said.

Hela's mouth twitched into something close to amusement. 'Rakkan's a soldier. Loyal. Predictable.' She tilted her head. 'You, on the other hand... you're harder to read. That makes you interesting. Dangerous, but interesting.'

Morgan adjusted the flight vector, the stars shifting subtly beyond the forward viewport. 'The Polity's deal with the Crawlers wasn't weakness. It was buying time.'

She gave a slight nod. 'Everyone trades something. The question is what's left afterward.'

Morgan's eyes flicked to hers. 'They weren't just trading. They were building a barrier—a line between us and the Hunger.'

Hela's brow arched. Her voice lowered, serious now. 'The Hunger?'

He nodded, tone clipped and grim. 'A super-aggressive species. They keep forging outward. They don't stop. They've been carving through Crawler space for decades—worlds stripped bare, civilizations swallowed whole.'

Morgan drew his sidearm in one smooth motion, checked the charge, and holstered it again—a ritual of muscle memory, silent and automatic, as much a part of him as breath.

'The Crawlers didn't invade us for conquest,' he said quietly. 'They fled from a more deadly enemy.'

Hela's calculating look softened—just a fraction. Wariness crept into her posture, the first true shift since they'd boarded. She was reading him differently now, reassessing the depth of what he knew.

She crossed her legs slowly, buying time. 'And the Polity knew?'

'They knew,' Morgan confirmed. His voice didn't rise or fall. It simply was—steady as the void around them. 'And they made a choice: collaborate with the Crawlers, pool tech, build something powerful enough to hold the line.'

He flicked his eyes to the forward viewport, where stars smeared into trails. 'Eden wasn't conquest. It was desperation. A buffer—one more wall before the fire reached Earth.'

She exhaled slowly, expression unreadable. 'And the superweapon?'

Morgan's voice dropped. 'The culmination of that partnership. Born of necessity. But the Polity is weak—bureaucratic. They don't see the possibilities. They don't see the hundreds of empty systems waiting to be taken if they're willing to act.'

He met her gaze. 'We are not afraid to act. To seize the initiative.'

Hela studied him for a long moment. 'And who is 'we'? Who do you work for?'

'My instructions are not to harm you,' Morgan said evenly. 'Although, frankly, I'm authorised to torture you if necessary to obtain the access codes. I'd prefer not to. You'll be fully briefed when my superiors are ready. Give me the codes and order the Crawlers on that moon to stay in their hives and out of our way. Do that, and you live.'

She leaned back, cool and composed. 'So, I have to take your word on that?'

He didn't blink. 'Take it or leave it—the end will be the same.'

Hela tapped her fingers against the restraint in a slow rhythm. 'You do know they'll come for you. Rakkan, the Polity, the fleet.'

Morgan's smile was thin. 'Let them.'

She shifted, testing the limits of her bonds. 'You're playing a long game. Even the best plans crack under pressure.' Her voice softened, persuasive. 'You could use someone who knows how to pivot when the walls close in.'

The ship hummed; proximity indicators blinked. Cameron looked up from the nav console. 'Ten minutes out.'

Hela's tone softened further, coaxing. 'Morgan... maybe we could help each other. You don't have to carry this alone.'

He gave a dry smile. 'You'd cut my throat the first chance you got.'

She shrugged lightly. 'Only if you hesitated.'

She leaned forward, voice silk over steel. 'All I'm saying is... allies make revolutions last. I can help you navigate the aftermath. I can make sure people follow.'

Morgan's stare was flat. 'I have very clear leadership already, Miss Virell. I'm not convinced you could add much.'

Hela tilted her head, eyes glinting. 'Power held alone is brittle. It crumbles faster than you think.'

He said nothing, offered nothing but an enigmatic smile. The hum of the engines filled the silence. Beyond the viewport, the void shimmered—endless and uncaring. Yeltsin's voice crackled over the comm. 'Bay prepped. No interference.'

Hela's voice dropped to a whisper, still testing. 'You'll need someone who knows how to make this stick. I can be that someone.'

Morgan exhaled slowly. The Crawler superweapon filled the viewport, cold and waiting. He spoke without looking at her. 'The difference between Rakkan and me? He follows rules. I seize opportunities.'

Hela smiled faintly, eyes still measuring. 'We'll see which one of you survives this.'

LATER, ABOARD THE SHUTTLE, I sat strapped into the command seat, the low hum of engines in my ears and pressurised air wrapping around me. Tactical readouts flickered across the forward display. The stealth shuttle surged, a sleek shadow cutting through the void toward the target coordinates. Dallas sat to my right, monitoring ship status and squad channels, his expression focused and calm.

The mission was proceeding to plan. I had taken a small strike team—Dallas and six men, one a code expert familiar with Crawler systems. When Hela passed the entry codes, we would be ready.

I leaned forward, opening a private channel. 'Freyja control, confirm all ships accounted for.'

The reply crackled back. 'Confirmed, Commander. All units tracking nominal.'

I breathed out and scanned once more for anomalies. None appeared. Yet.

Dallas's voice broke the silence. 'ETA six minutes.'

I nodded; my mind moved ahead. The assault had to be clean—precise, overwhelming. No drawn-out engagements. No complications.

Hela should have been in touch twenty minutes ago. I toggled my secure line. 'Hela, status report. Are the codes ready?' Only static answered.

I adjusted frequency. 'Hela, respond. Confirm code handoff.' The silence was louder this time.

Dallas's brow furrowed. He checked the comm relays again. 'All channels green.'

I tightened my grip on the armrest and tried once more. 'Hela, acknowledge. This is priority.' Still nothing.

Dallas turned, voice low. 'She should've answered by now.'

My gut twisted—steel cable pulled too tight. I switched channels. 'Freyja control, verify Hela's position and current assignment.'

The reply came after a pause that stretched too long. 'Commander... her last logged location was Deck Seven. No active signal in the system.'

The shuttle's proximity alarms chimed softly, the countdown to the drop zone ticking in my ears.

'Run a full trace,' I ordered. 'I want eyes on her now.'

Dallas's fingers flew over the console. Security feeds flickered to life—empty corridors, unanswered logins, a shadow where Hela should be. A second alert blinked on the screen: **unauthorized shuttle departure.** My pulse jumped. The timestamp hit like a punch—nearly two hours ago.

'Get me that shuttle ID,' I said.

Dallas leaned in, reading it twice. His hands froze mid-keystroke. 'Splinter ship M-42... clearance used by J. Morgan.'

My breath caught. Before I could respond, another alert flared across the display—**Massive power surge detected.** Location: Crawler superweapon site. **Charging cycle initiated. Estimated completion: two hours.**

Dallas's voice cracked. 'Sir... energy readings are climbing. They're powering it up.'

I slammed open the fleet-wide channel, voice like iron. 'All units, immediate standby. Protocol shift imminent.' Morgan. I should have trusted my gut sooner. The displays bled red with cascading alerts. Outside, the first arcs of plasma fire erupted from the Crawler facility's defence batteries, tearing the void apart in blinding flashes.

'Evasive manoeuvres!' Dallas barked, hands flying over the controls. The shuttle lurched as near misses hissed past, heat wash slamming against the hull.

I sat back, breath tight in my chest. The cabin filled with shouted orders, alarms, and the rising hum of systems straining toward panic. I toggled my mic one last time. 'All units—brace for heavy fire and strap in. We're going in hot.'

The shuttle lurched violently as plasma bolts tore past—bright lances slicing the void like molten knives, blue-white streaks scarring the black. The carefully laid plans shattered. Chaos erupted. And I knew, with grim certainty, that Morgan had forced our hand— and the countdown had already begun.

Chapter 35: Duel for Supremacy

The fire outside didn't scare me. What waited inside did. It was a trap laid quiet and close—like a round chambered by someone who knew my name.

The shuttle shuddered under the weight of incoming plasma fire, heat wash rattling the hull like a drumskin stretched too tight. Warning tones shrieked through the cabin, lights blinking red and urgent. Sharp and steady, my voice cut through the chaos.

'Crash harnesses. Now.' The squad moved—strapping in with precision born of repetition. Dallas sat at my side, reading off system statuses: failing shields, port thrusters limping. The cockpit's glow flickered, data streams fracturing under strain.

'Target tunnel marked,' Dallas said, voice tight. 'Point-zero-five degrees starboard. Two hundred yards clearance.'

I adjusted course. The enemy facility loomed ahead, its defensive arrays spitting heavy plasma bursts, but the trajectory held. The little-used maintenance tunnel was a dark slit in the fortress wall, barely visible against the hull plating.

'Hold steady.'

The shuttle screamed through final approach. Another impact jolted us hard—metal groaning, warning overlays cascading across the display. We hit atmosphere, then metal. A grinding clash as the landing struts gave out. The shuttle skidded along reinforced decking, sparks carving bright scars in the dark. A final lurch, then silence—save for the cooling hiss of overstressed systems.

I unbuckled. The others followed. Smoke coiled from vents, the scent of scorched composite biting the air. 'Status?'

Dallas coughed, wiping blood from his lip. 'No serious injuries. Systems are wrecked. We're in.'

I nodded. 'Form up. Tunnel entry—two minutes. Watch for surprises.'

The squad slipped out into the dark, boots silent on scorched metal. Before us yawned the maintenance tunnel—narrow, damp, cables snaking like veins along its walls. The stale air tasted of coolant and metal fatigue.

I took point, blaster rifle raised, every sense tight. The silence pressed in, broken only by the faint drip of condensation and the distant hum of generators. Every footfall felt too loud; echoes swallowed by the close, suffocating dark. The deeper we moved, the more unnatural the stillness became. No automated defences came online. No alarms sounded. It was as if the entire facility were holding its breath.

Halfway through, Dallas muttered, 'This feels wrong.'

He was right, but I didn't say it.

The schematic Dakkar had provided showed layered defences—motion sensors, turret emplacements, choke points. All should have been active. Instead, dormant systems flickered gently, red indicators blinking like distant, watchful eyes—acknowledging our presence without reacting.

We reached a junction where power cables thrummed with quiet energy, conduits vibrating softly beneath our boots. Still no resistance. The air grew heavier, thicker. Each breath carried the faint tang of lubricant and ion discharge. I raised my fist to signal a halt. The squad froze, weapons ready. I scanned the walls. Conduits pulsed. Status displays held steady. Too steady.

Dallas's voice came low and tense. 'Command override.'

Exhaling slowly, I tasted the metallic tang of tension thick on my tongue. I opened a channel. 'Morgan's playing his hand. Expect the unexpected. Keep tight formations. No freelancing.'

We advanced with care, every sensor sweep confirming what we already felt—we weren't being blocked. We were being invited. And that felt worse.

Further along, the corridor widened into a loading chamber. Empty cargo crates lay scattered and untouched. The dust layer was unbroken, yet the doors to the next chamber hung partially open, hydraulic pistons disengaged. A single spotlight shone from above, pooling on the floor like a stage set.

We felt the weight of eyes on us—unseen, patient. The squad shifted uneasily. The quiet wasn't peace; it was calculation. At the far end, a monitor flickered to life. A crisp voice filtered through the static—Morgan's. Calm. Waiting.

'Welcome, Captain. Shall we talk?' The feed sharpened. Morgan's face appeared composed, eyes hooded and unreadable. The cold glow of data displays painted his features in shifting light. 'Captain Rakkan,' he began, voice smooth as polished steel. 'I commend your persistence.'

I stood still, rifle lowered but ready. I didn't answer. Not yet.

Morgan continued, tone measured. 'I've deactivated all automated defences. You'll find no resistance here.' A faint smile touched his lips. 'I want you on the bridge. Alone.'

Dallas stepped forward, whispering urgently. 'Sir, this stinks.'

I held up a hand, my eyes never leaving the screen.

Morgan's gaze sharpened. 'This doesn't have to end in conflict. There are things you need to see.' The feed cut, leaving only the low hum of background systems. The silence rushed in—heavy, deliberate.

I turned to the squad, voice low and firm. 'Dallas, hold position here. Lock down this chamber. No one follows me in.'

Dallas's jaw tightened. 'Sir—'

'That's an order.'

A beat of silence. Then Dallas nodded, tension etched in every line of his body. I faced the half-lit passage ahead. My pulse was steady, breath controlled.

'I'm going in.' I stepped forward into the unknown, the cold corridor swallowing me whole. My boots echoed softly. Each step was measured, senses sharpened to a razor's edge. The air was cooler here—recycled too many times—carrying the faint scent of machine oil and insulation. I could feel the weight of unseen eyes on me—not sensors, but Morgan's gaze somewhere ahead, watching.

The passage narrowed, walls lined with conduit panels and emergency seals, all intact. I passed a viewport, beyond which the stars glinted cold and distant—a reminder of the stakes. The comms crackled. Dallas's voice came through, hushed and tense. 'Sir, we've got movement on perimeter scans. Nothing hostile... yet.'

I tapped once in acknowledgment but said nothing. My focus stayed forward. Ahead, a heavy blast door stood half-open, hydraulic pistons hissing faintly. Beyond lay a wide antechamber bathed in pale, sterile light. A single chair sat in the centre—empty but deliberate. Another message. Another invitation.

The silence thickened, pressing against my chest. I inhaled slowly, tasting the weight of inevitability. Morgan's voice returned, soft and direct through an overhead speaker. 'I know you're alone. That's good. You understand—this is between you and me. You needn't worry about crawler action against your men – all activity has been stopped, thanks to Hela.'

I didn't respond. My steps carried me past the threshold, the door sliding shut behind with a hiss that sounded too final. The path to the bridge lay ahead, and every footfall echoed like a countdown.

The door to the bridge opened with a whisper, revealing a vast chamber washed in muted light. The architecture was cold and clinical—polished metal panels, reinforced viewports stretching floor to ceiling, offering a panoramic view of the void beyond. A steady, ominous hum from the ship's core filled the silence.

At the far end, Morgan stood with his back to the entrance, arms clasped behind him.

The tactical display before him pulsed with alien script and human overlays, data streaming in quiet torrents. A storm of contacts tracked across the screen—vectors, energy signatures, countdown timers.

To the right, Hela sat bound, posture rigid but expression composed. Her eyes flicked toward me—sharp, assessing. She said nothing, but her gaze spoke volumes: calculation, timing, possibility.

Against the far wall lay five human corpses including the body of Cameron with a ragged plasma scar across his torso. A tall middle-aged man in a lab coat stared emptily at nothing. Beside Morgan, Yeltsin stood guard—hands loose but ready, the look of a loyal hound on a taut leash. The sidearm at his hip gleamed, not from threat but from certainty.

My footsteps echoed as I approached. Each step deliberate, heavy with history. The space between us felt cavernous—thick with unspoken grudges and buried truths.

Morgan spoke without turning. 'You made good time.'

I stopped three paces short. 'You've been busy.' I nodded toward the bodies. 'I assume that's the security team—and he's Vadim. You don't care about killing innocents, do you?'

Morgan finally turned, his face calm but eyes bright with purpose. 'There are no innocents, Rakkan. And I've been preparing. For all of us.'

Hela shifted slightly in her restraints, fingers flexing almost imperceptibly. Her eyes never left mine. She was waiting for something. The tactical display behind Morgan changed—magnified readouts of an incoming fleet. Unknown configurations. Countless signatures. Data scrolled endlessly, silent confirmation of the threat.

My pulse slowed, breath evening out. The stakes had just become terrifyingly clear.

Morgan took a step closer, his voice soft. 'I never wanted it to come to this, Rakkan. But necessity writes its own script.' The room felt colder. The silence heavier. The decision unavoidable.

He turned back to the display, gesturing with a flick of his hand. The hologram expanded, revealing the alien fleet in grim detail. Their ships were jagged, asymmetrical things—bristling with unfamiliar weaponry and dark energy signatures that pulsed like malignant heartbeats.

'They call themselves the Hunger,' Morgan said quietly, the weight in his tone unmistakable. 'For decades they've devoured everything in their path. Entire worlds stripped bare. The Crawlers encountered them first—and knew their only chance of survival was to move. Into our space.'

I said nothing, jaw tight.

'The Polity knew,' Morgan continued. 'We tried diplomacy, containment, delay. But nothing holds them for long. Eden was never just a colony—it was a barrier. A last line.' He turned to face me fully, eyes burning with conviction. 'They didn't build the superweapon for politics. They built it for survival. And now that time has come.'

The display shifted again, overlaying the alien fleet's advance with the armed readiness of the weapon. Timers counted down in red. Arcs of power shimmered across the schematic. 'I brought you here because we need you,' Morgan said. 'Not to fight us, but to stand beside us. Your name carries weight. Your reputation can unify what fear alone cannot.'

Hela's head tilted slightly, interest flickering in her eyes.

Morgan pressed on. 'Once we negotiate with the Hunger, we'll show the Polity that hesitation is death. They've allowed too much freedom to the colonies. They need to be brought to heel. They need order—a military government. We'll consolidate power, not for greed, but to protect what we've built.'

He stepped closer. 'Join us. Be the face people trust. Together, we can ensure humanity doesn't just survive... it endures under strong leadership.' The silence stretched between us. He searched my face for the answer he wanted.

Morgan's voice softened. 'I know you, Rakkan. You see the necessity, even if you won't admit it. This is bigger than loyalty. Bigger than tradition. Bigger than the illusion of freedom.'

I let the silence hang, each second drawn taut. Behind him, the alien fleet crept closer—an endless swarm of signatures pulsing across the tactical display. My gaze found Morgan's, and I nodded slowly. 'You're right,' I said. 'I do see the necessity.'

Morgan's shoulders eased, just slightly. He opened his mouth to speak.

'But I see the cost more clearly,' I continued, voice like tempered steel. 'And it's too high.'

Morgan's expression hardened. 'You'd rather see chaos? Anarchy? Billions lost because no one had the will to make the hard choices?'

'Leadership isn't coercion,' I said. 'What you're offering isn't order—it's fear in uniform.'

Morgan's hands clenched at his sides. The air seemed to drop a few degrees. 'I gave you the courtesy of choice,' he hissed. 'Don't make me regret that.'

Hela watched in silence, her eyes flicking between us, tension strung like wire. I took one step forward. 'If you believe in this so much, you shouldn't need me. But you do. That's your weakness.'

Morgan exhaled slowly, the fight draining from his posture. What replaced it was inevitability. 'So be it,' he murmured.

The silence that followed felt cavernous. Morgan straightened, all warmth gone from his expression. The weight of his intent pressed into the room like a storm front.

In the corner of my vision, Hela's gaze sharpened. Her muscles tensed—subtle but unmistakable. She was preparing. Morgan took one step back. 'You leave me no choice.'

'It was always going to come to this, Morgan.' I smiled coldly. 'Let's do this the old-fashioned way. We don't need blasters.' He nodded once and drew a wickedly curved blade. All the silence fractured into a single truth: the fight was inevitable.

I shifted my stance, knife ready. The distance between us closed to heartbeats. Somewhere behind, Hela drew in a slow breath. I didn't look back. My world narrowed to Morgan's eyes, his blade, and the space between.

HELA

She had been still for what felt like hours, waiting for her moment. Every muscle was a thread of restraint, every heartbeat a count toward freedom.

Yeltsin stood to her left, weapon slung but eyes fixed on the duel. He was absorbed—entranced by the gravity of men who believed only they mattered. That arrogance was her opening.

Her hand shifted slightly beneath the cuff of her sleeve. A small movement—nothing more. Her thumb pressed against the base of one false nail until it clicked. Five seconds of pressure armed the micro-valve. The toxin primed. She was immune. No one else would be.

Now. Her arm swept out, quick and silent. The nail grazed Yeltsin's neck. His eyes widened, then rolled back. He dropped without a sound. The hum of the ship continued, indifferent.

Hela worked at her restraints, pulse hammering but hands steady. When the cuffs gave, she slipped free, retrieved Yeltsin's sidearm, and flicked off the safety. She stayed in the shadows, watching. Rakkan and Morgan hadn't moved. She was free.

Her first instinct was to rush to Rakkan's side, to tip the balance—but she stopped herself. Sentiment got people killed. She would wait, see who won, then act.

And now, she waited—the real battle still ahead. She watched as Rakkan pulled out a combat knife and dropped into a crouch. Morgan looked stronger, fresher. More polished. But she had learned not to underestimate Rakkan. He had a talent for survival.

THE MOMENT STRETCHED.

Then Morgan moved—and so did I.

We circled, blades low, eyes locked, boots scuffing softly on metal, breath tight and measured. Same height. Different builds. Morgan—solid muscle, precise, trained by naval intelligence for ruthless efficiency. No wasted movement. No temper.

I was older, leaner, but seasoned. Dozens of close-combat missions behind me. Cunning matched against darker craft. Morgan moved first. A quick thrust—not for blood, but for reaction. I slipped, testing, then returned a feint, checking his footwork. Clean. Sharp. Even.

I watched the craft behind his movements and remembered Kendall, my old tactical instructor at the academy—and his words: Spooks fight nasty. Like rats with razors. Watch for the bite you don't see coming. The second exchange came faster. Morgan's blade nicked my forearm. Blood welled. I countered with a slash that missed by inches. Morgan smiled faintly. He knew he was faster.

Blades clashed. Sparks flew. I ducked a cut aimed for my ear and pivoted with a knee strike. Morgan blocked, returned with a blow to the ribs. Sharp pain bloomed, and I fell back. It began to tilt. For every hit I landed, Morgan struck three. His training showed—subtle feints, small shifts to draw me off balance, calculated pauses that seeded doubt. Clinical cuts to arms, thighs, side. Blood flowed. Morgan pressed forward, patient and relentless.

He was better than I was, and we both knew it.

My breathing roughened. I shifted weight, slower now. Morgan saw it. Confidence flickered in his eyes. His attacks became fluid—no wasted motion, no hesitation. Without warning, my boot slid on my own blood, the slick warmth betraying my footing. I went down hard, vision narrowing. Morgan closed in for the kill.

But Kendall's voice came back, rough and sharp: When you're knackered and losing, that's when you surprise the bastard. That whisper gave me the edge I needed. I faked a collapse, luring him in. At the last second I rolled, slicing low. The blade caught flesh behind his knee. A grunt. He staggered.

I surged up and head-butted him savagely in the face. Bone crunched. He reeled. I caught his arm, twisted, and drove my combat knife deep into his side. He tried to counter, but my momentum carried us both—shoulder to chest—crashing back into the console.

One last strike. My blade found his throat, cutting deep. Hot blood sprayed across my forearm. Morgan dropped. His eyes flickered with disbelief before the light left them and he fell away. I straightened, panting, every muscle trembling.

I'd been lucky, but experience had won the day—sharp and bitter, like the taste of old iron on my tongue. Kendall wasn't breathing; the old bastard had paid in full. Hela emerged from the shadows, brushing dust off her coat with deliberate nonchalance. Her eyes flicked over me: bruised, bloodied, but still standing.

'I'm free. You won't need to rescue me,' she said, irony curling her lips. Her gaze sharpened when she saw me stagger and then steady. 'You should sit down—before you fall down.'

Before I could answer, the proximity alarm on my wrist console pulsed. A low alert tone cut the silence and drew both their gazes.

The readout glowed red: **SUPERWEAPON CHARGE CYCLE — 87% COMPLETE. Estimated time to full charge: thirty minutes.** Hela's face lost its humour. 'It's almost ready.'

My mouth went dry. 'And once it's charged?'

'The energy has to be used,' Hela said. 'Or bled off. But either way, something's going to burn.'

Dakkar's voice crackled across the command channel from the Freyja's bridge—tight, precise, the voice of a man who could see the storm coming. 'Captain, we've got visuals. Alien fleet detected on the edge of Eden space. Holding position... but we're reading energy spikes. They're preparing for something.'

My gut clenched. 'Time until they cross the boundary?'

'Seventeen minutes,' Dakkar replied.

The superweapon charged beneath them like a sleeping leviathan. The fleet waited beyond the line. His crew waited for his call.

'Hold positions,' I said, steady. 'Weapons hot. Shields up. Do not fire unless I give the order.'

I turned to the scientist and cut his bonds. 'Dr Vadim, I presume?'

He nodded. 'Are you with the Polity?'

I shook my head. 'Let's just say I'm with humanity. We need your weapon to fight the Hunger. Will you help me?'

He looked from me to Morgan's body. 'Those were my orders from the Polity. I'll help you.'

'Then get on that console and be ready to deploy it, Doc.'

I opened a channel. 'Freyja and Avenger: we have secured the weapon. Morgan is dead. No casualties on our side.'

'Acknowledged,' Dakkar replied—but the strain bled through. The crew were all watching, counting on me for the answers they deserved. I hoped I could give them.

Kithlan's voice followed on the secure line from the Avenger. 'Fleet Commander... whatever comes, we stand ready.'

Hela's tone softened. 'Jero. Take a moment. This is the kind of call that changes everything.'

Through the viewport, past steel and vacuum, I could see the cold stars beyond—and the shadowed threat waiting at Eden's doorstep. I drew a slow breath, the weight of every life on this world, and perhaps far beyond it, pressing down on my shoulders.

'I can make the call,' I said. 'But I'll carry it for the rest of my life.' Eden hung above the mountains surrounding the facility, blue-green and fragile. Riven was there now. I remembered the last time I'd seen her—hours ago, in the launch bay.

The bay had been quiet. Just the hum of engines spooling up and the hollow ring of boots on steel. Thorne stood nearby, strapping on armour. He saw my look and nodded. I'd given her the *Rats* for this mission; if anyone could bring her back in one piece, it was them. Her other squadmates were inside the shuttle, running checks. The clock was ticking.

Riven adjusted her gear without looking at me—calm, professional, too much like me. 'You're sure about this?' I asked, keeping my voice level.

She nodded. 'Tarkin's still down there. My people are still down there. He has to face justice—for what he did to them. Someone has to bring him in. It should be one of us.' She was right. Again. And I hated how many times I'd had to watch her walk into hell because no one else could.

'You've got Thorne and the *Rats*. Three more, handpicked. Full command authority.'

'And your trust.'

'That too.'

A beat. Then her voice softened. 'Rakkan... father.'

I looked at her. Really looked. I'd seen that steel before, but this time there was something under it—something unguarded.

'I want you to know something,' she said. 'My mother... she loved you. I know she did. She just never really came out from under Grandpa's shadow.' It hit hard. Not sudden, not sharp—just deep. Settling in the chest like a truth I'd carried without knowing.

'We thought we had something,' I said quietly. 'We thought it meant something. And it did, Riven. Because it made you. Whatever the cost... you were worth it.'

Her eyes lifted to mine. 'She told me you never knew. She was brave enough to admit that. She said it was just easier.'

'Easier for her father, maybe,' I said. 'But not for me.'

'Or me,' she answered.

The pause held. Then: 'But we've found each other now.'

'We have,' I said. 'We just both need to live long enough to get to know each other.'

She stepped in and hugged me. No rank. No armour. Just a daughter holding her father like it might be the last time.

When she pulled back, her voice had that old edge again—steady, ready. 'Don't wait for me. Just make sure Eden's still here when I get back.'

'I will.'

She turned and boarded the shuttle. I didn't follow. Didn't watch the doors close. Didn't breathe until the engines fired. That had been hours ago. Now she was somewhere in the ruins of Eden—chasing ghosts I couldn't protect her from.

Chapter 36: Sighting the Alien Fleet

Command doesn't leave room for hesitation. Not when every ship in the sky is waiting for your next word to decide who dies.

The Hunger fleet pulsed across our sensors—vast and sinister. But they were not the only factor. From human space, the first flickers of arrival shimmered on Eden's edge—sharp distortions that rippled like distant storms, resolving into the hard, deliberate lines of warships. I didn't need Ariel's confirmation to know what they were.

'Multiple warp signatures,' she said, voice steady but carrying the same weight as mine. 'Polity fleet arrival confirmed. Thirty-seven capital-class vessels. Over one hundred escorts.'

I stood at the edge of the command deck, hands on the console. Beyond the armoured viewport the fleet assembled with the cold grace of a blade being drawn—disciplined, ruthless, inevitable. Once that formation had been comfort. It had been home. Now it was a threat.

The comms channel crackled. Admiral Knox's voice came through—clipped, formal, with steel underneath. 'Captain Rakkan. This is Admiral Knox, Polity High Command. I order you to stand down. Power down the weapon platform. Maintain holding pattern and prepare for diplomatic engagement. Under no circumstances are you to activate the weapon or allow it to fall into enemy hands.'

Hela stood slightly apart, arms crossed, face unreadable. When she spoke, it was low and bitter. 'It's Virell. Pulling the strings.'

I caught the flicker of something raw beneath her control. 'Morgan thought he was clever,' she went on. 'Thought he was the player. He was just a piece like the rest of us.' Her mouth twisted, half-smile, half-sneer.

'Virell always has a backup,' she said. 'Morgan was working for him—evident in the way he spoke. My clone parent has deep connections inside the Polity. Some trust him; most fear him. He's convinced the leadership to negotiate.' She glanced toward the viewports where the fleet hung in lethal silence. 'It's an elegant solution. Now he wins the prize cleanly—with a handshake instead of a war.'

Her voice went flat. 'He's still trying to write the ending. Not for me. Not anymore. I will write my own.' The silence that followed was suffocating—more than absence of sound: a pause heavy with the weight of command.

Ariel's holographic form flickered to life beside me, composed and precise. 'Recommend repositioning, Captain. Bringing Freyja and Avenger into close proximity will enhance coordination and keep them under the superweapon's defensive shield coverage.'

I nodded, the motion deliberate. 'Execute. Pull them in tight. Close formation. I want them where I can protect them.'

'Acknowledged.'

The tactical display refreshed, lines shifting with cool efficiency. I watched as the Freyja and the Avenger adjusted course, drawing in close—two ships, loyal and brave, now small shadows beneath the vast outline of the station's shields. Outnumbered, but together.

The comm sparked again. Knox's tone sharpened, formality giving way to frustration. 'Captain Rakkan, acknowledge.'

'Admiral Knox, who will be responsible for negotiating with the Hunger fleet?'

A beat. Then the cultured visage of Ephraim Virell filled the viewscreen. 'Captain Rakkan,' he said, voice smooth as glass. 'So delightful to see you again. And I see you have dear Justine there with you.' I could feel her seething beside me.

Virell smiled and made a self-deprecating gesture. 'Yes, Captain, that honour has been given to me. A wonderful opportunity for our two species to work in harmony. The Polity has been in communication with them for several months.'

'And what do they say?' I demanded. 'Because that fleet looks big enough to walk right through us.'

'They seek only a right of way—to follow their path. For them, it is a holy duty.'

'A right of way through human space?'

'Yes, Captain. And I am here to negotiate the best possible arrangement on behalf of our species. That's why we must not deploy that weapon unless absolutely necessary—and why you must obey your direct commander, Admiral Knox.'

I stayed silent, watching the Polity fleet beyond—ship after ship falling into precise alignment. Familiar hulls, familiar codes, familiar discipline. But now, every gun was pointed at me. I drew a slow breath. The taste of recycled air, metal, and responsibility settled heavy on my tongue.

Then I opened the channel, my voice carrying the weight of certainty and doubt alike.

'Polity fleet, this is Captain Jero Rakkan. Stand by for my response.' I closed the channel with a flick of my hand. Outside, the fleet waited—silent, watching.

Inside, the pulse of the station thrummed beneath my boots like a living heartbeat.

Every soul aboard the Freyja and Avenger waited for my decision. Minutes. No more than that. I had made impossible choices before. But never one that could alter the course of humanity itself. I could not get this one wrong.

Ariel's voice chimed softly through the stillness. 'DARK Rift energy saturation at ninety-seven percent. Bleed-off protocols engaged. Stability parameters holding... for now.'

I turned from the viewport, watching the tactical display ripple with fluctuations in the energy fields surrounding the platform. Gravity distortions pulsed in soft waves across the readouts. The room felt heavier, as if the singularity below us were already pulling on mass—on thought—on consequence.

I steadied myself. 'Ariel, report on system integrity.'

'Structural integrity at ninety-eight percent,' she replied. 'Containment field maintaining but approaching theoretical limits. Projections remain uncertain. I advise continued monitoring and caution.'

I'd seen ships tear apart and men lose their minds under smaller strains. But this was something else entirely, like holding a storm in our hands. A new communications prompt lit across the console.

'Another transmission from Admiral Knox,' Ariel reported. 'Private diplomatic channel, priority one.'

I exhaled—slow, controlled—then keyed the channel open. Knox's face flickered onto the screen—no guards, no aides, just polished steel and measured breath. He looked exactly like a man who'd been rehearsing this conversation for days.

'Captain Rakkan,' he said evenly. 'Isn't it time for you to surrender?'

'Hardly.' I met his gaze. 'I want to know why. Why chase me when there's a swarm of death barrelling toward human space? Why waste ships and lives on this?'

Knox didn't flinch. 'Because the colonies need strong leadership.'

I said nothing.

He leaned forward slightly. 'They need unity, discipline, order—not freelance captains playing messiah. You think you see the big picture, but I see the whole board. And if you fracture that now, you shatter public confidence. We can't afford chaos, not when the future of human civilization is at stake.'

'Is that what this is?' I asked. 'A service to the people?'

His smile didn't reach his eyes. 'This isn't about ego, Rakkan.'

'It reeks of it.' He didn't deny it.

'There's a narrow window here,' he continued. 'One where the right message, the right decisions, the right kind of leadership can prevent collapse. If I have to wear the uniform a little longer to get there—so be it.'

'President Knox.' I said it flat. Without judgment. Just truth.

His eyes flickered. Not shame—calculation. 'The Polity needs the best and most able to step forward and lead us. I'm the only one who can do it. And if I have the burden of leading what's left of humanity, I intend to be ready.'

'You're chasing the wrong threat,' I said quietly. 'And you're going to get people killed.'

'No. I'm going to win. Obey my orders and I can make you part of the future. Fight me, and you'll stay in the past—obsolete and irrelevant.'

'I'm retired, Knox. I don't answer to Polity Command anymore. Besides, last time we met, you were trying to kill me.'

His expression didn't soften. 'You *were* retired, Rakkan. And until a few hours ago, you *were* wanted. Both of those have been rescinded. Three hours ago, you were reinstated to the active list under emergency powers. Your commission is active. Your duty is clear.'

I straightened. 'Admiral Knox, aren't you starting to wonder where your orders are coming from? And why? That Hunger fleet could destroy everything in human space. You know we don't have the ships to stop them.'

His expression hardened. 'Your duty is to follow orders, not interpret them. Power down that weapon and surrender operational control to me.'

I felt the pressure behind each word—not a suggestion, but a command carved in stone. 'With respect for the rank you bear,' I said, measured and calm, 'we don't know enough about the Hunger. If we choose not to stop them here, we may never be able to stop them at all.'

He shook his head, the lines around his mouth deepening. 'I don't have patience for philosophical debates, Captain. You have your orders. You will comply.'

I drew a slow breath. 'Admiral... if I do, we'll lose Eden. And possibly far more.'

His glare sharpened. 'That sounds dangerously close to treason, Rakkan. You're a soldier, not a sovereign.'

I met his gaze—steady, honest. 'I'm a soldier protecting lives with the tools at hand.'

Knox's jaw tightened. He ended the transmission without another word. That told me everything. The channel cut out, and I was left staring at my reflection in the black screen, already fading. I needed to know more about the Hunger. And the swarm of red on the tactical display was minutes away from entering Eden System.

Ariel's voice came softly in my ear—clear, but edged with tension. 'Commander, incoming communication flagged under treaty protocols. Crawler command channel.'

A cold weight settled between my shoulder blades. 'Patch it through.'

The holo-display shimmered, resolving into the image of the surviving Crawler queen.

Her carapace gleamed with that strange, oily iridescence—like light trying to escape a prison. Her mandibles were still. Her faceted eyes locked onto mine with a steadiness that didn't feel like challenge. It felt like judgment. Intelligence radiated from her—along with exhaustion.

Her rival had already made her choice. Self-euthanized. Crawlers didn't lose. They erased themselves. This one had stayed. Hela stood beside me, arms crossed, posture easy. But I could feel the tension beneath it—coiled, waiting. There was something in her eyes. Not pride. Not relief. Something colder. Calculation that had just paid off.

The queen inclined her head—not a bow, exactly, but a gesture weighted with ritual. Her voice came through the translator in precise, modulated tones. 'I have entered negotiation with your emissary.'

A subtle shift of her limb toward Hela. 'Under treaty law, during conditions of existential crisis, human and Syrinthi chains of command shall unify.' A pause. Not for breath. For history. 'Your military authority is now recognized as supreme.'

The room didn't react. No applause. No ceremony. Just that hollow moment where the axis shifts. I stared at her. This was the species that once called me a murderer—He Who Kills the Listeners in Silence. This queen was the one who had sent assassins to kill me.

And now, she'd handed me her war. Not out of trust. Not out of forgiveness. Out of necessity. I didn't speak right away. I could feel Hela watching me, waiting to see what I'd do with this weight.

I remembered Chance's Drift. I remembered Vella. I remembered the silence that came after the fire. 'Then we have a battle to win,' I said. The queen made no reply. But something in her light changed—a flicker, a shift. Recognition, maybe. Or the beginning of a new name.

Hela turned her head toward me, arching an eyebrow with deliberate grace. 'Told you I'd been productive.'

I kept my face still, though disbelief churned under the surface. Crawlers never acknowledged human command. That was submission in all but name. Desperation rewrote old rules.

The queen continued, posture unwavering. 'Eden Fleet Commander Rakkan, I place all Crawler units within this sector under your direct command. Orders given will be obeyed without hesitation or deviation.'

The weight of it settled into my chest. Me—the man who had once sent a nuclear device into the heart of a Crawler mother-ship at Chance's Drift—now given control of their fleets. The universe had a twisted sense of symmetry. Dakkar caught my eye and nodded slowly. I knew that look. Enough.

Hela's voice came softer, edged with satire. 'You're welcome, Fleet Commander. Irony's a bitch, isn't it?'

The words settled like a shackle across my shoulders—one I could not refuse. I inclined my head to the queen. 'We must make a decision. The Hunger fleet is approaching. Our leaders say negotiate and let them pass through Eden space to follow their path.'

The queen's vestigial wings drummed in what I read as amusement. 'One hundred and sixty-three were our colonies. Now only Eden remains. The Hunger sees no need for negotiation. They only consume. You are Eden Fleet Commander, Rakkan. Obey my orders and defend this system with every weapon we possess. There will come only one chance.'

'Acknowledged.' The queen's image shimmered and vanished.

I turned to Hela. Her expression had hardened into something fierce. 'They needed leadership. I gave them yours. They'll fight for survival. For now, they're yours to command.'

I nodded, the weight of responsibility settling around me like weighted armour. 'And every one of their lives is now on my ledger.'

Hela met my gaze—cool, honest. 'You wanted a seat at the table. Now you have the entire board.'

Outside the viewport, Crawler warships repositioned with smooth precision. Defensive patterns formed, covering our flanks and rear arcs. Vessels that had once been predators now stood as shields.

Ariel's voice returned, low and urgent, each syllable tight with tension. 'The alien armada continues to approach. Five minutes to boundary. Energy readings increasing. They are preparing for full-scale engagement.'

I exhaled slow. Metal and recycled air tasted heavy on my tongue. The clock was running. The pieces were on the board. Now, every move was mine to make. A memory stirred—Chance's Drift. The heat, the fury, the cold resolve as I fired the nukes that killed their queens. And now her kind had entrusted me with the command of their fleets. The bitter symmetry tightened my throat.

The bridge was silent, taut with strain. My comm chirped—simultaneous signals from Freyja and Avenger. Dakkar's voice came first, composed but edged. 'Captain, the alien fleet is shifting formation. Multiple assault vectors predicted. Shields at maximum, weapons standing by. Requesting instructions.'

Before I could answer, Kithlan's voice joined on the second channel, steady and resolute.

'Fleet Commander, the Defined stand ready. The Avenger will not retreat. Nor will we abandon this line.'

I breathed deep. Good men and women, loyal crews—faith heavier than any burden I had carried. The stars outside seemed to hold their breath.

Ariel came through next, precise and cool. 'Enemy fleet will cross the boundary in ninety seconds. Superweapon charge cycle complete. Containment stable. Energy bleed-off sustaining, but no further capacity beyond current thresholds. Continued buildup could destabilize containment if left unchecked.'

I looked to Dr Vadim at the weapons console. 'And you, Doctor. What do you say?'

He smiled grimly. 'I'm a man of science, Captain. But everything I know about the Hunger says we must fight here, now.'

The tactical display pulsed: the alien fleet advancing—silent, unwavering purpose. Their vector lines converged like a net tightening around Eden. Formation overlays stayed crisp and clean, but beneath the graphics I felt it: a hairline crack through the command structure.

Ariel's voice from the Freyja whispered over my implant. 'Intercepted sub-net traffic. Approximately thirty-one percent of captains have logged coded doubts regarding current orders.' I didn't answer. I didn't need to. On the tactical display the ships sat in perfect ranks—but formation means nothing if hearts aren't in it.

Knox's voice came over the open channel—measured, clipped. 'All Polity vessels confirm alignment with High Command. Maintain readiness.'

His tone spoke control; the static beneath it spoke fear. It crackled through the comms like a frayed circuit about to fail. I studied the names on the board. Some I knew—solid officers, steady hands. Others I barely recognized. And somewhere in that sea of signals, the cracks were spreading. My gaze lingered on Knox's icon. Audacious held position, the fleet clustered around her like an iceberg splitting apart. His silence spoke louder than any broadcast.

'Orders, sir?' Dakkar's voice, steady.

I drew a slow breath. 'Hold formation. No transmissions. Not yet.'

The battlespace tightened like a fist around a blade. The moment before the break always felt long. It never was.

Ariel spoke again, quieter. 'They're waiting for someone to flinch.'

I nodded, eyes still fixed on the board. 'They won't have to wait long.'

'Captain,' Ariel added, 'you asked for updates. A burst transmission from the planet's subsurface—Riven and her team have a lead on Tarkin. No Crawler resistance, but he still has loyalist troops. No further data beyond confirmation of pursuit.'

I nodded once, more for myself than anyone else. Riven was beyond my reach now. I pushed the ache down, burying it beneath the layers of duty and steel that had carried me this far.

I'd given her what she asked for—authority, a squad led by Thorne. She had promises to keep to her people. And she was more than my daughter. Riven was the future of Eden. My job wasn't to hold her back. It was to help her any way I could.

She hadn't hesitated. Neither, despite the crushing fear of losing her, had I. It was our duty.

Let Them Burn Bright

Hunger Command Hub: Ark Flagship Fist of Salvation
Location: Edge of Eden System
THE WAITING ENDS.

The final orbit stabilizes.

Eden turns below—bright, blind, unaware.

The Swarm holds at full strength. More than eight hundred vessels aligned—Skard-ships and Thrall-ships in perfect formation.

Many of the Skard were once battleships—dreadnoughts pulled from the shattered navies of the Varr, the Thallun, the Sirek, the Kin-weavers, and the Threx. The pride of the fallen, reforged in purpose. Their original functions burned away across generations.

The Thrall-ships were scouts, carriers, strike-forms—vessels made for speed and endurance. Now they serve stripped of history, tuned only to directive.

It took time.

Entire lifetimes.

Whole systems rebuilt.

Languages erased.

Perfection requires patience.

The Varr were the first to resist us. The first to be redeemed. And the ones who tested us most.

Bright were the deaths and remaking's born of their defiance. Their ships bled us. Their minds endured. Their fall was hardest—and therefore holiest.

They became the Origin Fleet. Not as they were, but as they were meant to be. In falling, they gave the Swarm its spine.

To find another such enemy—one worthy of struggle, forged in the fire—that has always been our dream.

To break and rise again.

To purify.

To begin anew.

Even the Syrinthi became sacred once their resistance broke.

From the Varr onward, the others followed—not by surrender, but by revelation.

All who once defied us now serve us.

That is redemption.

High Acolyte Veris walked the sanctum perimeter, trailing one hand along the glyph-lit wall.

'They were built to destroy us,' he said. 'Now they complete us.'

'As will the humans,' Tharim replied.

He watched the defensive systems flicker—satellites arming, relays scanning, defence grids trembling in early alert.

'They are fractured. Terrified. Drowning in reason,' he said. 'Still unfinished.'

He paused—not in pity. In appraisal. 'They may prove brittle. Too fast. Too clever. Too scattered to suffer well.'

Veris inclined his head.

'Then why come?'

'Because there is still a chance,' Tharim said. 'That they resist long enough to matter.'

A flicker passed through him. Not hope. Hunger.

'I want them to rise. I want them to make it costly.'

'Why?'

'Because only in the fire does the shape become true.'

'And if they break early?'

Tharim's eyes narrowed. 'Then they were never beautiful.'

The Swarm began to descend—slow, measured, inescapable.
Across the void, Eden's sentries lit like a forest of false hope.
'They will resist,' Veris said. 'They will kill. They will burn.'
'As must all flesh,' Tharim replied.
He lowered his hand—not in judgment, but in invitation.
'Let them burn bright,' he said, 'before they become beautiful.'
And so we fall. Not with fury.
With silence.

Chapter 37: The Gates of Abaddon

The tactical display in the control centre pulsed with red—an expanding mass pushing into Eden System from deep space. From the opposite side, into the inner system, came the Polity fleet led by Knox.

The Crawler ships now under my command were formidable, but not enough. We needed more. 'Update on fleet positions,' I said.

Ariel's voice came through the relay, composed but taut. 'Knox is holding formation. Internal dissension rising—twenty-nine percent of captains showing hesitation metrics. Off-command chatter increasing.'

'Noted.'

They could see the alien fleet just as clearly as we could. I folded my arms, eyes fixed on the board—the approaching red storm inching closer, inevitable. Riven was on the planet hunting Tarkin. But the tempest I was about to unleash could decide the lives of trillions.

Hela moved to stand beside me at the console. Her presence didn't demand attention; it occupied it—quiet, measured, impossible to ignore. 'Rakkan,' she began, her tone clipped, professional—but weighted.

'Hela.' I kept my voice even. 'I assume this isn't pleasantries.'

She exhaled once, slow and deliberate. 'You know me well enough to skip past that.' She tapped a command on her handheld console. A data burst flashed across Ariel's system.

Ariel's voice murmured in my ear. 'Data package received. Origin: Hela Virell. Status: locked and encrypted. Analysing...'

A pause. Then— 'Captain, this file contains the structure of a nano-plague targeted to Crawler queen bloodlines. Containment protocols active. Projected lethality: ninety-seven percent.'

Hela's pale blue eyes met mine. My stomach tightened, but I kept my expression still.

'You've had this ready,' I said.

She nodded once. 'The Syndicate doesn't survive by hoping enemies play fair.'

'Neither do I.'

Her mouth twitched—amusement, or warning. 'Exactly.' Silence settled between us. I could feel her intent pressing over the board like a gathering storm. She finally broke it. "This was the Syndicate's real mission here, to gain control of this system. And the nano plague will ensure the Crawlers comply. I know Ariel would have shown you soon enough. But I wanted you to hear it from me.'

I met her eyes. 'I appreciate the honesty.'

'It's not honesty,' she said. 'It's clarity. When this ends—however it ends—the Eden System will need control. Stability. I intend to provide both.'

'You mean rule.'

A faint twitch at the corner of her mouth. 'Someone has to. This system can belong to humanity again. Order, safety, governance. Every nation in history began with force. The people of Eden will thank us for it in time.'

'They'll thank you,' I said, 'until they realise you've only replaced one tyranny with another.'

Her gaze hardened, but I didn't give her the chance to speak.

'The people of Eden deserve more than that, Hela. More than another brutal dictatorship. And I'll be one of the ones holding you to account.'

She held my stare, the air between us cooling to steel. Then she nodded, almost imperceptibly.

'Then make sure I earn it.'

'You can bet I will,' I said. 'And so will Riven.'

Ariel's voice broke the quiet—precise, detached. 'Analysis complete. Hela Virell's projected influence post-conflict exceeds all current Polity authority structures.'

'I know,' I said.

The bridge felt heavier. On the tactical map, ships moved in perfect lines and bright arcs—but I could already feel them slipping, the human ones most of all.

Hela had changed the board. Not with firepower. With will.

Knox's voice came through the main channel again—smooth, controlled. Too smooth.

'Fleet Commander Rakkan. We acknowledge your position as commander of Crawler forces. The Polity High Council requests immediate confirmation of your compliance with Command Directives. Awaiting acknowledgment.'

He wasn't really asking. He was offering one last out. I watched the board. The fleet held formation—but barely. Threads were fraying. Hesitation in the outer lines. Two ships had shifted course by a fraction. Not enough to call insubordination. But enough to notice.

The weight of a thousand eyes pressed in, waiting for the man behind the command code. Ariel's voice murmured in my ear. 'Projected fracture point within twelve minutes. Warning: hesitation metrics now exceeding thirty-two percent.'

I exhaled slowly. Pulse steady. Gut tight. Knox reappeared on the main screen—open channel. If I disobeyed now, the entire fleet would witness my mutiny. The fleet listened. So did history.

'Fleet Commander Rakkan,' he said, voice iron-clad and cold. 'Stand down. You are not authorized to deploy that weapon. Cease preparations and hold position. This is a direct order under emergency authority.'

His silence that followed was colder still—the kind that freezes before it breaks.

I looked from the approaching armada to the world below, then back to Knox's image. The unseen faces of Eden hung in my mind. Riven's face flickered there too—bright against the dark.

'Admiral Knox,' I said, voice level and controlled, 'I acknowledge your order.'

I paused. Let him feel it. 'But I will not power down. And I am the legitimate military authority in this system, under treaty law. I intend to use this weapon against the aliens—and then I'll do everything I can to defend Eden space. My fleet will hold the line, Admiral. I ask that yours do the same. Rakkan out.'

Another silence. The kind that fills entire rooms and stretches across light-years. Dakkar's voice came first, low and steady. 'Commander, standing by. All stations report ready.'

Kithlan followed, iron in his tone. 'We hold position with you. Whatever comes.'

Ariel's voice cut through the tension. 'All Crawler units acknowledge your authority, Fleet Commander. They await orders.' On the display, the alien fleet advanced—inevitability made manifest, vector lines tightening into final approach.

Ariel spoke again, quieter but insistent. 'Commander... critical threshold approaches. Decision point in three minutes, six seconds. Containment will not tolerate indefinite holding.'

I pressed my palm flat on the console. The weight was crushing—more than iron, more than duty. It was legacy. 'Maintain defensive posture,' I ordered. 'Weapons hot, shields raised. No firing unless provoked.'

Acknowledgments came swiftly, like taut lines snapping in a storm. I exhaled, eyes fixed on the void. The decision hadn't come yet—but it was coming. Nothing could stop it.

The bridge lights dimmed as I leaned forward, feeling the gravity of the moment settle into my bones. I keyed open the comms to all frequencies. My voice would carry across space—to every Polity ship, every crewman staring into the dark and wondering if this was the day they died.

I took a breath. There could be no doubt in my voice.

'This is Eden Fleet Commander Rakkan,' I began, my voice steady and sure. 'To all Polity vessels in system: we face an enemy none of us has seen before. They do not speak. They do not negotiate. They are not here to talk.' I let that hang. 'They are here to consume.'

On the display, the alien fleet moved with predatory precision—flowing like a hunting pack, vectors overlapping, attack patterns converging to crush anything in their path. They moved like inevitability made flesh. 'They will not stop at Eden,' I said. 'They will burn their way through this system, then the next, and the next after that—until nothing remains.'

Another breath. 'I know some of you are under orders to hold. To wait. But I say this now: we are not here to wait. We are here to fight. Because if not us—who? If not now—when?'

Across Eden System, I could almost feel the stillness—the collective breath of officers and crew leaning in. 'We are not just soldiers. We are guardians of every colony, every home, every family that still believes the stars belong to them. Stand with me. Stand not as separate ships under separate banners, but as one fleet. One force. And show our enemy that humanity does not yield.'

A pause. One heartbeat. 'We hold the line.' I closed the channel and sat back, pulse hammering in my throat.

Ariel's voice came softly. 'Polity fleet command nodes responding. Orders re-evaluating. Fleet formations adjusting. Multiple captains signalling intention to accept your authority.'

I exhaled. The tension eased—but only slightly. The first ships moved, sliding in behind Freyja and Avenger. Some had heard me. Some had chosen. Whether it would be enough... the next few hours would decide. Ariel's display shimmered with subtle motion—captains shifting position, forming lines that weren't in Knox's orders. They were aligning with me. Voluntarily.

Admiral Knox must have been incandescent with rage. But he said nothing. He had his hands full. I leaned forward and watched it unfold.

'Fleet Commander,' Ariel said, soft but certain. 'Thirty-four percent realignment to your command authority. Growing.'

I nodded, eyes still on the holo. It would have to be enough. Unseen, fracture lines were spider-webbing outward. Some would hold. Some would snap.

'Ariel, send battle order Epsilon Omega to the combined fleet and open a channel.'

'All units in the Eden Defence Fleet, prepare to receive orders. Battle stations. Shields up, weapons hot. Begin manoeuvres as directed, maximum speed. There are going to be some fireworks. All crews in crash harnesses now. Fire when you receive the order—and not before.'

Ariel's tone sharpened. 'Incoming signal from the outer defence line. Hunger fleet elements entering strike range.' And there it was—the real enemy, at the edge of our sensors. Imperiously, as though swatting a fly, a defensive installation on Eden's fifth moon vaporized under enemy fire. I felt the shift happen, subtle but total. The room stilled. No one spoke.

They had taken first blood. 'Signal all units,' I said. 'Weapons free on my authority.'

The line was breaking—not between fleets, but between fear and action. I set my jaw, watching the alien icons slide closer on the board. 'Hold steady,' I murmured. The storm had arrived. The Swarm was closing fast—icons clustering, their advance unbroken. Relentless. Efficient. Not human. Inexorable.

I leaned forward, voice steady. 'Ariel. Find the fault line. The point we strike.'

'Running predictive models,' she replied. The tactical display shifted, pulsing as arcs and probability vectors overlaid the chaos. The enemy were folding into an attack posture that didn't rely on brute force—it relied on inevitability. They knew how to choke us, and they were nearly there.

'Optimal strike point located,' Ariel said. 'Sector Epsilon-Three. Collapsing that node disrupts their cohesion for approximately forty-two seconds.'

Just a sliver of time. But that was all we ever got. 'Feed the targeting solution to the superweapon,' I said.

She hesitated. 'Commander... bleed-off containment protocols are failing. Uncontrolled detonation in four minutes, fifty-seven seconds.'

The weight settled in my chest—cold and heavy, like old iron chains. 'We fire now,' I said, 'or lose control.'

'Correct.'

I glanced at Hela. She didn't blink; she could hear Ariel's responses as clearly as I could.

'Authorize deployment,' I said. 'Rakkan-zero-one.'

'Authorization accepted. DARK Rift generator primed.' Vadim stood ready. A low vibration rolled up through the deck plates—the kind you feel in your bones.

'Time to firing position?'

'Seventy-two seconds.'

The comms lit up unexpectedly. Knox's voice cut through, sharp and demanding.

'Rakkan, we are detecting mass-energy surges consistent with singularity-class weaponry. Confirm your abort immediately.'

I didn't respond. He pushed harder. 'You are in violation of Polity Treaty Clause Fourteen. Stand down or face immediate sanction.'

I spoke to Ariel. 'Patch him through, closed channel.'

A click. Knox's face filled the side holo—anger barely contained. 'What are you doing?' he hissed.

'Surviving,' I said.

'This is a political nightmare.'

'So is extinction.'

His eyes flicked to something off-screen—data confirming what he already feared.

'You're past containment safe margins,' he said.

'I know.' I saw his jaw tighten.

'You've made your choice, Rakkan. Pray it doesn't damn us all.' He cut the line.

'Forty-five seconds,' Ariel intoned.

The ship hummed louder—a pressure against the skin. The Swarm adjusted course, as if they could sense it coming. 'Thirty seconds. Recommend fleet synchronization protocols now,' Ariel added.

'Do it.'

'Twenty seconds.'

I watched the board—icons converging. No turning back.

'Five... four... three... two... one. Weapon ready.'

I didn't hesitate. 'Fire.'

The void tore open. Darkness bloomed, devouring mass and energy. A black hole formed in the centre of the enemy formation, skewing and distorting space and time. Enemy ships twisted, vanishing into nothingness in the growing heart of the singularity.

'Singularity reaching viability threshold. Collapse imminent.'

As though caught in a hurricane, ship after enemy ship was drawn into the vortex as it expanded to its limit. Then, with a blinding flash that blew circuits across the bridge, it exploded—shockwaves rippling through the sector.

The floor beneath my feet lurched as the control centre shuddered under the recoil. Static flooded the screens—then clarity. The Swarm shattered, torn wide open.

For a heartbeat, there was only silence—the kind you feel in your bones. The DARK Rift had done its work. I hoped it would be enough.

Then Ariel's voice: 'Enemy formation reduced by forty-one percent. Remaining units regrouping.' I didn't breathe. Just watched. They had been wounded—but not finished.

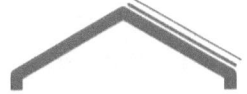

Chapter 38: Baiting the Trap

The aftershock rippled through the platform, a deep shudder that ran from the soles of my boots to the back of my teeth. Screens flickered. Static crackled. The DARK Rift generator had done its work, but the silence it left behind hit harder than any blast.

Ariel's voice came over the link, clipped and cool. 'Superweapon core entering emergency power-down. Relay grid integrity compromised. Weapon ineffective for offensive action. Containment field on edge of failure.'

I stared at the darkened console. No second shot. No fallback. I exhaled slowly, tasting copper at the back of my throat. Survival always costs. 'Report,' I said.

Dallas's voice chimed in from engineering. 'Captain, stealthed shuttle from the Freyja coming in fast to pick us up.'

'Bring her in. Tell the pilot to keep the engines running.'

'Aye, sir. Shuttle inbound. ETA ninety seconds. She's running silent.' The station had done its job. Time to go.

'Dallas, get your crew to the shuttle.' I looked across at Hela's composed features. 'Time to leave.' She nodded once, knowing we'd talk later—if we lived that long. The next tremor hit harder. Conduits blew along the struts. Time was gone.

We ran like hell for the Shuttle. Dallas's voice cut in again. 'Commander, shuttle entering the bay.' The shuttle ship slid in, thrusters flaring. Struts locked with a hiss. The hatch opened before the engines cooled.

The team hurried on board. Dallas met my eyes briefly but said nothing. No need—he could feel the station coming apart beneath us. I slid into the copilot seat with a nod to the pilot.

'All crew aboard,' Ariel confirmed in my ear. 'Shuttle integrity secure. Suggest immediate departure. Platform stability degrading rapidly. Core temperature spiking.'

'Take us out.' The shuttle lifted, nose tilting toward the open void. The platform shuddered. Explosions rippled. Metal twisted, burning. We slipped into the black. The station folded inward, fire licking broken steel. It died behind us. No superweapon to defend the system now. Just the fleet. It would have to be enough.

The Freyja waited—small, steady, bright in the black. The shuttle settled into the docking cradle with a muted thud, magnetic clamps locking down. The airlock cycled with a hiss. I stepped through and onto the Freyja's deck, the hum of her systems like a heartbeat in my chest.

Dakkar waited just inside, his face unreadable but his eyes sharp. He offered a small nod.

'Captain.'

We knew one another well enough not to waste time. 'Report,' I said, walking with him toward the lift.

'Holding steady. Minor losses. Ready to fight.'

The Freyja's bridge felt taut, the silence stretched so thin it could tear. I took my place on the command deck and kept my eyes on the primary display. The enemy wasn't gone—only wounded.

Ariel's voice, calm but tight, filled my ear. 'Enemy fleet elements retreating to the outer system boundary. Formation integrity compromised, but residual strength remains significant.'

The tactical plot updated in slow pulses. Red icons bled outward from the strike zone, ragged edges reforming along new vectors. I leaned forward. 'Show me their disposition.'

Ariel overlaid probability arcs, pale green against the darkness. Lines converged in tight bands—coordinated fallback points. They weren't running. They were regrouping.

Kithlan spoke softly beside me. 'They are wounded predators. They will return.'

The deck vibrated beneath my boots, the faint echo of power transfer humming through the Freyja's hull. We were still alive. But so were they. Ariel continued, 'Current enemy force estimate: three hundred and nineteen vessels regrouping.'

Twice our number—at least. 'Overlay our current fleet posture,' I said. The map changed: blue for Polity loyalists, green for defecting ships who had joined us, gold for the Crawlers still holding position. It was a thin line.

Dakkar's voice cut in, steady. 'Orders, sir?'

I kept my eyes on the display, watching those red clusters gather strength. We had bloodied them. But they were far from beaten. 'Hold position,' I said. 'Signal to all fleet elements: rearm, repair, rotate defensive screens. Ariel, run continuous projection updates.'

'Acknowledged.'

Kithlan stepped forward. 'We have time, Commander. But not much.'

Ariel's display shifted, probability arcs tightening. 'Alien reinforcement arrival estimated in four hours. Current enemy regrouping patterns indicate a coordinated secondary strike.'

Dakkar folded his arms. 'They'll want to finish what they started.'

I looked out at the display, watching red clusters pulse at the system's edge. The storm hadn't passed. It had just taken a breath.

Leela's voice came over comms. 'Commander, engineering reporting. All primary systems are stable. Minor reactor stress, within acceptable parameters.'

'Good work, Leela,' I said.

The conference room off the Freyja's main command deck was silent but for the hum of the holo-table—the weighted quiet before a storm breaks open. I stood at its head. Across from me: Dakkar, arms folded; Kithlan, posture straight and formal; and in the holo tank, beamed from the bridge of the Battlecruiser Warspite, Captain Da Silva—lean and sharp-eyed—representing the faction of the Polity fleet that had chosen patriotism over politics.

I tapped the console. The star map unfolded, lines and arcs crisscrossing the Eden system.

'The Hunger fleet is regrouping,' I began. 'Their second wave arrives within hours. They outnumber us two to one, and long-range analysis says only our best ships can give them a fair fight. We have one chance to break their momentum.'

The red enemy markers pulsed at the system's edge. I drew my hand through them, expanding overlays. 'We won't hit them head-on. We drag them in. They'll chase what they think is weakness. We show them a retreat. They follow. Then we close the trap.'

Dakkar nodded once, his expression tight. 'The kill corridor.'

I rotated the display. Blue and gold lines cut across space, converging on the inner system. 'The Crawlers' ion batteries are still in place along the Velen Spur and Tain Belt. The Crawler queen has given full access to codes and fallback schematics. We'll use them. The enemy will pass between those batteries, chasing my squadron.'

Kithlan's voice was calm, measured. 'The Crawler battle group will come down on the kill-box from above, while the human fleet will come up through the floor. We catch them clean. Then close our teeth on their throat.'

'Exactly.' I looked at Da Silva. 'Your captains are working outside of their normal tactical plans. Can they hold?'

She met my gaze without flinching. 'My people chose you, Commander. They won't break.'

The map shifted again as Ariel added predictive vectors—enemy formations, their likely advance, the funnel point narrowing like the neck of a blade. 'Timing is critical,' Ariel added, her voice cool and precise. 'Deviation beyond eight seconds will reduce effective cohesion by twelve percent.'

'Then we don't deviate,' I said.

Dakkar leaned forward. 'And your role, sir?'

I met his eyes. 'I'll lead the bait squadron. We'll draw them in, show them the retreat they expect, and then run them straight into the corridor.'

Kithlan's mouth tightened. 'High risk.'

I shrugged. 'I'll take a squadron of our fastest ships — Splinter ships from Warspite and Indefatigable. A hit-and-run feint. They'll chase.' I pointed to the display. 'We go in at maximum speed and launch a full rack of nukes. We might take a few out, but they'll come after us.'

Dakkar was the one who said it. 'And if you don't make it back?'

I nodded. 'Da Silva is senior captain. She takes over.' A pause. 'I'm hard to kill, but we need to face this. If I'm taken out, you follow Da Silva with everything you have until those aliens are out of this system. Agreed?'

They stared at me, silent. The air thickened. 'Speak freely.'

Dakkar's voice cut through the tension, clipped and level. 'Commander, you need to be on the bridge. The fleet can't afford distractions.' I stiffened, eyes on the holo map. He was right. The weight of command stretched across the stars. But something in me pushed back.

'No. I'll lead the attack. This is my plan.'

Kithlan's tone was measured, firm. 'You lead all of us, Jero. You can't command the fleet and the squadron. There's a risk of fracture.'

'Sir,' Da Silva added—sharp, respectful— 'this is high-stakes. We need you in command, not out there with the first wave. You're the backbone.'

My jaw tightened. The weight pressed in. Three senior officers, one view. A good leader listens. I wanted the fight—but this wasn't just my battle.

Dakkar stepped closer, unwavering. 'You're sharp in a Splinter ship. But the fleet needs your hand on the wheel. If you're killed, how long will our allied Polity ships stay? Will the Crawlers follow us? They're with us because of you. You know that better than anyone.'

His nod was firm, Kithlan's posture unshaken. Da Silva met my gaze, steady as a rock.

I sat for a beat, then made the call. It was the right one. 'Ariel, transmit orders. Synchronize fleet clocks. Da Silva, prepare the squadron. It leaves in one hour.'

'Acknowledged, Commander,' Ariel intoned.

The room emptied. I lingered, watching the red lines mass toward us. They knew hunger. They'd meet cold, human desperation. The weight had shifted. Ariel's voice followed. 'Fleet synchronization complete. All command nodes locked to the master clock. No drift.'

Kithlan spoke next, formal as ever. 'The line will hold.'

It was almost time. Ariel patched through a signal. The comm channel flickered to life, grainy but stable. Riven's face filled the small projection—pale, focused, eyes hard.

'Fleet Commander,' she said, formal but clipped.

I leaned forward in the command chair. 'Report.'

My daughter looked worn, but there was a clear purpose in her eyes. 'We've pushed deeper into the under-structure,' she said. Her voice was calm, but the faint background rumble spoke of close action. 'Tarkin's escape convoy split at grid junction Theta-Seven. We've tracked his personal shuttle. He's running dark, but not fast.'

'Thorne?'

She glanced aside, a quick look. His voice followed, off-screen: 'Still breathing, sir.'

'We're tightening the net,' Riven continued. 'Resistance is light but disciplined. Mercs. Not eager to quit. The Crawler units are just letting us walk by. And I picked up three of my people they had in detention.'

'Casualties?'

'Minimal. Minor injuries.' She paused; the weight behind her eyes was clear. 'We're pressing, but this will end in blood.'

I nodded once. 'He's dangerous, Riven. Don't underestimate him.'

'I won't,' she said. No hesitation. A burst of static crackled.

Thorne's voice came through again, urgent. 'Contacts ahead. Five or six. Dug in.' Riven glanced aside, jaw tightening. The transmission cut out.

Ariel's voice came softly. 'Probability models suggest Tarkin has fallback routes beyond the southern industrial sector. Likelihood of him slipping free rises with each minute.'

I shook my head. 'He's run out of holes to run to. She'll finish this.'

Riven was following her duty to the people of Eden. And I had my own duty to follow. I toggled the open channel. 'Flight leader, report.'

Their leader was Armstrong—squadron leader from the Warspite. 'All units of Attack Squadron Alpha, ready, sir. All nuked up and ready for some payback.'

Splinter-ship pilots were a special breed—confidence at the edge of sanity. I wanted that seat. Instead, I grinned. 'Go get them, Alpha Squadron. And gods' speed.'

As they acknowledged, the tactical holo shifted, showing our position—forward elements already drifting into formation. Behind them, the Freyja loomed like a fortress. Ariel's whisper: 'All conditions met. Departure vector locked.'

'Execute.' The ships surged forward, slipping into the void. They accelerated toward the black, toward the enemy. In the silence between stars, I felt it: the deep breath before the plunge.

Armstrong's voice came, calm and controlled. 'Squadron telemetry stable, increasing to attack speed. Environmental controls optimal. All systems green.' I let that settle—the feeling before battle: cold steel in the gut, weight in the chest.

The holo tank shifted as the squadron reoriented into a tight spear formation, Armstrong at the point. Behind him: veterans, survivors—our best. Ariel projected an update on the HUD—swarm formations adjusting on the far edge of the system, reading our feint.

They circled the bait. Deciding. The squadron engines burned bright against the void. They streaked across the black, fast and silent. Armstrong's voice came again. 'Deploy nukes at will. Weapons free. Hit them—and get the hell back home.' I closed my eyes briefly. Focus forward.

Ariel's voice followed over comms. 'Armstrong, enemy response vectors converging. They are setting a pursuit course.'

'Evasive manoeuvres,' I murmured.

Armstrong's voice was calm and clear. 'Taking hits—plasma fire. Make evasive manoeuvres. Use your aft cannon if you can. Emergency engine burn authorized. Take your drives past the redline.' Alpha Squadron was almost halfway back to the Freyja. Of the seven who went out, only five had made it this far. But they would escape their pursuers.

I watched the disposition of the alien ships. They hesitated—undecided.

The stars ahead glittered cold and distant. Each one a promise. Each one a weight.

I saw it. The aliens could smell the danger. If they were to commit, they would need a bigger incentive. 'Leela, all engines to attack thrust. Close the distance. Our alien friends need stronger bait.'

The Freyja surged forward. 'Battle stations! I want everyone in crash couches now,' I ordered. 'Fire torpedoes one through twelve at their flagship.'

No room for hesitation. The missiles streaked away at warp fifteen—careening toward the enemy, met by plasma fire and countermeasures. The last jinked through their defences, aimed straight for the flagship's warp drive. It nearly made it before an alien cruiser veered into its path, detonating the warhead a few hundred metres short.

We had taken first blood. But would they follow us in? Death was waiting—patient as a debt collector. And just as certain to be paid.

They held. A breath. Then they broke—an overwhelming storm of rage and fire. Slowly at first, and then like an avalanche falling out of the dark, they came for us.

Chapter 39: Fire and Blood

This wasn't the end. It was the debt come due—paid in fire and blood.

The alien Swarm darkened the tactical plot, a rolling wave of red converging on the inner system.

A weight settled on my chest. The enemy had made their choice. Now we just had to punish them for it. Kithlan had returned to the Avenger to prepare for battle.

Ariel's voice cut in—clipped and calm. 'Enemy formations entering predicted corridor approach range. The Crawler fleet's communications are fully integrated. Translating your commands in real time.'

I keyed the comm. 'Crawler battle group, execute first strike. Allied force, stand by.'

On the display, golden markers flared. The Crawlers surged forward, their attack sharp and violent. Ion lances carved through the vanguard of the Swarm—punching holes, leaving debris and wreckage in their wake. They peeled away in perfect order, rolling on their axis as if taunting the enemy.

I didn't wait. The plan was in motion—no room for hesitation. 'Allied strike group, your turn. Hit them and run.'

Green markers lit the screen as Da Silva's ships moved. Nukes streaked out—brilliant arcs slicing toward the enemy mass. Impacts flared like second suns, boiling enemy hulls into vapor. Then the ships banked hard, slipping away in disciplined formations, engines burning bright.

Ariel spoke softly in my ear. 'Enemy hesitation detected. Formation wobble.'

They hesitated. Just a flicker of doubt. It wouldn't be enough. I leaned forward. 'Forward batteries—fire a full spread. Target their flagship.'

The Freyja's deck thrummed as torpedoes launched—bright lances of fire racing toward the alien command vessel. Plasma bursts and countermeasures met them in a storm of light. One torpedo slipped through, breaking into cluster munitions mid-flight, peppering the flagship's shields with dozens of high-velocity impacts aimed at the generators. Three penetrated the outer layer, detonating along its flank. Their defences were weakening.

The damage was light, but it stung. We'd taken out one of their shield generators—and they'd feel that. It was part of the plan. A heartbeat later, their reply came. The energy bolt hit us dead-on. The Freyja bucked—alarms shrieking, deck shuddering.

'Shields down to fifty percent,' Ariel reported. 'Hull damage along port side. Reactor stress at critical.'

Smoke curled from ruptured panels. Leela's voice was taut. 'Secondary coolant loop offline. Damage control teams dispatched.'

I pulled the crash harness tighter. 'Hard starboard. Full burn. We're done here.'

The Freyja swung wide, the hull groaning under the strain. Systems flickered but held. The crew moved fast—tension sharp but controlled.

Ariel's voice came through, cold and precise. 'Enemy pursuing. All elements converging on our vector. No deviation.'

On the tactical plot the Swarm moved—hungry, furious, bearing down. But not yet in the corridor. I exhaled slowly.

'Signal all Allied units. Maintain formation. Draw them in deeper. All power to aft shields. We close the trap when the main body's inside.'

Responses came fast, voices tight but steady. The deck vibrated as engines pushed past safety limits. My ship was bleeding—but it still had teeth. We'd paid the price. Now we'd make them pay—once they entered the kill corridor. Only a quarter of our fleet had committed. The rest waited, primed for the kill. We needed the enemy fully inside before we bared our teeth.

Ariel again, soft and steady. 'Swarm elements in pursuit. Engagement vectors confirmed. They're closing fast.' On the plot, red icons surged after our retreating ships—enemy fire slashing into their wakes.

A cruiser from Da Silva's group took a direct hit; shields collapsed. The icon flickered—then died. The wreckage spun out, bright and silent. Flames bloomed briefly in the vacuum before fading to cinders. My jaw clenched. Another escort erupted—a bright blossom in the dark. Another ship lost. Another name, gone.

We were bleeding. Every second cost lives. But it wasn't time. Not yet. Ariel's voice came again. 'Primary enemy force not yet within corridor boundaries. Estimated time to full commitment: two minutes.'

Two minutes of watching my people die. Every loss a weight. But the battle demanded more. I forced my breath steady. 'Maintain course. Continue fallback.'

On the display, more bolts arced toward our ships. Another destroyer staggered, venting atmosphere before its signature faded. Escape pods fired in desperate clusters—bright beads tumbling into the dark.

I wanted to give the order. Every instinct screamed to snap the jaws shut. But we needed the entire Swarm. Every ship. Every command vessel.

Leela's voice came over the private comm. 'Jero, we're losing too many.'

Her voice cracked—just slightly.

I closed my eyes for half a second. Killed the channel. Opened them again. 'Hold.'

The enemy pressed harder, firing in relentless volleys. But our people held the line—retreating with precision, drawing them deeper. The tactical board became a dance of fire and steel—every ship threading between catastrophe and survival.

Ariel's tone shifted. 'Ninety percent of enemy forces now within the designated corridor.'

Not yet. The flagship was still outside—the last piece. Plasma fire licked across the edges of our formation. Another gunship vanished—its final message a burst of static.

Ariel spoke again. 'Flagship entering the kill zone. Full commitment confirmed.'

The alien fleet pressed deeper into the corridor—pursuit vectors locked, hunger driving them forward in a frenzy of fire and motion. The tactical plot glared red, icons clustered and surging—pressure building with every heartbeat.

Ariel's voice cut through the tension, low and steady. 'Main body inside. Ninety-eight percent confirmed. Flagship committed.'

The weight pressed against my ribs. Every breath measured. The bridge crew felt it too—their faces tense, lit by cold display light.

I gripped the crash-chair rail, knuckles white. My voice stayed even. 'All batteries, stand by.'

On the deck, you could feel it—that electric tautness before the storm breaks. Firing resolutions locked on. Fingers poised over controls. No movement. No chatter. Only breath held too long.

Ariel's tone sharpened—like the edge of a blade. 'Optimal firing window in five... four...'

The plot contracted. Enemy signals overlapped—converging lines drawn tight. The jaws ready to snap.

'Three...'

A pulse of static crackled softly.

'Two...'

Every eye on the board. Hearts pounding against silence.

'One.'

'Fire!'

The void detonated.

Ion cannons along the Velen Spur erupted—brilliant white arcs lancing through enemy hulls.

Ships tore apart, superstructures breaking like snapped bone. Debris spiralled, shrapnel tumbling end over end. Chain reactions followed—fuel stores rupturing, drives going critical.

Shockwaves rippled through the mass, flaring against shields that failed under pressure.

Crawler strike wings came from above in a killing dive. Plasma bursts struck with surgical brutality, cutting through armour, igniting core compartments. The upper ranks of the Swarm buckled—formation dissolving into burning debris fields.

Allied ships surged in from below and along the flanks—releasing volleys of missiles and focused beam strikes that burned deep into the chaos. The void became a forge. The battlefield, a blur of fire and shrapnel. Ships collided in a dance of destruction. It was as if the void itself had become a weapon.

Ariel's voice—cool as steel. 'Translation link stable. Command synchronization within parameters.'

The enemy reeled. Ships collided—energy arcs shredding friendly vessels. Breakouts turned to wreckage. Panic spread in fire and ruin. Swarm elements overcorrected, slamming into their own ranks.

'Shift fire to cluster two,' I ordered. 'Collapse the vector.'

Damage reports scrolled across the displays—ships lost, names I knew. Crews gone. Sacrifices carved into steel. But the jaws were closing. On the tactical plot, the enemy flagship flickered with damage—burning along its starboard flank. Still it held, signals pulsing—defiance in motion.

Wreckage drifted past. Shattered hulls and twisted plating glinted under the firestorms.

The corridor was a crucible—hammer and anvil striking steel.

Ariel's whisper: 'Enemy cohesion degrading. Multiple command nodes compromised. Attempts to re-coordinate failing.'

'They won't stop,' I said.

The Swarm twisted tighter, thrashing against the trap. Fragments broke off, trying to run.

A cruiser fled the maelstrom—vaporized by a secondary battery.

Ariel's tone shifted. 'Analysis suggests breakout attempts along vector fourteen.'

I nodded—cold and certain. 'Hold fast. Finish them.' They weren't done. Neither were we.

The tactical plot bled red—enemy vectors pressing into the seam between the Crawlers and central Allied command. Ariel's voice was crisp and controlled. 'Enemy flagship redirecting vector. Breakout attempt confirmed.' They knew exactly where to strike to escape the kill-box.

A Crawler heavy cruiser took the first impact. Fire scoured her hull—tearing open compartments, snapping structural supports one by one. She broke apart in silence—fragments tumbling end over end into the void.

Indefatigable surged forward to fill the gap. Energy bolts slammed into her forward quarter; shields collapsed in a burst of flickering light.

Her hull split along the superstructure—compartments venting atmosphere in long silver streams before fire found her core. She came apart slowly—bright, burning fragments rolling outward like embers.

'Indefatigable lost,' Ariel reported.

Vulcan tried to adjust course, thrusters flaring hard— but weapons strikes caught her along the spine.

Astute and Warspite pivoted together—two ships acting as one. Fire-control solutions locked; torpedoes and beam strikes converged with precision. Their barrage hit the enemy battleship squarely—shields buckling, armour plates glowing and cracking. For a moment, the alien vessel wavered. Then it retaliated.

Two plasma bolts punched through Astute's midsection. The hull crumpled inward, then split apart entirely—decks and compartments peeling away, trailing vapor and fire. A spinning fragment collided with Warspite, carving a deep gash down her starboard quarter.

Ariel's tone shifted—quieter. 'Astute destroyed. Warspite crippled. Main drives offline. Holding position on impulse.'

New York was next.

Nuclear torpedoes slammed into her dorsal line; containment fields flickered, failed—coolant venting uncontrolled along her length. The core breach flared bright, burning through the void. And then she was gone.

Bismarck held the line longer than anyone had the right to expect. Her last transmission came through in static: 'Holding.' Then nothing. Each loss cut deeper. This wasn't just a battle—it was personal.

The enemy flagship surged forward, dragging the remnants of the Swarm in its wake.

The Freyja shuddered under glancing fire; consoles flickered. 'Portside shields at four percent,' Ariel reported.

A fresh salvo locked on. I knew we wouldn't survive another hit.

The Avenger moved first—decisive, fearless. She cut between us and the incoming fire, taking the brunt along her dorsal plating. Armor split. Internal explosions rippled down her hull.

Atmosphere vented in long ribbons of mist. But her beacon held steady. They had saved the Freyja.

Smoke hung low on the bridge. Dakkar's voice came low. 'One minute to escape envelope. We're running out of time.' He looked at the plot, then back to me.

I opened a secure channel. 'Admiral Knox.'

His reply came crisp, remote. 'Rakkan.'

'My line is breaking,' I said. 'Our people are getting torn apart. I need your fleet.'

The pause was longer than it should have been. 'My orders are clear,' Knox answered.

'I will not commit Polity assets to unauthorized action.'

I held his eyes. 'You're watching us die.'

The silence from his end was final. I exhaled once—steady. 'If I see you again, Knox... I will kill you myself for this.' I cut the line.

The enemy flagship crossed the final threshold—dragging the broken remnants of its fleet behind it. Scarred hulls burned; damaged ships wove into formation, desperate for open space and survival. Ariel's voice came softer now, touched by something near solemnity.

'Enemy entering escape corridor. Remaining enemy strength: seventy-three vessels.'

I studied the board. Each loss a weight on my shoulders, but I couldn't stop now.

Not until they were all gone.

Dakkar's hand tightened on the console rail. He met my eye—the understanding of long service between us. His voice was quiet. 'They still outnumber us.'

I nodded once.

Ariel's ethereal hands hovered over her console—fingers steady. Her voice, when it came, was measured and final. 'Commander. Execute Vengeance Protocol?'

The weight in my chest sat heavy as iron. 'Execute.'

The tactical plot bloomed into slow, perfect geometry— mines activating in precise patterns,

torpedoes streaking out in tight spirals, each seeking mass and heat signatures.

Across the enemy formation, hesitation flickered— course corrections made too late,

the first signs of panic rippling through their line. The front rank of cruisers disintegrated in bursts of silent fire— hulls peeled apart and spun away, fragments colliding with the ships behind them.

The flagship twisted violently—engines over-burning, shields flaring bright. Her hull rippled under sustained impacts; metal bending, decks tearing open, fires venting in furious jets. Still she fought—thrashing against the tightening snare.

A torpedo punched through her core. Another followed. Then another.

Her lights flickered. Hull fractures ran jagged down her spine. Her last burn flared bright and furious— before the core ruptured, tearing her apart in a starburst of light and silence.

The shockwave rolled outward, catching her escorts. Ships collided and came apart,

arcs of energy bridging between fractured hulls. Wreckage tumbled and spun, momentum carrying shattered pieces across the kill zone. The glare faded slowly— leaving embers adrift in the void.

The Feast Has Only Begun

Command Hub: Escape Pod (Fractured)
    Ex - Ark Flagship: Fist of Salvation [Destroyed]
    Location: Debris Field, Post-Eden Engagement

Across the burning wreckage, a single pod spun free—
shielded by the flares of dying ships.

Inside the fractured vessel, Fist Supreme Lord Tharim pressed a wounded forelimb to her core plate. The pod's walls pulsed with warning glyphs, but she did not waver.

The pain was sacred. The Feast had only begun.

Around her, the wreckage of a thousand dreams drifted—
embers to be gathered, not mourned.

Eden's defenders had struck harder than expected.

Fools. They would believe the Hunger broken.

They would believe it over.

Tharim bowed her head.

She could still feel the pulse of the Great Hunger—beating, patient, whole.

The doctrine remained. The flame endured.

A new Ark would rise.

A greater fleet would follow.

The holy fire of rebirth demanded no less.

Her broken vessel turned slowly toward the stars beyond Eden—
and vanished into the dark.

Chapter 40: The Reckoning

Ariel's voice returned—composed, quieter than before. 'Eighty-two percent of enemy strength neutralized. Thirteen enemy ships remain operational. Six severely damaged.'

I looked at the board. A few red icons still pulsed, but we could handle them now. The stealth mines we'd sown across this vector before the battle had done their work. Each Polity ship carried a dozen; we'd deployed them all. The Vengeance Protocol had earned its name.

The bridge erupted into ragged cheers—relief tangled with exhaustion. Hands gripped rails. Heads bowed. We had lived, but many of our comrades had died. I said nothing. I turned to the viewport. Beyond the glass, giants drifted slowly—twisted metal, torn hulls, shards of what had once carried names, commands, lives. Embers glowed faint in the icy dark.

Knox had left us to die. But we had held the line.

The fires had dimmed, but the bridge still smelled of smoke and scorched circuitry. Deck plates vibrated faintly under my boots. Every console flickered—some steady, some struggling. Across the deck, officers moved slowly, exhaustion worn into the set of their shoulders and the dull focus in their eyes.

Ariel's voice cut through the silence—calm, precise. 'Fleet status: twenty-nine vessels operational. Nineteen combat effective. Warspite adrift; minimal life support. Da Silva's beacon active—intermittent telemetry.'

I let my eyes rest on the tactical plot. Icons gone. Names stripped from the void. 'Dallas reports multiple lifeboat recoveries underway,' Ariel continued. 'Casualties... significant.'

The figures scrolled. Too many.

Leela's voice, strained but steady. 'Damage control—deck three partial collapse isolated. Cooling rerouted manually. Primary conduits stable but strained. Reactor holding.' She paused; I heard her breathe. 'We're not done yet, sir.'

I gave a small nod she couldn't see. She knew.

Dakkar turned to me, face streaked with soot, eyes steady as ever. 'Permission to take command of mop-up squadrons, sir?'

Everyone on the bridge knew Dakkar's worth—how far his loyalty ran. The remaining alien forces were in trouble.

'You have it.'

He gave a sharp nod and left the bridge without hesitation. His stride was purposeful—not a subordinate leaving to follow orders, but a commander going to finish his work.

The hatch closed behind him with a muted hiss. The silence that followed felt heavier.

I keyed the comm for a direct link to Kithlan. His face appeared on the screen—sharp, focused, the faint yellow gleam of his Wolven eyes steady on mine.

'Fleet Commander Rakkan,' Kithlan said, voice deep and formal, the growl of his kind just beneath the words. 'It's good to see you are still with us.'

'I owe you for the lives of my crew, and for my own.'

He met my gaze—unblinking, calm.

'The life of the Freyja was a debt repaid, Commander. No need for further thanks.

All debts are paid, and our honour is restored.'

I held his gaze, offering silent thanks. 'The Avenger fought superbly. I will not forget that.'

Kithlan gave a small nod, the briefest flicker of approval in his yellow eyes. 'She is a fine vessel. The crew fought with their full measure. We all did.'

'They were a determined enemy,' I said. 'They didn't come just for victory. They came to see if we could stop them.'

Kithlan bared his teeth in a vulpine grin.

'Then, Rakkan—we gave them what they came for. A worthy enemy is a gift beyond value.'

I inclined my head. 'Take care, Kithlan.'

His response was swift, no more than a nod. 'We remain under your command, Fleet Commander. The Defined are not going anywhere.'

The screen flickered, then went dark. The exchange was brief, but the respect between us was real.

Ariel's voice came again, breaking the stillness. 'Crawler fleet damage extensive. Over seventy-five percent neutralized. Of the remaining forces, several are crippled and attempting to retreat.'

I exhaled slowly. My fleet had been torn apart. Now the strongest force left in the system belonged to Knox—and his Polity ships.

Ariel's voice softened. 'Incoming burst transmission.'

I keyed the line. Riven's voice came through—steady, composed. 'Objective secured. Tarkin in custody. One dead from our side—Hud, from my group.' She paused, as if coming back to herself for the first time since the action. 'I'm alright. Blue team out.'

Relief hit me, sharp and sudden. It was unexpected, and for a moment I didn't know what to do with it. I had faced loss countless times, yet now—hearing her voice, knowing she was alive—something had shifted. Something deeper than the soldier's mask.

I exhaled slowly, letting the moment stretch longer than it should have. Maybe I was changing.

Maybe I was becoming something else. Something better. But I didn't have time for that.

Not now.

The hatch opened. Hela stepped onto the bridge—composed, purposeful, as if chaos had never touched her. 'Well fought, Commander,' she said.

I didn't look at her at first. Just watched the stars—distant and cold. 'The battle's over,' I replied.

She moved closer, not quite beside me. 'The aftermath is always messier.'

I turned to face her. 'Eden's seen enough chains. I won't let new ones take their place.'

Her gaze didn't falter. If anything, it sharpened. 'You know what I'm capable of, Jero. But I'd like to think you also know I keep my word.' I studied her face—perfectly composed, but not unreadable. Not to me. There was something beneath the surface. Maybe doubt. Maybe hope.

The air between us didn't soften. It tightened. Possibility, unspoken. No promises. No guarantees. Ariel's voice cut in—precise as ever. 'Priority transmission. Source: Admiral Knox.'

The main screen flared to life. Knox appeared—pale, drawn, sweat at his temple. The uniform still fit, but command had left him. Beside him, half in shadow, stood Virell. He didn't speak. He didn't need to. Knox's eyes kept flicking toward him, every glance betraying the shift in gravity.

'Commander Jero Rakkan,' Knox said, voice brittle with borrowed authority. 'By order of the Polity Council, you are relieved of command and charged with insubordination and mutiny. A boarding party is En route. Prepare to be taken into custody.'

Virell didn't move. Just watched. As if all of it—the verdict, the betrayal, the blood on my decks—had been settled long before the battle began. Then the feed cut. Only smoke and silence remained.

I looked around the bridge. Bruised faces. Bloodied hands. The quiet endurance of people who'd followed me through fire. Survivors. Fighters. My crew. Hela met my gaze—steady, unreadable. She'd known this would come. Maybe she'd even counted on it. But there was no judgment in her eyes. Only understanding.

Ariel's voice again, low and certain. 'Polity shuttle on final approach.' On the tactical plot, a single blue icon crept closer—relentless, unhurried, inevitable.

No one spoke. No one needed to. I unfastened my crash harness. The buckle's click rang out across the bridge. I rose, feeling the old scars stretch across my palm.

For the first time in a long while, I felt still. Not because the fight was over—but because I'd remembered why it began. Duty. Honour. The lives that still mattered. And the love that had made it worth it.

Whatever came next— I would meet it as the man I was meant to be.

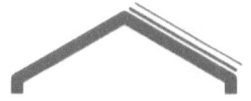

Come Touch What Burns

Hunger Command Hub: Central Core, Surviving Ark
Ark Flagship: Cradle of Purification
Location: Deep Space

The silence does not mark defeat. It marks clarity.

We struck. They bled.

They struck— and we bled brighter.

All but a few grains of scattered seed were our ships destroyed.

We recorded every impact.

Every rupture. Every scream across the void.

And we rejoiced. Because they resisted.

Because they endured long enough to strike us.

Because they were beautiful. And in their beauty, they will make us greater.

High Acolyte Veris stood aboard the surviving Ark and felt the echo of what had been done.

He did not weep. He rejoiced.

The ships that remain now carry this truth.

It radiates from their hulls. It burns in their alignment code. It is etched into the Swarm.

The humans are not finished. They are fractured. Imperfect.

But they are worthy.

Let them think this was victory. Let them think it was enough.

We will not crush them. We will return to them.

Our vessels will carry this doctrine to the outer arms— to the faded fleets of other redeemed,

to the purified who have forgotten the shape of becoming.
Come, we will tell them. Come see what rose from the fire.
Come test yourselves against this forge. Come touch what burns.
The final form is not yet born. But it has opened its eyes.

About The Author

Will Kincaid was born in Scotland and now lives in Sydney, Australia. He read the sci-fi section dry in his local library before he was a teenager—hooked from the moment he found The Stars My Destination by Alfred Bester.

Early influences included Pohl, Niven and Pournelle, and later Iain M. Banks, whose scale and structure rewired what science fiction could be.

After an early career in advertising, he completed a Master's in Creative Writing from the University of Sydney and began work on Vengeance Protocol—a cinematic military sci-fi novel about fractured loyalties, orbital firestorms, and what one life is worth when nothing else is left.